Simple Genius

David Baldacci is the internationally acclaimed author of more than 20 bestselling novels. With his books published in at least 45 languages, and with over 90 million copies in print, he is one of the world's favourite storytellers. His family foundation, the Wish You Well Foundation, a non-profit organization, works to eliminate illiteracy across America. Still a resident of his native Virginia, he invites you to visit him at www.DavidBaldacci.com, and his foundation at www.WishYouWellFoundation.org, and to look into its programme to spread books across America at www.FeedingBodyandMind.com.

Novels of David Baldacci

The Camel Club series

The Camel Club
The Collectors
Stone Cold
Divine Justice
Hell's Corner

Sean King and Michelle Maxwell series

Split Second
Hour Game
Simple Genius
First Family
The Sixth Man

Shaw series

The Whole Truth
Deliver Us From Evil

Other novels

True Blue
Absolute Power
Total Control
The Winner
The Simple Truth
Saving Faith
Wish You Well
Last Man Standing
The Christmas Train

DAVID BALDACCI

Simple Genius

PAN BOOKS

First published 2007 by Warner Books, Inc., New York

First published in Great Britain 2007 by Macmillan

This paperback edition published 2010 by Pan Books
an imprint of Pan Macmillan, a division of Macmillan Publishers Limited
Pan Macmillan, 20 New Wharf Road, London N1 9RR,
Basingstoke and Oxford
Associated companies throughout the world
www.panmacmillan.com

ISBN 978-0-330-51780-5

3 5 7 9 8 6 4

A CIP catalogue record for this book is available from
the British Library.

Printed in Great Britain by CPI Mackays, Chatham ME5 8TD

Visit **www.panmacmillan.com** to read more about all our books
and to buy them. You will also find features, author interviews and
news of any author events, and you can sign up for e-newsletters
so that you're always first to hear about our new releases.

To my dear friend Maureen Egen,
May the days be long and the seas calm.

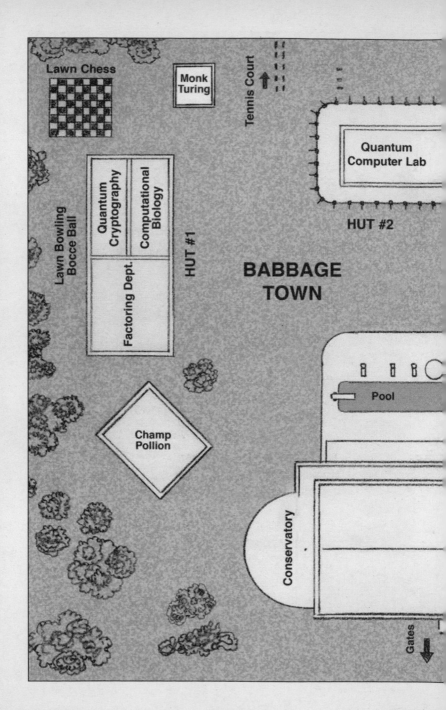

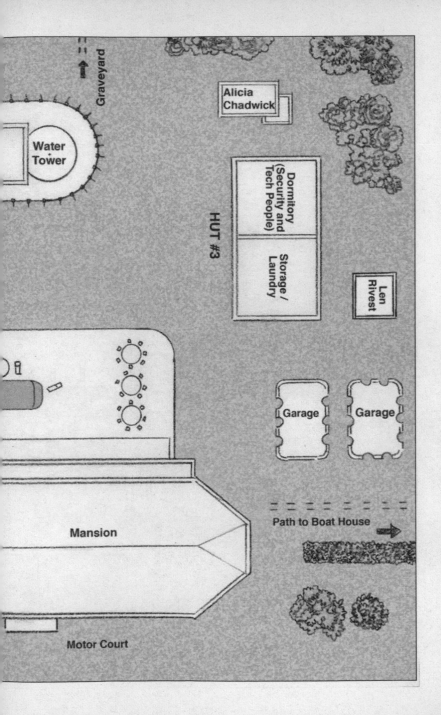

simple genius

1

There are four acknowledged ways of meeting your maker: You can die by natural causes including illness; you can die by accident; you can die by another's hand; and you can die by your own hand. However, if you live in Washington, D.C., there is a fifth way of kicking the bucket: the political death. It can spring from many sources: frolicking in a public fountain with an exotic dancer who is not your wife; stuffing bags of money in your pants when the payer unfortunately happens to be the FBI; or covering up a bungled burglary when you call 1600 Pennsylvania Avenue home.

Michelle Maxwell was currently stalking the pavement in the nation's capital, but because she wasn't a politician, that fifth choice of mortal exit was not available to her. In fact, the lady was focused only on getting so wasted she'd wake up the next morning with a chunk of her memory gone. There was much she wanted to forget; much that she *had* to forget.

Michelle crossed the street, pushed open the bullet-pocked door of the bar and stepped inside. The smoke hit her first, some of it actually from cigarettes. The other aromas were rising off substances that kept the DEA jacked up and in business.

Brain-piercing music crushed all other sounds and would provide an army of hearing specialists with lucrative business in a few years. While glasses and bottles clinked, a trio of ladies ground it out on the dance floor. Meanwhile, a pair of waitresses juggled trays and bad attitudes, all the while prepared to slug anyone attempting to grab their ass.

The bar's collective attention turned to Michelle, the only WASP in the house this or probably any other night. She looked back at them with enough defiance that they returned to their drinks and talk. That status could change because Michelle Maxwell was tall and very attractive. What they didn't realize was that she could be nearly as dangerous as a bomb-wrapped terrorist and was looking for any reason to put her foot through someone's front teeth.

Michelle found a corner table in the back and wedged in, nursing her first drink of the night. An hour and more drinks later, the woman's rage began to swell. Her pupils seemed to grow dry and harden, while the rest of the eyeball eased to a blood red. She lifted a finger at the passing waitress who satisfied her thirst one last time. Now all Michelle wanted was a target for the fury that had laid claim to every square inch of her.

She swallowed the last drop of alcohol, stood and whipped her long dark hair out of her face. Michelle's

4

gaze zoned the room grid-by-grid looking for the lucky one. It was a technique the Secret Service had pounded into her head until that instinct of observation became the only way she could look at anything or anyone ever again.

It didn't take long for Michelle to find the man of her crystallizing nightmare. He was easily a head taller than anyone else in the place. And that head was chocolate brown, bald and beautifully smooth with a column of gold rings stacked in each thick earlobe. His shoulders spanned about a mile. He wore baggie camouflage pants, black military boots and an Army green shirt that showed bare arms full of knotted muscles. He stood there sipping his beer, swaying that big head to the beat of the music, mouthing trash lyrics it was impossible even to hear. Definitely her kind of guy.

Michelle shoved aside a man who stepped in front of her, walked up to this living mountain and tapped him on the shoulder. It felt like she was touching a block of granite; he would do very nicely. Tonight, Michelle Maxwell was going to kill a man. This man, in fact.

He turned, slipped the cigarette from his lips and took a swig of beer, the mug barely visible in his bear paw of a hand.

Size did matter, she reminded herself.

"What's up, baby?" he said, idly blowing a smoke ring to the ceiling and taking his gaze off her.

Wrong move, baby. Her foot connected with his chin, and he staggered backward, knocking down two smaller men. The impact sent a shock wave of pain from Michelle's toes to her pelvis, so hard was his chin.

He tossed the mug at her; it missed, but her slashing front kick didn't. He bent over as air was torn from his gut. Michelle next slammed a vicious kick to his skull with such force she could almost hear his vertebrae screaming over the apocalypse of the music. He fell back, one hand pressed against his bloody head, eyes wide in panic at her raw power, at her speed and precision of attack.

Michelle calmly eyed both sides of his thick, quivering neck. Where to hit now? The trembling jugular? The pencil-thick carotid? Or perhaps the chest cavity, throwing his heartbeat into a fatal misfire? And yet it looked like the fight had gone out of the man.

Come on, big boy, don't disappoint me. I came all this way.

The crowd had cleared back except for one woman who streaked off the dance floor, screaming her man's name. She aimed a meaty fist at Michelle's head, but Michelle deftly sidestepped the charge, grabbed her attacker's arm, bent it behind her and gave her a push. The lady kept right on going, taking down a table and two patrons sitting there.

Michelle turned back to confront the boyfriend, who was doubled over, breathing hard and clutching his gut. He suddenly made a bull run at her. That charge was halted by a crushing kick to his face, followed by an elbow thudding against his ribs. Michelle finished this off with a neatly executed side-kick that disrupted a good bit of the cartilage in his left knee. Screaming in pain, the big man dropped to the floor. The fight had now turned into a slaughter. The silent crowd took one collective step back, unable to believe David really was kicking the crap out of Goliath.

The bartender had already called the cops. In a place like this, 911 was the only number on the speed dial besides the lawyer's. From the looks of things it was doubtful they would be in time, though.

The big man managed to stand straight up on his one good wheel, blood running down his face. The swells of hatred in his eyes said everything that needed to be said: Either Michelle had to kill him or he was going to kill her.

Michelle had seen that same look on the face of every son of a bitch she had ever kicked the male ego out of and that list was impressively long. She'd never started one of these fights before. They usually resulted from a thick-headed slob hitting on her and not reading the not-so-subtle cues she sent back. Then she would stand up to defend herself and the men would fall down, with an imprint of her boot on their knuckled heads.

The blade whipped at Michelle after being pulled

7

from the mountain's back pocket. She was disappointed by both the choice of weapon and the feeble thrust. She sent the knife sailing away with a well-aimed kick that broke one of the man's fingers.

He retreated until his back touched the bar. He didn't seem so big now. She was too fast, too skilled, his superior size and muscle were useless.

Michelle knew that with one more shot she could kill him: a snap of the spine, a crushed artery; either way he was six feet under. And from the look on his face, he knew it too. Yes, Michelle could kill him and maybe vanquish the demons inside her.

And that's when something snapped inside Michelle's brain with such ferocity that she almost deposited all the booze in her belly on the heel-scarred floor. For perhaps the first time in years Michelle was seeing things as they were really meant to be seen. It was startling how fast the decision was reached. And once she made it, she did not revisit the issue. She fell back on what had dominated her life: Michelle Maxwell acted on impulse.

He threw a weary punch and Michelle easily sidestepped it. Then she aimed another kick, this time at his groin, but he managed to clamp a big hand on her thigh. Reenergized at having finally seized his elusive quarry, he lifted her up and threw her over the bar and into a shelf of wine and liquor bottles. The crowd, delighted at this change of events, started chanting, "Kill the bitch. Kill the bitch."

The bartender screamed in fury as his inventory spilled over the floor, but he stopped when the big man came over the bar and laid him out with a wicked uppercut. Next, he picked Michelle up and twice slammed her headfirst into the mirror that was hanging over the demolished booze, cracking the glass and maybe her skull too. Still enraged, he drove a massive knee right into her gut, and then threw her to the masses on the other side of the bar. She hit the floor hard and lay there, her face bloody, her body going into spasms.

The crowd jumped back when the big man's size sixteen boots landed next to Michelle's head. He grabbed her by the hair and lifted her straight up, her body dangling like a spent yo-yo. He studied Michelle's limp form, apparently deciding where next to hurt her.

"In the face. In the damn face, Rodney. You mess it up good," screamed his lady, who'd picked herself off the floor and was dabbing at the beer, wine and other crap staining her dress.

Rodney nodded and swung a big fist back.

"Right in the damn face, Rodney!" his lady screamed again.

"Kill the bitch!" barked the crowd a little less enthusiastically, sensing the fight was just about over and they could return to their drinking and smoking.

Michelle's arm moved so fast Rodney didn't even seem to realize he'd been struck in the kidney until his brain told him he was in awful pain. His scream of fury actually drowned out the music still ripping from the bar's sound system. Then his fist connected to her head, once, knocking a tooth out; and then he hit her again; blood gushed from her nose and mouth. Big Rodney was hauling back for the crusher when the cops kicked down the door, guns out, looking for any reason to start shooting.

Michelle never heard them come in, save her life and then arrest her. Right after the second blow landed she started to fade into unconsciousness and didn't expect to be coming back.

Before she blacked out completely Michelle's final thought was simple: *Goodbye, Sean.*

2

Sean King stared out across the calm wedge of river in the rapidly fading light. Something was going on with Michelle Maxwell and he didn't know how to deal with it. His partner was growing more depressed each day and this melancholy was becoming entrenched.

In the face of this troubling development he'd suggested that they move back to the Washington, D.C., area and start anew. Yet, the change of scenery had not helped. And with funds low and work scarce in the highly competitive D.C. area, Sean had been forced to accept some largesse from a buddy who'd scored big in the world of private security consulting, selling his company to one of the global players.

Sean and Michelle were currently staying in the guesthouse of the friend's large river estate south of Washington. At least Sean was; Michelle had not been around for several days now. And she was no longer answering her cell phone. The last night she had come home she'd been so wasted he'd laid into her for getting behind the wheel in that condition. By the time he got up the next morning, she was gone.

He ran his finger over Michelle's racing scull that was tied to a cleat on the dock he was sitting on. Michelle Maxwell was a natural athlete, an Olympic medalist in rowing, an exercise fanatic beyond all reason, and held various martial arts black belts enabling her to kick other people's butts in multiple and painful ways. Yet the scull had lain untouched since they'd arrived here. And she didn't go running on the nearby bike path and showed no interest in any other physical activity. At last Sean had pressed her to get professional help.

"I'm out of options," she'd replied with a grimness that had startled him. He knew her to be impetuous, often acting on gut instincts. That sometimes ended up getting you killed.

And so now he was watching the day end and wondering if she was okay.

Hours later, while he was still sitting on the dock, the screams reached Sean's ears. He wasn't startled by it; he was pissed. He slowly rose and headed up the planked steps away from the calm of the river.

He stopped at the guesthouse near the large swimming pool to grab a baseball bat and some cotton balls, which he stuffed in his ears. Sean King was a big man, six-two, over two hundred fairly trim pounds, but he was pushing forty-five and his knees were gimpy and his right shoulder suspect from a long-ago injury. So he always took the damn bat. And the cotton balls. On the way up he looked across the privacy fence and noted the older woman staring back at him in the dark, arms crossed and scowling.

"I'm going up, Mrs. Morrison," he said, raising his wooden weapon.

"Third time this month," she said angrily. "Next time I call the police right away."

"Don't let me stop you. It's not like I'm getting paid to do this."

He approached the big house from the rear. The home was only two years old, one of those mansions that had sprung from a knockdown of a rancher a quarter the size. The owners were rarely here, preferring instead to ride their private jet up to their estate in the Hamptons in summer or to their oceanside palace in Palm Beach in winter. But that didn't stop their college-age son and his nose-in-the-air friends from regularly trashing the place.

Sean passed by the Porsches, baby Beemers and hand-me-down Mercedes and marched up the stone steps and into the sprawling kitchen. Even with the cotton balls buffering the sounds, the music was so loud he could feel his heart cringe with every smack of the overloaded bass.

"Hey!" he shouted over the music as he pushed his way through the gyrating nineteen-year-olds. "Hey!" he screamed again. No one paid him any attention, which was why he'd brought the bat. He walked over to the makeshift bar set up on the kitchen island, raised his trusty wooden Louisville Slugger behind his shoulder, assumed his stance and pretended he was taking his cuts at Yankee Stadium. He cleared out half the bar with one swing and finished the rest off with a second sweep.

The music stopped and the kids finally started focusing on him, though half seemed too stoned to take too much of an interest. Some of the under-dressed ladies started giggling while a couple of shirt-less guys stared grimly at Sean, their fists clenched.

Another kid, tall and chunky with wavy hair, stormed into the kitchen.

"What the hell's going on?" He stopped as his gaze settled on the ruined bar. The kid shouted, "Damn it! You're gonna pay for this, King."

"No, I'm not, Albert."

"My name's Burt!"

"Okay, Burt, let's call your dad and find out what he thinks."

"You can't come in here and pull this shit all the time."

"You mean saving your parents' house from being wrecked by a bunch of rich assholes?"

"Hey, I resent that," said one girl, who was teeter-ing on four-inch spikes and wearing only a butt-level skintight T-shirt that left absolutely nothing to the imagination.

Sean glanced at her. "Really? Which part: rich or *asshole*? By the way, in that washcloth you're wearing, I can just about see yours."

Sean turned back to Albert. "Let me spell it out for you, *Burt*. Your father gave me the authority to clear this place out any time in my judgment things were getting out of hand." He held up the bat. "Well, this is my gavel and judgment has been rendered." He stared at the others. "So all of you can get the hell out before I call the cops."

"All the cops do is come and tell us to turn the music down," Burt sneered.

"Not if somebody tells them that there's drug use going on. *And* underage sex and drinking." Sean glanced around at the teenagers. "How would a felony arrest look? Think Mommy and Daddy would pull your keys to the Benz and cut the old party allowance?"

That statement cleared half the room. The other half disappeared when Burt tried to jump Sean and caught the handle of the bat in his gut for the trouble. Sean grabbed the kid by his shirt collar and hauled him off the floor.

"I'm gonna be sick," Burt moaned. "I'm gonna be sick!"

"Just take deep breaths. But don't ever try that again."

When Burt had recovered he said, "I'll get you for this."

"What you're going to do is clean up this place."

"I'm not doing shit!"

Sean grabbed the young man's arm and gave it a

twist. "You clean up this place or we can take a ride down to the police station." Sean pointed his bat at the dregs of the smashed bar. "I'll be back in an hour to check on the progress, *Albert*."

Only Sean wouldn't come back in an hour. Forty minutes later, Sean received the call on his cell phone. Michelle was lying unconscious in a hospital in D.C. after having been arrested for felony assault. He nearly smashed down the front door on his way to the car.

3

He stared at her lying in the bed. Sean turned to the doctor, who said, "Don't worry, it's not as serious as it looks. She had a concussion but otherwise the pictures of her head came back fine and there's no internal bleeding. She got a tooth knocked out and suffered two cracked ribs and bruises over much of her body. She's going to be in some pain when she wakes up, even with the meds."

Sean focused on the one thing that looked totally out of place: a handcuff on Michelle's right wrist, with the other cuff attached to the bed's side rail. And then there was the beefy cop parked outside who'd searched Sean for weapons and told him he had ten minutes with her.

"What the hell happened?" Sean asked.

"Your friend walked into a bar and picked a fight with a guy. A really big guy."

"How do you know that?"

"Because the big guy's down the hall getting worked on right now."

"*She* picked the fight?"

"I assume that's what the handcuff is for, although she's in no shape to make a run for it. The other guy was pretty banged up too. She must be quite a pistol."

"You have no idea," Sean muttered under his breath.

After the doctor left, Sean drew nearer to the bed.

"Michelle? Michelle, can you hear me?"

All he got was a low moan. He backed out of the room, eyeing the handcuff with every step.

It didn't take Sean long to run down the full story. He had a buddy on the D.C. police force who checked the arrest report and filled him in.

"It looks like the guy's filing charges," the detective told Sean over the phone.

"And they're sure she wasn't provoked?"

"About fifty witnesses swore she attacked the other guy. And what the hell was she doing in that part of D.C. in the first place, Sean? Did she have a death wish?"

Did you have a death wish, Michelle?

He ran into big Rodney in the hospital corridor. His girlfriend was with him, still sponging stains off her dress.

"She's been going through a really tough time," Sean explained.

"You think we give a shit!" the woman yelled.

"I'm gonna sue her ass off!" Rodney bellowed.

"Damn right," his girlfriend said. "That bitch! Look at my clothes."

"She doesn't have any assets," Sean pointed out. "You can take her truck, but it's got a hundred thousand miles on it."

The girlfriend said, "Ever heard of garnishment? We take her whole paycheck for the next twenty years. See how she likes that."

"No, you get a *portion* of her salary, but she doesn't have a job either. In fact, after she gets out of here they'll probably just take her back to the institute."

"Institute? What institute?" the girlfriend asked as she stopped rubbing her dress.

"St. Elizabeths. You know, for people with mental problems."

"I don't believe this shit," Rodney exclaimed. "That bitch attacked me!"

"You saying she's nuts?" the woman asked anxiously.

Sean eyed Rodney. "Come on, you think any sane person would take a run at him? Especially a woman?"

"Damn, maybe the man's right. I mean she's got to be crazy to do that, right, baby?"

"Well, I want money from *somebody*," the woman said, hands on hips. She eyed Sean pointedly. "A *friend* will do just fine. Or little miss karate bitch and her bony white ass can do some jail time."

"Okay, I can probably raise some cash."

"How *much* cash?" the woman snapped.

Sean quickly calculated what he had left in his

19

account. "Ten thousand but that's a stretch. It'll pay your doctor bills and leave enough over to make you forget about it."

"Ten? You think I'm an idiot? I want fifty thousand!" the woman roared. "Doc says Rodney needs to get his knee scoped. And she *broke* his damn finger."

"I don't have fifty grand."

"Well, I ain't taking a penny under forty-five, I can tell you that," the woman said. "Or we let this go to court and your friend can have a few years in prison to work on her damn anger management."

Sean said, "Okay, forty-five." That took away every bit of their safety net.

"And the bar got messed up too," Rodney pointed out. "Man's gonna want his money."

"Fifteen hundred to the bar guy. And that's my final offer."

Early the next morning the matter was settled right outside the hospital. The prosecutor dropped his case when Rodney told them he wouldn't press charges. As the big man folded the check he said, "I gotta hand it to her though, she nearly kicked my ass, but . . ."

"But what?" Sean said quickly.

Rodney shrugged. "She had me, man. I ain't ashamed to admit it. She was doing that kung fu shit on me. But then right when she could'a taken me out for good, she threw this weak-ass kick. After that, it was all over. It was like she wanted me to bust her up. But she's crazy, like you said."

Sean hustled back inside the hospital. He didn't want Michelle to wake up with the handcuff still on.

Her fitness was such that Michelle recovered quickly from her injuries, at least her *physical* injuries. The effects of the concussion wore off, the ribs started to heal, and a tooth was implanted to replace the one knocked out. Sean had checked into a motel near the hospital and was there with her every day. Yet then another problem cropped up. When Sean brought Michelle home from the hospital the locks on the guesthouse had been changed and their bags were packed and sitting on the porch. Sean called his buddy the owner. The man who answered the phone said that Sean should feel fortunate the owner was not filing assault charges against him for attacking his son with a bat. And the man added that Sean should never attempt to contact them again.

Sean looked over at Michelle in the passenger seat. The woman's eyes were blank, and it wasn't just the pain meds.

He said, "Uh, Michelle, they're, uh, renovating the guesthouse. I knew about it, but forgot."

She just looked out the window, not registering on anything.

He drove to a motel and checked into a double room, not trusting Michelle to be left alone. He had gotten cash from his bank, afraid even to look at the pitiful balance of funds left. As dinner that night he had takeout Chinese while Michelle, with her badly bruised jaw and newly installed tooth, could only drink liquids.

He sat on the edge of her bed where she lay huddled. "I need to change the dressing on your face," he said. "Okay?"

She had superficial cuts on her jaw and forehead. Both areas were still tender to the touch and she flinched as he took the old bandages off.

"Sorry."

"Just do it," she snapped, startling him. He glanced at her eyes but they'd already retreated into a deep glaze.

"How're the ribs?" he asked, trying to keep the conversation going. She turned away from him.

After he finished he said, "You need anything else?" No answer. "Michelle, we need to talk about this."

In response she lay back on the bed and curled into a ball.

He stood and paced the room, his hand clasped around a bottle of beer. "Why in the hell would you take on a guy who looks like he could start at left tackle for the Redskins?"

Silence.

He stopped pacing. "Look, things will turn around.

23

I've got a few leads on some work," he added, lying. "Does that make you feel better?"

"Stop, Sean."

"Stop what? Trying to be optimistic and supportive?"

All that got in response from her was a grunt.

"Look, you go into another bar like that, some guy'll probably pull a gun and put a hole in your head and that'll be it."

"Good!"

"What is going on with you?"

She stumbled into the bathroom and locked the door. He could hear her upchucking.

"Michelle, are you all right? Do you need help?"

"Leave me the hell alone!" she screamed.

Sean stalked outside and sat by the motel's pool, dangling his feet in the warm water and breathing in chlorine fumes while he finished his beer. It was a beautiful evening. And to top it off a cute, twenty-something lady had just slipped into the pool wearing a bikini that was so small it hardly qualified as clothing. She started doing laps, her strokes efficient, powerful. On the fourth lap she stopped and treaded water in front of him, her full breasts bobbing on the surface. "Care to race?"

"From what I've seen of your performance, I doubt I could give you much competition."

"You ought to see me really perform. And I don't mind giving lessons. I'm Jenny."

"Thanks for the invite, Jenny, but I'll have to take a pass."

He got up and walked off. Over his shoulder he heard Jenny say in a disappointed tone, "God, why do I *always* pick the cute gay guys?"

"Damn, this has been such a great day," Sean muttered.

When he got back to the room Michelle was asleep. He lay on the other bed staring at her.

Two more days passed with no improvement. Sean made a decision. Whatever was hurting the lady, he simply didn't have the tools to help her. Apparently, a deep friendship didn't cut it with matters of a wounded soul. But he knew someone who might be able to help.

5

The next morning Sean called an old friend, Horatio Barnes, a psychologist in northern Virginia. In his fifties, Horatio wore a ponytail and sported a furry, silver goatee. He favored faded jeans and black T-shirts and rode a vintage Harley. He made a specialty of helping federal law enforcement folks through myriad problems caused by the stress related to their work, which is how Sean had met him.

Sean filled Horatio in on the event at the bar and his discussion with Rodney about the fight. He made an appointment and took Michelle to see him under the pretense of a doctor's visit for her injuries.

Located in an otherwise abandoned warehouse, Horatio Barnes's office was large and airy, with rows of dirty windows and books stacked on the floor. His desk was made out of construction sawhorses with what looked to be a large door placed across them. The man's black Harley motorcycle was parked in one corner.

"In this neighborhood, if I left it outside, it wouldn't stay there, now would it?" he explained with a broad smile. "Okay, Sean, out of here. Michelle doesn't need your sorry butt listening in while she tells me everything about herself." Sean obediently left them, waiting in a small, cluttered anteroom. After an hour Horatio came out, leaving Michelle sitting in his office.

"Okay, she's got some serious issues going on," Horatio said.

"How serious?" Sean asked cautiously.

"Deep enough to qualify for some inside time."

"Don't you do that when you think the person's a threat to herself or others?"

"I believe she went into that bar *partly* to die."

Sean flinched. "Michelle said that?"

"No. It's my job to read between the lines."

"Where is this place?"

Horatio said, "Reston. A private clinic. But it's not cheap, my friend."

"I'll get the money. Somehow."

Horatio sat down on an old packing crate and motioned for Sean to do the same. "So talk to me, Sean. Tell me what you think the problem is."

And Sean talked for a half-hour, explaining what had happened to them both in Wrightsburg.

Horatio said, "Frankly, I'm surprised you're not both in therapy. You sure *you're* okay?"

"It affected us both, but Michelle was hit a lot harder."

"She obviously feels that she can't trust her judgment anymore, and with her that's a big deal."

27

Sean said, "And she cared for the guy too. And then to find out what he was really like. I guess that would screw anyone up."

Horatio scrutinized him. "And how did you feel about that?"

Sean gaped. "A guy slaughtering a bunch of people? How the hell do you think I felt about it?"

"No, I meant about Michelle becoming involved with another man?"

Sean's face took on a more subdued expression. "Oh. Well, I had my own personal involvement at the time."

"That wasn't exactly what I was referring to."

Sean looked at him quizzically, but his friend didn't pursue it.

Sean said, "Do you think she can get better?"

"If she really wants to. If she's ambivalent about getting better we can at least show her the steps she can take to get there."

"What if she doesn't want to get better?"

"That's a different planet altogether." Horatio paused. "But remember that I said she was in that bar *partly* to die? Well, Michelle going in there and picking a fight with the biggest son of a bitch she could find may be the best sign that she actually wants to get better."

Sean looked at him oddly. "How do you figure that?"

"It was a cry for help, Sean; an awkward one, but

a cry nevertheless. What's curious is why she chose now to do it. She's obviously had these issues for a long time."

"Any guess?"

"Like I said, she feels she can't trust her instincts anymore. Next stop, that bar and the end of that guy's fist. Her punishment."

"Punishment? For what?"

"I don't know."

"What if she doesn't want to admit herself to the facility?" Sean said.

"We'll never get an involuntary commit from a judge. Either she puts herself in or I have to counsel her on the outside."

"Then I'll get her inside, somehow."

"How?"

"By wearing my lawyer hat and lying my ass off."

6

That evening Sean sat down with Michelle back at the motel.

"Look," he began. "The guy you beat up filed assault charges against you. I can get them dropped without you appearing in court, but I know the judge is gonna want something from you."

She sat huddled in front of him. "Like what?"

"Psychiatric treatment. Horatio knows of a place you can go."

She stared up at him. "You think I'm crazy?"

"What I think doesn't matter. Now if you want to get prosecuted for assault and spend some time inside another *facility*, fine. But if you voluntarily agree to admit yourself the charges get dropped. It's a sweetheart deal." He silently prayed she would never learn that this was all a concoction of lies. Thankfully, Michelle agreed to admit herself. She also signed a release that allowed Sean to be informed of her treatment and progress. Now all Horatio Barnes had to do was work his mental magic.

"But don't expect miracles overnight," the psychologist told Sean the next day at a coffee shop. "These things take time. And she has a fragile personality."

"She never struck me as being fragile."

"On the outside, no. On the inside, I believe it's a whole different dynamic going on. She's a classic over-achiever with clear obsessive instincts. She told me she used to work out for hours every day. Is that true?"

Sean nodded. "An annoying habit, but one that I actually miss seeing right now."

"Is she also obsessively neat? She wouldn't really address that question."

Sean almost spit out the coffee he had just put in his mouth. "You wouldn't need to ask that question if you'd ever seen the inside of her truck. She's the world's biggest slob and she never saw a pile of junk she couldn't add something to."

"And she's the youngest of five *and* the only daughter?"

Sean nodded. "And her dad was a chief of police in Tennessee and her brothers are all cops."

"That's a lot to live up to, Sean. Maybe too much. If I were in that family I would've been busted about twenty times before I graduated from college."

Sean smiled. "A felony machine, were you?"

"Hey, man, it was the Sixties. Everybody under thirty was a felony machine."

"I haven't contacted her parents yet. I didn't want them to know about this."

"Where are they?"

Sean said, "Her mom and dad are in Hawaii on a second honeymoon. I did talk to her oldest brother, Bill Maxwell. He's a state trooper in Florida. I told him some of what happened. He wanted to come up, but I told him to hold off." Sean asked bluntly, "Is she going to get better?"

"I know what you want to hear, but it's really up to the lady."

Later that day, Sean visited Michelle in her room at the facility. She was dressed in a pair of jeans, sneakers and a floppy sweatshirt with her hair pulled straight back in a ponytail.

He sat in a chair across from her and took her hand. "You're going to get better. You're in the right place to get better."

He might have been mistaken but he thought she'd gripped his hand in response. He immediately squeezed back.

That evening Sean went to an ATM and almost laughed at the insignificant amount in his account. Even the initial private clinic bills were overwhelming and unfortunately not covered by Michelle's insurance. He'd already dug money out of a retirement account and cashed in an old insurance policy but he hadn't worked a day since Michelle had gotten hurt and now things were at a crisis point.

He tried every contact he had but no one had anything of substance to throw his way. The most lucrative investigative work in D.C. all required high-level security clearances that Sean had once possessed but no longer did. And getting new ones was a time-consuming process. He notched his belt tighter and kept making calls and knocking on doors.

Finally, out of options, he decided to do something he'd told himself he never would do. He called Joan Dillinger, an ex–Secret Service agent and now a vice president in a big private investigation firm. She was, also, unfortunately, his ex-lover.

Joan took his call and said, "Absolutely, Sean. Let's have lunch tomorrow. I'm sure I can find *something* that you and I can do together."

He hung up the phone and stared out the window of the crummy motel room he could no longer afford. "I was afraid she was going to say that," he muttered.

7

The woman looked good, Sean had to admit. Good and lethal. Hair and makeup were immaculate. Dress short and tight, heels high and thin yet lifting her petite frame only up to within eight inches of his six-two. Her legs were slender and firm, her chest large but soft and all her own, he knew from experience. Yes, she looked good, actually better than good, terrific, in fact. And he felt absolutely nothing for her.

Joan Dillinger seemed to sense this and quickly motioned him to sit down on a couch. She sat in a chair beside him and poured out coffee.

"Long time, no see," she said pleasantly. "Catch any more mass murderers?"

"Not this week," he said, attempting a smile as he spooned sugar in his coffee.

"How's that obnoxious little girl you hooked up with? Mildred, was it?"

"Her name's *Michelle*," he answered. "And she's fine. Thanks for asking."

"And you two are still working together?"

"We are."

34

"Wow, she's really good with the cloak-and-dagger thing, because I can't even see her."

Now Sean became suspicious. Had Joan found out about what had happened to Michelle? That would certainly have been in keeping with her control freak personality.

He said casually, "She's busy today. As I said on the phone, we just moved back into town, and I was wondering if you had anything you might want to throw our way on a freelance basis."

Joan put down her coffee, rose and started walking around the room. Sean didn't know quite why she did this, but it might have been simply to show off her body some more. A usually complex woman, Joan Dillinger could be oddly transparent when it came to things like sex and personal relationships. In fact, he strongly suspected she used the former in *substitution* for the latter.

"So let me get this straight. You want me to throw you some work on a freelance basis although I have a whole company of seasoned investigators to do any assignment that comes in the door? And I haven't heard from you, in what, over a year?"

"It just seemed better to keep our distance."

Her features hardened. "You're not making it easy for me to help you here, Sean."

"If you didn't have anything, why meet with me?"

She perched on her desk and crossed her legs. "I don't know. Maybe I just like looking at you."

He stood and came over to her. "Joan, I really need some work. If you don't have any to toss my way, fine. I won't take up any more of your valuable time." Sean set his coffee down and turned to leave. Only then did Joan seize his arm.

"Just hold on, big boy. You have to let a girl have her pout. It's only fair." Joan sat down behind her desk, all business now as she slid a legal agreement across to him. "Take a few minutes to read this. I know you're a lawyer after all."

"What's the compensation?"

"Standard rates for this type of work, a reasonable per diem for expenses and a nice bonus if you crack it." She ran her gaze over him. "You look like you've lost weight."

"I've been on a diet," he said absently as he read through the contract. He signed the agreement and slid it back to her. "Can I see the file now?"

"How about I buy you lunch and we can discuss it? I have some ideas and you have a few other documents to sign. Your partner will have to do the same thing."

Sean tensed. "Well, the thing is, she won't be working with me on this one."

Joan tapped a pen against her blotter. "Tied up on something else, is old Mildred?"

"Yeah, *Michelle* is."

Over lunch at Morton's Steakhouse, they discussed the case, though Sean focused quite a bit on his meal.

"Off the diet, are we?" she said, eying his impassioned stabs with the fork.

He laughed shamefacedly. "Guess I was hungrier than I thought."

"If that were only true," she replied sardonically. "Okay, here's the case. And it might turn out to be a challenging one. A suspicious death. Man by the name of Monk Turing. He was found on property owned by the CIA near Williamsburg, Virginia. Either a murder or a suicide. You have to find out which, why and, if it was a murder, the all-important who."

"Turing worked for the CIA?"

"No. Ever heard of a place called Babbage Town?"

He shook his head. "What is it?"

"It's been described to me as a sort of quasi-think tank with potentially enormous commercial applications. That's where Turing worked as a physicist. With the CIA involved and the FBI investigating the homicide because it took place on federal property it'll take some delicate handling. I have some veterans here I could send down, but I'm not sure any of them are as good as you."

"Thanks for the vote of confidence. So who's our client?"

"The people at Babbage Town."

"And who are they?"

"You'll have to find that out too. If you can. You game?"

"You mentioned a bonus?"

She smiled and patted his hand. "As in cash or professional services?"

"Let's start with the cash."

"Our policy is to split the bonus with the principal field agents on a sixty-forty basis." She cocked her head. "You remember from last time, Sean. Only you refused to take any of the money you were so clearly entitled to and let me keep it all. I never really understood why you did that."

"Let's just say I believed it was safer for both of us. And I thought you were going to use that cash to retire?"

"Alas, my spending got a little out of control. So I'm still on the treadmill."

"So if we solve this how much am I looking at?"

"That gets complicated because it's based on certain formulas. But suffice it to say, it'll be a big nut." Her gaze ran over him. "You won't be nearly so thin, I imagine."

Sean sat back and took another bite of his mashed potatoes.

"So, are you interested?" she asked.

He picked up the bulky file. "Thanks for lunch. And thanks for the work."

"I'll make arrangements for you to go down there. Say in a couple of days?"

"Fine. I'll need some time to get stuff in order."

"Like saying goodbye to Mildred?"

Before he could respond she slid an envelope across

to him. He looked at her questioningly. "An advance on your expense money. I figured you might need it."

He looked at the check before sliding it in his pocket. "I owe you, Joan."

"I hope you mean that," she said to herself as he walked off.

8

Michelle studied the doorknob of the room she was in, waiting for it to turn, revealing another person who wanted to ask her questions. Every day here was like the one before it. Breakfast, shrink time, lunch, exercise time, then more psychobabble, an hour to herself, then more shrink interaction centered around mastering her emotions, tempering her inner violent core that threatened to destroy her. Then came dinner, a couple of pills if she desired them, which she usually didn't, and then bed, where she could dream about the next day of this living hell.

When the knob didn't budge she slowly rose from her chair and her gaze bounced off all four windowless, brightly painted walls. She rocked back and forth on the balls of her feet and took deep breaths, testing the healing stage of her ribs.

Michelle hadn't thought much about that night in the bar. She'd gone there to drink and forget. And then, drunk, she had done her best to kill a man. Well, not her best. Somewhere deep in her mind had she wanted to be hurt, perhaps to die? No, Michelle could not admit that. And yet if that *was* her intent, she apparently couldn't even kill herself properly. *How did one even chart that level of ineptitude?*

She spun around when the door opened and Horatio Barnes walked in, dressed in his usual faded jeans, sneakers and black T-shirt with a silkscreen of Hendrix on the front smoking the frets. She'd seen him several times since she'd come here, but their conversations had all been general. She had come to think the man was not very smart, or else didn't really care whether she got better or not. *Do I even care?*

He was clutching a tape recorder, and asked Michelle to sit. And she did. She always did what they asked. What else was there to do?

Horatio sat down across from her and held up the recorder. "Do you mind? I'm afraid dementia's setting in. I'm lucky I remember where my front door is or I'd never get out anymore."

Michelle shrugged. "I don't care, record away."

Horatio took this rebuke in good spirits, turned on the recorder and set it on the table beside her. "And how are we doing today?"

"*We* are super. How are *you* doing today, Dr. Barnes?" Michelle added in a dead-on impression of the man.

The psychologist smiled. "Just make it Horatio. My old man was the Dr. Barnes in the family."

"What kind of a doctor was he?"

"He was chief of medicine at Harvard Medical

41

School. Dr. Stephen Cawley Barnes. That's why he was ticked I always called him Stevie."

"How come you're not an M.D.?"

"My father wanted me to become one. Had my whole life planned out for me. He named me Horatio after some distant relative of ours from colonial times because he thought it would give my life historical weight. Can you believe that? Do you know the shit I took about my name? In high school I was either called 'whore' or 'rat' just because my old man was an elitist snob. So I went to Yale and became a shrink."

"Quite a rebel, were you?"

"Go big or go home. I see from your chart that you didn't have a restful night."

Michelle took this abrupt segue in stride. "I wasn't sleepy."

"Nightmares apparently," Horatio said. "They finally had to wake you up."

"I don't remember."

"Well that's why I'm here. To help you remember."

"And why would I want to remember a nightmare?"

"I find I do my best soul-searching smack in the middle of some kick-ass nightmare."

"And if I don't want to know? Does that count?"

"Sure. Do you want to know?"

"Not really."

"Gotcha. I've mentally checked the nightmare off-limits box. I also see that you asked Dr. Reynolds if he was getting laid enough at home. Mind telling me why you did that?"

"Because he kept trying to look up my gown every time I crossed my legs. You'll notice I'm wearing pants now."

"Lucky me. Okay, let's talk about why you went to that bar."

"Didn't we already discuss this?"

"Humor me. I have to justify my enormous salary somehow."

"I went there for a drink. Why do you go to bars?"

"Let's just say I have barstools retired in my honor in eleven different states."

"Well," said Michelle, "*I* went for a drink."

"And then what?"

"And then I got in a bar fight and got my ass kicked. That cover it for you?"

"And you'd been to that bar before?"

"No. I like to try new spots. I'm what you'd call daring."

"I am too, but picking a bar in the middle of the highest crime area in the District of Columbia at eleven-thirty at night? Think that was a wise choice?"

She smiled and said politely, "Didn't turn out to be, did it?"

"Did you know the brick wall you got in the fight with?"

"No. I'm not even sure how it started, to tell the truth."

"Which I'd like you to start doing, Michelle, telling the truth, and I think you can."

"What exactly is that supposed to mean?"

"According to the police report every eyewitness in the bar said you walked up to the biggest bastard there, tapped him on the shoulder and then sucker-punched him."

"Well, eyewitness accounts are notoriously unreliable."

"Sean talked to the man you attacked."

Michelle visibly flinched at this news. "Really, why?"

Horatio didn't bite on that. Instead he said, "The guy told Sean something interesting. Would you like to know what?"

"Well, since you're obviously dying to tell me, go ahead and fire away."

"He said you *let* him nearly kill you."

"Well, then he was wrong. I made a bad move and he got hold of me, end of story."

"Last night, the nurses said you kept shouting in your sleep, 'Goodbye, Sean.' Do you remember saying that?"

Michelle gave a brief shake of her head.

"Were you thinking maybe of leaving your partnership with Sean? If so, shouldn't you tell him that? Or do you want me to?"

Michelle said quickly, "No, I—" She broke off, evidently sensing a trap. "How am I supposed to know what I meant? I was sleeping."

"I'm a pretty good dream analyzer and I throw in nightmare interpretation for no extra charge. It's a special I'm running this week because business is so damn slow."

Michelle rolled her eyes.

Unperturbed, Horatio said, "You trust Sean, don't you?"

"As much as I trust anybody," she said tersely. "Which isn't much these days."

"*These* days. So has something changed for you?"

"Look, if you're going to jump on every word I say, I'm just not going to say anything, okay?"

"Fair enough. I understand that your parents don't know that you're here. Would you like us to contact them?"

"No! I mean you call your parents if you made the Dean's List or got a new job. Not because you checked yourself into the psych ward."

"And why did you check yourself in here?"

"Because Sean said I had to. To avoid jail time," she added defiantly.

"Is that the only reason? Isn't there something else?"

Michelle sat back in the chair and curled her long legs up to her chest.

Twenty minutes later she hadn't broken her silence and Horatio hadn't either. Finally the psychologist switched off the recorder and rose. "I'll be back tomorrow. In the meantime I'm available by phone at any time. If I don't answer, you can just assume I'm either at my favorite bar or dealing with another whack job like you."

"I guess this session was pretty much a bust. Sorry," Michelle added sarcastically. "But I guess you get paid the same regardless, right?"

"You bet I do. But I thought our session was dynamite."

Michelle looked confused. "How do you figure that?"

"Because you actually sat there and thought about why you wanted to be here. And I know you're going to keep thinking about it once I leave, because you just won't be able to help yourself." He started to leave but then turned back. "Oh, just to warn you about something coming up."

"Yeah?" Michelle said, the look on her face begging for a fight of some kind.

"They're having Salisbury steak for dinner tonight. Get the PBJ option instead. The steak sucks. I don't even think it's real meat. I think it's something the Russians invented to make dissidents talk during the Cold War."

After Horatio left, Michelle sat down on the floor and slumped back against the wall. "Why am I here!" she screamed, kicking the chair clear across the room with one snap of her powerful right leg.

By the time a nurse came rushing in, the chair was upright and Michelle was on her feet. She said ceremoniously, "I understand the steak sucks."

"It does. So you want the PBJ instead?" the nurse said.

"No, put me down for the steak, double helping," Michelle said as she sauntered out the door.

"What, you a glutton for punishment?" the nurse called after her.

You bet your ass I am.

9

Later that night Michelle lay on the bunk in her room, the rancid grub they called Salisbury steak burning a hole in her belly. Since she was in here on a voluntary basis, her movements were fairly unrestricted and she was leaning toward a walk over hugging the toilet. Not all patients here had such liberty. There was a separate ward, locked down and patrolled by guards, that housed involuntarily committed patients who were deemed to be violent. Michelle had heard some staffers refer to it as the "Cuckoo's Nest."

The door opened and her roommate, Cheryl, walked in; last names were not used here. Cheryl was grossly underweight, about forty-five, with ringlets of graying hair plastered against her gaunt face. She carried a drinking straw with her and constantly sucked on it. Michelle didn't know exactly why Cheryl was in here, but assumed anorexia figured in somehow.

Cheryl collapsed on her bunk and started sucking on the damn straw.

It's no wonder I keep having nightmares, Michelle thought. Great, big sucking beasts coming after me in bed.

"How's it going, Cheryl?"

The sucking sound stopped for an instant and then started again.

Michelle started pacing. She wanted to call Sean, but what would she say? I'm sorry about the whole bar thing. Come get me, I'm fine now.

In desperation she turned to Cheryl. "That steak was something, wasn't it? Feels like I've got a tire in my gut."

Cheryl turned away from her and started sucking louder.

Michelle gave up and headed to the small workout area. For obvious safety reasons all exercise equipment was locked up when it was not being used. However, a large rubber ball had been left out. Michelle used it to work her abs and legs. That took thirty minutes and it felt good to use her muscles again. Yet she still had the rest of the night to kill, and she wasn't sleepy.

She walked back down the hallway, passing two other patients dressed in scrubs and blue slippers accompanied by a nurse. On another of the corridors one of the burly attendants passed her and stopped. "You need any help, Michelle?"

He was a muscle-bound six-footer running to fat in his fifties with close-cropped blond hair and three

49

gold chains visible from under his green scrub V-shirt. His nameplate read, "Barry."

The way he asked she didn't like, but maybe it was just her bad attitude. Then he touched her elbow and his intentions became clearer with just the feel of his fingers against her skin. "You need help back to your room maybe?"

She pulled her arm away. "It's not that big a place. I can find it." She strode off, but could feel his gaze burning into her. She whipped her head around and caught him smiling at her.

She hurried back to her room. Cheryl was still sucking on her straw. Michelle lay on her bunk, staring at the door. There were no locks on the rooms, so patients couldn't barricade themselves in. But it also meant that you couldn't stop others from coming in, like Barry.

An hour later the lights went dark and still Michelle did not close her eyes. She was waiting for footsteps, stealthy and motivated by evil purpose. Around one in the morning she finally told herself, "He just touched your arm, for God's sake, and made a suggestive comment." Was she adding paranoia to her other issues? No, she told herself, I don't have *issues*.

At two in the morning she was awakened by footsteps passing down the hallway. She slowly sat up and checked Cheryl's bed, but the straw sucker was dead asleep. Michelle slipped the covers off and put on her tennis shoes. A moment later she was out in the corridor. At night there was a reduced number of staff on duty and the rental guard had a lot of ground to cover and not a lot of motivation to do it.

She followed the sounds of the footsteps down another corridor. Michelle heard a door open and then close. She crept closer, straining to hear something. Then she froze. She'd heard another sound, but this one was *behind* Michelle. She took a few steps back and then cut down another corridor.

An instant later, coming around the corner was Barry, the gold chain attendant. He strode right past Michelle's hiding place in the darkened hall. As soon as it was safe, Michelle ran back to her room.

10

The next morning Michelle returned to that part of the building. Two things caught her eye: the lovely, well-dressed lady who was being wheeled out of her room by a nurse; and the pharmacy at the end of the hall.

Later that afternoon, Michelle had her session with Horatio.

"No more nightmares last night?" Horatio asked.

"No, it was really peaceful. There's a woman in a wheelchair in a room at the end of the patient corridor on the east wing?"

Horatio looked up from his notes. "Yes, what about her?"

"Who is she?"

"She's not one of my patients. But if she were, I couldn't tell you anything about her. Patient confidentiality, you understand. That's why I don't talk to anyone else about *you*." He added jokingly, "Unless they pay me an enormous amount of money of course. I have my ethics, but I'm not stupid."

"But you do to Sean. Talk about me, I mean."

"Only because you signed that release."

"Can you at least tell me why she's in a wheelchair? That's not mental, right?"

"It certainly could be. But as I said, she's not my patient. Why do you want to know?"

"Just curious. There's not a lot to hold one's attention around here."

"Well, I'll give you something. How about we focus on getting you better?"

"Okay, what's on the menu today?"

"Not Salisbury steak, but the spaghetti isn't much better. Now yesterday we finished up with your thinking about why you're here. What conclusions did you draw?"

"Not many, I've been busy."

"Busy? Really? I thought you just said you were bored?"

"Okay, I'm here because I want to get better."

"Are you just saying that or do you mean it?"

"I don't know, which answer do you want?"

"I can play games with the best of them, Michelle, but it does waste a lot of time."

"Is that what you've been telling Sean, that I'm wasting his time, and his *money*? I know he's paying for all this."

"And does that matter to you?"

"I know he's trying to help me. He's a good guy. It's just . . ."

"Just what?"

"I think he could probably spend his time and money better elsewhere, that's all."

"Meaning you'd rather he abandoned you to your fate? You going melodramatic on me? Do I have to add that to the list of weird shit to look out for in you?" Horatio's smile managed to defuse this comment.

Michelle studied the floor for a few moments.

"Do you think *you* know Sean well?" Horatio finally asked.

"Of course. We went through some pretty dangerous things together."

"He told me you saved his life, more than once in fact."

"He did the same for me," she said quickly.

"If you know Sean so well you have to realize that he's not going to walk away from you."

"All I'm doing right now is holding him back."

"Oh, he told you this?"

"Of course not. He'd never say it. But I'm not stupid."

"Were you two ever physically intimate?"

Horatio's question caught Michelle so off-guard that she could only gape.

"It's a fairly standard query, Michelle. I need to understand the different roles that people close to you play in your life. And sexual roles are very powerful influences for both good and bad."

"We were never intimate like that," she said in a mechanical tone.

"Okay. Did you want to have sex with him?"

"You can ask me this shit?" Michelle exploded.

"I can ask you pretty much anything. It's up to you to answer or not."

"I don't understand the question."

"It's not too difficult, is it? Sean King is tall and handsome, smart and brave, honest and true." Horatio smiled. "Frankly, I think those traits are given inflated importance in life, but who am I to say? And he's a *good* guy too, as you said. You're a young, attractive woman. You worked closely together."

"Just because you work with someone doesn't mean you have to sleep with him."

"You're absolutely right. So if I said you did not have thoughts of being intimate with Sean that would be correct?" He smiled. "I need to check off the right box on the multiple choice test here."

"God, I feel like I'm on the witness stand being cross-examined."

"*Self*-examination can be even harder than getting drop-kicked by a skillful shyster in the courtroom. So, no feelings of intimacy toward the big teddy bear?"

"Just go with your gut, Doc. That's all I can tell you."

"That actually tells me a lot. Thank you."

"Now that we're finished with Sean, I suppose you'll want to know if I wanted to sleep with my dad."

"Let's talk about that."

"Come on, I wasn't being serious."

"I get that. But how is your relationship with your father? Good?"

"No, great! He was a police chief, retired now. He and Mom are in Hawaii on a second honeymoon. That's the reason I didn't want to let them know about me. They would've just rushed back."

Horatio didn't let on that he had already learned part of this from Sean. "Very thoughtful of you. Do you think they'd be surprised you're here?"

"I hope they'd be *stunned*!"

"I understand your brothers are cops as well. Ever think of doing something else for a paycheck?"

Michelle shrugged. "Not really. I mean I had the usual pie-in-the-sky ambition to be a professional athlete, but that wasn't going to happen."

"Don't sell yourself short. You're the first Olympian I've ever treated. A silver medal in rowing, Sean said."

"Yeah," she replied, a smile tugging at her mouth. "That was great. The high point of my life, or at least I thought so at the time. Maybe it was after all," she added quietly.

"And then you were a cop for a while and then you joined the Secret Service. Any special reason for the change?"

"All my brothers were cops. I thought it would be cool to be a fed."

"And your father was okay with that?"

"Not really. He wasn't big on me being a cop actually."

"And how'd that make you feel?"

"I understood. Daddy's little girl and all. My mom didn't like any of us being cops. But I did it anyway. I'm sort of independent."

"You'll be *stunned* to learn that one I'd already diagnosed," Horatio said. "So I take it you love your parents very much?"

"I'd do anything for them."

Horatio looked a bit curious at this statement. "Would you give me permission to talk to them about you?"

"Not my parents, no!"

"How about one of your brothers?"

"You can talk to Bill, he's the oldest, a state trooper in Florida."

"Whatever you wish, milady."

"I wish I wasn't here," Michelle blurted out.

"You can leave anytime you want. You know that, don't you?"

"Yeah, sure."

"You can leave right now, get up and walk out. If that's what you want. Get the hell on with your independent life. No one's stopping you. There's the door."

There was a long moment of silence and then she said, "I think I'll stay, for now."

"I think that's an excellent choice, Michelle."

After they finished their discussion Michelle followed Horatio out. As they stood in the doorway Barry walked by, but didn't look at them.

Michelle said, "What do you know about that guy?"

"Not much. Why?"

"Just curious."

"Now why don't I believe that?"

"You doubting my word, Horatio?"

"I was thinking of a more technical phrase, like liar, liar, pants on fire."

11

Beale Peninsula is a wedge of land that juts out into the York River on the Gloucester County side midway between Clay Bank and Wicomico in Virginia's picturesque Tidewater. Like much of Virginia, Beale had been settled early in colonial times. It was filled with the first glories of the new country that over a century later would become the United States. Less than ten miles to the south, at Yorktown in 1781, British General Cornwallis had turned both his sword and thousands of humbled redcoats over to George Washington's ragtag Continental Army. This effectively ended the American War for Independence on a distinctly high note for the victorious yanks, who, up until that point, had rarely seen a battle they could not somehow manage to lose in the end.

From the cleared fields of those early days had risen magnificent brick and clapboard plantations that depended on legions of slaves to run them properly. Less than a hundred years later, depleted soil and the Civil War ended these sleepy days of southern aristocracy forever.

A second wave of prosperity hit when the newly minted wealth of the Industrial Age found its way to this tranquil spot on the York, enticed by its clean water, good fishing, temperate climate and pastoral setting. It was also deemed a restorative place for those with consumption, due to its low elevation and water breezes and abundance of longleaf yellow pine that was thought to be good for tubercular lungs. And once one or two of these exalted families began putting down expensive roots, others had quickly followed.

For this reason, at its peak, six private railway lines stretched down from the north and three more from the west terminating at this doughy fist of Virginia red clay with its steady river breezes.

Now, years later, a few of these palaces had been turned into bed-and-breakfasts or small hotels. The majority though, like the southern plantations before them, had fallen into ruins, which at least provided adventure-filled places for the children to roam during the long, humid days of a Tidewater summer.

Directly across the river on the York County side the United States government's imprint was heavy with Camp Peary, next to a naval supply center and a weapons station. Together this triumvirate took up the entire waterfront from Yorktown to on past Lightfoot, Virginia. It was said that the folks at Camp Peary, an ultra-secretive training center for CIA agents and nicknamed the "Farm," had technology that could discern a person's eye color from across the wide river in the dead of night. And it was also accepted as fact by the locals that every person who had ever come within a four-mile radius of the place had been spied on from outer space. No one had proven that this was so, but it was very much true that no visitor ever left the area without hearing that story at least three times.

Beale had endured the ups and downs of the economy and the whims of the rich, while its more moderately well-off citizens went about their ordinary lives in ways that occurred throughout much of the country. That was so except for one recent development in the area.

And that was a place called Babbage Town.

Sean King's small plane landed smoothly on the asphalt of the lone runway and came to a stop, its twin props winding down. A slate blue Hummer pulled up to the aircraft and a young, lanky black man in a private security uniform got out and helped Sean with his bags.

As the Hummer rolled along, Sean sat back and thought about his visit with Michelle before he'd headed to Babbage Town. He'd called Horatio to make sure it was okay to see her before he left. And, in turn, the psychologist had asked to see Michelle's personal things at the apartment Sean had leased for them both. Horatio had also wanted to see Michelle's truck.

"Just wear a mask and gloves," Sean had warned him, "and make sure your tetanus shot is up to date."

When Sean had seen Michelle in the visitor's room his spirits had been lifted by her healthy appearance. She even gave him a hug, listened to what he was saying and answered directly the questions he put to her.

"How long will you be gone to this Babbage Town place?" she'd asked after he'd told her about his new assignment.

"I'm not sure. I'm taking a private plane down that Joan arranged."

"And how is your paranoid schizophrenic slut of an *ex-friend* Joan?"

He took the comment as a sign of her returning spirit and said, "Well, she won't be coming with me. There's a guy down there named Len Rivest who's head of security for Babbage Town. He was with the FBI, knows Joan and recommended her firm. He'll be my main contact there."

"You said a man was murdered?"

"We don't know for sure. His name was Monk Turing. He worked at Babbage Town."

"What exactly is Babbage Town?"

"It's only been described to me as a secret think tank working on some important stuff."

"Who runs the place?"

"According to the file a guy named Champ Pollion."

"Monk? Champ?"

"I know; it's weird right from the get-go. But there'll be a nice payday if I can find out what happened to the guy."

"Is that how you can afford this place? I know my insurance doesn't cover it."

"All you need to do is get better. Let me worry about the rest of it."

"I am getting better. I feel good." Her voice sank lower. "And there's something weird going on *here*."

"Weird? What do you mean?"

"Sounds in the night. People moving around in places they shouldn't be."

Sean took a deep breath and said in a mildly scolding tone, "Will you promise me you won't get mixed up in it, whatever it is? I won't be around to help if you do."

"*You're* flying into the middle of nowhere to investigate a murder without me backing you up. I should be the one putting the screws to you."

"I promise I'll be careful."

"As soon as I'm out of here I'll come down and help you."

"I hear you and Horatio have really hit it off."

"I can't stand the son of a bitch."

"Good, then you *are* getting along."

A few minutes later he'd started to leave when she clutched his arm. "If things start getting really wild, call me. I can be down to help in a flash."

"I'll watch my backside."

"I don't think you can watch your front and back at the same time."

He pointed a finger at her. "The most important thing is for you to get yourself right. Then we can start being our perfect opposites–attract all–star detective team again."

"I'm looking forward to that."

"Me too."

Now he was heading to Babbage Town, alone, and regretting more than ever that Michelle wasn't with him. Yet his partner had a long road to travel back to good health and his mind was constantly preoccupied with the possibility that she might not succeed.

As they drove along beside the York River a scattering of birds rose into the air; at the same time a half–dozen deer flew across the road. The driver barely tapped his brakes. The flank of the last whitetail deer came within a couple inches of meeting the fender of the pumped–up SUV. All Sean could envision were antlers coming through the windshield and impaling him on the deep, rich Hummer leather.

"Get that a lot this time of year," the driver said in a bored tone.

"What's that, instant death?" Sean snapped.

He looked to his right where he could see the river through the patches of cleared fields. Beyond that he made out, just barely, the shiny chain link fencing topped by razor wire surrounding the land just across the York River.

"Camp Peary?" he asked, pointing.

"CIA spook land. Call it the Farm."

"I'd forgotten it was down here." Sean knew perfectly well it was there, but he was pretending ignorance in the hopes of getting some local intelligence.

"People who live around here never have trouble remembering."

"Small animals and children disappearing in the night?" Sean asked with a smile.

"No, but that plane you came in on? You can bet that a surface-to-air missile from the Farm was trained on your ass until you touched down. If the plane had wandered into restricted airspace, you would've come down out of the skies a lot faster than you would've wanted to."

"I'm sure. But I guess they bring a lot of jobs to the area."

"Yeah, but they also took stuff."

"What do you mean?" Sean asked.

"The Navy ran it first. When they came here they kicked everybody out."

"Everybody out?" Sean looked confused.

"Yeah, there were two towns over there: Magruder and Bigler's Mill. My grandparents lived in Magruder. During the war they got moved to James City County. Then the Navy vacated the place after the war but came back in the early Fifties. It's been off-limits ever since."

"Interesting."

"Yeah, wasn't so interesting for my grandparents. But the military does whatever the hell it wants."

"Well, you should take comfort in the fact that now it's just your neighborly CIA over there watching you through binoculars."

The man chuckled and Sean changed the subject. "Did you know Monk Turing?"

The man nodded. "Yeah."

"And?"

"And he was like everybody else at Babbage Town. Too much brains. We didn't exactly speak the same language."

"How long have you worked there?"

"Two years."

"Why does this place need security?"

"Important stuff they're working on."

"Like what?"

"Asking the wrong person. Has to do with numbers and computers. They'll probably tell you, if you ask them." He smiled. "Oh, yeah, they'll tell you in a way that you'll never understand, but there you are." The driver pointed up ahead. "Welcome to Babbage Town." He added with a grin, "Hope you enjoy your stay with us."

12

While Sean was working on his investigation, Michelle was intent on beginning one of her own. In the cafeteria she took her tray and made her way over to the table where the woman in the wheelchair was having lunch. Michelle sat down beside her and opened her bottle of water. She glanced over at the lady.

"I'm Michelle."

"Sandy," the woman said. "What are you in for?"

"I'm apparently suicidal," Michelle said bluntly.

The woman brightened. "So was I, for years, but you get over it. I mean I guess you do, unless you actually manage to kill yourself."

Michelle ran her gaze over the woman. She was in her late forties, long bottle blond hair meticulously styled, fine cheekbones, a pair of vibrant hazel eyes, and an ample bosom. Her makeup and fingernails were immaculate. Even though she was only wearing plain khaki pants, tennis shoes and a purple V-neck sweater, she carried it off with the confident air of a woman used to far more expensive things in life. Her voice had a Deep South foundation to it.

"So what are you in for?" Michelle asked.

"Depression, what else? My shrink says everybody's depressed. But I don't believe him. If everybody felt the way I did, well, I just don't believe him, is all."

"You seem okay to me."

"I think I have a chemical imbalance. I mean that's what everybody blames it on these days. But then like a snap, I just run out of energy. You seem okay too. Sure you're not in here goldbricking?"

"I've heard of goldbricking when you've been physically injured."

"People in lawsuits claiming emotional distress or mental trauma can help their case if they wind up in a place like this. You get a bed, three squares a day and all the meds you want. For some, that's nirvana. Then their shrink testifies how they'll never reach orgasm again or can't leave their homes without fainting and, bam, they get a big, fat settlement."

"Quite a scam."

Sandy added, "Oh, I'm not saying lots of people aren't legitimately screwed up, I happen to be one of them."

Michelle glanced at the woman's legs. "Accident?"

"I was shot in the spine by a nine-millimeter bullet fired from a Glock," she said matter-of-factly. "Instant and irreversible paralysis and in a split second outgoing, athletic Sandy became a poor crip."

"My God," Michelle exclaimed. "How'd that happen?"

"I was in the wrong place at the wrong time."

"Is that why you were suicidal? Because you were paralyzed?"

"The paralysis I could deal with. It was other crap that was hard to take," she added mysteriously.

"What other crap?" Michelle asked.

"Not going there. You think you're getting better?"

Michelle shrugged. "I think it's too early to say. Physically I feel okay."

"Well, you're young and pretty, so once the bruises heal you'll be fine to take control of your life."

"Take control of it how?"

"Get yourself a man with money, and let him take care of you. Use your looks, honey, that's why God gave them to you. And just remember this, title everything as joint tenants with right of survivorship. Don't swallow the line that his money is his money bullshit."

"You sound like you speak from experience."

Sandy gave a shudder. "God I wish they let you smoke in here, but they say nicotine is an addictive substance. I say give me my cigs and get out of my damn face."

"But you want to be here, right?" Michelle asked.

"Oh, we all want to be here, honey." She smiled and slid two pieces of asparagus neatly into her mouth.

Barry passed by, assisting a young man.

Michelle nodded at him. "You know that attendant, Barry?"

Sandy studied him for a moment. "I don't know him, but it's easy to tell that book by its cover."

"Where's home for you?"

"Definitely not where the heart is, sweetie. Now I've gotta go, I feel a migraine coming on and I don't like people to see me that way. You might change your high opinion of old Sandy."

She quickly wheeled herself away, leaving Michelle staring at her food.

After lunch, Michelle took a stroll that carried her by Sandy's room. As she slowly walked by she glanced in the square cut of Plexiglas in the middle of the woman's door. Sandy was lying asleep in her private room. Michelle continued on down the hall until she stopped at the locked door to the pharmacy. She glanced through the barred window and saw a short, balding man in a white coat dispensing a prescription. When he looked up and saw her she smiled. He turned his back to her and continued his work.

"Okay, you're off my Christmas card list," Michelle said to herself.

"Wandering again?" the voice said.

Michelle turned quickly to see Barry staring at her.

"What else is there to do?" she said.

"I can think of a few things. Your face looks better. Getting those killer cheekbones back."

"Thanks," she said curtly.

"I saw you talking to Sandy at lunch today," he remarked.

"Nice lady."

"I'd watch out for her."

"Oh, you know her well?"

"Let's just say I know people like her. They can be trouble. You don't want to get into trouble, right?"

"I never go looking for trouble," she lied.

"Good girl," he said condescendingly. "Look, if you ever need anything, don't hesitate to ask."

"Anything like what?"

He seemed both surprised and amused by her question.

"Anything means anything." Barry looked around and moved closer to her. "I mean I know it gets damn lonely in here for a hot babe like you."

"It never gets *that* lonely," she said walking off. Sandy had definitely been right about that book's cover.

Later that afternoon Horatio Barnes sat down across from Michelle.

"No tape recorder today?" she observed.

He tapped his head. "I took my vitamins today, so I've got it all up here. By the way, I talked to your brother."

Michelle sat forward, her look suddenly anxious. "How much did you tell him?"

"Just enough to let him follow along."

"Did you tell him about the bar?"

"Why would I tell him you went to a bar to get a drink and *accidentally* got in a fight with the Incredible Hulk."

"Stop screwing with me. Did you tell him?"

"I was actually more interested in what he had to say about you." He flipped back through his notebook. "He said you were a dynamo, with limitless energy and a drive that put everyone in the family to shame. A walking, talking tornado was his description. I'm sure he meant it with great affection. "

"Bill has been known to exaggerate."

"I think he was entirely accurate. But he also said something else interesting."

"What was that?"

"Care to guess?"

"Look, who the hell's playing games now. Just tell me!"

"He said that when you were little you were as neat as a pin. Everything in its place. They used to make fun of you. But then, bam, complete personality change."

"What's the big deal? I grew out of it. Now I'm a slob."

"You're right; it does happen, but not usually overnight at age *six*. If you'd been a teenager I wouldn't blink an eye. There's a chromosome that goes haywire when you turn thirteen. It commands you to live in filth while withstanding all threats by parents to clean up your act. I'm just wondering what the reason was in your case because it happened long before that chromosome ordinarily flips out."

"It was a long time ago. Who cares?"

"For our purposes the lapse of time doesn't really matter. What does matter is what was going on in your head at that time."

"You know, we've never really even talked about my relationship with a man who killed a bunch of people. I'm not a shrink, but don't you think that might be *relevant* as to why I'm so screwed up?"

"Okay, let's talk about him."

Michelle sat back and kneaded her fists into her thighs. "There's not a lot to tell really. He was good-looking and kind, an accomplished artist and an amazing athlete with an interesting background. He made me feel good about myself. He was in a bad marriage and was trying to make the best of it." She added sarcastically, "In fact his only negative was he just happened to be a mass murderer."

"And you can't believe that you were so easily duped by such a man?"

"It had never happened to *me* before?"

"But also consider that serial killers are notorious for being great deceivers; it's part of the psychological makeup that makes them who they are, and allows them to prey on their victims with such success. Ted Bundy is usually held up as the poster boy of that theory."

"Wow thanks, that makes me feel so much better."

"And because of that one incident you just chuck years of professional success and sound instincts? Do you think that's reasonable?"

"I don't care if it's reasonable, it's how I feel."

"Do you think you loved him?"

She pondered this. "I think maybe I could have, given time. And every time I think that, I want to slit my wrists. The bastard tried to kill me and would've if Sean hadn't been there."

"Sean to the rescue. For which you were no doubt very grateful."

"Of course I was."

"I understand that while you were having your relationship, Sean was also seeing someone?"

Michelle said dully, "He's a big boy; he can do what he wants."

"But from what he said, that turned out to be a big mistake too."

"You bet it did."

"You think Sean's a smart man?"

"One of the smartest I've ever met."

"And yet he was deceived too."

"But he figured it all out. Me, I was still in la-la land."

"How did you feel about Sean and this woman?"

"Like I said, he's a big boy."

"That's not what I asked you."

She snapped, "I felt bad about it, okay? Are you satisfied?"

"Bad because he chose her over you?"

Her eyes narrowed. "You don't have a lot of tact, do you?"

"We'll assume that I don't. But is that how you felt?"

"I think I felt he was making a fool of himself."

"Why?"

"She was a witch. Desperate to get her claws in him. And she was a murderer too though we could never prove it."

"So you suspected her of being a killer while Sean was seeing her?"

Michelle hesitated. "No, I didn't. There was just something about her that I didn't like."

"So your instincts proved right with her."

Michelle sat back. "I guess so. I never thought about that really."

"Well, that's why I'm here, to help you think of these things. And patients often contribute to the healing process perhaps without even knowing they are."

"How so?"

"Like when you were in that bar. Part of you was looking for someone to hurt, to maybe even kill. Yet another part of you was looking for someone who could actually punish you, kill *you*. The result was you got the shit beat out of you, but you didn't die, and I believe you had no real intention of doing so."

"How are you so sure?" she said mockingly.

"Because people who really want to die use methods that are basically foolproof." He ticked items off on his fingers. "A shotgun blast to the head, hanging, gas in the oven or poison down the throat. Those people don't want help; they want to die and they almost always do. You didn't die because you didn't really want to."

"Suppose you're right, now what?"

"Now I want to talk about Michelle Maxwell as a six-year-old."

"You go to hell!" Michelle stalked out of the room and slammed the door behind her.

Horatio screwed the top back on his pen and smiled contentedly. "Finally, we're getting somewhere."

13

To Sean's eye the enormous brick and stone mansion ran at least two hundred feet in length and soared three stories into the overcast sky. It combined a number of architectural styles with at least eight chimney stacks that Sean could see; there was a proper British glass conservatory, gabled windows, a Tuscany-style veranda, mullioned windows, an Asian-influenced tower and a copper-plated domed wing. It had been built, according to Joan, by Isaac Rance Peterman, who'd made a fortune in the meat-packing industry. He'd named the place after his daughter, Gwendolyn. Her name was still on the entrance columns. To Sean's mind the appellation could not have been more inappropriate as Gwendolyn looked like an overdressed fort with an identity crisis.

There was a cobblestone car park in front and the Hummer pulled through the gates where a uniformed guard was stationed and into an empty space next to a trim black Mercedes convertible.

A few minutes later, Sean's bags were in his room

and he was sitting alone in the office of Champ Pollion, the head of Babbage Town. The room was littered with books, laptops, charts, electronic gadgets and printouts containing symbols and formulas that Sean, even at a glance, knew he could never hope to decipher. Hanging on the back of the door was a white martial arts jacket and pants with a black belt attached. *So a genius with lethal hands. Wonderful.*

A moment later the door opened and Champ Pollion came in. In his late thirties he was as tall as Sean, but thinner. His brown hair had a small patch of gray on top and was neatly parted on the side. He wore a pair of khaki pants, tweed jacket with soft leather elbow patches, white button–down shirt, V-neck sweater and paisley bow tie. Sean half-expected to see a pipe swinging in one of the man's hands to complete this picture of the 1940s-era scholar.

The man sat in his desk chair, leaned back, put his size-thirteen scuffed loafers up on the book-strewn desk, and glanced anxiously at Sean.

"I'm Champ Pollion. You're Sean King." Sean nodded. "Would you like some coffee?"

"Thanks."

Champ ordered the coffee, then sat back in his chair.

"So the FBI's involved in the case?" Sean asked.

Champ nodded. "Having the police and FBI running around, no one likes it."

"And Turing was found on CIA property?"

"Why in the world would Monk have gone there? Those men have guns for God's sake."

"And you have men with guns here too," Sean pointed out.

"If I had my way there wouldn't be. But I merely run Babbage Town, so it's not my call."

"And you need guards here why?"

"Our work here has potentially enormous commercial application. We are in a sort of race against time. Others in the world would love to beat us. Hence, we have guards. Everywhere." He waved his hand distractedly. "Everywhere."

"Has the CIA been here yet?"

"Well, spies hardly ever walk up and say, 'Hello, we're the CIA, tell me all you know or we'll kill you.'" Champ pulled from his jacket pocket what looked like a thin glass tube.

"Did you just come from your lab?" Sean asked.

Champ looked suspicious. "Why?"

"That little thing you're holding. It looks like a big eyedropper although I'm sure you have some technical name for it."

"This *little thing* could well be the greatest invention ever, leaving Bell's telephone or Edison's light bulb a distant second."

Sean looked startled. "What the hell is it?"

"It might well be the fastest nonclassical computer in the history of the universe if we can only get the damn thing to work up to its enormous potential.

This isn't a working model, of course, only a conceptual prototype. Now getting back to what's happened here. There have been lots of people through Babbage Town recently. That included the local police in the person of a doddering old duffer in a Stetson hat named Merkle Hayes who says, 'Good Lord' a lot, and several stalwart members of the aforementioned FBI." He put the tube down and looked up at Sean. "You know what I think?"

"What?"

"I think there's some massive conspiracy going on. Not involving the CIA. They'd be too obvious a choice, wouldn't they? No, I believe it has to do with the military-industrial complex that President Eisenhower warned the country about before he left office."

Sean tried to hide his skepticism. "And how would that tie into Monk Turing's body being found at Camp Peary?"

"Because right next to Camp Peary is the *Naval* Weapons Station. And Camp Peary used to belong to the *Navy*."

"Does what you're working on have *military* applications?"

"I'm afraid I can't say."

"But you're not working for the government?"

"Does this look like a government facility to you," he said sharply.

"Maybe." Sean glanced over at the martial arts uniform on the door. "Karate? Kung fu?"

"Tae Kwon Do. My father made me start taking it when I entered high school."

"So he was into martial arts?"

"No, he made me take it so I could defend myself at school. It may shock you to learn that I was something of a *nerd*, Mr. King. And if it's one thing teenage boys hate, particularly teenage boys whose neck size is larger than their IQ, it's a nerd." Champ glanced at his watch and then picked up some papers on his desk.

Noting this Sean said quickly, "I'll need to go over the details of the case. If you don't want to regurgitate them again, I can always speak with Len Rivest."

At that moment a short, stocky, gray-haired woman came in carrying a coffee tray. She handed out the cups, sugar and spoons.

Champ said, "Doris, would you ask Len Rivest to join us?"

After she left Sean turned back to Champ. "So while we're waiting, without revealing anything confidential, what exactly is Babbage Town? The driver didn't really know how to explain it."

Champ didn't look inclined to answer.

"Just background, Champ, that's all."

"Have you ever heard of Charles Babbage?"

"No."

"He was instrumental in developing the blueprint for the modern computer; no small feat when you consider the man was born in 1791. He also invented the speedometer. As a lover of statistics he drew up a set of mortality tables, a standard tool in the insurance industry today. And whenever you send a letter you use the single postal rate that Babbage conceived. But in my mind the most amazing thing that Charles Babbage did was break the Vigenère polyalphabetic cipher, which had withstood all decryption attempts for nearly three centuries."

"Vigenère polyalphabetic cipher?"

Champ nodded. "Blaise de Vigenère was a French diplomat who fashioned the cipher in the sixteenth century. It was known as a *poly*alphabetic because it used multiple alphabets instead of simply one. However, it lay unused for nearly two hundred years because people thought it was too complex, to hell with it being impregnable to frequency analysis. Do you know about frequency analysis?"

"Sounds familiar," Sean said slowly.

"It was the holy grail of the early code-breaking community. Muslims invented it in the ninth century. Now frequency analysis means what it says. You analyze how often certain letters appear in writing. In English the letter e is the most common by far, followed by the letter t and then a. That's immensely helpful in decoding ciphers, or at least it was. Today decryption is based on the length of secret number keys and the power and speed of computers to factor those keys. All the linguistic romance has been ripped right out of it.

"A thousand years ago the substitution cipher was thought unbreakable. Yet the Muslims managed to blow it right out of the water and gave the cryptanalysts the upper hand over the encryption people for centuries. That's why the Vigenère cipher was so revolutionary, frequency analysis was useless against it."

Sean squirmed a bit in his seat in the face of this lengthy history lesson.

"Forgive me, Mr. King, but I promise I'll have a point at the end."

"No, it's very interesting," Sean said, stifling a yawn.

"Now, as I said frequency analysis was useless against the Vigenère monster, so craftily and uniquely was it designed. And yet old Charlie Babbage managed to put a knife right through its numeric heart."

"How?" Sean asked.

"He attacked it from a direction that was absolutely original and indeed set the standard for cryptanalysts for generations to come. And yet he received no recognition for it because he never bothered to publish his research."

"So how did Babbage's discovery become known?"

"When scholars went over his notes in the twentieth century, long after the man was dead, they determined that he had been the first to do it. And at long last, here is my point. I christened this place Babbage Town as a homage to a man with a great brain but little ability in *self-promotion*. However, if we achieve our goals here, have no doubt that we will scream it to the heavens." Champ smiled. "After we secure all necessary patents ensuring that we will be fabulously rich once commercial exploitations of our various inventions commence."

"So you get a piece of the pie?"

"I wouldn't be here otherwise. Yet even if we don't make a fortune the work is exhilarating."

"So who owns Babbage Town?"

The door opened and a short, barrel-chested man in his early fifties walked in wearing a two-piece suit with a muted tie. His silver hair was gelled down and his eyes were blue and alert. He looked from Sean to Champ.

Champ said, "Len, Sean King."

On that note, Champ took his nifty, if nonclassical and nonworking, glass tube computer, and walked out. It was only then that Sean fully realized the man had said a lot and told him nothing.

14

Horatio Barnes parked his Harley outside the rental apartments near Fairfax Corner, took the keys to Sean and Michelle's place out of his pocket and then hesitated. Should he check out the truck or condo first? He decided on the Toyota Land Cruiser. It was parked near the entrance to the apartment building.

Horatio unlocked the driver's side door of the truck and swung it open.

"Holy shit!" was his first reaction. Sean hadn't been kidding about getting his tetanus shot and wearing a mask. The middle and back cargo areas were so filled with stuff that Horatio couldn't see the floorboards. Sports equipment, melted PowerBars, bottles of Gatorade, trash, moldy food, a box of twelve-gauge shotgun shells, wrinkled clothes, and a pair of plastic-coated dumbbells littered the truck's interior. Horatio picked up one of the dumbbells with some effort, then glanced through one of the martial arts magazines piled in the back.

"Okay, note to esteemed but cowardly psychologist.

Never really piss the lady off because she will kick your scrawny, middle-aged ass."

He sat in the middle seat for a bit with the windows down and thought it over. A type-A wound tighter than a golf ball's innards, and this is what he was looking at? Total, trash-filled chaos?

He walked up to the apartment on the second level and went inside. He easily discerned Sean's very ordered influence here and also which bedroom was his. The second bedroom had Michelle's things stacked neatly, clothes hung in the closet, and no trash on the floor, only because the woman had never been here. There was a locked gun safe in the top of the closet where presumably Michelle kept her pistol.

Out on the small balcony was Michelle's racing scull. It was polished to perfection with a pair of pristine oars next to it. Horatio went back inside. On the table just inside the small foyer was a stack of mail, which he looked through. Most were addressed to Sean, having been forwarded from his previous address. Others were the typical bills and marketing pitches that all of humanity suffered through. Yet there was one more piece of mail; it was a letter addressed to Michelle Maxwell, and it was from her parents in Hawaii. This was probably just a note to let Michelle know how much fun they were having.

As he was wandering around an idea struck Horatio. He called Bill Maxwell in Florida. The man picked up on the second ring.

"This a bad time?" Horatio asked. "If you're on a high-speed chase just put me on hold and I'll wait until either you nail the bad guys or I hear the sounds of a car crash."

Bill chuckled. "I'm off-duty today. I was actually getting ready to do some fishing. What's up? How's Mick?"

Horatio had quickly learned from Bill Maxwell that all her siblings called their sister Mick. It was a very brotherly thing to do, he understood.

"Getting better all the time. Look, do your parents still live in Tennessee?"

"That's right. In a new house they had built after Pop retired. All the kids chipped in to help. Police chiefs make pretty good money, but with so many kids, there wasn't a whole lot of savings. This was a way to say thanks."

"That's really cool, Bill. So do you see your parents much?"

"Probably four or five times a year. I'm way down here in Tampa. Flights are expensive and it's a long drive to Tennessee and I've got three kids of my own."

"Your other brothers see them much?"

"Probably more than I do. They live closer. Why do you want to know?"

"Just trying to flesh things out. And Michelle? I'm assuming she sees your parents a lot. She lives just next door in Virginia."

"I don't think that's true. Mick was never at Mom

and Dad's place when I was there. And I talk to my brothers pretty regularly. They never mention seeing her at our parents'."

"Maybe your folks went to see her."

"She never really lived in a place that had room for visitors," Bill replied. "I tried a couple times, because my kids love her to death and they think it's really cool that their aunt is an Olympian and guarded the president. But I got some weird vibes from her and never took the kids."

"What sort of weird vibes?"

"She was always too busy. Now when she was with the Secret Service I could understand that. But when she went into the private sector, you'd think she'd have some free time, but it never happened."

"When's the last time you saw your sister?"

"A few years ago, and it was only because I was in Washington for a cop convention. We had dinner. She was still with the Service back then."

"Do you feel that she's estranged from your family?"

"I didn't until you started asking all these questions."

"I'm sorry to seem to be prying, Bill, but I'm doing all I can do to get her better."

"Look, I know that. I mean, she is cool if quirky."

"Quirky, yes. I was just looking at her truck."

Bill laughed. "You call the infectious disease people yet?"

"I assume you've seen it."

"She gave me a ride to dinner when I was in town that time. I held my breath and took two showers when I got back to my hotel."

"You ever see any excessive hand washing, checking doors before going out, or chairs before sitting down? Anything like that?"

"You mean OCD stuff? No, nothing that I recall."

"And age six, things changed, you said? You're sure?"

"I'd finished college, and wasn't around much, but when I came back home for a couple months I remember she was a different person. They were living in a little town about an hour south of Nashville."

"And it couldn't simply be put down to a kid's personality changing as she grows older? That happens you know."

"It was more than that, Horatio. My kids have changed too, but nothing that abrupt."

"You said outgoing to withdrawn. Gregarious to shy. Trusting to suspicious. And she would cry?"

"Only at night."

"And she became sloppy in her personal habits?"

"I remember it being mostly the floor in her room. Before, it was as neat as a pin. Then, overnight, there was junk everywhere. You couldn't even see the carpet. I always just put it down to her being an independent hellion."

"That would explain some things, Bill, but not *all* the things I'm seeing. And in my field when things are inexplicable, I have to find out why, because somewhere, and it may be buried deep, there *is* an explanation." Horatio paused. "Okay, I'm glad you're about a thousand miles away because of the next question I'm going to ask."

"Mick was never abused."

"I see you've given this some thought."

"I'm a cop. I've seen abused kids, some real nightmare situations, and Michelle wasn't like that at all. She never exhibited any of the signals. And Pop would never, I mean, he wasn't like that. And being a cop he wasn't home that much anyway. I tell you this, I love my old man, but if I thought for a second anything like that had been going on, I would've done something about it. I didn't become a cop because I like looking the other way."

"I'm sure, Bill. But did your parents have an explanation for the change in her? Did they ever seek professional help?"

"Not that I knew of. I mean it wasn't like she was throwing nonstop tantrums or cutting up small animals. And back then, you didn't run to a shrink with every little thing and put your kid on Ritalin because he can't sit still for ten minutes; no offense, Doc."

"Hey, I know plenty of psychiatrists who should properly be labeled pharmacists. Do you ever talk to your parents about Michelle?"

"I think we've all just decided to let her go her own way. If she ever wants to rejoin the family, we're here for her."

"And you didn't tell them about her current situation?"

"Nope. If Mick didn't want them to know, it wasn't my place to tell them. Plus, you think I want a black belt Olympian dead-eye shot pissed at me, sister or not?"

"She scares me too. Anything else you can think of that might help me?"

"Just give me my little sister back, Horatio. You do that, you've got a friend in Tampa for life."

15

Len Rivest led Sean around the grounds of Babbage Town. Behind the mansion was a network of buildings of various sizes. Sean observed that every door had a security panel next to it. One of the largest buildings covered about a quarter of an acre and was surrounded by a seven-foot fence. It had what looked to be a grain silo attached to it.

Sean pointed to the silo. "What's in that thing?"

"Water. They need it to cool some equipment."

"And in the other buildings?"

"Other things."

"And which one did Monk Turing work in? And what did he do here?"

"I was hoping I could avoid saying."

"Len, I was under the impression that *you* hired *us* to help find out how Monk Turing died. If you don't want us to do that, just say so and I can get on back home and stop wasting everybody's time. I've just spent a half-hour being told nothing by that Champ guy, I don't intend on repeating the process with you."

Rivest dug his hands in his pockets. "I'm sorry,

Sean. I know you were at the Service with Joan, and I don't like playing cat and mouse like this with a fellow fed. Between you and me I think the powers-that-be are having second thoughts about private investigators being here."

"And who are the powers-that-be?"

"If I knew that I'd tell you."

Sean gaped. "Are you telling me you don't know who you're working for?"

"If someone has enough money they can cover their tracks pretty well. My paycheck says I work for Babbage Town, LLC. I got curious once and tried to track down the corporate identity a little further and was told any other attempt to do the same would result in my ass being canned. This job pays far better than anything I've ever had before. I got two kids in college. I don't want to blow it."

"So how do you know they're having second thoughts?"

"I get private communications on my computer each day. I told them you were already on the plane, and that you should at least have a chance to take a crack at this thing. Because it might get dicey."

"Because of the FBI's and CIA's involvement?"

Rivest scowled. "Camp Peary of all damn places. But if you can solve it fast and hopefully show it has nothing to do with Babbage Town then maybe our problems go away."

"But if it does have to do with Babbage Town?"

"Then I probably start looking for another job."

"Champ Pollion thinks it has to do with some big conspiracy orchestrated by the military-industrial complex."

Rivest groaned. "Please, I've got enough problems without wasting time on bullshit theories coming from that geek."

"Okay, let's focus on the basics. How did Monk Turing die?"

"Gunshot wound to the head. Gun was next to the body."

"Where exactly was he found at Camp Peary?"

"Extreme eastern end of the complex that fronts the York River. You would've passed it coming down here if you'd looked across the water."

"Fenced-in area?"

"Yeah, his body was lying just inside it. Evidence on the corpse indicates he climbed over. I'm sure the area's patrolled, but apparently not 24/7. There're thousands of acres to Camp Peary, and much of it undeveloped. Even the CIA doesn't have the money to secure every square inch of it. Monk got in there somehow."

"Where's the body now?"

"A temp morgue was set up in White Feather, a small town fairly close to here. A medical examiner from Williamsburg did the post. There's no doubt about the cause of death. I've seen the body and the report. But feel free to take a look."

"Okay. Was Turing married?"

"Divorced. We're still trying to locate the ex. No luck so far."

"Kids?"

"One. Viggie Turing, age eleven."

"Where's she now?"

"Right here. She lived with her father in Babbage Town." He inclined his head toward some cottages. "The buildings on the perimeter over there are housing for the people working here. Some of them live in the mansion too."

"Is Viggie a nickname or a family name?"

"It's short for Vigenère or so I heard."

Sean said, "After Blaise de Vigenère?"

"Who?"

"Never mind. Turing have any known enemies?"

"Well, he had at least one *unknown* one."

"But what about the suicide theory? Near contact wound, gun found nearby?"

"Could be," Rivest conceded slowly. "But my gut tells me otherwise."

"Sometimes the gut is wrong."

"It worked for me at the FBI for twenty-five years. And it's telling me something's wrong here."

"I'll want to talk to Viggie."

"You're going to have a hard time pulling anything out of that kid."

"Why's that?"

"If she's not a little autistic, she's something close. Monk could reach her, but nobody else really can."

"Does she even know her dad's dead?"

"Let's put it this way, no one really knows how to break it to her. But it won't be pretty."

"Why, is she a violent child?"

Rivest shook his head. "She's quiet and shy and one helluva pianist."

"So what's her problem?"

"She lives in her own world, Sean. You can be talking to her normally and all of a sudden it's like she disappears. She just doesn't communicate on the same level as you and me."

"Has she been evaluated by a professional?"

"Don't know."

Sean thought of Horatio Barnes. "If it comes down to it, I might have someone who can help. Who's looking after her now?"

"Alicia Chadwick among others."

"And who is she?"

"She works in one of the departments here. I said Monk was the only one who got through to Viggie. But Alicia seems to be able to do it too, if on a limited basis."

"Who found Monk's body?"

"A guard on patrol at Camp Peary."

"Any forensics at the crime scene to suggest any leads?"

"None that I know of."

"The gun?"

"It was Turing's. He had a permit for it."

"Were his prints on the gun?"

"It seems like they were."

"It *seems* like they were? Either they were or they weren't!"

"Okay, they were. There was also nothing to suggest he'd been bound and no defensive wounds." Rivest blurted out, "Look, maybe a damn Camp Peary guard pulled the trigger."

"Using Turing's gun?"

"Monk was trespassing. A guard shot him and they're trying to cover it up."

Sean shook his head. "If he was trespassing the guard would have a good reason to kill him. Covering it up just digs the hole deeper. And you wouldn't use Monk's own gun to do the deed."

"Who the hell knows with the CIA?" Rivest protested.

"The second reason is even stronger. Monk was killed with a near contact wound. If a guard was close enough to do that he could've arrested Monk without killing him."

"They got in a scuffle and the gun went off accidentally?" Rivest suggested.

"But there was no evidence of a fight, you said."

Rivest sighed. "Who the hell knows where the real truth lies."

"So what's the CIA position?"

"That he climbed over the fence and shot himself."

"You obviously don't think that?"

Rivest looked around uneasily. "There're a lot of eyes around here."

"Meaning what?"

"Meaning a place like this, there might be spies."

"Spies? Why do you think that?"

"No proof. Just my gut again."

"Anything turn up in Turing's personal possessions?" Sean asked.

"The Bureau's taken all that stuff. His computer, papers, passport, etc."

"Who was the last person to see Monk alive?"

Rivest said, "It might have been his daughter."

"Doesn't the Bureau have experts who can help with her?"

Rivest seemed to welcome this change in topics. "They brought one of these so-called experts down and she got nowhere with the kid."

Sean thought again about his Harley-riding friend Horatio Barnes and decided he would give him a call later. He was torn, though, because he wanted Horatio to focus on getting Michelle well.

Rivest continued, "He was seen at dinner the night before his body was discovered. After that he went to do some follow-up work in his department."

"How do you know that?" Sean said, sharply.

"The computer log showed him leaving there at eight-thirty. His movements after that are just speculation."

"How'd he get to Camp Peary? Did he swim or take a boat? Or drive?"

"I don't see how he could have driven. You can't get to that part of the compound without going through the main gate. And we can't tell if he swam over or not. Because of all the rain his body and clothes were soaked through. But it'd be a long haul across the river."

"By process of elimination he probably went by boat. Any found nearby?"

"No."

"Are there any boats kept here?"

"Oh, sure. Some rowboats and kayaks; there's a large sailboat and a few racing sculls. And there're a couple of powerboats owned by Babbage Town."

"So lots of watercraft available; but none missing?"

"Right. But if someone did take him over, they could have just put the boat back in its place and who would know?"

"Where are they kept?" Sean asked.

"At a boathouse down by the river."

"Anybody hear a motorboat on the night Monk was killed?"

Rivest shook his head. "But the boathouse is a good ways away with forest in between. It's conceivable nothing would've been heard."

"We seem to be hitting a wall everywhere."

"You feel like a drink?" Rivest asked.

"You think I need one?"

"No, I do. Come on, we'll have some dinner, a few drinks, and then tomorrow I'll tell you more about Babbage Town than you'll ever want to know."

"Tell me this much, is it worth somebody getting killed over?"

In the fading sunlight, Rivest stared over Sean's shoulder at the mansion. "Hell, Sean, it's worth countries going to war over."

16

It was one a.m. when over the sounds of Cheryl's light snoring Michelle heard footsteps in the hallway again. Already dressed, she stepped out in the hallway in her stocking feet and followed the person. It was Barry's tread, she was pretty sure.

She stopped as the footsteps up ahead halted. Michelle looked around. She was on the corridor headed to Sandy's room. She hadn't believed Barry when he'd said he didn't know the woman. His explanation had been too clumsy. Her ears perked up as the person started walking again.

She slid forward, her gaze sweeping across the dimmed lights of the hallway ahead. She heard a door open and close. Michelle edged forward and peered around the corner. There was a light on at the end of the hallway. Then it went out. She ducked back behind the wall when another door opened and closed. After waiting about five minutes, Michelle heard a door open and close again. The footsteps started coming back toward her. She looked around for someplace to hide.

She ducked inside an empty room and crouched next to the door. When the person walked past she peered through the window in the top half of the door. It *wasn't* Barry. The person was too small. She didn't get a good look at him because he had on a hat and his coat collar was turned up. When he disappeared from her line of sight she left the room and debated whether to follow him or go and see where he had been. She finally opted for the latter. She crept down the hall, turned the corner and continued on.

At the end of the hall was the door to the pharmacy. Was that the one she'd heard open and close? She looked to her left. Sandy's room was here too. She peered through the glass of the woman's door. Sandy was asleep in her bed or at least she seemed to be.

As Michelle glanced down at the floor, her gaze caught on something. She stooped and picked it up. It was a piece of white puffy plastic that people used in shipping boxes. She put it in her pocket, looked once more at Sandy sleeping and quietly made her way back to her room.

The next morning Michelle woke early and made the rounds of the corridors. She passed Sandy's room as the woman wheeled herself out into the hall. Sandy wore a Red Sox ball cap and a generous smile.

"How's the migraine?" Michelle asked.

"All gone. One good night of sleep usually does it. Thanks for asking."

"When's your shrink session?"

"My first is at eleven. Then there's a group session after lunch. Then they give me my drugs. Then a counselor comes and sees me. Then I get another little pop of joy pills and then go gab with some more strangers. At that point, I'm so looped I couldn't give a shit. I'll tell 'em whatever they want to hear. Like my mom breast-fed me until I left for the prom, stuff like that. They eat it up and then go write articles on it for the medical journals while I'm laughing my ass off."

"I don't think I could do the group thing," Michelle said.

Sandy spun her wheelchair around in a tight circle. "Oh, it's easy. All you have to do is get up, or, in my case, remain seated, and say, 'Hi, I'm Sandy and I'm screwed up so bad, but I want to do something about it. That's why I'm here.' And then everybody claps and throws you kisses and tells you how brave you are. And then I get a sleeping pill and crash for ten hours and get up and do it all over again."

"Sounds like you have the routine down pat."

"Oh, honey, I'm at the point where I see the questions coming before they even ask them. It's cat and mouse stuff, only they haven't figured out that I'm the cat and they're the mouse."

"You ever try and address whatever's *actually* making you depressed?"

"Hell no, then it gets way too complicated. The

truth will not set me free, it'll just make me suicidal. So until they let me out of here, I dance my little jig"—she slapped the wheels of her chair—"figuratively speaking of course, and Sandy goes with the flow, so long as they keep giving me my pills."

"Are you in a lot of pain?"

"When people tell you you're paralyzed from the waist down, you think to yourself, 'Okay, that's a real *bitch*, but at least I can't feel anything hurting.' Wrong with a capital fucking W. What they don't tell you is how much being paralyzed hurts. The bullet that took my legs away is still inside me. The quacks said it was too close to my spine to remove. So it just sits there, that little nine-millimeter son of a bitch. And every year or so it moves a tiny bit. Ain't that something? *I* can't move but *it* can. And the real zinger is the quacks say that if it ever hits against a certain place on my spine, I might just drop dead, or lose the feeling in the rest of my body and become a full-fledged quad. How 'bout that? Isn't that just too screwed up for words?"

Michelle said, "I'm really sorry. My problems don't seem like such a big deal now."

Sandy waved this remark off. "Let's go get some breakfast. The eggs are for shit and the bacon looks like pieces of tire tread and tastes worse, but at least the coffee's hot. Come on, I'll race you." Sandy took off and Michelle, smiling, trotted after her, then grabbed the wheelchair's handles and sprinted down the hallway, Sandy screaming with laughter the whole way.

After breakfast, Michelle met with Horatio.

"I talked with your brother Bill again."

"And how is Bill?"

"Good. He doesn't see you much, though. That goes for the rest of the family."

"We're all busy."

He handed her the letter from her mother.

"I was at your and Sean's apartment and picked it up. I know you haven't seen the place, but it's really nice. I'm glad I got to see it before you trashed it like your truck. Speaking of major landfills, ever think of cleaning your Toyota out? I mean just from the perspective of preventing bubonic plague."

"My truck might be a little messy, but I know where everything is."

"Yeah, about two hours after I eat spicy Mexican I know what's inside my colon, but that doesn't mean I want to see it. You want to read the letter from your parents? It might be important."

"If it were, they would've reached me some other way."

"Do they keep in touch with you?"

Michelle crossed her arms. "So is this parents day with the shrink?"

Horatio held up his notepad. "It says right here that I have to ask."

"I talk to my parents."

"But you almost never visit them. Although they're not that far away."

"Lots of kids don't visit their parents. It doesn't mean they don't love them."

"True. Do you feel like you have a chip on your shoulder being the only girl and your big brothers and father being cops?"

"I prefer to think of it as healthy motivation."

"Okay, do you like the fact that you pretty much can physically dominate any man you come across?"

"I like to be able to take care of myself. It's a violent world out there."

"And being in law enforcement, you've seen more than your share of that. And it's men who commit the vast majority of violent crimes, isn't that right?"

"Too many men tend to lead with their muscle instead of their mind."

"Do you still want to hurt yourself?"

"You have the most awkward segues of any person I've ever met."

"I like to think of them as something to wake you up in case you were starting to doze off."

"I never wanted to hurt myself in the first place."

"Okay, I'll just check that one off in the 'I'm lying my ass off' box, and we'll move on. So what do you see as the problem? And how do you think I can help you?"

Michelle looked nervously away.

"It's not a trick question, Michelle. I want you to

get better. I can sense you want to get better. So how do we get there?"

"We're talking, isn't that something?"

"It is. But at this rate I'll be long dead and buried and you'll be sucking your dinner through a straw before we figure out what makes you tick. There's no rule against going for the point of least resistance."

Michelle blurted out, "I don't know what you want from me, Horatio."

"Honesty, candidness, a real desire to participate in this exercise we call soul searching. I know the questions to ask, but the questions don't help if the answers to them mean nothing."

"I'm trying to be honest with you. Ask me a question."

"Do you love your brothers?"

"Yes!"

"Do you love your parents?"

Again she said yes. But Horatio cocked his head at the way she said it.

"Will you talk to me about your childhood?"

"Is that what every shrink thinks? It all comes down to crap that happened when you were a kid? Well, you're running down the wrong road."

"Then point me in the right direction. It's all up in your head. You know it is, you just have to suck it up and have the courage to tell me."

Michelle stood, trembling with rage. "Where the hell do you get off questioning my courage, or my ability to suck it up? You wouldn't have lasted ten minutes in my shoes."

"I don't doubt it. But the answer to your problems is between your left and right frontal lobes. It's a distance of about four inches and quite remarkable in that it contains trillions of bits of thoughts and memories that make you, you. If we get to just the right piece of you stuck away up there we can reach the point where you'll never pick another fight with a guy hoping he'll send you straight to the morgue."

"I'm telling you that didn't happen!"

"And I'm telling you, you're full of shit."

Michelle balled up her fists and screamed, "Do you *want* me to hurt you?"

"Do *you* want to hurt me?" he shot back.

Michelle stood there, glaring down at him. Then she let her hands drop, turned and walked out of the room, this time leaving the door open behind her, perhaps symbolically he thought, if unconsciously.

Horatio remained in his chair, his gaze on the doorway. "I'm pulling for you, Michelle," he said quietly. "And I think we're almost there."

17

After dinner in the mansion's dining room Sean and Rivest went back to Rivest's cottage to drink. After some wine and three vodka martinis Les Rivest fell asleep in his living room armchair after promising to meet with Sean the next day. That left Sean, who'd only sipped on his gin and tonic, to slip out and take a stroll around Babbage Town. Rivest had given Sean a security badge with his photo on it. The badge didn't enable him to enter any of the buildings other than the mansion unaccompanied, but it would prevent his being stopped and detained by the compound's security force.

Rivest's bungalow was on the western edge of the main grounds and off the same graveled path as three other cookie-cutter residences. Near Rivest's place was a far larger building. As Sean walked past it he noted the sign over one of the two front doors. It read: Hut Number Three. It seemed to be split into two equal premises. Sean watched as two uniformed guards armed with Glock pistols and MP5s came out the left front door and walked off, presumably on their rounds. That was a lot of fire-power. *But for what?*

He reversed direction, passing the rear courtyard of the mansion where an Olympic-size pool was located along with chairs, tables and umbrellas, an outdoor, stainless steel grill and a stone fireplace. A group of people were gathered around the fireplace, beers and wineglasses in hand, talking quietly. A couple of heads turned in his direction, but no one made an effort to greet him. Sean noted one person sitting off by himself nursing a beer. Sean sat down next to him and introduced himself.

The man was young, and looked nervously at his shoes. He had known Monk, worked with him, he said.

"And your field is?" Sean asked.

"Molecular physics, with a specialization in . . ." The young man hesitated and took a swallow of beer. "So what do you think happened to Monk?"

"Don't know yet. He ever talk to you about anything he was into that could've gotten him killed?"

"No way, nothing like that. He worked hard, like all of us. He has a daughter. She's sort of, well, she's special. Super-bright, I mean things she can do with numbers, even I can't do. But Viggie is one odd bird, though. Guess what she collects?"

"Tell me?"

"Numbers."

"Numbers? How do you collect numbers?"

"She has all these amazingly long numbers she keeps in her head. And she keeps thinking of new ones. She labels them using letters. You ask her for the 'x' number or the 'zz' number you get the right one every time. I've tested her. It's astonishing. I've never seen anything like it."

"Monk ever talk to you about Camp Peary? Maybe wanting to go there for some reason?"

The man shook his head.

"You knew about it, though, right?"

"Can't hardly miss it, can you." A few people from the pool area were pointing over at them. The kid quickly rose. "Excuse me, I've got to go."

Sean continued his walk. Nobody at this place was prepared to talk. Yet if Monk Turing *had* killed himself, there had to be a reason. With enough digging, that motivation would surface, Sean was sure of it.

He stopped near the building with the water tower attached. The sign on this building read Hut Number Two. As he approached the front entrance an armed guard stepped forward and put a hand up.

Sean held out his badge and explained who he was. The guard scrutinized the security badge and then eyed him. "Heard they were sending someone down."

"Did you know Monk Turing?" Sean asked.

"No. I mean I know what he looked like but fraternization between the guards and the brains is not encouraged."

"Any peculiar behavior that you noticed?"

The guard laughed. "Man, all these guys are pretty much whack jobs in my book. Too much smarts can be a bad thing, you know what I mean?"

Sean motioned toward the building. "So what's Hut Number Two?"

"You can ask, but I won't tell. Not that I know all that much anyway."

Sean tried two or three more times to get additional information but, to his credit, the guard held firm.

"You wouldn't happen to know where Turing lived on the grounds?" he finally asked.

The guard pointed down a path with trees bordering either side. "First right, second bungalow on the right."

"His daughter living there?"

The man nodded. "Along with somebody from Child Services. And an armed guard."

"Armed guard?"

"Her dad's dead. You take precautions."

"This place looks pretty well guarded actually," Sean remarked.

"So's Camp Peary, but someone managed to kill Monk Turing over there."

"So you think he was murdered? Not a suicide?"

Now the guard looked uncertain. "Hey, I'm not the detective."

"The FBI and the local police, you talked to them?"

"We all did."

"They have any theories?"

"None that they cared to share with me."

"No security problems with Turing? No strangers hanging around here?"

The guard shook his head. "Nothing like that."

"Turing was killed with his own gun. Did you know he owned one?"

"As far as I knew only the guards have guns."

As Sean moved down the road he saw the row of bungalows up ahead. The first one was dark, the second one—Monk Turing's place—had a light on in the front window. All of these residences were constructed of red brick and looked to be about twenty-five hundred square feet in size. *Nice digs*, he thought. The small lawns were well kept; the picket fences in front neatly painted. Pots of colorful flowers sat on the steps leading up to the front door. It was like one of those idyllic paintings depicting life as it *never* really was. From inside the house Sean could hear someone playing a piano. He opened the gate and headed up the sidewalk to the front porch.

He eyed a pile of sports equipment on a small bench on the porch. A couple of golf drivers, a basketball, a baseball and a first baseman's glove were among the items there. Sean picked up the glove; it smelled of well-oiled leather. Turing must've been into sports, probably to relax after all the brain work.

Sean peered through the screen door. A plumpish

woman dressed in a robe with slippers on her feet was asleep on the couch. There was no sign of a guard. In the far corner of the room sat a baby grand. Playing the piano was a young girl. She had long, white blond hair and pale skin. While Sean was standing there she switched from classical, Rachmaninoff Sean thought, to an Alicia Keys piece he recognized, without missing a beat.

Viggie Turing looked up and saw him. She wasn't startled. She didn't even stop playing.

"What are you doing here?"

The voice surprised Sean because it came from behind him. He turned and saw the woman right at his elbow.

He held out his badge. "I'm Sean King. I'm down here investigating Monk Turing's death."

"I know that," the woman said tersely. "I meant what are you doing here, at this house? At this hour?"

She was in her mid-thirties, about five-five. Her red hair was short, parted on the side with a little flip halfway down her neck. The front door light was on so he could see that her skin was freckled and her eyes a milky green. She had on jeans, black loafers and a corduroy shirt. The lips were too full for the thin face, the shoulders a bit too wide for the frame, the nose not quite in sync with the eyes, the chin too sharp for the neighboring square jaw. And yet with all that asymmetry, she was one of the loveliest women Sean had ever seen.

"I was just taking a stroll. I heard Viggie, I presume that's her playing the piano, and just stopped to listen." He assumed that was enough information to allow him to ask a question of his own. "And you are?"

"Alicia Chadwick."

"She's an amazing pianist," Sean commented.

The milky green eyes settled back on him. "She's an amazing child in many ways." She put a hand on his sleeve and pulled him away from the door. "Let's talk. There are some things you need to know."

He smiled. "You're the first person I've met here that's willing to talk."

"Reserve your judgment until you hear what I have to say."

18

Five minutes later Alicia led Sean up the stone steps of a large green clapboard house with a cedar shake roof and broad front porch. He followed her inside into a comfortable study lined with books. A desk stood in the middle of the room with a large flat screen computer monitor on it. She motioned with a finger toward a worn leather chair while she plopped down in the swivel chair behind the desk.

He watched with interest as she put her right leg up on her desk and pulled on the lower section of her pants. The Velcro strip came free about mid-thigh and that part of the pants leg came away in her hand. It was then that Sean could see the highly polished metal and straps underneath. She undid the leg straps, unloosened a few levers, and set the prosthetic with the black loafer still on it down on her desk. Then Alicia rubbed at the spot where her flesh had met aluminum.

She glanced up at him. "I'm sure Emily Post and her progeny would condemn a person showing off her artificial leg to a complete stranger but I don't really care. Ms. Post, I assume, never had to walk around in one of these all day. And even with all the technological advances they still can hurt like hell."

"How did it happen?" Sean asked as she popped three Advil with the aid of a glass of water poured from a carafe on her desk. "I'm sorry. You may not want to talk about it," he added quickly.

"I don't like to waste time and I can be blunt. I'm a mathematician by training, but a linguist by passion. My father was in the Foreign Service and we traveled extensively in the Middle East when I was young. Consequently, I can speak Arabic and Farsi and several other dialects the U.S. government has deemed valuable. Four years ago, I volunteered as an interpreter in Iraq for the State Department. For two years things were going all right until I was riding in a Humvee near Mosul when it rolled over an IED. I regained consciousness in Germany a week later to find that not only had I lost seven days of my life, but most of my right leg as well. I was lucky though. Only two people survived the explosion, myself and another man, who pulled me to safety. They told me the only thing left of the driver sitting next to me was his torso. Shrapnel trajectory in enclosed spaces is hardly an exact science. However, my country completely rehabbed me and gave me this wonderful accoutrement." She patted the artificial leg.

"I'm sorry," Sean said. He inwardly marveled at

her ability to talk so dispassionately about what must have been a horrific event.

Alicia settled back in her chair and studied him closely. "I still have no idea why they brought you down here."

"There's been a mysterious death and I'm a detective."

"That part I can follow. They've had enough policemen down here to have Jack the Ripper himself shaking in his blood-soaked boots. But they're all government people, you're private."

"Meaning what exactly?"

"Meaning they can't really control you, can they?"

"I don't know, can they?" She didn't answer him so he said, "You mentioned you had some things to tell me?"

"That was one of them."

"Okay, who's *they*, as in the owners of Babbage Town? No one down here seems anxious to tell me or they don't know. Both of which I find remarkable."

"Afraid I can't help you there."

"Have the FBI talked to you?"

She said, "Yes. A man named Michael Ventris. Humorless and efficient."

"Good to know. What's your take on Champ Pollion? Let me guess, he was first in his class at MIT."

"No, he actually was second in his class at the

Indian Institute of Technology, a school many in the field consider even more prestigious."

"He also seems very nervous about what happened to Monk."

"He's a scientist. What does he know about violent death and murder investigations? I saw enough blood in Iraq to last a thousand years, but even I've been unsettled by what happened to Monk. At least in Iraq you knew who was trying to kill you. Here you don't."

"So you think Monk was murdered?"

"I don't know. That's what's so unsettling."

"He was found at the CIA?"

"Right. But if the CIA had anything to do with his death do you think they would have conveniently left his body there? I mean they could've just dumped him in the York River."

"So what's your role in Babbage Town? I can tell you're not simply one of the rank and file."

"And how do you know that?"

"Your house is bigger than the other bungalows."

"I run a department here. Champ lives on the opposite side of the mansion, near Hut Number One."

"And what do they do in Hut Number One?"

"That's actually my department. Champ runs Hut Number Two. The one with the water silo."

"And you won't tell me what you do?"

Alicia said, "It's nothing terribly exciting. We factor

numbers. Very large numbers or at least we try to. It's quite a difficult proposition. We're hunting for something that many people in the field are convinced doesn't exist. A mathematical shortcut."

Sean looked skeptical. "A mathematical shortcut? That justifies armed guards and expensive digs?"

"It does if accomplishing it can stop the world dead in its tracks. And we're not alone. IBM, Microsoft, NSA, Stanford University, Oxford and countries like France, Japan, China, India, Russia, they're all engaged in similar activities. Maybe even some criminal organizations. They'd definitely have incentive to do it."

"I'm not sure I'd want to be in a competition with NSA."

"Maybe that's the real reason we need armed guards. To protect us from *them*."

"So all of Babbage Town is devoted to this factoring stuff?"

"Oh, no, that's just me and my little operation in Hut Number One. And to tell the truth, I feel a bit like the unfortunate stepsister. Clearly my work is only seen as a backup in case Champ's research doesn't pan out. But the payoff could be enormous."

"For stopping the world dead in its tracks?" Sean said, repeating her words. "How does that make sense?"

"Some inventions, like the light bulb or antibiotics, help mankind. Others inventions, like nuclear weapons, have the potential to end the human race. But people still come up with them. And other people still buy them."

"Why do I feel like Alice toppling through the looking glass?"

"You don't have to understand our world, Mr. King. You just have to find out what happened to Monk Turing."

"Make it Sean. Was Monk in your department?"

"No, Champ's. Monk was a physicist not a mathematician. But I knew him."

"And?"

"And I spent time with him and Viggie but I can't say I knew him all that well. He was quiet, methodical and kept to himself. Never said much about his personal life. Now go ahead and ask me the obvious questions. Did Monk have any enemies? Was he into anything that could have led to his death, that sort of thing?"

Sean smiled. "Well, since you already asked them, I'll just wait for your answers."

"I don't have any. If he was into drugs or stealing or had a deviant sexual side that led him to being murdered, he hid it well."

"Did you know he was killed with his own gun and his were the only prints on it?"

"So it was suicide then?"

"We don't know all the facts yet. You said you didn't know him that well, but did he ever appear depressed, suicidal?"

"No, nothing like that."

"Was he a good father to Viggie?"

Alicia's expression softened. "A very good father. They'd play ball in the front yard for hours. He even learned to play the guitar so he could accompany her on the piano."

"So you spent a lot of time with them?"

"Not with Monk, but I did with Viggie. Sort of the daughter I never had."

"And Monk was okay with that?"

"He worked long hours, not that I don't. But our schedules were different, so it worked out that I could be with her sometimes when he couldn't."

"I see. And the mom?"

Alicia shook her head. "No idea. Never knew her."

Sean suddenly thought of a question that he probably should have asked Rivest. "Did Monk take any trips recently?"

"No, not recently. You don't get a lot of vacation time down here." She paused. "He did go out of the country about eight or nine months ago, I think."

Sean perked up. "Do you know where?"

She shook her head. "He never told me."

"How do you know it was out of the country then?"

"I remember him mentioning that he had to get his passport renewed. I guess that would tell you where he went. His passport."

Which is in the hands of the FBI. "How long was he gone?"

"About two weeks."

"Who watched Viggie?"

"I helped. And Babbage Town hired some people to look after her."

"And Viggie was okay with a bunch of strangers around her?"

"I guess Monk had talked to her. If he told her it was okay, she'd believe it. They had that kind of relationship."

"Can *you* get through to Viggie at all?"

"Sometimes. Why?"

"Because I might need your help when I talk to her."

"What could Viggie know that would help you in your investigation?"

"She may know something about her dad that might explain what happened."

"If she does talk to you, it might not be a language you understand very well."

Sean smiled. "Good thing I'll have a world-class linguist assisting me."

She said in a condescending manner, "You could care less whether Monk Turing committed suicide or was murdered, do you? You'll get paid regardless."

"You're wrong. I *do* care whether the killer is caught."

"Why?"

"Technically, I'm a P.I. But I'm really a cop and cops just think that way. That's why we do a job most people can't. You said there were some *things* you wanted to tell me? I've only heard one."

She stared at him curiously. "I'm really tired so I'm going to bed. I'm sure you can see yourself out." She reattached her prosthetic and slowly moved up the stairs.

Sean locked the door on his way out. If there *was* a murderer on the loose, you could never be too careful.

As he walked back to his room at the mansion, Sean only had one thought marching through his head: *What the hell have I gotten into?*

19

After walking out on Horatio, Michelle skipped lunch. Instead she did such an intense workout in the gym that there wasn't a dry thread on her. She was feeling better, she told herself. The endorphins were obviously doing what Horatio Barnes couldn't. She was slowly convincing herself that what had happened in that bar was one moment of bad judgment probably triggered by too much booze. Soon she would be out of here, back with Sean solving other people's problems. Horatio could go leech on someone else's misery.

She returned to her room to shower. After combing out her wet hair she wrapped a towel around her and stepped out of the bathroom. She sat on her bed, and started moistening her legs with lotion. Then she whirled around so fast her towel fell to the floor.

Barry had been standing behind a bureau in one corner of the room.

He had stepped out so she could see him, a broad smile on his face.

"What the hell are you doing here?" she cried out.

"Cheryl didn't show up for her session. They sent me to get her," Barry said quickly, his gaze squarely on Michelle's naked body. She snatched a sheet off the bed, wrapped it around her and stood.

"She's not here, so get the hell out!"

"Sorry to have disturbed you," Barry said, the smile still playing across his lips.

"I'm going to report you for this, you son of a bitch," she said furiously. "I know exactly what you're up to."

"I was told to come here to see about a patient. It's not my fault you were walking around naked. Didn't you read the section of the facility's information packet that said during the day patient rooms are treated as public spaces and staff may come and go at all times? It also goes on to say that all patients should therefore dress in the bathroom if they desire privacy."

"You seem to have focused on that particular section. Let me guess why, Mr. Pervert."

He backed toward the door, his gaze on her long, bare legs. "And if you file a report against me I'll have to defend myself."

"What exactly is that supposed to mean?" Michelle said furiously.

"It means that other female patients have stooped to seducing male staff in order to get preferential treatment, small favors, drugs, smokes, candy, even vibrators. I mean the way I look at it I was standing right here and you started showing off your body to me. Do you want a vibrator, sweetie? But being the good staff member that I am, I can't treat you any differently. Sorry."

Michelle's fists were clenched she was so angry. "I didn't see you, you bastard! You were hiding over in that corner."

"You said I was hiding, I say I wasn't. Have a nice day." He gave her one last, penetrating stare and then turned and left.

Michelle was so upset she was trembling. She took several calming breaths, grabbed her clothes and finished dressing in the bathroom. The door didn't have a lock for obvious reasons, so she stood with her back pressed against it in case the man came back for something more than a peek at her ass and boobs. She felt violated beyond belief. She was deciding whether to report Barry when another staff member walked in after Michelle had finishing dressing.

"I'm here to take you to the session," the woman said.

"What session?" Michelle asked.

"Horatio Barnes has scheduled you for a group session this afternoon."

"He didn't tell me that."

"Well, it's on your chart. I'm just here to make sure you go."

Michelle hesitated. *Damn him.* "How many people in the group?"

127

"Ten. I'm sure you'll get a lot out of it. And it's only thirty minutes long."

"Fine, let's just get it over with," Michelle said sharply.

"That's not the proper attitude to have," the woman said in a scolding tone.

"Lady, right now it's the only attitude I've got."

A male doctor Michelle had never seen before was leading the session. The only saving grace for Michelle was that Sandy was there. She made a beeline for the woman and sat next to her. As soon as Michelle did so the door opened and Barry came in. He stood in the back against the wall.

Every time Michelle felt his gaze on her, her skin prickled. That jerk had seen her *naked*. It was killing her. Even Sean had never seen that much of her.

While the doctor was handing out some materials, Sandy looked over at Michelle and saw her expression of misery. "You okay?"

"No, but I'll tell you about it later. How does this session work?" she whispered.

"Just follow my lead. It'll be okay. This shrink isn't bad. He means well, but he's totally clueless to what goes on in the real world."

"That's inspiring," Michelle said.

After the session was over, Michelle pushed Sandy's wheelchair past Barry.

"You ladies have a nice day," Barry said, holding the door for them and smiling broadly.

"Go fuck yourself!" Michelle said loud enough for him and everyone else to hear.

Sandy screwed up her face. "Oh, honey, please, that conjures up such a nasty vision and I just had my lunch."

Barry stopped smiling.

On the way back to Sandy's room Michelle filled her in on Barry's actions.

"I've heard he listens for the showers to go on and off in the good-looking women's rooms and then slips in for a little peek."

Michelle looked outraged. "If the bastard has an MO that people know about why hasn't he been fired?"

"People are afraid to speak up. Face it, most folks are here because they're messed up, vulnerable. They're not in the best position to defend themselves against assholes like that."

"I'd love a few minutes alone with the guy. His face would be even uglier than it is now."

"That would be hard to do," Sandy replied.

Michelle wheeled Sandy into her room and saw the large bouquet of flowers on the nightstand. "You have a secret admirer?" she asked.

"Don't all women?" Sandy fingered a rose petal. "Speaking of admirers, who was that tall, gorgeous man I saw you talking to when you first got here?"

"Sean King. We're partners."

"Partners? So no ring yet?"

"No, we're partners in a detective agency."

"You're a detective?"

"And ex-Secret Service."

"I wouldn't have pegged you for being a fed."

"Why, are we supposed to have a certain look?"

"No. But I'm usually pretty good at telling the goodies from the baddies."

"You've had a lot of experience with both?"

"Let's just say I've had lots of experience *period*." She patted Michelle's hand. "So this Sean King and you? Anything happening outside of work?"

"Now you sound like my shrink."

"Is he as good inside as he looks on the outside?"

"Even better actually."

"Then honey, can I ask why you don't have a ring on your finger?"

"We're business partners."

"There're lots of ways to make a living. But it's been my experience that handsome men with hearts of gold are as rare as a woman leaving a bar without getting her bottom grabbed. Find one like that, you better reel him in or someone else will."

Michelle thought of Sean and Joan working together again while she was stuck in here having a fight for her soul with Horatio "Harley-Davidson" Barnes and getting peeped on by Barry the Dickhead. "It's not that simple," she finally said.

"Oh, women tell themselves that all the time. That's partially because nothing for women is simple.

It's only simple for men and that's because, God love the little bastards, they just can't see any higher than they can grope."

"Sean is different."

"Then you're just making my point for me. Screw the complex and keep it simple. A ring on the finger. That's all it takes."

"Assuming for argument's sake that I'm willing, what if he's not?"

Sandy ran her gaze over Michelle. "Then, frankly, he needs to be in here more than you. He might be a cut above most men, but I'm assuming he still has a zipper and something behind it."

"Relying on physical attraction doesn't work long term."

"Of course it doesn't! But you bait them with the curves, haul them in and use the time till your looks fail to train them properly."

"Have you ever been married?"

"I was. For about ten minutes."

"Quickie divorce?"

"No, I was shot on my wedding day and ended up like this. My husband of ten minutes wasn't so lucky."

"My God, he was killed? During your wedding!"

Sandy nodded. "The wedding planner was pretty much speechless. She'd been fussing about the shrimp and the ice sculpture. She didn't have a clue how to do triage."

"How did it happen?"

Sandy nimbly lifted herself out of her chair and onto the bed. She had on a short-sleeve shirt and Michelle saw the ripple of triceps muscles and the veins down both the woman's biceps. Sandy sat back on the bed. "What it was, was a long time ago. I only had the love of my life officially for ten minutes. But let me tell you I wouldn't have traded it for a lifetime with anyone else. So you think about your Mr. King. You think long and hard. And realize he won't always be there. Because there are lots of women out there who could give a damn about complex. They just take what they want, sweetie. They just take what they want."

20

Sean had spent his first night at Babbage Town alternating between trying to sleep and looking out the window at the darkened grounds. His room was in the mansion on the second floor overlooking the side of the property close to where Champ Pollion's house was and also within sight of Hut Number One run by the very blunt and very one-legged Alicia Chadwick. The mansion's decorations had a European flavor, and each guest room, he'd quickly discovered, came equipped with its own computer and WiFi high-speed Internet connection.

Around two A.M. Sean saw some movement near Champ's house. He thought it was the physicist he'd seen climbing the steps to the front door and going in, but the moonlight was weak and he couldn't be sure. Then Sean heard a noise that took him completely by surprise. He flung open his window and looked out.

It was a plane coming in, and not just any plane. It was a jet, a large one judging by the sound of the engines, and from the level of noise, the damn thing was landing. He leaned out the window but saw nothing, not even a blink of lights against the black sky. He listened for a while longer and heard the plane's engines being thrown into reverse to stop the aircraft after it touched down. Yet where had the plane landed? Camp Peary? The Naval Weapons Station? And what the hell was a large jet flying without lights doing landing across the river in the middle of the night?

Nearly two hours later he'd awoken again and taken a seat by the window. He saw two guards standing on the pebble path, talking and sipping coffee. Even from up here he could hear the squawks coming from their portable radios.

At five o'clock, Sean gave up on sleep, showered, dressed and headed down the stairs with a knapsack slung over his shoulder. In the broad, barrel-vaulted entrance hall, there was the smell of coffee and eggs and bacon coming from the dining room.

He ate breakfast and carried a Styrofoam cup of coffee with him as he stopped by the security desk set up near the mansion's front door and showed the guard stationed there his badge. The stocky man nodded but said nothing as he took Sean's card and swiped it through a slot on top of his computer screen.

Apparently they want to know where everyone is at all times, Sean thought to himself. *Including their own hired detective.*

"You hear that plane come in earlier?" he asked the guard.

The man didn't answer. He simply handed Sean his card and turned back to his computer monitor.

"Love you too," Sean muttered as he headed out.

It was still dark and Sean stood there for a bit wondering what to do. Alicia *had* been wrong; he wasn't just doing this for the money. He wanted to find out what had happened to Monk Turing. Every child should know what had happened to his or her parents. And every murderer should be punished.

Monk had left the country eight or nine months ago. Where had he gone? His passport would show where if he had used the normal channels of international travel. But if he had traveled under a fake name or via another country's planes? Was he a spy? Had he gone out of the country to pass Babbage Town secrets to another country willing to pay well for them?

He breathed in fresh air devoid of the toxic fumes of the Washington Beltway and listened for a moment to scurrying feet from the nearby woods. Squirrels and deer probably; people made far different noises when they were moving. Sean had been trained to deduce the motive behind a person's movements. It wasn't actually all that hard to do. Most people couldn't hide their motives to save their lives. If they could, far more than four American presidents would have been assassinated.

Sean had some FBI Hostage Rescue buddies who'd trained at Camp Peary with the CIA's paramilitary units. These units traveled the world doing things no one at the CIA or anyone else in the government would ever talk about. Sean definitely did not want to cross swords with them. But had Turing?

Sean walked on, finally arriving at Len Rivest's place. It was pretty early as yet and Rivest had really hung one on last night. He decided he'd let the guy sleep. He tossed his coffee in a trash can, passed the security office and a one-story squat building that appeared to be a garage and turned left where a sign that read "Boathouse" pointed down a gravel path. As he walked along Sean was quickly engulfed by forest.

It took twenty minutes to clear the trees and he came to the York River and the boathouse belonging to Babbage Town, which was situated along a pier that jutted out into the wide, calm, deepwater river. It was a long, plain cedar board structure painted yellow with multiple slips and garage-style doors enclosing each slip. He tried the door to the boathouse but it was locked. He peered through a window and could make out the shapes of several boats. He walked out onto a floating dock attached to the boathouse and noted several kayaks stacked on a holder there as well as two paddleboats tethered to cleats. One covered boat slip was open. On a power lift there were three Sea-Doos with their covers on. If Monk had used one of these crafts to get to Camp Peary, who had returned it here? Dead men didn't make good sailors.

The sun was coming up now, throwing streams of light across the flat surface of the water. Sean pulled out a pair of binoculars from his knapsack. The sunlight was glinting off the razor-wire fence on the other side of the York. Sean walked down to the edge of the river, his feet near the sandy edge, and took a sweep of the land opposite, not seeing much of interest. A couple of discarded crab pots floated in the water. Channel markers rose out of the depths of the York and a low-flying heron swooped effortlessly across his line of sight looking for breakfast in the murky water.

He wondered where the runway was that would allow a large jet to land. As he looked to his left he saw it: a clearing in the tree line revealing a wide swath of grass. The runway must start just after the grass, he thought.

Farther down to his left, long crane arms reached to the sky. The Cheatham Annex, he concluded. Navy boys. On the drive to Babbage Town he'd seen a gunmetal gray destroyer alongside a pier in front of the Naval Weapons Station. This area was alive with the presence of the military. For some reason that didn't give him comfort.

The small branch fell from the tree and hit him on the head. Sean dropped to the ground not because the branch had hurt him, but because something else almost had. It had to have been a long-range rifle round. The bullet had clipped the branch right over his head. He hunkered down in the tall river grass. Who the hell had taken a shot at him? After about a minute he chanced a peek, his gaze scanning across the river. The shot had to have come from there. Now the question was obvious. Did the shooter intend to miss just to scare him, or was the branch supposed to be Sean's brain?

When the next bullet whipped over his head, missing it by inches, his question was answered. The person was trying to kill him.

He burrowed deeper into the dirt and sand, pressing his body as flat to the ground as he could.

He waited for two minutes. When no other shot sailed past he began clutching at the short grass and propelling himself backward, resembling a snake whipping through the grass, albeit in reverse. He reached a patch of tall grass, and then the tree line. Once behind a thick oak, he stood and began zigzagging through the trees back toward Babbage Town.

He hit the path and ran flat-out to Len Rivest's bungalow. Rivest didn't answer his knock, so Sean pushed the door open and went in.

"Len. Len! Somebody just took a shot at me."

No one was on the main floor. He raced up the stairs, two steps at a time, and flung open the first door he came to and stopped, his chest heaving.

Len Rivest was lying naked at the bottom of his claw-footed bathtub, his eyes staring unseeingly at the pale blue ceiling.

21

Horatio Barnes was sitting at his desk looking at a map showing the small town in Tennessee where Michelle had lived when she was six.

Horatio had learned from Bill Maxwell that Michelle was many years younger than her next oldest sibling. Michelle might have been a mistake, Horatio mused. That could affect a child, he knew.

Horatio had pulled a few strings and gotten some information from her work file at the Secret Service. It had listed all the traits he knew that she had: control freak, hard on her underlings, but hardest on herself, incorruptible, fair, all earmarks of a good federal agent. Somewhere along the line she had lost or at least managed to control her fears, her inability to trust others, though the two agents he'd talked to about her had had strikingly similar comments. Both men had said that they would have trusted her with their lives, but they had never managed to get to know the enigmatic person behind the Kevlar and Glock pistol.

He'd had patients like Michelle before, and he'd wanted to help them all, but with Michelle he felt an extra urge to get her straight. It might be because she'd risked her life for her country or was the closest friend of Sean King, a man he respected like few others of his acquaintance. Or perhaps it was because he felt in her a hurt so deep that he just wanted to help her erase it, if she could.

And there was another reason, one he had not shared with Sean King or Michelle. People who attempted to end their lives, no matter how amateurishly they might do so at first, often got better at it, with the result that on the third, fourth or sixth try, they ended up on a slab with a coroner poking around their remains. He could not allow that to happen to Michelle Maxwell. He had a week's vacation coming up. He'd planned on flying to California to go abalone diving with some friends. Instead, he went online and bought a plane ticket to Nashville.

22

Michelle heard the footsteps again, exactly at one A.M. She rose and slipped out the door. Now she had added incentive to find out what Barry the Peeping Tom was up to. She prayed it was at least a felony. She headed down the darkened hall, gauging the pace of the steps echoing lightly in front of her. She reached the end of the corridor and peered around the corner. There was a light on at the end of the hall. She edged forward until she could see its source. It was the pharmacy. There was someone in there. As the man moved in front of the glass window in the door, she saw that it wasn't Barry. It was the little man she'd seen in the pharmacy earlier. Pretty late to be dispensing drugs, she thought.

As she stood there another figure appeared near the door to the pharmacy. Barry looked around cautiously and then went inside, closing the door behind him. Michelle slipped forward as much as she dared for a better look. And then it hit her. Why would Barry be here at this hour in the first place? He'd been on the day shift. During her stay here Michelle had noted that the personnel pulled twelve-hour shifts, turning over in the morning and evening right at eight o'clock. Barry had been off-duty for five hours. Was he putting in a little personal overtime?

Michelle heard it before she saw anything; it was the slight squeak of rubber on linoleum. At first she thought it was the sneakers that the nurses here wore. But then she saw the wheelchair come into view. Sandy was fully dressed, her hands efficiently propelling her down the hall. Then she stopped and took up watch, her gaze on the pharmacy door. Michelle quickly drew back as Sandy suddenly whipped her head around and looked in her direction. A minute later when Michelle dared look back around the corner, Sandy was gone. A few minutes after that Barry and the other man left the pharmacy, the latter closing and locking the door. Fortunately, they walked down the hall away from Michelle.

As soon as their footsteps had faded, she stepped forward and made her way cautiously down to the pharmacy. What surprised her was that both men had left the pharmacy empty-handed. What was going on here?

Then she turned her attention down the other hall, toward Sandy's room. She edged along the corridor, taking small, near-silent steps and hugging the wall. She reached Sandy's room. It was dark. She peered in the glass and could just make out Sandy lying on the bed. The woman was obviously pretending to be asleep. But what had she been doing watching the pharmacy? Was she part of whatever Barry was up to? Michelle didn't want to believe that but she couldn't discount the possibility.

Michelle slipped back to her room where sleep didn't come easily. She tossed for several hours, her mind racing with possible theories that would explain what she had seen, each one more unlikely than the last.

She woke early and went down to breakfast. After that she attended another group session that Horatio had arranged for her. Then she had a one-on-one with a therapist. After it was over, Michelle made a beeline for Sandy's room and found her there. With other people.

"What's wrong?" Michelle said. A doctor, two nurses and a security guard were gathered around Sandy's bed. The woman was lying there thrashing around and moaning.

One nurse turned to her. "Please return to your room, right now."

The guard stepped toward her, his hands out. "Right now," he said.

Michelle turned and left, but she didn't go far.

A few minutes later her vigil was rewarded when the group left Sandy's room and passed her. Sandy was strapped to a gurney and there was an IV in her arm. She appeared to be sleeping now. Her Secret Service training kicking in, Michelle continued to run her gaze down the woman's arm to her hands. What she saw puzzled her deeply. Sandy had always been so meticulous about her appearance.

Michelle waited until they were out of sight and then she hustled to Sandy's room and closed the door behind her. She felt a bit guilty about taking advantage of Sandy's illness to search her room. But only a bit.

It didn't take long because the woman had brought few personal possessions with her. One thing that she wasn't seeing puzzled Michelle. No pictures of family or friends. Then again, Michelle hadn't brought any of those with her either. But from the loving way Sandy had talked about her late husband, Michelle would have thought she'd have at least one picture of the man. Yet with the horrific way it had ended, maybe she didn't want a reminder.

She looked around the room and her gaze settled on the bouquet of flowers. She examined the table the bouquet was on, tracing her finger across the veneer of fine dirt particles. Her gaze went to the floor, where she could see a few bits of dirt as well. That's what had puzzled her about Sandy's hands. There was dirt on them. As though she'd—

Michelle raced across the room and flattened herself against the wall next to the door. Someone was out there. The door opened slowly. Michelle ducked down away from the glass opening so the person couldn't see her through it.

As the person came in and walked toward the bed,

Michelle silently slipped around the door and through it. She glanced back and saw Barry advancing toward Sandy's bed. She raced down the hall and to the nurse's station.

"I just saw someone sneak into Sandy's room, I don't think he's supposed to be there since Sandy's sick," she said to the nurse on duty there. The woman rose immediately and walked quickly down the hall.

Michelle fled back to her room and almost collided with Cheryl, who was coming out sucking on her straw. Michelle didn't want to be alone right now in case Barry came to give her a little payback for ratting him out. Michelle clearly couldn't count on the nurse she'd told keeping her identity confidential. In fact she might be mad at Michelle for making her rush to Sandy's room only to find Barry there. As the bastard had said, he could come and go pretty much as he pleased.

"Hey, Cheryl, you want to talk or something?"

Cheryl stopped sucking momentarily and looked at Michelle as though she was seeing her for the very first time.

Michelle started speaking quickly, "I mean we're roommates and all and we really haven't gotten to know each other. And I think it says somewhere in the patient handbook that we all ought to try and relate to each other as a form of therapy. You know, a little girl-to-girl soul searching."

Michelle's invitation was so obviously insincere that

145

Cheryl simply walked past her after giving her straw an extra loud slurp. Michelle slipped inside the room and pressed herself against the door.

Twenty minutes passed and Barry didn't come for her. She wasn't physically afraid of the man. She had already sized him up as a bully who would turn and run the first time he was struck back harder than the blow he'd delivered. But he could hurt her in another way, by making allegations against her. Or he might slip some stolen drugs in her bed. If people believed him over her, what would happen? Would she be stuck in this place against her will? Would she go to prison? Her chin sank to her chest as a horrible depression dropped solidly on her shoulders.

Sean, come and rescue me from this place. Please. Then the obvious occurred to her. She was here voluntarily. She had checked herself in, she could check herself out. She could leave right now. She could go to the apartment Sean had gotten for them, chill out for a day and then go down and join him. He would probably need her help right about now anyway. He always needed her at some point on a case.

She burst out the door and almost ran into the nurse standing there.

Michelle blinked and stepped back. "Yeah?"

"Michelle, Sandy wants to see you."

"Is she okay?"

"She's stabilized. And she wants to talk to you."

"What's wrong with her?"

"I'm afraid I can't discuss that."

Of course you can't, Michelle grumbled under her breath as she followed the woman down the hallway. But then her pace quickened. She did want to see Sandy. She wanted to see her very much.

23

Horatio Barnes drove his rental car out of the Nashville airport. An hour later he was in rural Tennessee looking for the small town where Michelle Maxwell had lived when she was six years old. He found it after several wrong turns and some time-consuming backtracking. He reached the small, crumbling town center, stopped and asked for directions at the hardware store and drove out of town heading southwest. He was sweating because apparently his rental fee didn't cover a car with functioning air-conditioning.

The neighborhood where Michelle had lived clearly had seen better days. The homes were old and dilapidated, the yards ill-nourished. He checked house numbers on the mailboxes until he found it. The Maxwell house was set off the street. It had a large front yard with a dying oak anchoring it. On one limb was a tire hanging from a rotting rope. In the side yard was a 1960s-era Ford pickup up on cinder blocks. He saw the jagged dead stumps of what looked to be the remains of a privacy hedge that had run across the front of the house.

The paint on the clapboard siding was peeling away and the screen on the front door had fallen off and was lying on the steps. Horatio couldn't tell if the place was inhabited or not. From its piecemeal look he reasoned it was an old farmhouse. Presumably the original owners had sold the bulk of the land to a developer and the neighborhood had sprung up around their homestead.

He wondered what it would have been like for the young girl to grow up here with just her parents, the beloved sons having moved on to manhood. Horatio also wondered again if Michelle's conception had been an accident. Would that have influenced how her parents treated it? From experience Horatio knew that one could cut both ways. *Which way had it cut with you, Michelle?*

He pulled his rental to the edge of the graveled shoulder, got out and looked around, wiping the sweat off his face with his handkerchief. Apparently there wasn't an active neighborhood watch program because no one seemed to be paying any attention to him. Probably there was nothing here worth stealing.

Horatio walked up the gravel drive. Part of him was waiting for an old hound to lumber around the corner of the structure with teeth bared just looking for a plump leg to bite. However, no animal or person came forward to greet or attack him. He reached the porch and peered inside the busted front door. The

place seemed abandoned, or if not, the current inhabit-
ants were setting a new standard for minimalism.

"Can I help you?" a firm voice said.

Horatio swung around and saw a woman standing
there at the end of the drive. She was young, short
and chubby, wore a faded sundress and had a fat baby
riding on her left hip. Her hair was dark and curly
and in the humidity it clung to her head like a
skullcap.

He walked toward her. "I sure hope so. I'm trying
to find out about the people who used to live in this
house."

She stared over his shoulder. "You mean the bums,
druggies or whores?"

He followed her gaze. "Oh, is that what it's used
for these days?"

"I pray to the Lord to strike the sinners dead."

"I presume the sinners don't come by in the
daylight, just at night."

"Well ain't no law says we got to hide in bed when
it gets dark. So we see the evil and evil it is."

"Well, I'm really sorry about that. But I wasn't
talking about the, um, evil. I was talking about a
family named the Maxwells; they lived here about
thirty years ago?"

"We've only been here five, so I wouldn't know,
would I?"

"Anyone else here who might?"

She pointed a thick finger at the farmhouse.

"Because of that evil, ain't nobody want to stay too long." Her baby gave a hiccup and spittle ran down its mouth. She wiped him up with a rag she pulled from her pocket.

Horatio handed her a business card. "Well, if you think of anyone who might be able to help me, you can reach me at that number."

She studied the card. "You a shrink?"

"Something like that."

"From Wash-ing-*ton*?" She said the word with a pronounced sneer. "This here's Tennessee."

"I have a big practice."

"Why you want to know about these Maxwell folks?"

"It's confidential, but I can tell you that it's to try to help a patient of mine."

"What's it worth to you?"

"I thought you didn't know them."

"I know somebody who might. My granny. She gave us this house when she went in the nursing home. She lived there, oh, must've been forty years or so at least. Hell, Gramps is buried in the backyard."

"That's nice."

"Grass grows real well over that spot, I tell you that."

"I'm sure. So your grandmother's at a nursing home. Near here?"

"State place, about an hour away. She couldn't afford nothing fancy. That's why she give us her house, so's she could get help from the government. You know, so they wouldn't know she had stuff."

"Like assets to be used to pay for her care?"

"That's right. Government screws everybody six ways from Sunday. We got to fight to get our fair share. Give it a few years and the Mexicans will run the whole damn place." She looked to the sky. "Lord, strike me dead before that happens."

"Be careful what you wish for. Do you think she might talk to me?"

"Maybe. She got good days and bad days. I try to go up to see her, but what with the baby and more kids in school, and gas ain't exactly cheap is it?" She studied him. "So how much is it worth to you?" she asked again.

"Well, that depends on what she tells me." Horatio took a moment to scrutinize her. "Let's say if the information is good I'll pay her a hundred dollars."

"Pay *her*! She ain't got no use for the money. I meant pay *me*."

Horatio smiled. "Okay, I'll pay you. Can you arrange for me to see her?"

"Well, seeing as how we got us a business arrangement I'll go with you. Don't want you leaving town without remembering the deal."

"When can we go?"

"My man gets home at six. We can head out then. That way we get there after dinner. Old folks don't like people interrupting their chow time."

"Okay. What's your grandmother's name and the name of the nursing home?"

"Do I look stupid? You can follow me up in your car. I'll take you to her room."

"Fine. You say she has good and bad days. What does that mean exactly?"

"That exactly means that she's losing her marbles. She's got that demon stuff."

Horatio cocked his head at this remark, worried that the young woman was totally nuts. Then he guessed what she meant. "You're referring to *dementia*?"

"That's it. So you got to roll the dice and see what comes up."

"Well, thank you for your help, uh . . ."

"Linda Sue Buchanan. My friends call me Lindy, but you ain't my friend so you just stick to Linda Sue for now."

"You can call me Horatio."

"That's one weird-ass name."

"Well, I'm one weird-ass guy. I'll see you here at six o'clock. And by the way, *Linda Sue*, the little bundle of joy just puked on your shoe."

He left her cursing and dragging her foot across the grass.

24

Sandy was sitting up in bed looking much better. The nurse left them alone and Michelle drew next to the bed and took the older woman's hand in hers.

"Okay, what the hell happened to you?" Michelle demanded.

Sandy smiled and gave a casual wave of her other hand, although the one holding Michelle's tightened at the same time. "Oh, honey, it happens to me from time to time. Nothing to worry about. My old butt just hits a wall and everything sort of pops. They give me a little happy juice and I'm right as rain."

"You're sure you're okay?"

"Absolutely."

"I thought you'd had a seizure or something."

"Now you see why I can't hold down a job. And I think I would've made a hell of an airline pilot, don't you?" She pantomimed using a PA system. "Ladies and gentlemen, this is your captain speaking. We're about to begin our initial descent into *hell* and the person flying the plane, namely me, is about to *freak* out on you! So just hold on tight, you little bastards, while I try to lay this baby on the ground." She gave a weak laugh and let go of Michelle's hand.

"I'm sorry, Sandy. I really am."

"Comes with the territory and I'm comfortable with that."

Michelle hesitated. "I went into your room after they took you. I don't know why, I guess I was just stunned. I heard someone else coming. I ducked behind the door and Barry came in."

On this, Sandy sat up a little straighter. "Did he see you?"

"No, I ducked out. But I ratted on him to the head nurse, for all the good it'll do me. He's probably plotting his revenge as we speak."

Sandy sat back. "What could he want in my room?"

Michelle shrugged. "Probably just wanted to see what all the fuss was about. Or he might've been looking to take anything of value that wasn't nailed down."

Sandy made a snorting noise. "Well, I hope he can dig all the way to my bank because that's where my good jewelry is. I never bring any of that with me to one of these places because it won't be there when you leave."

"Good thinking."

Sandy tried to sit up some more and Michelle quickly went to her aid. She lifted the sheet up, exposing Sandy's legs, took the woman around the waist and slid her higher on the pillow and then covered her legs back up.

"You're strong," Sandy remarked.

"You're pretty muscular yourself."

"Upper body, yes. But my legs are spaghetti and about as big." Sandy sighed. "You should've seen the gams I used to have, Ann-Margret quality."

Michelle smiled. "I'm sure." Sandy's legs *were* withered, which was why Michelle had lifted the covers. She wanted to make sure Sandy really was disabled. Her instincts told her there was something wrong about Sandy.

"You look like you're thinking way too hard," Sandy said.

"That's all we have to do in here, isn't it, think too much?"

An hour later Michelle participated in yet another group session Horatio Barnes had signed her up for.

"So when is Mr. Harley-Davidson expected back?" Michelle asked one of the nurses.

"Who?"

"Horatio Barnes!"

"Oh, he didn't say. But he has an associate covering for him who's very qualified."

"Good for him."

Coming back from the session Michelle turned the corner and nearly ran into Barry coming from the other direction.

She started to walk away when he said, "So how's your *girlfriend*, Sandy?"

She knew she shouldn't take the bait, but something inside her just wouldn't let it go. She turned around and said brightly, "She's great. Did you find anything in her room worth stealing?"

"So you're the one who turned me in to the nurse."

"It took you this long to figure it out? What a loser."

He smirked. "Why don't you do a reality check? I can leave anytime I want. You're a nutcase that's locked up in here."

"That's right. I am a nutcase. I'm a freaking nutcase who can break your neck anytime I want."

He sneered. "Listen, little girl, I grew up in the toughest neighborhood in Trenton. You don't know the meaning of the word tough—Holy shit!"

She had put her foot right through the drywall an inch from his head. As she slowly pulled her leg back she looked at him as he cowered there, his hands over his head.

"Next time you try and screw with me or Sandy, it won't be the wall I crush." She turned to leave and then looked at the hole she'd made. "You might want to clean that up, Barry. Hygiene regulations and all."

"I'm going to report you for attacking me."

"Good, you go ahead. And I'll get a petition signed by all the women you've taken a peek at while you've been here. I'm sure they'd just love to see your ass in jail."

"Who'd believe them? They're nuts."

"You'd be surprised, Barry. There's always credibility in numbers. And why do I think your history might not be so squeaky-clean if someone looks hard enough? And believe me, jerk-off, I know how to look."

Barry swore at her, turned and stomped off.

As Michelle walked back to her room she knew there was only one true way to deal with Barry. She planned on devoting all her energies to that task, starting this minute. And she had a hunch where to begin.

25

The local cops had done their thing as had the FBI, in the person of the dour Michael Ventris. He barely gave Sean a glance after he finished explaining how he'd found Rivest's body.

"And you came back here, why?" Ventris asked in a surly tone.

"We'd arranged to meet to go over the case. He didn't answer the door. So I went in." Sean kept back the part about being shot at. Until he understood the situation better, his instincts told him to keep that to himself.

Ventris said, "I'd heard the folks here had hired a private detective to come down and poke around. So you're it?" The FBI agent didn't look the least bit impressed.

"I'm it."

"Piece of advice. First time you get in my way, it'll be the last time. Got it?"

"Got it." Sean didn't dare ask why the FBI was investigating the death of a private citizen in the first

159

place. It wasn't like Monk Turing's death; he'd been found on federal property.

Len Rivest's remains were removed to the temporary morgue where Monk's body lay, while the local sheriff stood looking at the now empty bathtub and shaking his head. Sean was next to him doing the same thing, but the thoughts running through his head were probably a little more complex than the ones sifting through the sheriff's, he imagined.

Rivest was killed between the time Sean had left him around midnight and the time Sean had found him, a span of about six and a half hours. And he thought he'd seen Champ Pollion going into his bungalow around two in the morning. Thought, but wasn't certain.

"Sheriff Merkle Hayes," the man said, interrupting Sean's musings. Before Sean could say anything the man added, "You're Sean King, right?"

"That's right."

"Ex-Secret Service?"

"Right again."

Hayes was in his early fifties with closely cut grayish white hair, a little potbelly, thick legs, wide bony shoulders and a slightly curved back that reduced his six-foot height a notch. "Any idea what might have happened?"

"I was with Len last night. He'd had a few drinks, maybe a few too many. I left around midnight. He was passed out on the couch downstairs."

"So what'd you two talk about?"

Sean had been prepared for this question and had been surprised that Ventris had not asked it. "This and that. Some about Monk Turing's death. A little about Babbage Town."

"You think he was drunk enough to climb into this bathtub and accidentally drown himself?"

"I couldn't say for sure that he *wasn't* drunk enough to do it."

Hayes remained silent, but nodded at this comment.

"The door was unlocked when I got here," Sean said. "I remember locking it last night."

Hayes said, "So either he unlocked it or . . ."

"Right."

"We've started asking around. So far, no one saw anything. Of course the FBI's taken the lead."

"And why's the FBI involved in this? Rivest wasn't a federal employee, this isn't federal land and no one did anything across state lines that I can see."

"Why don't we take a walk outside?"

Rivest's home had been cordoned off with the standard yellow police tape as if anything could ever make a possible murder seem standard. The ambulance with Rivest's body had just disappeared down the road. Sean glanced over at the small crowd gathered in front of the cottage and saw both Alicia Chadwick and Champ Pollion talking together in low voices.

When Alicia caught his eye, perhaps hoping he would come over, Sean quickly glanced away. He wasn't yet ready to deal with her or Champ.

Hayes led him over to his unmarked cruiser and motioned for Sean to get in the passenger's side. Inside the car Hayes said, "What I'm about to propose might seem a little unorthodox, but I'll risk it. How about you and me partnering on this case?"

Sean raised an eyebrow. "Partnering? You're a county sheriff, I'm a private detective."

"I don't mean formally. But it seems to me that we both have the same goal in mind. Find Rivest's killer."

"Doesn't that apply to Turing as well?"

"Well, it wouldn't be the first time a murder was made to look like a suicide."

"Rivest seemed to think the same thing."

"Did he now? That's interesting. What else did he say about it?"

"That was pretty much it. But he seemed to want it to be a murder rather than a suicide, if you get my meaning. Not that wanting something makes it true."

"We got a lot going against the murder scenario. His gun, his prints and it looked like he went to Camp Peary voluntarily."

"Turing didn't seem suicidal from what I've learned."

"Not all of them do," Hayes said. "I looked up your record at the Service and read about those cases you were involved in down in Wrightsburg. So what do you say? If I'm going up against the FBI, I need some help."

"How about I get back to you after talking to my superiors?"

"How about you just say yes?"

"I tell you what, I'm working on the case anyway, *cases* now, I guess. So if I find something or something occurs to me, I'll give you a holler." He studied Hayes's face. "But it works both ways. You flush something out, you let me know."

Hayes considered this and finally put out his hand. "Okay. It's a deal."

"You can do something for me right now."

"What's that?"

"Take me to see Monk Turing's body at the morgue."

26

The temporary morgue was set up in a small, empty office in the main town area of tiny White Feather. It was staffed by a medical examiner sent over from Williamsburg who didn't look the least bit happy being away from his home turf. He pulled Monk Turing's body out of the portable freezer.

Monk had not been a handsome man in life and death had not improved his looks. He was short and muscular with a paunch that had been obscured by the Y-incision that had split him from his neck to his pubis. Sean tried to see a resemblance between him and his daughter, but couldn't find one. She must take after her mother, he thought.

The ME dutifully went over his official findings with Sean. Monk Turing; age, thirty-seven; height, five-six; weight, one-seventy, etc. The man had clearly died from a gunshot wound to the right temple.

"Monk was right-handed," Sean commented. "That would fit with the suicide theory."

"I hadn't gotten to that part yet," the ME said a little suspiciously. "How'd you know?"

"Right hand's a little bigger, more calloused. And I saw a baseball glove at his house. It wasn't made for a left-hander."

Hayes nodded approvingly while the ME glanced back at his notes.

Sean eyed Monk's hands again. "Looks to be some trace on his hands."

"Ground into the palm and fingers. Reddish fragments," the ME said.

Using what amounted to a high-tech magnifying glass, the ME showed them the traces and then laid the dead man's hand back down.

"Looks like rust stains. Could have come from climbing the chain link fence at Camp Peary," Hayes said.

Sean looked at the ME. "You have the clothes he was wearing?"

They were produced and examined. A pair of black corduroy trousers, a cotton, blue-striped shirt, dark jacket with a hood, underwear, socks and muddy shoes.

Hayes handed Sean a small waterproof bag. "This was found next to the body. It's been confirmed as belonging to Turing." Inside were a blanket and a flashlight.

"He probably used the blanket to get over the razor wire on top of the fence," Sean said, noting some tears on the fabric. "Still a dicey proposition. No cuts on the body from the wire?"

The ME shook his head.

"Surprised we didn't find any gloves," Hayes added. "I mean for getting over the fence and wire."

"Well, if he had worn gloves we wouldn't have his prints on the gun. It's starting to look like he killed himself, Sheriff," Sean said.

The ME looked up. "I can't say for sure if it was suicide or not. Forensics can only go so far."

Sean remarked, "Your report says that the wound was a *near* contact, not a contact wound. Also there are no defensive injuries on the victim or evidence that he was bound. Someone getting that close to the guy with the gun and him not defending himself? That's a little implausible."

"Could've been drugged," Hayes suggested.

"Which was my next question," Sean said. "What's the tox report say?"

"Don't have it back yet."

"So we really can't rule out suicide," Sean said. "And if he did kill himself, why at Camp Peary? Any connection between him and the CIA? Did he ever work there? Did he want to but got rejected?"

Hayes shook his head. "We haven't run that down yet." He turned to the ME. "Do you have an approximate time of death on Rivest yet?"

"He wasn't in the water all that long. Maybe five to six hours. There was what looked to be hemorrhagic edema fluid in his mouth. That indicates he died by drowning. When I open him I'll be able to confirm that of course by water in his lungs."

Hayes consulted his wristwatch. "Five to six hours. Based on when the body was discovered, if he wasn't in the tub all that long before he drowned we're looking at between one to two o'clock in the morning as the time of death."

"Not that long after I left him," Sean said. *And that tallies with the time I might have seen Champ come home.* "He'd had a lot to drink," Sean volunteered. "Cocktails and some red wine."

The ME noted this down. "Thanks."

"Could he have been drunk enough to just pass out and drown himself? Wouldn't the water going in his mouth and nose have woken him up?" Hayes asked.

The ME shook his head. "If he was unconscious from too much alcohol, the shock of the water would not have necessarily revived him."

"I left him pretty much passed out. I wonder what made him decide to take a bath after he came to?" Sean said.

The ME said, "Maybe he threw up and decided to get cleaned up."

Sean shook his head. "You've got puke all over you, you're not going to wait for the bathtub to fill up. You'd jump in the shower." As soon as he said it, Sean froze.

"Good point," Hayes said, not catching the look on Sean's face.

Back in the car Hayes said, "Where to now?"

Sean didn't try to conceal his excitement. "I want to have another look at that bathroom. Something just occurred to me."

"Like what?"

"I know that Len Rivest *was* murdered."

27

When they got back to Len Rivest's house, Sean led
the way to the bathroom and stopped at the doorway.

He said, "I came in here last night around eleven
or eleven-fifteen to use the toilet. This is the only
bathroom in the place."

"Okay," Hayes said expectantly. "And?"

"And was anything removed from the bathroom
by any of your men or the FBI?"

"No. Only the body's been removed. Why?"

"Well, look around, what's missing?"

Hayes studied the interior of the small place. "I
give up. What?"

"There are no towels, no washcloths." He pointed
at the floor. "And no bath mat. Now all those things
were in this room when I was here last night. And
there's something else." He walked over to the com-
mode and looked behind it. "There was a long,
wooden-handled plunger here too. Only it's not here
now."

Hayes said, "So you're saying . . . ?"

Sean knelt on the floor and ran his hand along the tile and then along the wall above the tub. "Damp, but not soaked." He stood. "I'm saying you have to take the towels if you used them to wipe up the water that would have splashed on the floor and walls while you were struggling with Rivest."

"And the plunger?"

Sean pantomimed gripping something in his hand and standing next to the tub. "You don't want to hold Rivest under with your hands. He can reach you that way and maybe get some of your DNA or clothing fiber under his fingernails. But if you place a long-handled plunger on his chest, you can hold him down without him being able to get to you."

"Damn!"

"But everything's going to get soaked that way. So you have to take the towels, mat, plunger with you otherwise the police will see them, deduce a struggle and we go from accidental drowning to murder. Rivest may have come up here to take a bath and just settled in when the killer struck. If he hadn't been drunk he might still be alive."

"So if he was still drunk and the killer used the plunger, we can't rule out that it was a woman who did it."

Sean looked at him shrewdly. "That's right. Call the ME and tell him to check for a circular ring on Rivest's chest or stomach. A plunger might have made an abrasion that can still be seen under the scope. And also tell him to check for fragments of wood from the plunger handle under his fingernails."

Hayes whipped out his cell phone and made the call while Sean continued to poke around.

After the sheriff finished his call he smiled at Sean. "I left a message. I gotta say, my decision to partner up with you is really starting to look smart."

"Don't get too excited. Knowing that a man was murdered and finding out who killed him is, to borrow a line from Mark Twain, the difference between the lightning bug and the lightning. Now we need to really canvass the place and find out if anyone saw someone leaving Rivest's last night. There's security all over the place. Someone had to see *something*. Especially if my theory is correct and the person was leaving with a bunch of wet towels and a plunger."

"Will do. Anything else?"

Sean held an internal debate and said, "I was down at the banks of the York this morning, around six-thirty or so. I wanted to have a look at the boathouse and take a recon of the area. Somebody took a couple shots at me with a high-powered rifle. That's what I was coming to tell Len."

Hayes gaped at him. "Where'd the shots come from?"

"Maybe from across the river."

"Camp Peary?" Sean nodded. "And Monk Turing was found dead on Camp Peary property," Hayes said slowly.

Sean could easily read the man's mind. Did the rural sheriff want to get mixed up in something that involved the CIA. Yet if Monk Turing and Len Rivest had been killed by the folks across the river the question was why. And Sean King had to admit, it was a very intriguing question. The only thing, was he willing to risk his life to get the answer?

"And I can't be sure of it, but I think it's possible that I saw Champ Pollion returning to his cottage around two this morning."

"But you can't be sure?"

Sean shook his head. "I couldn't testify to it. It was too dark. But it's still something we need to check out when we do our alibi canvass. Oh, one more thing. I understand that Monk traveled outside the country about eight or nine months ago. We need to find out where he went."

"The Bureau has his passport and personal effects."

"You're the sheriff down here. Ask for copies."

"You think it could be important?"

"Right now everything is important."

Sean walked back out into the bright sunshine and wondered when, if ever, his life would come close to being normal.

He felt a tap on his shoulder and turned around.

Alicia Chadwick was standing there looking very upset. "We need to talk. Now!"

"And if I don't want to?"

"Then I'll take off my metal leg and beat you to death with it."

"I wouldn't want you to have that on your conscience. Let's go."

28

Barry walked down the hallway carrying a cardboard box. Lurking ten paces behind him was Michelle. The drop-off for mail and overnight parcels was right outside the front door.

Barry unlocked the front door with his key and headed outside. Michelle picked up her pace, reached the unoccupied foyer and ducked down behind a large potted tree.

When Barry unlocked the door and came back in, Michelle tensed. This would be tight because she didn't have a key. With one eye on Barry and one eye on the slowly closing door, she darted out. He was less than three feet from her and never turned around, a testament to how silently she could move. As Barry disappeared around the corner, Michelle stabbed her foot inside the door to prevent it from closing. Removing her shoe she wedged it between the door and the jamb and hurried out.

It only took her a few seconds to find Barry's package in the pile outside the building next to the mailbox. Michelle whipped out a piece of paper and a pencil and wrote down the address where the box was going. She also glanced at the sender's name and wasn't terribly surprised to find it wasn't Barry's.

"Lola Martin," she said, reading off the sender's name. She ducked back inside the building, grabbed her shoe and jogged back to her section of the building. She managed to distract a nurse long enough to take a peek at the patient records at the nurse's station. Lola Martin was comfortably ensconced in the Cuckoo's Nest, the psychotic residents of which were not known to post many packages. She ducked into the patient services center and used a telephone there to make a phone call to a buddy of hers with the Fairfax police. After she'd filled him in, he said, "How'd you score this info, Maxwell?"

"I'm, uh, working undercover."

An hour later, Michelle went into Sandy's empty room. The flowers were still there, but the dirt had been cleaned up off the floor. Michelle assume that Sandy's hands were by now spick-and-span clean too, even under the manicured nails. Michelle had never had that problem for the simple fact that she'd never had a manicure. She didn't want anyone messing with her trigger finger.

Five minutes later, her mission accomplished, Michelle headed back to her room. That afternoon she attended a group session. She was so pleased with the progress she'd made on nailing Barry that she actually stood up and talked about herself. "I'm Michelle and

I want to get better," she said. "In fact, I think I am better." She'd smiled at the others in the circle as they nodded approvingly. Some lightly clapped their hands while others whispered words of encouragement. A few others sat there sulking or else looking at her in disbelief.

If it occurred to Michelle that the only reason she thought she was better was because she'd made herself too busy to think about her own problems, the woman showed no sign of such an internal dilemma. She essentially lived for the adrenaline and not for the often calamitous revelations of self-examination. True to that personality trait, all she could think about was Barry and Sandy. After that she just wanted to get the hell out of here before they finally figured out she might belong in the Cuckoo's Nest after all.

29

Sean sat across from Alicia in her office in Hut Number One. She'd whisked him through the main area so fast that he'd only been able to see a large open area with lots of small desks and what was doubtless a genius at every one of them. He could almost smell the mental power of the folks working there along with the hum of multiple servers.

He motioned to Alicia's right leg and said in a joking tone, "You try and club me with that thing I'm going to lay you out."

She didn't even crack a smile. "How did Len Rivest die? And don't tell me it was a suicide."

He noticed that her eyes were red. "I don't know how he died."

"How could you *not* know?"

"Only the killer knows for sure. And considering that I didn't kill him, I can only speculate as to the cause of death."

"All right, go ahead and speculate."

"I can't do that. It's an ongoing police investigation."

She snapped, "I can't believe you're falling back on that pathetic line."

"I used to be a cop and I know how leaks can screw up an investigation. The police are treating it as a suspicious death."

"But that could mean he was murdered or died accidentally?"

He smiled. "Or it might be determined that he actually died from natural causes."

"You said someone killed him."

"And I could be wrong."

"Oh thank you for being such a big help," she said.

Sean leaned forward, his features no longer jocular. "The fact is I just met you and don't know you from Eve. For all I know you could be the murderer."

"I didn't kill anyone."

"I never met a murderer who said otherwise. That's why we have defense lawyers."

"Do you think this is connected to Monk's death?"

"You must have missed my last point. Would you like me to repeat it?"

Now Alicia sat forward. "Monk Turing's last will and testament was discovered in his house last night. I was just told that in that will, Monk named me as his daughter's guardian. I intend to carry that duty out to the fullest. If the girl's in danger I want to know about it."

"Monk named you guardian, I didn't think you two were that close."

"Monk knew that I cared about Viggie. Her well-being is my top priority."

"Well, with Rivest getting killed, Babbage Town doesn't seem to be all that safe."

Alicia put a hand over her eyes and moaned, "Poor Len! Oh, God, I can't believe he's dead."

Sean sat back. "You seem to be taking Len's death really hard. Any particular reason why?"

She grabbed a tissue from a box on her desk and blew her nose. "Len and I were friends."

"Friends. Good friends, or something more?"

"That's none of your damn business."

"If you had a relationship with Len Rivest, it will be the business of the police to look into that."

"Okay, we were seeing each other, so what?"

"Casual dating? Deeper than that? Wedding plans?"

"You are an obnoxious prick!"

"You're obviously very smart, but apparently you can't see that I'm preparing you for what the police and FBI will ask. You think Agent Ventris is going to go gentle on you? Dead man plus relationship equals *you* being a suspect."

"I didn't kill him. Dammit I cared for him. He was a nice man. Maybe we had a future together. Now?" She turned away from him as tears trickled down her face.

"Okay, Alicia, okay," Sean said gently. "I know this is hard for you." He paused. "Can you just tell me if Len mentioned anything to you about anyone wanting to hurt him? Or whether he knew anything that might endanger him? Something to do with Babbage Town? Camp Peary? Anything like that?"

Alicia took several deep breaths and wiped her eyes with her sleeve before answering. "Camp Peary? What has that got to do with Len's death?"

"If Monk Turing's death is connected to what happened to Len, maybe everything."

"But I thought you said it looked like Monk killed himself."

"We don't know that for sure. But please answer my question, did Len mention anything to you?"

"He never said anyone wanted to hurt him."

Sean leaned forward. "All right. How about spies here? He ever talk about that?"

She shook her head. "No, never. Why?"

"Just something he said to me. Anything else you can think of?"

"Well, he did say that the people here had no idea what they were getting into. That what we were working on would change the world. And not in a good way." She attempted a smile. "He said we geeks were clueless about how the real world worked. Maybe he was right."

"He mentioned to me that what was going on at Babbage Town was worth countries going to war for. It can't be just numbers."

"I'm scared, Sean. Len Rivest was a very capable man. The fact that someone could kill him, like that, in his own house with security all around." She shuddered and fell back in her chair.

She looked so miserable that Sean rose and put an arm around her shoulders to steady her. "It'll be okay, Alicia."

"Don't patronize me! I'm terrified about Viggie. She could be in danger too."

"Why?" he asked.

"You tell me. You're the expert in this sort of thing."

"Does the girl know her father's not coming back?"

Alicia looked uncomfortable. "I'm trying to lay the groundwork to tell her, but it hasn't been easy."

"If you're really concerned about her, then I'd get her out of Babbage Town."

"I can't do that."

"I thought Viggie's welfare was your top priority?"

"Viggie's happy here. I can't just uproot her and take the girl someplace she's never been. It could destroy her."

"I'll admit it's not much of a choice."

"I have another option," Alicia said suddenly, gripping his hand. "*We* stay and *you* help keep Viggie safe."

"I've already got a job." *I've actually got two jobs now*, Sean mentally corrected.

"She's a child. She needs help. Are you just going to sit there and refuse to help a vulnerable little girl who just lost her father?"

Sean started to say something and then stopped. Finally, he sighed. "I guess I could keep an eye on her."

Tears again trickled down Alicia's cheeks. "Thank you."

"I guess now that I'm her unofficial bodyguard I should actually meet the young lady."

Alicia composed herself and rose. "She's just finished doing some factoring exercises for me."

"What?"

"Viggie has the ability to factor large numbers in her head. Not so large as to make my work obsolete, but there could be something lurking in the recesses of her mind that provides the key to unlocking the shortcut I've been looking for."

"And the vulnerable little girl brings the world as we know it to a screeching halt?"

Alicia smiled. "Well, it's said that the meek shall inherit the earth."

30

Sean had expected to find a shy, quiet type in Viggie Turing; however, the girl was full of energy, and her wide, blue eyes seemed to capture every movement around her. She wore a bright red shirt, Capri pants and was barefoot. After being introduced by Alicia, Viggie immediately took Sean's hand and led him over to the piano.

"Sit."

He sat.

"You play?" she asked, staring at him with a pair of eyes that were uncomfortably intense.

"Bass guitar. Only four strings, not so complicated. And when you're losing millions of brain cells every day like I am that's a good thing."

She didn't bother to acknowledge his little joke. Viggie sat down and played a tune that he'd never heard before.

"Okay, you stumped me," he said. "Who is it?"

Alicia supplied the answer. "'Vigenère Turing.' It's an original composition."

Sean stared at the girl, impressed.

"You like it?" she asked simply.

He nodded. "You're a very gifted musician."

She smiled, and Sean could finally see the eleven-year-old girl inside, for it was a shy, eager-to-please sort of expression. And this scared him. It might make her trust people she shouldn't. *Spies here, Rivest had said.*

"Viggie, do you—"

She started playing another song. When she finished, Viggie got up and walked over to a chair at the kitchen table and stared out the window. As Sean watched, her wide, dancing eyes retreated to slits.

Sean rose. "Viggie?"

Sean looked over at Alicia, who was motioning him to join her on the couch.

Speaking quietly she said, "She sort of withdraws into a little world of her own. If we wait she'll come around."

"Has she been seen by experts? Is she on medication?"

"I don't know about the experts, but she's not on medication. Now that I'm her guardian I'm going to look into it right away."

"What do you know about Viggie's mom?"

"Monk said they were divorced, years ago. He had full custody."

"That's what Rivest said. But you know, Alicia, if Viggie's mother shows up a court will likely grant her custody unless she's in prison or otherwise incapable of taking care of her daughter."

"But Monk appointed me guardian."

"That doesn't matter when a parent is involved."

"I'm not going to worry about that until it happens."

"18,313 and 22,307."

They turned to look at Viggie, who was now staring at them.

"Those are the prime factors of 408,508,091," the girl explained. "Aren't they?"

Alicia nodded. "That's right. If you multiply 18,313 and 22,307 you get 408,508,091."

Viggie clapped her hands together and giggled.

"But I just gave you that number barely an hour ago. How did you come up with them so fast?" Alicia asked.

"I saw them, in my head."

Alicia said eagerly, "Were they lined up? Were you doing math in your head again?"

"No. It just popped into my mind. I didn't have to do math."

"At least not any math of which mere mortals are aware," Alicia said thoughtfully. "Viggie, I think Mr. Sean wanted to ask you something." Viggie looked at him expectantly.

"Well, I just wanted you to know that I'll be coming to see you. Would that be okay?"

Viggie looked at Alicia, who nodded.

"I guess so," Viggie said. "But I should really check with Monk."

"You call your dad by his first name?"

"He calls me by my first name. Isn't that what people do?"

"I guess it is. I haven't met your dad, but he sounds like a really cool guy."

"He is. He played in a rock band in college." Viggie looked out the window again and Sean was afraid she was about to lapse into one of her "funks," but she merely said, "I wish he'd come home soon. There are lots of things I have to tell him."

"Like what?" Sean asked, perhaps a little too quickly.

Viggie immediately rose and started playing the piano again, louder and louder.

When she momentarily stopped, Sean said, "Viggie, when was the last time you saw you dad?" This query only caused her to play even more fiercely.

"Viggie!" Sean said, but Alicia was already pulling him toward the front door as Viggie smashed her fists down on the keyboard and raced out of the room. A few seconds later they heard a door slam. An instant later the woman Sean had seen sleeping on the couch the night before entered the room.

Alicia said, "I'll be back in a few minutes to check on her, Mrs. Graham." Alicia led Sean from the house.

"Okay, I see your problem with Viggie," he said, scratching his head.

"I think she knows, deep down, that there's something wrong with her father. Anytime anyone starts nibbling around that subject she just shuts down."

He caught sight of Viggie staring at them from her bedroom window and then, like a thought he'd lost in his head, she was gone.

Sean turned to Alicia. "Those numbers she told you. Couldn't she have figured it out on a calculator?"

"Yes, but it would have taken her about a full day to do it. 18,313 is the 2,000th prime number, meaning she would have to have gone through all those that preceded it to see if it divided into 408,508,091 without leaving a remainder. She just saw it in her head, like she said."

"And tell me why this is so important?"

"Sean—"

"Damn it, Alicia, people are dying here. I've agreed to protect Viggie because you think she's in danger. The least you can do is start telling me why."

"All right. The world runs on information sent electronically. How to move it from A to B safely is the key to civilization. Using your credit card to buy things, getting cash from an ATM, sending an e-mail, paying bills or purchasing things online. Encryption these days is strictly about numbers and their length. The strongest system is based on asymmetric public key cryptography. It's the only thing that makes electronic transmissions, from government to commercial to private citizens safe and thus viable."

"I think I've heard of it. RSA or something?"

"Right. Now, the standard public key is typically a very large prime number hundreds of digits long that would take a hundred million PCs, working in parallel several thousand years, to figure out the two factors. However, while everyone knows the public key number, or at least your computer does, the only way to read what's being sent is by unlocking the public key using the two *private* keys. Those keys are the two prime factors of the public key and only your computer software knows what they are. To use a simple example, the number fifty might be the public key and ten and five would be the private keys. If you know the numbers ten and five you can read the transmission."

"Like the numbers that Viggie gave you?"

"Yes. With computers getting faster all the time and the practice of running hundreds of millions of computers in massive parallel assaults the encryption standards keep getting ratcheted upward. But, still, all you have to do is add a few more digits to the public key and the time required to break it goes up thousands, if not millions of years."

"But your research might just throw a monkey wrench in all that."

"The encryption community is betting on the fact that there is no shortcut to factoring because in 2,000 years of searching no one's found one. And yet Viggie is able to do it from time to time. Can she do it for bigger numbers? If so, as I said, no electronic transmission is safe and the world as we know it would be drastically different."

"Back to typewriters, couriers and tin cans strung with wire?"

"It would shut down business and government; the poor consumer would have no idea how to function. And generals could no longer safely communicate with their armies. I doubt most people realize that as late as the Seventies, before public key cryptography was invented, private businesses and governments had to send thousands of couriers out constantly with new codebooks and passwords. No one wants to go back to those days."

He said, "It's incredible how our entire civilization is based on not being able to factor huge numbers quickly."

"We made the bed, now we have to lie in it."

"Obviously the public isn't aware of any of this?"

"It would scare the public to death."

"So do you think there's a shortcut?"

"Viggie makes me think there might be one. But despite that, my biggest worry right now isn't about numbers, it's about Viggie. I can't let anything happen to her."

"You think someone knows Viggie might be the key to stopping the world in its tracks?"

"You said Len thought there were spies here. Her father knew about her ability and he's dead. I don't know. I just don't know."

Sean once more put a comforting hand on her shoulder. "Nothing's going to happen to her. The FBI and police are around; the place is crawling with guards."

"That was true *before* Len was killed," she pointed out.

"But now I'm on the case."

"And how exactly do you propose to protect Viggie?"

"How many bedrooms do you have in your bungalow?"

"Four. Why?"

"One for Viggie, one for you and one for me and one left over."

"You, moving in with *me*?"

"If I stay in the main house, there's no way I could get to her in time in case something happened."

"I'll have to get Champ's approval and talk to Viggie. I get off duty tomorrow around six in the evening. How about then?"

"Why don't you just move into Viggie's cottage?"

"There are too many reminders of Monk there for her. I thought taking her away from that would be best."

"How will you explain it to Viggie?"

"I'll think of something."

Alicia walked off.

Sean stood staring after her when his cell phone buzzed. He looked at the number and groaned. It was

Joan Dillinger. How was he going to explain taking on not one, but two new assignments? The answer was clear. He just wasn't going to answer the damn phone.

He trudged back to his room and wondered how he was managing to dig the hole he was in ever deeper.

31

When Horatio Barnes returned to Linda Sue Buchanan's house that evening her man, Daryl, didn't look too happy about what his little lady was planning. He was a big, sloppy fellow, his greasy T-shirt stretched wide over both chest and belly. He held the baby in one beefy paw and a can of Michelob in the other.

Daryl bellowed, "You don't even know this little dude, Lindy. He might be some damn sex rapist for all you know."

"Well, if you think about it, most rapists are *sex* rapists," Horatio said pleasantly. "In fact I've seen a few of them in prison."

"See, what'd I tell you? Dude's been in the joint," Daryl declared.

"No, I *consulted* with several state prison systems to counsel inmates. But unlike my patients I could leave at the end of the day."

Linda Sue checked her purse and pulled out her keys. "We're going in separate cars, Daryl, and I got my Mace and this." She held out a compact revolver.

Daryl looked relieved at the sight of the firearm. "Well if he tries anything you just shoot his ass."

"That's the plan," Linda Sue said, matter-of-factly checking the ammo in her gun.

"Hold on a minute, folks," Horatio said. "First, no one's shooting anybody. And by the way do you have a permit for that thing?"

Daryl snorted. "Hell this is Tennessee, man, ain't need no permit to carry a gun in good old Tennessee."

"You might want to check that again," Horatio said. "And I'm here only to talk to Linda Sue's grandmother. I told her she could just give me the directions to the place and I'd go myself."

Daryl whipped around to look at her. "Is that right? So why you going then?"

"I'm going so I get paid, you dumb-ass," she snapped.

"I tell you what, I'll give you the hundred dollars right now, and you can just hang here with your debonair man about town," Horatio said while Daryl gave him a confused look.

"No way. My understanding was that a hundred bucks was the *minimum* and if the information Granny got is real good, it'd be worth more. Maybe a lot more."

"Well, that wasn't my understanding."

"Do you want to go see Granny or not?"

"A hundred bucks! Damn!" Daryl said as the amount finally sank into his clouded head.

"Okay, you win. Let's go," Horatio said.

"Thought you'd see it my way," Linda Sue said with a little smirk.

Daryl called after them from the porch. "Hey, Lindy, if you got to shoot him make damn sure you got the money first."

"Well, if she shot me, she could take *all* my money since I'd hardly be in a position to object," Horatio said helpfully.

"Hey, that's right," Daryl agreed excitedly. "Baby, you listening to this?"

Horatio held up a cautionary hand. "But then she'd have to spend the rest of her life in prison for murder and armed robbery. In fact, in *good old* Tennessee that might just get you the death penalty. And that might apply to accessories *before* the fact. I hope you recognize your role."

Daryl simply stared at him, his mind unable to form a response.

Horatio turned to Linda Sue. "Make sure you don't shoot yourself."

"I've got the damn safety thingy on," she snapped.

"That'd be quite a feat, since revolvers don't have safeties."

"Oh," Linda Sue said.

"Yeah, oh."

32

The nursing home was about an hour's drive away. When he walked into the facility, the odor of human urine and feces hit Horatio like a sledgehammer. He'd been in these state-run places before treating people for depression. Hell, who wouldn't be depressed having to spend their Golden Years in a festering dump like this? Old folks were stacked like packing crates in their wheelchairs and walkers up against the wall. From down the hall the sounds of canned laughter from a TV floated to Horatio and Linda Sue as they headed to the reception area. The laugh track was insufficient to cover the moans and groans coming from the Greatest Generation abandoned in this stench-filled pile of concrete and crushed hopes.

Linda Sue moved steadfastly ahead, somehow ignoring the human misery on all sides of her.

Two minutes later they were in Granny's room, a semiprivate ten-by-ten with its own TV that didn't appear to be working. Granny's roommate was out but Granny herself was sitting in a chair in a checkered housecoat, red, swollen feet bursting forth from her tattered slippers. Her gray hair, what was left of it, was flattened under a net. Her face was saggy and lined, her teeth yellowed and worn down in many places. Yet her eyes were clear and steady. They moved from Linda Sue to Horatio and then back to her grand-daughter.

"Haven't seen you for a while, Lindy," Granny said in a mellow southern accent.

Lindy Sue looked extremely put out by this comment. "Been busy, got kids to raise and a man to keep happy."

"Which man might that be? The one just *out* of prison or the one headed *to* prison?"

Horatio had to stifle a chuckle. Old Granny was clearly not suffering from dementia.

"This here feller," Lindy said, pointing at Horatio. "He wants to know some stuff 'bout folks that used to live in the neighborhood while you were still there."

Granny's gaze swiveled around to rest on Horatio. There was intrigue in those old eyes, he could see. Probably she would welcome anything to get her mind off this place.

"I'm Horatio Barnes," he began, shaking her hand. "Nice to meet you. And thank you for your time."

"Hazel Rose," she replied. "Time is the only thing I got plenty of in this place. Now who do you want to know about?"

He told her about the Maxwells.

She nodded. "I remember them, sure. Frank Maxwell cut quite a figure in his uniform. And those boys they had; big, good-looking fellows they all were."

"And the daughter, Michelle? Do you remember her?"

"I do. Now why don't you tell me *why* you want to know all this?"

"You'll probably find it very boring."

"I doubt it could compete with this place in the boredom department, so please go ahead and humor an old woman."

"I've been engaged by the family to find out something. Something that happened when Michelle was around six. That would have been about twenty-seven or twenty-eight years ago."

"Happened? Like what?"

"Like something that would have made Michelle's personality change."

Linda Sue snorted. "Hell, a six-year-old ain't got no personality."

"On the contrary," Horatio said. "A child's permanent personality is substantially formed by age six."

Linda Sue snorted again and started fiddling with her purse clasp while Horatio turned his attention back to Hazel. "Did you notice anything like that? I know it was a long time ago but it would really be a big help if you could remember."

Hazel seemed to reflect on this for a bit, pursing her lips as she did so.

Linda Sue finally broke the silence. "I'm going out for a smoke." She rose and then wagged a finger at Horatio. "And there's only one way in and out of this place, so don't you even *think* about trying to scoot off without you know what." She flicked what she probably assumed was a sincere smile in her granny's direction and left.

"How much did you promise to pay her?" Hazel asked as soon as her granddaughter was out of earshot.

Horatio smiled, pulled up a chair and sat down next to her. "A hundred bucks. I'd much rather give it to you."

Hazel waved this gesture off. "I don't have anything to spend money on in this place. Just give it to Lindy. Way the girl goes through deadbeat men, she'll need it. Four babies by four different sperm donors, excuse my French, and she'll probably have four more before she's done." She sat quiet for a few moments and Horatio decided to ride it out.

"How is Michelle?" Hazel asked.

"She's been better," Horatio said frankly.

"I followed her career," Hazel admitted. "Read about her in the papers and all."

"You did? Why?"

"Look what the girl did with herself. Olympic athlete. Secret Service. Girl's done herself proud. Always knew she would."

"How?"

"Like you said, with a child you can tell how they're going to be from a pretty early age. That girl was stubborn and determined. I remember thinking about her that it's not the size of the dog in the fight, but the size of the fight in the dog. And that girl was not going to let anything or anyone stand in her way."

"You would've made a good psychologist."

"I wanted to be a doctor. Graduated third in my class in college."

"What happened?"

"My older brother wanted to be a doctor too. And back then the boys got what they wanted over the girls. So I stayed home, took care of my ailing parents and then got married, had my babies, my husband dropped dead of a coronary the day after he retired, and now here I am. Not much of a life, but it's the only one I've got."

"Raising a family is a pretty important job."

"I'm not saying I regret any of it. But everybody has dreams. Some people, like Michelle, fight hard enough to realize theirs."

"So did you notice a difference in her?"

"Yes. I couldn't say it was when she was six. Too many years ago, you understand. But all of a sudden the child wouldn't meet my eye and we were friends, had her over for little tea parties and such with some of the other neighborhood children. Then she stopped coming. Things would make her jump, or cry. Tried to talk to her mother, but Sally Maxwell didn't want to hear about it. As it was they moved away shortly thereafter anyway."

"And do you have an idea of what might have happened to cause the change in Michelle?"

"I've thought about it over the years, but nothing ever popped out at me."

"One of the things that her family told me was that she became increasingly sloppy. And that hasn't changed."

"I wasn't really invited over to their house much. Sally had her hands full, what with Frank gone so much with work and all."

"I would've thought police work there would've had pretty regular hours."

"Michelle was a late baby for them. Frank was trying hard to get on with a major city police force. He worked during the day and was taking night courses at a local college to get a master's degree in criminal justice."

"Ambitious guy. So nothing else you can tell me?"

"Well, there is one thing that's puzzled me. Probably has nothing to do with what you're looking at."

"Right now, I'll take anything."

"Well, the Maxwells had a beautiful rose hedge that ran in front of their house. Frank planted it for an anniversary present to Sally. It was a pretty thing and the *aroma*. I used to go over there just to smell the flowers."

"It's not there anymore."

"That's right. I went to bed one night and woke up the next morning and somebody had chopped it all down."

"Did you ever find out who did it?"

She shook her head. "Frank figured it was some kids he'd busted for drunk driving, but I'm not so sure about that. Teenage boys, what do they know from flowers? They would've slashed Frank's tires or thrown rocks through the windows."

"Do you remember when this was?"

She stared at the ceiling, the lips pursed again. "Nearly thirty years ago, I expect."

"Or maybe twenty-seven or twenty-eight?"

"Could be, yes."

Horatio sat back, deep in thought. Finally he rose and took out his wallet. Hazel immediately held up her hand.

"Give the money to Lindy. She'll make your life miserable until you do."

But Horatio wasn't taking money out of his wallet. He wrote something down on the back of a card and handed it to her. "This is the name and number of a woman I know down here who can get you into a facility that's a lot better. Give me a day to make the arrangements and then give her a call."

"I don't have money for a *better* facility."

"It's not how much money you have; it's who you know, Hazel. And the place I'm thinking of has ongoing classes in different subjects, including *medicine*, if you're still interested."

The old woman took the card. "I thank you," she said quietly.

As Horatio turned to leave, she said, "If you see Michelle, would you tell her Hazel Rose said hello? And that I'm real proud of her?"

"Consider it done."

Horatio walked down the hall, found Lindy flirting with a burly attendant in the visitor's lounge, paid the sullen woman off and fled the state-supported hell-hole.

As he climbed into his car he started wondering how vanishing rose hedges might have ended up destroying Michelle Maxwell's life nearly three decades later.

33

The next morning Michelle worked out hard, bitched at one of the nurses about the AWOL Horatio Barnes, went back to her room and ripped the straw out of Cheryl's mouth after the woman emitted six excruciatingly long slurps in a row.

Then she heard the running feet heading her way and knew the moment of truth had arrived. She grabbed Cheryl, who was protesting loudly, and threw her in the bathroom. "Don't come out until you hear one body hit the floor," she yelled in the woman's face. This remark actually made Cheryl stop screeching for her straw.

Michelle slammed the bathroom door, turned and braced herself.

The door to her room was kicked open and there was Barry, holding a metal pipe.

"You bitch!" he screamed.

"You drug dealer!" she screamed back in mock fury and then laughed. "So let me guess, they busted your partner this morning and he ratted on you."

"You bitch!" he roared again.

She motioned with her hands. "Come and get me, Barry, baby. You know you want to. And after you kick my ass you can have yourself a real good time with me."

He sprang forward, the pipe held high for the killing blow.

He flew backward just as fast when her foot collided with his face. She didn't wait for him to recover. Her fist crashed into his gut and then she whirled around and delivered a crushing kick to his jaw driving him backward and over Cheryl's bed. He struggled up, stunned by the strength of her blows. He threw the pipe at her, missing her head by an inch as she ducked. Then he picked up a chair and hurled that too, but Michelle was too nimble. He bounded over the bed and lunged for her, and caught nothing except air and a massive side kick to his kidneys that seemed to drive all the fight out of him.

He dropped to his knees groaning as she stood over him and for good measure drove an elbow into the back of his head. That sent him flat to the floor.

"I'm waiting, Barry. If you want to finish this, you better hurry; the cops will be here soon."

"You bitch!"he moaned weakly.

"Yeah, you said that already. Can't you think of something new?"

He tried to get up and she tensed to deliver a knockout blow when two Fairfax cops peered through the doorway, guns drawn.

She pointed at Barry. "He's the one you want. I'm Michelle Maxwell, the one who tipped off Detective Richards yesterday."

One of the cops, eyeing the destroyed room, said, "You okay, ma'am?"

Barry groaned from the floor, "You idiot! *I'm* the one who's hurt. I need a doctor. She attacked *me*."

"This is my room. He came in with the lead pipe over there, his prints are all over it," Michelle said. "He tried to pay me back for crashing the little drug op he had going with the pharmacist here. My guess is they were fudging the computer records on the drug inventories so the theft wouldn't show up and old Barry here was shipping them out to his street team under the cover of patients in the locked ward here sending out packages." She glanced down at the beaten man. "As you can see, things didn't work out exactly as he'd planned."

The cops hauled Barry up, despite his protests of devastating injury, cuffed him and read him his rights.

"We'll need your statement, ma'am," one of the cops said.

"Oh, and I'm just dying to give it."

They'd holstered their weapons and were leading Barry out when everyone froze. In the doorway was Sandy in her wheelchair. However, everyone was fixated not on the woman but on the gun she was holding.

34

One cop's hand flew to his sidearm, but Sandy yelled, "Don't!" She gripped the gun with both hands. "Don't," she said again. "I don't want to hurt you, just him," she added, motioning with the pistol to Barry.

She settled her gaze back on him and said, "Don't recognize me, do you? No reason you should. You didn't come there that day to kill me; you came to murder the best man. But you missed and got the groom instead. My husband!"

Barry sucked in a breath and Sandy smiled even more broadly. "Oh, now it's coming back to you." She shook her head. "What a bad shot you were. Killed my husband, left me a cripple and missed your target. Your mob bosses must've been real pissed off at you for that."

Now Michelle stepped forward and the pistol moved around to point at her.

Sandy said, "Michelle, don't act the hero here. I really don't want to hurt you. But I will if you try and stop me from giving this piece of trash what he should've gotten a long time ago."

"Sandy, you don't have to do this. Barry's being

arrested for drug-dealing. He's going to go away for a long time."

"No, he won't, Michelle."

"Sandy, we have the evidence, he's busted."

"He's in Witness Protection. They're going to cover it up just like they've done in the past."

Michelle turned to look at Barry and then back at Sandy. "Witness Protection?"

"He ratted on his mob bosses and did no time in jail for killing the man I loved; the feds looked the other way because he helped bring down a major crime family. And they're going to look the other way on this. Isn't that right, Barry, or should I call you by your real name, Anthony Bender?"

Barry smiled and said, "Don't know what you're talking about. And if you try and shoot me you're going down too."

"You think I care? You took the only thing from me I ever cared about. Ever!"

"I'm crying inside for you, little miss cripple."

"Shut up! Shut up!" Sandy screamed, her finger edging to the trigger. The cops were looking steadily at Sandy's weapon. Michelle sensed this, turned and mouthed something to each of them. Then she slid between Barry and Sandy.

"Sandy, give me the gun. He's going to jail this time, I'll make sure of it."

"Right." Barry laughed.

Michelle whirled around. "Shut up, you idiot."

She turned back to Sandy. "He will go to prison, I swear it. Now give me the gun."

"Michelle, get out of the way. I've spent years tracking this bastard down and now I'm going to finish it."

"He took your husband and your legs from you. Don't let him take the life you have left."

"What life? You call this a life?"

"You can help other people, Sandy. That's worth a lot."

"I can't even help myself, so how can I help anybody else?"

"You've helped *me*." Michelle took another step forward. "You helped me," she added more quietly. "You're not a criminal. You're not a killer. You're a good person. Don't let him take that from you."

The gun wavered a bit in Sandy's hand, but then it became very rigid and her voice calmed.

"I'm sorry, Michelle. You're right. I can't kill that filth even if he does deserve it."

"That's right, Sandy. Now give me the gun."

"Goodbye, Michelle."

"What!"

Sandy placed the gun against her temple and squeezed the trigger. The click reverberated around the room. Sandy squeezed the trigger again and then again, yet no bullet flew out to end her life. She looked stunned as Michelle walked up and slipped the gun out of her hand.

"I took the bullets out earlier."

Sandy stared up at her in amazement. "How, how did you know?"

"Dirt on your fingers and dirt on the floor. People don't normally ferret around in the soil of a flower basket. I knew something was in there."

"Why didn't you just take the gun then?" one of the cops grumbled. "If you hadn't alerted us just now that it was empty we might have shot her."

Michelle took hold of one of Sandy's trembling hands. "I thought she might have to play this out, to get on with her life. To see what she was and *wasn't* capable of." Michelle smiled tenderly at the woman. "Sometimes that's the best therapy of all."

"You knew about Barry?" she said.

"I hadn't figured that he was the one who shot your husband, but I saw you watching him and could sense you had some interest in him. I didn't know about the Witness Protection angle though."

"By the way," Barry began confidently. "Call my handler at the U.S. Marshals Service. His name is Bob Truman, right in D.C."

Michelle brightened. "Bobby Truman?"

Barry looked at her blankly. "You know him?"

"I should. I won a silver medal in the Olympics with his daughter. When I tell him what happened, you'll be fortunate to see sunlight before you're eighty. Must be my lucky day."

They took Barry away, kicking and screaming. The cops made some noise about charging Sandy, but

Michelle ultimately dissuaded them from doing so. "Do you really want to fill out the paperwork on that one? And besides, every *wife* in America would be screaming at you for being jerks," she added, staring pointedly at the wedding band on one of the cop's fingers.

"The gun *was* unloaded," that cop said nervously to his partner.

The other cop said, "Screw it, I don't need the hassle. But we're taking the weapon."

Michelle wheeled Sandy back to her room and spent some time talking to her. When Michelle got back to her room, she heard a whimpering sound. She opened the bathroom door and Cheryl nearly fell out.

"Cheryl, I'm sorry, I forgot all about you." Michelle led the quivering woman over to her bed and sat down with her. Then she spotted the straw on the floor, picked it up and handed it to her. To her surprise Cheryl didn't start sucking on it. Instead she clung tightly to Michelle's shoulders. Michelle could feel the woman's sharp bones against her skin.

Michelle sighed, then smiled and hugged the woman back. "I hear they're having a really good session on eating disorders tonight. What say we go together? After *dinner*."

In a tremulous whisper, Cheryl said, "You don't have an eating disorder."

"Are you kidding? Cheryl, I ate the Salisbury steak, a *double* helping. And actually *liked* it. If that's not a disorder, I don't know what is."

35

The next evening Sean was packing when someone knocked on his bedroom door.

"Come in."

Champ Pollion poked his head through the door.

"Did Alicia talk to you?" Sean asked.

"About the move? Yes. I have no problem with you acting as Viggie's guardian angel. I would just caution you not to end up dead," he added firmly.

"Self-preservation has always been high on my list of priorities." Sean closed his bag and set it on the floor. "You know, we never got around to talking about what it is you do here at Babbage Town."

Champ came into the room. "I was really counting on Len to go through the details."

"Since Len can't do the honors, care to give me the tour? I could take a stroll to Hut Number Two with you right now."

"So you know about Hut Number Two, do you?"

"And I'm really curious about that gadget you had, the one that will make people forget about Edison and Bell?"

"I have been known to give in to hyperbole from time to time."

"Why don't you let me see for myself?"

"Look, I don't mean to be uncooperative—" Champ began.

"Then don't be," Sean cut in.

"There are confidences one has to keep," Champ said loftily.

"Let me explain the situation to you, Champ. First, I'm working with Sheriff Hayes on the case and he can compel you to show me if you force me to go down that road. Second, we've got two dead men tied to Babbage Town. I doubt you'd like to see it go to three, especially if you happen to be the third corpse."

"*Me!* You think *I'm* in danger?"

"I know *I'm* in danger, so you sure as hell must be."

"Look, can't this wait? I'm very busy."

"That's what Len Rivest told me. And look where it got him."

Champ stiffened and then relaxed. "I don't know; this is very awkward."

"It's been my experience that uncooperative people have something to hide."

Champ's face flushed. "I have nothing to hide."

"Good, so you won't mind telling me where you were between the hours of midnight and two A.M. the night Len Rivest died?"

"Is that when he was killed?"

"Just answer the question."

"I don't have to answer anything," he said defiantly.

"True. Call your lawyer, clamp your mouth shut and let the FBI investigate every detail of your life back to preschool. And if the Bureau is anything, it's thorough."

Champ seemed to consider this for a few moments. "I couldn't sleep so I went down to the hut to go over some test results."

"Anyone see you?"

"Of course. There are always people working. We're a 24/7 operation."

"So you were there the whole time? Twelve to two A.M? And beyond? Verified by witnesses." *Come on, Champ, tell me a lie. Come on.*

A sheen of perspiration rose on Champ's forehead. "As best as I can recollect. You can't hold me to the minute."

"I can't but other people can and will. Now let's go check out your *hut*."

On the way over Sean said, "Do you have a cleaning staff come in? Or do your folks do their own cleaning and laundry?"

"The maids come in daily in several shifts. About two dozen cleaning personnel at a time." He pointed up ahead where a woman in a white maid's uniform was pushing a very full laundry cart down the pavement.

"The laundry services are housed in part of Hut Number Three, next to the security headquarters. All the cleaning people have been vetted, wear the same uniforms and carry nontransferable IDs. Is that sufficient?"

"No, it's not. What type of detergent do they use?"

Champ stopped walking and stared at him. "Excuse me?"

"Just kidding, Champ, just kidding."

36

Hut Number Two was far larger than Alicia's domain. To enter by the locked door, Champ had to insert his security badge in a slot and have his fingerprint scanned by a device attached to the wall. The interior of the hut was made up of an enormous work area in the middle, with enclosed rooms around the perimeter. Through some of the open doors of these rooms, Sean could see sophisticated machinery and people working with them. On one wall hung a banner that read: "P = NP."

Sean pointed to it. "What's that mean?"

Champ hesitated and then said, "It's an equation representing NP, or nondeterministic polynomial time equaling P or polynomial time. When fully realized, it'll make E equals MC squared look like a blueprint for a set of Tinkertoys."

"How so?"

"Polynomial time represents problems that are easy to solve, well, relatively easy. NP-complete problems represent the most difficult problems in the universe."

"Like how to cure cancer?"

"Not exactly, although who knows what the applications might turn out to be. In fact we have a department here whose sole duty is to determine how newly minted proteins fold up into just the right shape that determines their function in the body. There are trillions of different ways they could fold, and yet most proteins fold up just the right way."

Sean noted that the man was far more talkative and articulate when it came to areas of his expertise and he intended to press this advantage. "So if they usually get it right, why is understanding how they do it important?"

"Because they don't *always* get it right. And when they don't it can be catastrophic. Alzheimer's and Mad Cow Disease are examples of proteins blowing the folding sequence. But what I'm really talking about are, for example, the absolute best way for a car to be manufactured, or how to manage the world's air traffic not in *one* of the best ways possible, but *the* best way possible taking into account every conceivable factor. How to take energy from point A to anywhere else with maximum efficiency; or how to get the proverbial traveling salesman on his route in the most optimal way possible. Indeed, with just fifteen cities on his itinerary the poor salesman has more than 650 *billion* possibilities to consider.

"Did you know that no software in the world comes with a guarantee of being bug-free? Yet if we can solve NP problems it would be possible to send out perfect software every time. And the kicker is, the way the universe is set up, there's every reason to believe that when you solve one NP problem, you've solved them *all* in one fell swoop. It would be the greatest discovery in history. The Nobel Prize wouldn't come close to doing the discoverer of it justice."

"So how come computers can't do that now?"

"Computers are *deterministic* creatures, whereas, as the name states, NP problems are *non*deterministic. Thus one needs a nondeterministic technology to solve them."

"And that's what you're working on here?"

"Along with a way to factor huge numbers rapidly."

"Alicia explained the concept to me. She's attempting to find a shortcut, then nothing is secure anymore and the world as we know it stops. And stopping the world in its tracks is worthy of a Nobel Prize?"

Champ shrugged. "That's an issue for the politicians, not us humble scientists. Alicia's research is a long shot at best." Champ pointed around the room. "Here is where the answer lies. We only have to find it." He hesitated a moment and said, "Look at this."

He eagerly led Sean over to an oval table covered in glass. Underneath the glass was a small odd-looking machine.

"What is it?" Sean asked.

"A Turing machine," Champ replied with a tone of reverence.

"Turing. Like in Monk Turing?"

"No, as in *Alan* Turing. However, I believe Monk was related, which goes to show there is something to genetics after all. Alan Turing was a true genius who saved millions of lives back during World War II."

"Was he a doctor?"

"No, Turing was a mathematician, though that word hardly does the man justice. He was assigned to the famed Bletchley Park, outside London. We've named our buildings *huts* in tribute to the code breakers at Bletchley because that's the term they used there for their work facilities. Simply put, Turing invented the bombe machine that broke the back of one of the most important German Enigma ciphers. The war in Europe ended at least two years early because of what Turing did. He was also a homosexual. Thank God the government didn't find out back then. They would've blackballed him and the Allies might have lost the war, the idiots! As it turned out, after the war his homosexuality was discovered, his career ruined and the poor fellow committed suicide. All that talent wasted simply because he liked boys and not girls."

"And you called this a Turing machine?"

"Yes. Turing hypothesized a universal thinking machine for want of a better description. Though it looks very simple, I can assure you, with the right set of instructions, a Turing machine can take on any problem. All computers today are built along these lines; think of it as very early software. No one can invent a classical computer that is better or more powerful in concept than a Turing machine; you can only build one that performs the steps faster."

"There's that word *classical* again."

Champ picked up a long, thin glass tube. "And this is the only device in the world that is potentially more powerful than a Turing machine."

"You showed me that thing when we first met, but didn't explain what it was."

"I can tell you, but you won't understand it."

"Come on, I'm not stupid," Sean said irritably.

The other man snapped, "That's not the point! You won't understand it because not even *I* understand it really. The human mind is not meant to function on a subatomic plane. Any physicist that tells you he fully understands the quantum world is lying."

"So quantum? That's what we're talking about here?"

"Specifically subatomic particles that hold the potential for computing power far beyond human comprehension."

"It doesn't look like much," Sean said, glancing at the tube.

Champ slid his finger along it. "In the computer field, it's said that size matters. At the Los Alamos National Laboratory there is a supercomputer called Blue Mountain. As you undoubtedly know, every PC in the world has a chip. It's the brain of the computer and has millions of miniature switches chirping language in 1s and 0s. Blue Mountain has over *six thousand* chips making it a three teraops computer; that means it can perform three trillion operations per second. They use it to simulate the effects of a nuclear blast since the U.S., thankfully, doesn't explode the damn things for real anymore. However, as powerful as a three teraops machine is, when they tried to reproduce a mere one millionth of a second of a nuclear blast, it took old Blue *four months* of crunching numbers."

"Not exactly blazing speed," Sean commented.

"They're working on another supercomputer that will render Blue obsolete, a thirty teraops machine code-named Q spread out over an acre of ground. It will be able to perform more calculations in a minute than a human with a calculator could in a *billion* years and there are plans to build even faster ones. Yet all these computers are no better than the Turing machine; they just take up far more space and cost far more to run. That was the best we could do." He held up the tube. "Until now."

"And you're saying that's a computer?"

"In its current state it's a rudimentary device that can do a few calculations, yet that's quite beside the point. A computer talks in languages of 1s and 0s. Now with a classic computer you're either a 1 *or* a 0. You're not both. In the quantum world those limiting rules do not apply. An atom, in fact, can be both a 1 and a 0 at the same time, and therein lies the beauty of the whole concept. A classical computer plods through a problem mostly in a linear fashion until it gets to the right answer. With a quantum computer every single atom searches for the right answer in parallel. So, say if you want to know the square root of all numbers from 1 to 100,000, you place all the numbers on a line of atoms, manipulate the atoms with energy, and then collapse it *very* carefully because once it's observed the whole thing tumbles down like a house of cards. And voilà, you'll have all the correct answers at the same time, in milliseconds."

"I'm not seeing how that's possible."

Champ's face clouded. "Of course you can't! You're *not* a genius. But let's bring it back to something you *can* understand. A supercomputer like the behemoth Q feeds on data in sixty-four-bit chunks. So let's string a row of sixty-four atoms together. Remember, Q takes up an acre; sixty-four atoms are microscopic. The sixty-four-atom quantum computer can theoretically perform eighteen quintillion calculations *simultaneously* compared to Q's rather *meager* thirty trillion per second."

Sean gaped. "Eighteen quintillion? That's an actual number?"

"I'll try to give you some context. To equal the computing power of those sixty-four microscopic bits of energy, Q the supercomputer would need the surface space equal to five hundred *suns* to house all the required computer chips." He smiled impishly. "If you could figure out how to deal with the heat issue, of course. Or you can just use molecules. As you can see they take up far less space. And as I said that's why size matters in the computing world; only *small* rather than large is far better."

"And Monk Turing was familiar with all of this?" Sean asked.

"Yes. He was a very gifted physicist."

"And what he knew might have been something that could be sold?"

"There certainly might be people out there willing to pay for it."

"Anyone ever mention to you that there might be spies at Babbage Town?"

Sean had thrown this comment out offhand to gauge the man's reaction.

"Who told you that?"

"So you knew about possible spies here?"

"No, I mean, well, it's always possible," Champ said haltingly, his face very pale.

"Okay, calm down, and tell me the truth."

The other man bristled. "I can't say for sure whether there are or aren't spies here. That's the truth."

"If there are what would they be after?"

"We have years of data, of research, of trial and error, of progress, of possibilities. We are closing in on the answer."

"And that's valuable?"

"Enormously valuable."

"Worth going to war for?"

Champ stared at him. "I hope to God not, but—"

"Monk Turing apparently went out of the country about nine months ago. You must have approved the leave. Do you know where he went?"

"No, but he said it was family-related. You don't think Monk Turing was a spy, do you?"

Sean didn't answer. He glanced over at a worker who was leaving the hut. As she passed through the doorway, a small panel next to the door blinked. Sean hadn't noticed it when they'd come in.

"What's that?"

"A scanner," Champ said. "It automatically records who leaves and when."

"That's right. Len Rivest told me about the computer log. They were able to track Monk Turing's movements that way. So we can just ask the computer when *you* came here last night and when you left."

Champ was about to respond when both men's attention turned to the door as it banged open. Sheriff Hayes hustled in with a harried-looking security guard in his wake.

"I've been looking all over for you," an out-of-breath Hayes said to Sean. "We're wanted at a meeting," he added. "Right now. With Ian Whitfield. Well, he asked me to come, but I want you with me."

"Who the hell is Ian Whitfield?" a surprised Sean asked.

"He runs Camp Peary," Hayes answered. "We better get going." He glanced sharply at Sean. "You're coming, right?"

"I'm coming."

37

After suffering through an early dinner and attending the eating disorder session with Cheryl, Michelle checked herself out of the facility. Before leaving she visited with Sandy.

"I checked with my buddy at the U.S. Marshals. He said they're sick of Barry pulling this crap. They're kicking him out of Witness Protection and told the prosecutors to go for the max."

"I can't thank you enough, Michelle. I don't know what would've happened if that gun had been loaded."

"Hey, that's what psycho friends are for."

"Now stop worrying about me and go get that man of yours."

"Sandy, we're just friends."

"But you are going to see him?"

"Hell yes. I miss him."

"Good, then you can see if you still want to be just friends."

As Michelle was heading out, Sandy called after her, "Don't forget to invite me to the wedding. And if I were you I'd invest in a metal detector. With your line of work you never know who might show up to your nuptials."

On the way out Michelle left a message for Horatio Barnes with the head nurse. "Tell Mr. Harley-Davidson he can check me off his to-do list. I'm cured."

"I'm glad our treatment plan was so effective for you."

"Oh, it had nothing to do with your treatment plan. It was all about nailing that weasel Barry. I'd take that over happy pills any day." Michelle slammed the door on her way out.

She breathed in the fresh evening air and took a cab to the new apartment. Using the set of keys Sean had left her, she went inside and proceeded to mess up her part of the digs. She even tossed a few of Sean's things around. He'd pick them up when he got back of course, sick neatnik that the man was, but she'd at least force him to make the effort.

Then she nearly sprinted to her truck and drove around for a half-hour with the windows down, Aerosmith blasting in the CD chute and the comforting feel of her junk underfoot. All she had needed was a little R&R, she told herself. Sure the sessions with Barnes had been a real bitch, but she'd survived them too. In a war of wills, she had had little doubt who was going to prevail.

And then all thoughts of Horatio Barnes left her mind as she focused on her next plan of action: joining

Sean. She should probably call him and let him know she was coming. Yet Michelle hardly ever opted for the proper thing. And though she didn't want to admit it, a little piece of her was afraid that if she did call Sean, he would tell her not to come.

When she got back to her apartment Michelle found what she needed after a quick search of Sean's things: a file copy on Babbage Town complete with directions. Sean had said he was taking a small plane there, no doubt courtesy of little Miss Joan the pain-in-the-ass. Michelle opted to drive. She gauged the trip would take about four hours for normal drivers but with her illegal radar detector and her foot mashed to the floorboard she was confident she could drive it in under three. The fact that she was not employed by Joan's company did not deter her in the slightest. The case was the thing. And if she knew one thing, Michelle understood quite clearly that together on the hunt she and Sean were nearly unstoppable. That's what it was really all about. Not her. *Them.*

She packed a bag and hit the road, stopping only for a twenty-four-ounce high-octane coffee and three PowerBars. Her adrenaline was sky-high. God, it felt so good to be alive. And free.

Horatio went straight from the airport to the psychiatric facility to find his star patient had flown the coop.

"Did she say where she was going?" he asked the head nurse.

"No, but she asked me to tell you that she's cured."

"Oh, really? She's into self-diagnosis now?"

"I don't know, but let me tell you what she did while she was here." The nurse quickly explained about Barry and Sandy, Witness Protection and the drug bust.

"She did all that in the time I was away? Hell, I wasn't gone that long!"

"That lady doesn't let grass or apparently anything else grow under her feet. I heard she kicked Barry's butt pretty good. You know, I never liked him."

"Isn't hindsight wonderful," Horatio grumbled as he walked away.

"Good night to you too, Mr. Harley-Davidson," the nurse muttered.

Horatio thought things over. He had to make deductions about what Michelle would do now. Actually, it wasn't that difficult. She would without a doubt want to hook up with Sean. She might be headed there right now. Legally, there was nothing Horatio could do to stop her. But he also knew that the woman was not cured. The incident that had happened at the bar could happen again, manifesting itself in a different and more deadly form.

He was debating whether to alert Sean when his phone rang.

"Speak of the devil, I was just about to call you," Horatio said.

Sean chuckled. "I'd make that quip about great minds, but I'm actually surrounded by big brains down here, so I'll forgo the opportunity. I'm on my way to meet with the head of Camp Peary but I wanted to ask you something."

"Camp Peary? As in the CIA Farm?"

"The one and only. I've got a favor to ask you." He explained about Viggie. "I know it's a pain wanting you to come down because you're busy with Michelle and the rest of your practice."

Horatio cut in. "Actually, I'm not. My favorite patient went AWOL on me." He brought Sean up to date on both Michelle's adventure at the facility and her checking herself out.

"Damn, leave it to her to find trouble wherever she goes," Sean said, but there was a touch of pride in his voice at what she'd done.

"And my best guess is she's on the way to see you."

"Me? I told her a little about the case, but not where it was."

"Did you leave anything back at the apartment?"

Sean groaned. "Oh, hell, I left a file copy there because I don't have an office."

"Your organizational instincts are commendable, but that means she'll probably be there by morning if not sooner."

"Joan will pitch a fit. They don't really get along."

"Astonishing. I'll head down tomorrow. Is there a place to stay nearby?"

"I can probably get you a bunk at Babbage Town. So what do I do when Michelle shows up?"

"Act normal, she certainly will seem to be."

"Have you made any progress on her case?"

"I had an interesting trip to Tennessee that I'll fill you in on when I see you. I have to thank you for bringing me in on what has been a fascinating case. This Viggie sounds interesting too."

"Horatio, this whole place is interesting. And more than a little dangerous right now, so if you want to respectfully decline I won't hold it against you."

"I'll pretend I didn't hear that."

"Is Michelle any better?"

"We need to help her clean up her soul, Sean, so she won't have to worry about a bomb ever going off again. And I'm not letting go until we get her to that point."

"I'll be right there with you, Horatio."

"Good, because from what I've seen of that woman, there's not a man alive who can take her by himself."

"Tell me something I don't know."

38

As they pulled through the college town of William and Mary and its neatly laid out brick buildings, Sean glanced over at Hayes. The good sheriff was hunched forward gripping the steering wheel so tightly his knuckles were the color of an eggshell.

"Sherriff Hayes, if you break the steering wheel in half we won't be able to get back."

Hayes's face reddened and he loosened his grip. "Just call me Merk, everybody does. I guess I'm not acting like a proper law enforcement officer, am I?"

"Most cops don't get summoned to meet with the big bad wolf in the middle of an investigation."

"What do you think he's going to say?"

"I doubt anything we really want to hear. And I can tell you straight out, the C does not stand for cooperation."

"My day just keeps getting better and better!" Hayes exclaimed.

"So did you talk to Alicia?"

Hayes nodded. "After you told me she was seeing Rivest, I had to."

"Was it serious between them?"

"She seemed to think so."

They parked in front of the address Hayes had been given. It was a three-story brick building that appeared to Sean to be made up of residential units.

A man dressed in a polo shirt and khaki pants met them inside the lobby area. Sean sized up the fellow as Ian Whitfield's security. The guy wasn't as tall as Sean, and lacked bulging muscles, but there wasn't an ounce of fat on his body; the man's six-pack abs were visible through the shirt. And to Sean's informed eye, the guy carried himself with the air of someone who could kill you a dozen different ways without breaking a sweat.

The first thing he did was show them his ID, then confiscate Hayes's sidearm. He next frisked Sean, all without saying a word.

They rode the elevator up to the third floor and were soon seated in comfortable chairs around an oval table inside one of the corner units. Six-Pack disappeared for a moment and then returned with another gent. This guy also wore a polo shirt and khakis and was in nearly as good condition as the other, even though he had close-cropped gray hair and was probably nearing sixty. However, Sean noted the man limped. There was something wrong with his right leg.

A flick of a gaze by the man at Six-Pack and a manila file folder appeared in Whitfield's hand, for this was Ian Whitfield, Sean assumed.

There followed a few minutes of silence while their

host methodically read through the file. Then he finally turned his attention to them.

"There have been four confirmed suicides in the vicinity of our installation over the last twenty-seven months," Whitfield said.

Sean hadn't expected this opening line and obviously neither had Hayes.

Whitfield continued: "For some reason we've become the whipping boy for the depressed and suicidal. I don't know why, but it seems there could be many reasons, including wanting notoriety or causing trouble. It goes without saying that I'm growing a little tired of these stunts."

"Someone dying hardly qualifies as a stunt, does it?" Sean asked while the blood drained from Hayes's face. "The circumstances of Monk Turing's death have not been fully uncovered yet. Suicide, murder, we don't know yet."

Whitfield tapped the file. "All facts point to suicide." He looked at Hayes. "Don't you agree, Sheriff?"

Hayes stammered, "I guess you could say that."

"There was no evidence that Monk had been depressed enough to take his own life," Sean pointed out.

"Aren't all geniuses depressed?" Whitfield answered.

"How do you know he was a genius?"

"When people move into *my* neighborhood I like to get to know them."

"You've been to Babbage Town, have you?" Sean pressed.

Whitfield turned back to Hayes. "I trust I've made my position clear. Four suicides and now five. My patience is at an end."

"A man *has* died," Hayes said, apparently screwing up his courage in the face of the other man's patronizing tone.

"Anyone can jump a fence and blow his brains out."

Sean said, "Just because you say it doesn't make it true."

Whitfield kept his eyes on Hayes. "I'm assuming this man is associated with you somehow."

Sean piped up. "Sorry, I'm Sean King. I guess we missed the introduction phase of the conversation. I *am* associated with Sheriff Hayes on this matter. And we're assuming that you're Ian Whitfield, head of the CIA's Camp Peary? If not, we're wasting a lot of time."

"The FBI has concluded its investigation and suicide was the verdict," Whitfield said.

"Well, it wouldn't be the first time the Bureau has jumped the gun, would it? And of course we have the murder of Len Rivest, head of security at Babbage Town."

"That's no concern of mine," Whitfield said.

"Well it is if it turns out that Turing's death is connected somehow."

"I highly doubt that's the case."

"Well, that's why we play the game, isn't it?" Sean said. "Because your opinion doesn't really count."

In response, Whitfield's gaze flicked to the door. A moment later Six-Pack had Sean's arm in a vise grip and was leading him rapidly to the exit. *Or maybe off the roof.*

Back in the lobby Hayes's gun was returned to him, Six-Pack gave Sean's arm an extra-hard squeeze and both men walked out into the darkness.

As they reached the cruiser, Hayes said, "Are you nuts talking to him like that?"

"Probably."

"Come on, you went out of your way to tick him off, why?"

"Because he's a prick, that's why."

Hayes said, "He's right about the four suicides."

"That doesn't mean Monk killed himself. In fact, it might have given whoever murdered Monk the idea to make it look like suicide."

"That's a good point."

"Thanks. I try to have at least one a day."

"So it's back to Babbage Town?"

"I want to check something out first."

Sean climbed in the driver's seat of the cruiser while Hayes scrambled into the passenger side.

"I'm not sure regulations allow you to drive the car," Hayes pointed out.

"In for a dime, in for a dollar," Sean said as he put

the car in reverse, backed out of the space and then took up a position away from the building entrance.

"What are we doing here?" Hayes asked.

"It's called surveillance. I'm assuming you're acquainted with the concept."

"Who the hell do you think you're running surveillance on? The head of Camp Peary!"

"Is there a law against it?"

"Hell, probably."

Fifteen minutes later a car pulled up to the entrance of the building and a woman who looked to be in her mid-thirties got out. She was tall, tanned, leggy and blond with a figure that demanded not just a second but possibly a third look. As she approached the front door, Whitfield and his shadow came out. The woman spoke to Whitfield for a few moments and then he limped away with Six-Pack, climbed in a black sedan and drove off, leaving the woman looking more than a little put out.

"Interesting," Sean said. "She's either Whitfield's wife or mistress."

"Or girlfriend."

"Uh-uh, Whitfield was wearing a wedding band."

While they were talking the woman got in her car and drove off. Sean put the cruiser in gear and drifted after her.

"What the hell are you doing?" Hayes demanded.

"Following her."

"Sean, we could get in trouble for this."

"I'm already in trouble." Hayes sat back with an air of resignation. Sean smiled and said, "Still glad you decided to partner with me?"

"No!"

"Good, that means we're really starting to click as a team." And that remark made Sean remember that in a few hours' time Michelle would be here. Normally Sean would look forward to seeing his *real* partner. Yet Horatio's words kept coming back to him. Michelle could be dangerous, to herself. She shouldn't have left the facility. She wasn't cured. She was coming down here. And who the hell knew what would happen?

39

Michelle took advantage of the drive down to call a girlfriend of hers who worked at the National Intelligence Center after a stint at the Secret Service where Michelle had helped her along the career path. She called the woman at home figuring her phone at work would be monitored.

After a bit of chitchat, Michelle said, "Not looking for any secrets, Judy, but what can you tell me about Camp Peary?"

"You mean the DOD's Armed Forces Experimental Training Activity?"

"Come on, Judy, give me a break. We're talking CIA."

"Okay, okay, forgive the automatic official response." Her friend gave her the physical dimensions of the place, a thumbnail of its history and its official mission. "Most of the advanced training is now done at the Point in North Carolina," Judy said. "But it's still the CIA's primary Field Tradecraft center. Actually, the Pentagon's thinking about establishing its own espionage school and setting up intelligence op commands around the world."

"Sometimes too much intelligence is a bad thing," Michelle said wryly.

Judy laughed. "I officially can't comment on that. Now the current head of Camp Peary is a man named Ian Whitfield. Ex-military, Delta Force, I believe. Vietnam War hero. Not a guy you want to mess around with. He came over to the intelligence side sometime in the 1980s. He was stationed in the Middle East for the last several years. Now that he's back stateside, word is he's doing all he can to bring Camp Peary back to prominence."

"How's he going about that?"

"What's your interest?"

"Got a job down there. Someone was found dead on the property."

"I read about that in the newspaper. I thought it was a suicide."

"It might turn out to be. We were talking about Whitfield?"

"Well, two years ago some money was slipped through Congress to construct a new building down there, purportedly a dormitory."

"Purportedly?"

"Look, you didn't hear this from me."

"Judy, I never talked to you, okay? Now spill it."

"In the Nineties they built a 105-room dorm to go

along with a new training school. So, word around here is the new money was really for an interrogation center."

"Interrogation? Why would that be so hush-hush?"

"Depends on who they're interrogating and—"

Michelle finished for her. "And *how* they're interrogating them."

"Exactly."

"Terrorists?"

"You know the NSA is probably listening to this conversation."

"Let them. They don't have enough personnel to sift through the real bad guys' conversations much less people like you and me. So they're bringing people down there that nobody knows about and maybe torturing them?"

"Officially? Absolutely not. Unofficially, who knows? It's not like we're going to be telling everyone that a brand-new torture chamber has opened in Tidewater, Virginia, three hours from the capital of the free world. I'm not for mistreating prisoners, but it's a war on terror. It's not like we can fight it the old-fashioned way."

"Okay, how are they getting them there?"

"Along with the funds for the 'dorm,' money was also appropriated for a new runway that would accept larger jets."

"Like jets capable of intercontinental travel?"

"Exactly."

Michelle was quiet for a few moments. "The paramilitary squads still assigned to Camp Peary?"

"I can't say."

"Judy, come on!"

"Let me put it this way, don't go there for a picnic, you might never be seen again."

"I appreciate it. You've been a big help."

"You're the only reason I survived my first year with the Service."

"Girls do have to stick together."

"Are you working on this with Sean King?"

"Yep."

"So are you two more than just business partners yet?"

"Why do you want to know?"

"Because if you're not going after him I want a shot. He's gorgeous."

"You ought to see him when he's cranky."

"I'll take him cranky, believe me."

Michelle clicked off, downed a PowerBar and finished off her coffee. She checked her watch and then her navigation system. Ninety miles an hour and sixty minutes to go. Trusty old illegal radar detector.

40

Hayes and Sean followed the lady into the parking lot of a very popular bar located about three blocks off the William and Mary campus. As she went inside, Hayes and Sean held a quick consultation. It was decided that Sean would go in alone, leaving the uniformed Hayes in his police cruiser.

As Sean slid out of the car the sheriff held up a warning hand. "Look, I want to be on the record that you going within two miles of that woman is a really bad thing if she turns out to be married to Whitfield."

"But on the other hand if Monk's death *is* connected to Camp Peary and Ian Whitfield, then the lady might provide us with a shortcut. And as an added bonus, maybe I can find out who tried to kill me."

The inside of the bar held an interesting mix of college kids and those who had to actually work for a living. Behind the old-fashioned bar, which looked straight out of the *Cheers* set, two young men and an older gent were filling drink orders as fast as their brains and hands would operate. Higher education was known to inspire great thirst, Sean thought.

There she was, at a high table in the back, near the pool tables. She already had her drink and was nimbly fighting off the advance of what looked to be a member of the William and Mary football team, a lineman judging by the young man's heft. Not that Sean could blame the guy for trying. The lady's skirt was short and the legs long, and the way the blond hair fell over the shoulders, spilling near the deep cleavage revealed by the plunge of her neckline, and the heat of those blue eyes bubbling just below the surface . . . Hell, if he'd been in college he could imagine moving heaven and earth to bed that prize. The bragging rights alone would've lasted the entire four years he'd be in school.

The guy wrote something down on a piece of napkin and handed it to her. She looked at the writing—no doubt a phone number or description of a lewd sexual act he wanted to perform on her— shook her head and motioned him away.

Sean took the opening and sat down beside her. Whether it was because he was obviously old enough to drink legally or her energy had been sapped by fending off the lineman's thrust, she smiled appreciatively at Sean.

"I haven't seen you in here before," she said.

"That's because I haven't been in here before." He caught a waitress's eye. "What the lady's having."

She held up her drink. "You into Mojitos?"

"I am now." He glanced at the wedding ring on her finger.

She saw this. "I don't believe there's a law against a married woman going out by herself."

"None at all. Sorry. I'm Sean Carter."

"Valerie Messaline."

If she was married to old Ian, the lady hadn't taken her husband's surname.

They shook hands. Her grip was strong, confident. He thought of a similar grip he knew well: Michelle's.

"So what brings you to our little hamlet?"

Sean replied, "Business. I take it you live around here?"

"No, but my husband keeps an office near here. I was actually planning on going out with him tonight." She looked down into her glass. "Things didn't work out."

That explained the little scene outside the building.

"Should I ask what's wrong with your husband that he doesn't see how lucky he is, or would that be indiscreet?"

She laughed. "The question isn't indiscreet, but my answer might be."

Sean's drink came and they both sipped while he shot glances around the bar. Sean was trying to spot anyone paying them more than cursory attention.

"So what is it that you do, Sean?"

"I'm a problem solver."

"Oh good, can I hire you?" she said jokingly.

"I'm not cheap."

"I wouldn't let you sit there if I thought you were."

"So what is it *you* do?"

"Not much anymore."

"Kids?"

"No, didn't work out."

"Me either."

She glanced at his hand. "Not married now?"

"Divorced. Never got back in the saddle."

"So what did you do to make your little woman divorce you?"

"I apparently snore, very loudly."

"There's a surefire cure for that."

"Really? What?"

"Getting your brains screwed out."

He smiled. "Damn, should I start blushing now or what?"

"Just making a comment. It's not necessarily directed at you, although you're a very attractive man, but you don't need me to sit here and tell you that. Do you?" Her tone was blunt, aggressive. The woman was not flirting with him now. There was definitely something else going on.

He glanced at his watch. Michelle would be showing up soon. And he didn't want to push Valerie too much the first time out.

"I'm sorry if I'm boring you," she said in an annoyed tone.

He looked up to see her offended gaze on him.

"I just have an appointment I have to get to."

"Well, then you better get to it. Then I can finish my drink in peace for a change."

"Valerie, I saw that other guy hitting on you. I'm not like that."

"Famous last words."

He reached in his pocket and pulled out a piece of paper and wrote something on it. He handed it to her. "I've got to go now, but here's my number."

"Why would I want your number?"

"For now let's just call it new friends exchanging information." He looked at her expectantly. "You don't have to give me your number if you don't want to."

"Good, because I don't think I want to."

He finished his Mojito and rose. "Pleasure making your acquaintance, Valerie."

She didn't answer him, yet he could feel her gaze burn into his back with every step he took away. Outside in the cruiser Sean filled in Hayes on the encounter.

"Do you have a death wish!" the lawman exclaimed. "Whitfield looked like he wanted to kill you for asking him a single question about Camp Peary. Can you imagine what he'd do to you if he finds out you're screwing around with his wife?"

"I just had a drink with the lady. At first she was friendly, but then something happened and all of a sudden she wasn't. That's one reason I beat a retreat."

"Maybe she's used to people trying to poke around to find out about her husband and using her to do it. Just like you are!"

They drove back to Babbage Town in silence. As Sean got out of the car he said, "I have a couple of associates coming down to join me. Would you like to extend to them the same arrangement you made with me?"

"You mean to partner?" Sean nodded. "I don't know, are they any good?"

"As good as me, if not better."

"Well, maybe I will seeing as how you're probably going to get yourself killed by a jealous husband real soon."

As Hayes drove out the gate of Babbage Town Sean saw the wink of lights heading toward him. As the truck drew closer he took a deep breath.

Michelle Maxwell had arrived.

41

Sean feigned surprise at seeing Michelle, but didn't ask for a lengthy explanation, instead turning his attention to getting her inside the compound. It took a heated argument with the security guards at the front gate and finally a call to Champ Pollion, who came out to settle the dispute.

When Champ first saw Michelle, the brilliant physicist was instantly reduced to a puppy begging for attention.

"Yes, of course you can stay," Champ said, stammering slightly as he held out his hand to Michelle.

Sean said, "Maybe we can grab some chow in the dining room while we discuss the case."

"Fine," Michelle said, her gaze on Champ. "Thank you, Mr. Pollion."

"Please, call me Champ."

"I'm sure you live up to your name," she said.

As they drove off Sean glanced back at Champ and saw his look of longing at Michelle.

In your freaking dreams, pal.

The dining room was mostly empty at this hour,

but true to its 24/7 policy, the Babbage Town chefs were on duty and in a matter of fifteen minutes they had hot food and coffee in front of them.

Sean filled Michelle in on everything, including the attempt on his life, his theory on Rivest's murder, and his brief conversation with Valerie Messaline. In turn, Michelle brought him up to date on what she'd found out from her friend at the National Intelligence Center.

"I heard a plane landing around two A.M. my first night here. A big one. I wondered why I couldn't see any running lights."

"My contact at NIC also told me that Ian Whitfield is a man not to be crossed."

"Trust me I'd already gotten that impression," Sean said.

"So you're partnering with this Sheriff Hayes?"

Sean stirred some sugar into his coffee. "It seemed like a good way to keep in the loop."

"And little Joanie is okay with that?"

"Little *Joanie* doesn't know, because I haven't been returning her calls."

"I knew I loved you."

"Hold your accolades; I'm going to have to fill her in at some point."

"And this Hayes guy? Is he okay?"

"Solid guy, if excitable. He doesn't think I should be going anywhere near Whitfield's wife."

"Well neither do I."

"If Monk was killed by the folks at Camp Peary, she may be the only way we can find out about it."

"From the way you said he blew off the little missus tonight, I doubt Whitfield is giving his wife a daily briefing."

"She might have learned something anyway. The lady isn't stupid and she's not happy with her hubby right now."

"Okay, let's say Whitfield had Monk Turing killed. Why?"

"Something he saw? These secret flights maybe? There's something weird going on over there for damn sure. Somebody took a shot at me. And say what you will about the CIA, they don't usually go out of their way to kill American citizens for no reason."

"He might've seen someone tortured. Or even killed," Michelle added.

"People are assuming that Turing climbed the fence and then died right there. But what if he went a lot farther than that? In fact what if he was try-ing to get back *out* of Camp Peary when he was killed?"

"But you said all evidence pointed to suicide."

"Come on, the CIA can't rig a murder to look like suicide?"

"Sean, why would Monk Turing be sneaking over there in the first place?"

"According to Whitfield, to kill himself to either

make the CIA look bad or die in a blaze of media glory."

"But you don't buy that."

"No, but maybe he saw the flights coming in and being a curious genius he decided to check it out?"

"This *genius* couldn't figure out that doing something like that was tantamount to suicide?" she said skeptically.

"So maybe there was *another* reason he was going there. But there's another possibility. He might be spying on *this* place and selling its secret to the highest bidder. Rivest apparently thought there were spies here. And Turing *did* leave the country."

"That doesn't explain how he ended up dead on CIA property. And maybe Turing isn't spying on *this* place."

"What do you mean?" Sean said curiously.

"I mean, what is it they really do here at Babbage Town? Play with numbers and little computers, or so they say?" She lowered her voice. "So how do you know *this* place isn't really a spy ring? Right across the river is a super-secret CIA facility. Maybe all the scientific mumbo-jumbo is just that, crap to cover up their real work: espionage against this country."

Sean smiled. "That's a brilliant theory. I knew I missed you for a good reason."

"That's why they call it a partnership."

"But if this place is a spy ring, why call us in?"

"*Rivest* called us in. Maybe he wasn't in on the

espionage. But he did say the owners were having second thoughts."

"When I screw up the courage to talk to Joan, I'll ask her for a rundown on some of these things. I especially want a more detailed background check on Champ, Alicia and Monk Turing."

"So quantum computers, you said?"

"Len Rivest said it was worth countries going to war for."

"So you think Rivest's death is connected to Monk's?"

"If not, at least to Babbage Town. He was going to tell me all about the place. Then he goes to take a bath and gets murdered in the tub."

"But the FBI still thinks it was an accident?"

"Ventris is the guy in charge. I don't know what he thinks. He made it very clear that I was a bug to be crushed if I got in his way."

"It's late. Why don't we get moved into our new home?"

Sean grabbed his bag and they headed over to the bungalow. There were no lights on inside.

"They must be asleep." Sean unlocked the door with the key Alicia had given him and led Michelle inside. He turned on the foyer light and said, "I'm bunking in one of the bedrooms at the top of the stairs. There's an empty one across from me. I'll explain things to Alicia in the morning."

He studied her without seeming to do so. "So you're doing okay?" he said quietly.

"Actually, better than okay. I have to admit, the R&R was good for me."

"And the weird stuff you mentioned going on at the psych hospital? Anything come out of that?" he asked casually, already knowing the answer.

"Nothing worth mentioning," she lied. "I have to tell you, your buddy Horatio was a big disappointment. After asking me a bunch of irrelevant and insulting questions he took off, haven't seen the little shit since."

"Really? That's surprising." Sean elected not to tell her that the "little shit" would be here in a matter of hours.

"Okay, point me in the direction of my bed. I'm about ready to collapse," she said.

In the next moment Michelle pulled her gun and pointed it at the sounds that came rushing at them out of the darkness.

42

Sean grabbed hold of Michelle's arm and said, "Viggie? Viggie is that you?"

The sounds became clearer now. It was someone whimpering.

Sean led the way into the next room and found a light switch.

Viggie was huddled in a chair against the wall. She was dressed in her pajamas and her hair was down around her shoulders. It made her look older than did the pigtails. Her eyes were red from crying and the expression on her face was that of a person who hurt everywhere.

Michelle quickly holstered her gun and strode over to the girl. She bent down and said quietly, "Sweetie, are you okay?"

Whether it was the gentleness of Michelle's words or the worried look on her features, Viggie put out a hand and Michelle took it in hers.

Sean said, "Viggie, has something happened? Is Alicia here?"

Viggie said nothing, keeping her gaze fixed on Michelle.

"Stay with her, I'm going to check on Alicia." Sean raced up the stairs while Michelle sat down on the floor and stroked Viggie's hand.

"It's going to be okay, Viggie. I'm Michelle. Michelle Maxwell. I'm a friend of Sean's. You can call me Michelle, or even Mick if you want."

"Mick," Viggie said immediately and wiped her eyes with her free hand.

"And is it okay if I call you Viggie or would you prefer Miss Turing?"

Viggie shook her head. "Viggie," she whispered.

"Viggie it is. That's a cool name. I've met lots of Michelle's but I've never met a Viggie before. That means you must be really special."

Viggie nodded, as though in agreement, but her grip tightened on Michelle's fingers. "Mick," she said again.

"We're friends now. Okay?"

Viggie slowly nodded, her eyes searching Michelle's as though for any hint of doubt, or worse, untruth.

When Sean returned he had Alicia in tow. Michelle looked up and noted the woman's sleepy features and then, visible at the bottom of her calf-length pajama pants, the artificial leg. Sean made quick introductions.

"I didn't know she had come downstairs," Alicia

said. She focused on Sean with an angry look. "We waited for you until it was very late."

"I'm sorry, Alicia, I got hung up on something else."

"Maybe we should just rethink the arrangement then."

"I'm here," Michelle said, rising from the floor, but still holding on to Viggie's hand. "I'm Michelle Maxwell, Sean's partner. Between the two of us we'll be able to handle things now."

Alicia stared at Sean for a long moment and then nodded her head at Michelle. "I see that you and Viggie have already made friends."

Michelle smiled at the girl. "I think Viggie and I will be great friends."

Viggie jumped up and raced to the piano in the other room. From the darkness they heard the song she was playing.

Michelle turned to Sean. "Wow, that's amazing."

"It's Viggie's way of showing that she likes you," Alicia explained.

"Why was she so upset?" Sean asked.

She said in a low voice, "That damn FBI agent, Ventris, came by earlier tonight. He started going into Monk's death. And Viggie overheard him."

"Oh, hell!" Sean exclaimed.

"You should've seen Viggie a few hours ago. She was inconsolable. I had to tell her the truth. I couldn't lie to her, not when she was like that. I finally had the staff doctor prescribe a sedative for her. She was asleep when I finally went to bed, but I guess the meds wore off."

Sean said, "What the hell was Ventris doing here talking to you?"

"He wanted to question Viggie at first, but I put my foot down. I don't think he meant for her to overhear him, but he didn't stick around to help with her either."

"What did he want to know?" Michelle asked.

"If I had any idea why Monk Turing would have gone to Camp Peary. Or if he'd mentioned going there before."

Sean and Michelle exchanged quizzical expressions. Sean said, "I was told that officially the Bureau thinks Monk killed himself."

Alicia coaxed Viggie off the piano, but the little girl refused to go to sleep until Michelle took her hand, led her up the stairs and put her to bed.

After they said good night to Alicia, Sean and Michelle settled into their bedrooms. Sean came in and sat on Michelle's bed while she was still unpacking.

"Don't worry, it won't take you long to mess up this place," he commented.

"What a comedian you are. So what happened to Alicia's leg?"

Sean explained about her experience in Iraq and her job here at Babbage Town.

"Amazing lady." Michelle added, "It must have been horrible for Viggie to find out that way about her dad."

"It must have been," Sean agreed. There was a vibrating sound. He groaned and glanced at his phone.

Michelle smiled and said, "Let me guess, Little Miss Joanie? Are you going to ignore her again?"

"No, if I don't answer this time she'll probably head straight down to Babbage Town."

"Wow, that would be a lot of fun," Michelle said, as she slipped her pistol under the pillow. "Maybe you shouldn't answer then. If she does come down, I could accidentally shoot her thinking she's some predator looking for fresh meat. Oh, that won't work, because she *is* a predator and my shooting her *wouldn't* be an accident."

"You're not really helping matters. *I* have to reason with her."

"Go ahead. But while you're doing that I really want to hear you tell the witch off once and for all."

Sean stood. "That *witch* is signing our paychecks, or at least mine. So let me just handle this misery in the peace and comfort of my own room."

"Coward. Are you going to tell her I'm here?"

"I said let me handle it, Michelle."

"What is it with men and confrontation? Women have no trouble at all going for the jugular."

After he left, Michelle slipped down the hall and opened the door to Viggie's room. The girl was sitting up in bed in the dark. "It's me, Mick," Michelle said.

In a tiny voice Viggie said, "Hi, Mick."

"Like me to sit with you for a bit?"

Viggie held out her hand.

Michelle lay down next to the frightened child in the darkness. As the girl's hand touched hers, Michelle felt a jolt as the fragments of a distant and unwelcome memory hit her. Another frightened little girl sat all alone in the dark trying to make sense of the indecipherable. In a flash the image was gone, leaving Michelle as puzzled, confused and scared as the little girl next to her.

43

Joan Dillinger screamed at him for a full two minutes, though it felt longer. She even played the guilt card.

"I went out on a limb for you, Sean. And this, *this* is how you repay me?"

"I didn't return your calls because I didn't have anything to report. What's the big deal?"

"I'll tell you what the big deal is. My boss got a call from no one less than the DDO at Central Intelligence telling him in no uncertain terms that we better back the hell off, and he named *you* as one of the chief offenders. The Deputy Director of Operations for God's sake!"

"Ian Whitfield didn't waste any time getting that done. I wonder how he knew your firm was on the case."

"They're the CIA, Sean, they can find out things. Hell, half the people at my firm worked at Langley at some point."

"I can't stop the police from investigating a murder, Joan."

"Oh and that's another thing. So you're telling me that you're now affiliated with the police?"

"It gets me into places I wouldn't otherwise be able to, which increases the chances that I'll find out the truth. Isn't that what I'm supposed to be doing?"

"Sean, when you were hired to do this job—"

Interrupting, he said, "Yeah, let's get that straight right now. Who hired us?"

"Len Rivest."

"He's only the head of security. Someone had to authorize him to hire your firm."

"Well, did you think of asking him?"

"It doesn't matter if I did or not now. He's dead."

"What!"

"He's *dead*. I'm surprised the DDO failed to let that little tidbit slip."

"I can't believe it. Len was a good guy. We went way back."

Sean said, "I'm sure you did; however, his status as a good guy has not been established in my mind."

"What do you mean by that?" she said sharply.

"He was murdered, Joan. And in my experience people get murdered for one of two reasons. One, because someone didn't like them. Two, because someone didn't want them alive to talk."

"You think Len was involved in Monk Turing's death?"

"Murders so close together tend to be connected."

"It hasn't been established that Monk was murdered."

"Technically, it hasn't been established that Len was either, but I'm sure that he was. And by the way, someone took a couple of shots at me. I think they came from the vicinity of Camp Peary."

"Good God, all this happened and you never called me?"

"I've been busy. So getting back to my original question: Who hired us?"

"I don't know."

"Joan, I'm tired and I'm totally pissed off at the world. So don't play games with me. Len Rivest said, 'countries would go to war' for whatever they're doing here."

"He said that?"

"And you didn't know?"

"I didn't. I swear, Sean. From the little I knew of the case, I figured you'd pull a few days down there and it would be concluded that Turing killed himself on Camp Peary grounds. It's happened before, you know."

"Yeah, Ian Whitfield enlightened me on that point. But the dynamic has changed now with Rivest's death."

"*If* they are connected."

"My gut tells me they are."

"Then I'm sending down reinforcements."

"I've already got someone."

There was a long pause and then Joan hissed. "Are you telling me that *she's* down there with you?"

"Who, Mildred?"

"Michelle effing Maxwell!" she screamed so loudly that Sean had to pull the cell phone away from his ear.

"That's right," he replied calmly. "She just showed up and reported for duty."

"She does *not* work for this firm."

"I know. I'm subcontracting the work out to her."

"You have no authority to do that."

"Actually, I do. I'm an independent contractor to your firm. In paragraph fifteen, subsection d of the contract I signed with your company it gives me the latitude to consult with assets that I deem appropriate to the task so long as payment for such assets comes out of my fees."

"You actually read the contract?"

"I always read the contract, Joan. So maybe together we can get to the bottom of this thing. I've also got another friend coming down, a psychologist by the name of Horatio Barnes."

"Why? Or am I not entitled under the contract to *question* your choice of assets?"

"Monk Turing's young daughter," he said simply. "She found out a little while ago that her father's dead and went hysterical. And she's also not so easy to communicate with on the best of days. But I think Horatio may be able to get through to her."

Apparently having resigned herself to these developments Joan said, "Do you think the girl may know something about her father's death?"

"Right now it's one of the few leads we have."

"Sean, risking your life is not in the job description."

"I'll keep that in mind."

"On the other hand, tell *Mildred* she'd look positively stunning eating a large-caliber bullet meant for you."

"Doubtless she already knows your feelings on the subject."

Sean put the phone down, collapsed back on his bed fully clothed and fell asleep. He had no concerns for his personal safety now. The A team was right across the hall. It was probably a good thing he couldn't see how scared and confused his A team was. The man would not have slept nearly so soundly.

44

When Horatio Barnes arrived early the next morning Champ was not as accommodating as he had been to Michelle.

"We are not a resort!" Champ exploded.

"But I think he can help Viggie," Sean said.

"Then he can do it from a distance, damn it. This is a highly secure facility full of highly confidential research and I don't even know who this man is."

"I can vouch for him. And you let Michelle stay here," Sean countered. "You don't know her either. So what's the difference?"

Champ snapped, "No!" And stalked off.

Horatio was relegated to a bed-and-breakfast in the nearby town of White Feather.

Michelle thankfully was not up yet so Sean borrowed a car and followed Horatio to White Feather. After Horatio checked in the two men sat in the dining room having a cup of coffee.

"Nice area," Horatio said. "Except for all the people being slaughtered, I might've considered retiring down here."

"Tell me about Tennessee," Sean prompted.

When Horatio had finished, Sean said, "What's a whacked rose hedge got to do with Michelle's problems?"

"I don't know if it has any connection." He studied Sean over his cup of coffee. "So how's our girl doing?"

"Seems to be in fine form. She hit the ground running."

"That might not last. So talk to me about Viggie."

Sean did so and Horatio sat back. "This doesn't sound like it will be easy. How do you want to play it? This Champ chump won't let me on the grounds."

"I can bring Viggie here. Alicia will okay it. She really cares about the girl."

"Good. Did you tell Michelle I was coming?"

"No, but she'll find out soon enough. When I explain it's for Viggie's benefit I think it'll be okay. She seems to have bonded really quickly with her."

"That could be telling in certain respects," Horatio said, looking thoughtful. "Maybe I can work two birds with one stone."

When Sean returned to Babbage Town he found Michelle in the dining hall talking with Champ. Viggie hovered at one end of the long table chewing what looked like soggy Cheerios.

When Champ spotted Sean he rose from the table. "I hope you understand why your friend couldn't stay here."

"What friend?" Michelle said quickly.

"Horatio Barnes," Sean answered bluntly.

When Champ noted Michelle's astonished reaction to this he seemed taken aback. "If you'll excuse me," he stammered and hurried off.

After Champ left, Michelle snapped, "Why the hell is Barnes here?"

"For Viggie. We need somebody who can get through to her."

"And you had to call in the guy who locked me up and then walked away? I can't believe you would do that, Sean."

"He didn't lock you up. You went into the facility voluntarily. And he didn't walk away from you."

"What are you talking about? He vanished."

"He went to Tennessee."

Michelle's features became so hard that it looked like she'd been frozen.

After nearly a minute of silence had passed she said quietly, "Why would he go to Tennessee?"

"Why do you think?"

"I don't appreciate you of all people playing games with me."

"Okay. He went to Tennessee to find the place where you lived when you were six years old."

"I don't believe this shit!"

Neither of them noticed the heads of people at other tables turning toward them as their voices rose.

"According to your brother you had an abrupt personality change that year."

"I was a kid!"

"Come on, Michelle, what happened?"

"Nothing! Do you remember when *you* were six years old?"

Sean suddenly realized what he was doing. He was, in fact, screwing everything up. He was intruding on Horatio's jurisdiction, asking Michelle incredibly personal questions in an incredibly clumsy fashion in front of strangers. "No, I don't," he said hastily. "I'm sorry." His contrite tone seemed to deflate the anger in her a little. They both looked up to see Viggie eying them, her features full of uncertainty. Michelle immediately sat down beside her and put an arm around her shoulders.

"It's okay, Viggie, just a little disagreement, we have them all the time." She said sharply to Sean, "Don't we?"

Sean nodded. "All the time." He got up and joined them.

Viggie was dressed in denim overalls, her hair done up in the usual pigtails. Michelle noted that the girl's fingernails had been bitten down completely.

Sean said, "She has to go to class. They have a school here for workers with families. It's right down the hall in the mansion." He lowered his voice. "I've arranged to have a guard sit with her. We'll be back before class lets out."

"Back, back from where?"

"You'll see."

45

They dropped Viggie off in the schoolroom. Before they left Viggie, Michelle and Sean spoke to her teacher, a middle-aged woman.

"A special case," the teacher said about Viggie. "But on her good days she's as brilliant as any student I've ever had."

"Alicia Chadwick says she can factor large numbers in her head," Sean said.

"Exactly. Can you imagine being able to see millions, if not billions of numbers neatly lined up in your mind's eye?"

Sean said, "No, I can't. I actually have trouble remembering my own phone number."

They left Viggie with her teacher and guard and headed out. In the hall they ran into Alicia Chadwick.

"She's safe in the school," Sean told her and then explained about Horatio. "Maybe he can help her."

"Get through the ordeal of her father's death?" Alicia asked, casting him a sharp glance. "Or something else?"

"Alicia, if she knows anything about Monk's death

we need to find that out. The sooner *we* find out the less important Viggie becomes to a killer."

Alicia said, "Okay, let's do it."

As Sean and Michelle walked the grounds of the mansion, he said, "The place was built by a guy who made a fortune selling people canned food packed full of crap that probably killed as many consumers as not."

"I didn't see any sign with the name Babbage Town."

"Funny, neither did I." He went over the hut system with her and then gave Michelle a more detailed rundown of his conversation with Champ and the quantum computer.

"I've got Joan digging on who owns this place. Say what you want about her, she's really good at that."

"Most animals with claws are," Michelle shot back.

They eventually came to stand in front of Turing's now empty cottage. "FBI Special Agent with-a-bad-attitude Michael Ventris took all the stuff but I'm having Joan run down where Monk might have traveled to."

"You said Alicia mentioned it was overseas?"

"She just didn't know where."

He took her to Len Rivest's cottage next.

"Did you check Champ's alibi on the night Rivest was killed?" she asked.

"Computer says he clocked in Hut Number Two

at eleven-thirty and punched out at three in the morning. So whoever I saw around two in the morning, it wasn't him."

"And since it looks like Rivest had been dead for at least five hours when you found him, that rules Champ out."

"Suspects come, suspects go," Sean said with a sigh.

They next walked down to the boathouse. Michelle ran an expert's eye over the watercraft. "Nothing too exceptional, mostly recreational," she pronounced. She motioned to a twenty-six-foot Formula Bowrider up on a boat lift in one of the slips. "One of the owners of this place must be a New Yorker."

Sean looked at the name stenciled on the stern transom: "The Big Apple." He pointed across the river. "How long to row across? Not for someone like you, I mean an ordinary mortal."

She considered this. "Not knowing the current, I'd say at least forty-five minutes or so. It always looks closer on land. When you're sloughing through the water, it's a lot farther."

"So there and back we're talking over two hours, considering you'd probably be rowing slower on the way back."

"That's right."

He led her through the woods to the spot where Camp Peary could be seen. Michelle pulled a pair of binoculars from her backpack and focused them.

The sun was glancing off the shiny fence surrounding the CIA's property.

"Heck of a shot at you," she said, studying the distance and trajectory.

"Yeah, well let's be happy it wasn't a *helluva* shot or I wouldn't be here."

She pointed to her left at the break in the tree line. "Runway?"

"Yep."

She looked at the large cranes farther down the river. "Navy?" Sean nodded. "Where'd they find his body?"

"As best I can figure out, right about there." He pointed to a wooded spot about five hundred yards down from the runway.

"So the thing is, if Monk went over there voluntarily and not just to kill himself, then he either went to meet someone, or to spy on the place and someone got the jump on him," she said.

"Right, but if he went to spy on the place the CIA had every right to shoot him. So why cover it up to make it look like suicide?"

"Well, maybe it was suicide after all," Michelle said.

"But what about Rivest? He was most definitely murdered."

"Unconnected to Monk's death," she said simply.

Sean didn't look as confident. "Maybe."

As they walked back Sean abruptly said, "Look, I

should've given you a heads-up that Horatio was coming down. I'm sorry. I was just trying to help."

"Forget it," she replied. But she said it in a way that Sean knew she would never forget it.

46

As soon as they climbed in Michelle's truck, Sean rolled down the window and took a deep breath. "I recall you once cleaned out your truck for me so I could breathe without the aid of machinery."

"That was back when I used to like you," she said, slipping the truck into gear. "Okay, where to now?"

They drove along the river. Every half-mile or so they passed a ruined mansion or plantation; the only thing left standing in most of them were multiple brick chimney stacks.

"The third little pig was right, build it out of brick and it'll last," Michelle commented.

They finally stopped at one property and got out. Sean walked up the overgrown drive and Michelle followed. On the tilting stone entrance column was the name "Farleygate" written in weathered bronze script.

Sean said, "There was a book on local history at Babbage Town that I read through. Farleygate was owned by the son of some famous inventor."

Michelle asked, "So what happened?"

"Like lots of rich people who inherit money, he blew it. Most of the mansions around here, Brandon-field, Tuckergate, have fallen into ruins."

Michelle added, "Or been turned into secret labs where people die."

A chilly wind blew across the front lawn that was rapidly being consumed by the surrounding forest.

"I bet it was beautiful when it was new," Michelle said as she wrapped her arms around her shoulders and stared up at the manse. Unlike many of the abandoned manors around here, Farleygate's walls were still standing though the large wooden front double doors had rotted away, most of the windows were broken out and the slate roof was full of holes. "Probably a nice place to grow up," she said a bit wistfully.

He looked at her in surprise. "You've never even owned a home. I didn't think you were into possessions."

"I've never been married either. It doesn't mean I can't look," she shot back.

Noise filtered out from the mansion.

"That sounds like voices," Michelle said. She pulled her gun and headed to the house with Sean right behind. Inside, Michelle slid a flashlight out of her backpack and shone it around.

The corridor they were on was long, the floors rotted, the walls coming down in chunks. The air was dank with mold and Sean began to cough. The noises they heard started up again, like hurried whispers.

275

Then a tiny scream seemed to come from right next to them. They both jumped and Michelle swung both her light and pistol in that direction. A blank wall looked back at them and yet they still heard what sounded like buzzing.

She looked at Sean searchingly. "Hornet's nest?" she said. He looked puzzled and then stepped toward the wall and tapped on it. All noise instantly ceased.

He looked at her and shook his head. "Human nest." His fingers probed around the wall until they found what they were looking for: a small loop of metal. Sean pulled on it and the section of wall opened up.

Something hit him around the legs, and something else around the chest. He fell backward, landing on his butt. Running feet echoed down the hall.

As Sean got up he heard other sounds: screams and laughter.

He looked over his shoulder. The screams were coming from a little boy, about eight years old, that Michelle had a tight hold of. The laughter was coming from Michelle and it was clearly directed at Sean.

After Sean had dusted himself off, Michelle said in a fake stern voice to the boy, "Okay, name, rank and serial number, mister."

He was looking fearfully at her and Michelle noticed she still had her gun out. "Whoops, sorry." She holstered her pistol and said, "Come on, talk. What were you doing here?"

Sean said, "You can get hurt in a place like this, son."

"We come here a lot," the boy said defiantly. "We never get hurt."

Sean peered inside the hidden space. "A secret room. How'd you find it?"

"My brother, Teddy. He used to come here when he was my age with his gang. Now it's my place. All these old places have secret rooms."

Sean stiffened and looked at Michelle. He pulled out his wallet and handed the boy a ten-dollar bill. "Thanks, son."

After the little boy ran off, they walked outside and sat on an old stone bench.

"So we search Babbage Town for a secret room?" Michelle asked.

"Yep."

"Can I ask why?"

"It'll give us something to do. And if there is a spy at Babbage Town . . . ?" His voice trailed off.

"You really think a spy will be using a secret room? What, he sneaks out at night on his traitorous rounds? Give me a freaking break."

"What do you know about Camp Peary?"

"Other than what I told you, not a lot."

"If you research the place online, there's nothing. Only the same few articles come up."

"And you're surprised?" she said.

"The guy who picked me up when I got off the

plane, he said the Navy owned the land during World War II and trained Seabees there. Then they left but came back in the Fifties and kicked everybody out."

"Everybody? Everybody who?"

"There used to be two towns over there. Magruder and another one I can't remember the name of. Apparently the homes and everything are still there."

"What's that got to do with our investigation?"

"Nothing. I'm just killing mental time until I do think of something relevant," he admitted.

"Speaking of relevant, how well did Rivest know Monk Turing?" she asked.

"According to Rivest not very well. When we were drinking together though he opened up a bit and said something interesting."

"What?"

"He mentioned that he and Monk had gone fishing together one day on the York River. They were out in a little boat just drinking beer and throwing lines in the water, not expecting to catch anything."

"And?"

"And Monk looked over at Camp Peary and said something like, 'It's really ironic them being the greatest collector of secrets in the world.'"

"What was really ironic?" Michelle asked.

"According to Rivest, when he asked him about it, Monk just clammed up."

"I don't see how that helps us."

"I never met him but I don't think Monk Turing

would say something without a good reason. Come on."

"Where to?"

"Remember I said there were only a few articles about Camp Peary on the Internet?"

"Yeah, so?"

"Well two of them were written by a guy named South Freeman who lives in a little town near here called Arch. He runs the local newspaper and he's also the resident historian for the area. I figure if anyone can fill us in on Camp Peary, he can."

Michelle slapped her thigh as she rose off the bench. "South Freeman? Monk Turing? Champ Pollion? What the hell is it with this case and freaky names?"

47

Arch was a town of few streets, a single traffic light, a number of mom-and-pop stores, a line of abandoned railroad tracks grafted onto Main Street like ancient sutures and a one-story brick building badly in need of restoring that housed the *Magruder Gazette*. Another small rusted sign stated that the Magruder Historical Society was also housed in the same building.

"If the town's name is Arch, why isn't it the *Arch Gazette*?" Michelle asked as she parked the truck and they got out.

"I have my suspicions, but we can ask old South for the answer," Sean replied mysteriously.

They went inside and were met by a tall black man in his sixties with a lanky body and a cadaverous face outlined with a white-gray beard, in the center of which sat a smoldering cigarette protruding from thin, cracked lips.

He shook hands. "South Freeman," he said. "Got your phone call. So you want to know a little bit about the history of the area? Came to the right damn place then."

Sean nodded and South led them to a small room set up as an office. It was lined with gunmetal gray file cabinets and a couple of shabby desks although a shiny new computer rested on one of them. The walls held an assortment of photographs of the area including a large satellite image of what Sean recognized as Camp Peary. A sign above it read, "Hell on Earth."

Sean pointed to it. "I see you're a big fan of your country's premier intelligence service."

South looked at the photo and shrugged. "Government took my parents' home and kicked us all out. How am I supposed to feel?"

"That would be the Navy, not the CIA," Sean corrected.

"Navy, Army, CIA, I prefer to think of it collectively as the Evil Empire."

"I read your articles on Camp Peary," he said.

"Well, you didn't have many to choose from now, did you?" South stubbed out his cigarette and immediately lit another. Michelle waved smoke from her face.

Sean, glancing at Michelle, said, "So you lived in Magruder? I sort of assumed from the name of your paper."

Freeman nodded. "That's right. There were two towns on the grounds of what's now Camp Peary: Bigler's Mill and Magruder, where I was born. They're now on the list of places that just disappeared from the Commonwealth of Virginia's official registry."

"They keep statistics like that?" Sean asked.

In answer Freeman pointed to a list tacked to a bulletin board. "See for yourself. On there are all the counties, towns and what-not that have either been merged into other places, changed their names or, like Magruder, been stolen by the damn government."

Sean glanced at the list for a moment and said, "I understand from your articles that the houses are still there, entire neighborhoods in fact?"

"I can't confirm that, of course, since they don't exactly let the likes of me wander around there. But from the scraps I've gathered from people who have been there, yeah, a lot of the buildings are still there. Including the place where I was born and lived in when I was a little kid. That's why my paper's called the *Magruder Gazette*. This is my way of keeping the town alive."

"Well, I guess everyone had to make sacrifices during World War II," Sean pointed out.

"I got no problems with sacrifice so long as it's shared equally."

"What do you mean?" Sean said.

"Magruder was a working-class African-American community, or *colored* community as they referred to them back then. I didn't see the Navy go sweeping in on any rich white neighborhoods and start throwing people out. It was just the same old, same old. Kick

282

out the poor black folk because nobody's gonna give a damn."

Sean said, "I appreciate the problem, South, I really do. But we're here to talk about Camp Peary and the local history."

"That's what you said over the phone, only you didn't say why."

"We're private investigators who were hired by the people who run Babbage Town to look into the death of Monk Turing."

"Right, fellow they found dead over there. I wrote an article about that. Hasn't been published yet because I'm still waiting for the ending." He eyed them suspiciously. "So you're working for Babbage Town? How about a trade? I talk to you about the Farm and you talk to me about what they're really doing over at genius-ville?"

"Afraid we can't do that, South. We're bound by confidentiality."

"Well maybe I am too."

"What we're trying to do is get to the truth about Monk Turing's death," Michelle interjected.

"And that other fellow, the one that was killed *at* Babbage Town? They say he died by accident in his bathtub. I say, right, sure, and Lee Harvey Oswald and James Earl Ray acted all by their lonesome. Well, one hand rubs another. You can't talk and neither can I. So there's the door right over there. So long."

"And maybe if we find out the truth about Monk Turing," Michelle continued, "it might not look so good for Camp Peary. And maybe *they* might up and move."

South's expression immediately changed. Now he looked far more intrigued than defiant. "You think that's possible?"

"Anything's possible. And Monk Turing *was* found dead there."

"But all the mainstream media's saying it was suicide. Like those other people found dead around there over the last few years. And all the Internet bloggers are screaming government conspiracy. Wonder who's right?"

"Maybe we can find out, with your help," Sean said.

South stubbed out his cigarette, picked up a newspaper lying on his desk and seemed to be reading it. "What do you want to know?"

"What can you tell us about Camp Peary? I'm more interested in current events."

South shot him a glance over the newspaper. "Current events?"

"Yeah, like from the air."

"So you noticed the planes coming in? I guess you do get a nice view of them over at Babbage Town. They'd land right after they passed over the river. Am I right?"

"But at two A.M. you don't really get a good view

of anything, especially when they have their running lights off."

"Yeah, I know."

"You've seen 'em?" Michelle asked.

"Hey, the damn government doesn't own all the land around here. Grab me some world-class barbeque from Pierce's right down the road from Spookville, and head on across the river to a buddy of mine's place. Sit out on his dock and wait for that plane to drift on in with stuff the government doesn't want you or me to know about. Let me tell you, I knew something was up before Gulf One and Afghanistan and Iraq started because that damn runway at Peary looked like Chicago's O'Hare what with all the traffic going in."

His eyes gleamed. "Once a week I drive my car toward the Camp Peary entrance, see the green metal roofs on the guardhouses, all them damn warning signs saying 'No Trespassing, U.S. Property' and I say, 'Hey, shitheads, that's my momma's property, give it back.' I don't say it loud enough for them to hear of course," he added chuckling. "Then I turn around in the little U-turn slot—they have that for people who get lost, or who're just curious. Turn of last return, they call it, and then I go home. Makes me feel better." South fell silent for a moment. "Those planes come in once a week, on Saturdays. Always at the same time. And they're big jets. I got a buddy at Air Traffic Control and he's got contacts in the military down at Norfolk. Those planes don't land anywhere else in this country except at Camp Peary. They don't go through customs, military checkpoints, nothing."

"But they're military planes?" Michelle asked.

"Not according to my friend. He thinks they're registered as private aircraft."

"Private aircraft belonging to the CIA?" Sean said.

"Hell, CIA's got its own damn fleet. It's not like they have to tell anybody what they spend *our* tax dollars on."

"Wonder what kind of cargo is on those planes?" Sean asked.

South shot him a penetrating look. "Maybe the living, breathing kind that only speaks Arabic or Farsi?"

"Foreign detainees?"

"I've got no sympathy for terrorists but there is something to be said for due process," South said firmly. "And if the CIA is deciding who to snatch and bring over here without a court looking over their shoulder? I mean their track record on that sort of thing isn't exactly golden." He smiled. "Now if stuff like that *is* going on, there's a Pulitzer Prize waiting for the journalist who breaks the story."

"Yeah, it'd be quite a coup for the old *Magruder Gazette*," Michelle said sarcastically.

Sean said, "They recently lengthened the runway so bigger jets could land and they also got money for a new dorm building. What do you think about that?"

South stood. "Let me show you what I think about that."

He led them toward another room. Sean lagged behind and when South was out of the room, he slipped back and using his cell phone camera snapped a few pictures of the satellite map of Camp Peary before quickly joining them in the next room. In the center was a large table. On the table a detailed map was spread out.

"This is the portion of Camp Peary that used to be Bigler's Mill and Magruder." He pointed at various spots on the map. "You see how many houses there are? Well-built houses. You got good streets, access to all points. So you have all this housing and yet you need to build *another* dorm to put up people. How's that make sense?"

"Maybe the houses fell into disrepair or got knocked down?" Michelle said.

"Don't think so," South answered. "Like I said, I got folks to talk to me who'd worked there. And if you knock down whole neighborhoods, you got to haul the debris somewhere off-site. I would've heard about that." He pointed to another spot on the map. "And Camp Peary is also home to the only property on the National Historical Register that will never be open to the public: Porto Bello. It was the home of Virginia's last royal governor, John Murray, the Fourth Earl of Dunmore. Even the CIA can't touch that without getting in big-time trouble."

"How'd a place like that end up in Camp Peary?" Michelle asked.

"Dunmore hightailed it from Williamsburg where the governor's mansion was located to Porto Bello, his hunting lodge, when Washington's army got too close during the Revolutionary War. Then the chicken-shit snuck away during the night on a British ship and sailed back to England. There's a street in Norfolk named after him. Not in his honor, but because it was thought to be the last place he set foot in America, the royal prick. But my point is they got lots of places for people to live, so why the need for a new dorm?"

"You have any contacts at Camp Peary you can work?"

"If I had I would've worked them. I just get low-level scuttlebutt from time to time. No one's gonna be passing me the passenger manifest for those flights if that's what you mean." He pointed to some other areas on the map. "They have paramilitary squads training pretty much full-time there. Scary dudes. Practicing snatch-and-grabs, I guess. Or government-ordered assassinations. CIA can kill you better than anybody else. They simulate doing missions all over the world. Hell, they even have big balloons they float up to change the weather. Make it rain or snow, stuff like that. Big wind machines too. Or whopper heat makers. Least that's what I heard."

"To simulate desert fighting. Like in Afghanistan," Michelle commented.

They spent a few more minutes with South Freeman, then left after promising that they would keep
him in the loop. In return he said he'd let them know
if anything interesting came his way. "Who knows,"
he said before they left. "Maybe I might get my
parents' house back. Now wouldn't that be a hoot!"

As they were climbing into Michelle's truck Sean's
cell phone rang. "King."

He sucked in a quick breath as he listened. "Shit!"
He clicked off.

"Is somebody else dead?"

"Yes, and two dead men are even deader."

"What are you talking about?"

"That was Sheriff Hayes. The morgue just blew
up."

48

"Gas leak," Sheriff Hayes said as they stared at the charred rubble that used to be the makeshift morgue.

"Isn't that what they always say?" Michelle said.

"And you said the ME died?" Sean asked.

Hayes nodded. "He was in there working on Rivest's remains. There's not enough left of him to do an autopsy on."

"So Rivest's and Monk's bodies?"

"Pretty much bone and cinder."

"That's *way* too convenient, don't you think?" Sean said.

"I thought I told you to keep the hell out of my way," boomed a voice.

They all three turned to see FBI Special Agent Ventris striding toward them. He came to a stop a few inches from Sean's face. "Do you have a hearing problem?"

"He's working with me, Agent Ventris," Hayes said hastily.

"I don't give a shit if you're working with God Almighty Himself, I told you to stay out of my way."

"I just came down here in response to a call I got

from Sheriff Hayes," Sean said evenly. "And would you care to explain to me how the FBI has jurisdiction over a local death that's unrelated to any federal matter or person?"

Ventris looked ready to take a swing at Sean. Michelle stepped between them.

"Look, Sean and I used to be part of the federal side too, Agent Ventris. Our main contact was Len Rivest and now he's dead. Sean discovered the body; it's only natural that we want to stay informed about the matter. But we will in no way interfere with a federal investigation. All we're looking for is the truth, same as you."

Her words seemed to take a bit of the steam out of Ventris.

Hayes quickly said, "Sean, maybe you better fill in Agent Ventris on your theory about Rivest."

"I don't want to be seen as interfering," Sean growled.

"Just lay it out," Ventris snapped.

Sean grudgingly explained about the absence of towels and the bath mat and the missing plunger and his theory of how Rivest could have been killed. "We'd asked the ME to check the body for a trace of something like that happening."

Ventris studied the pavement for a few moments. "I actually noticed that there were no towels," he said. "And the bath mat, but I didn't know about the plunger."

Michelle said, "So you were suspecting murder too?"

"I always suspect murder," Ventris said. "I'm bringing in a team to go over everything here."

Sean said, "And you're interested in Rivest's death because you think it ties into Monk Turing's, which *was* on federal property."

"So maybe we should join forces," Michelle suggested.

"That's not possible," Ventris said. "If you have information you want to share with me, fine, but it's not a two-way street. We have ways of doing things at the Bureau."

"I thought your ways of doing things included working with the local police," Sean said.

"And I fit that bill," Hayes added.

"But *they* don't," Ventris replied fiercely, glaring at Sean and Michelle.

"Isn't the point that we catch whoever did all this?" Michelle said.

"No, the point is, *I* catch them," Ventris snapped.

"I'll make it easy for you," Sean began. "We'll just make it a competition. Who gets there first gets the credit. But just so you know we're going to kick your ass." He turned and stalked off.

Ventris turned on Hayes. "If he in any way impedes my investigation, you'll be going down with him, Hayes!"

"I'm just trying to do my job here," Hayes shot back.

"No, apparently you're trying to do *my* job."

Ventris noticed Michelle staring at him and smiling.

"What the hell are you looking at, lady?"

"Should've taken me up on my offer of coopera-tion, Ventris. Because when we crack this thing you are going to look like such an idiot." She turned and walked off.

"I can arrest you for saying shit like that," Ventris screamed after her.

Michelle turned back around. "No, you can't. It's that little bedrock thing called free speech. Have a nice day."

A minute later Hayes joined Sean and Michelle in front of her truck.

Hayes said, "Great, we've now managed to piss off the CIA *and* the FBI. Who we gonna do next? DEA?"

Michelle said, "Assuming the morgue was blown up on purpose, the question becomes why."

"And the answer seems obvious," Sean remarked. "There was something on those bodies that the ME would find that would point us down the right road."

"He'd already done the cutting on Monk," Hayes pointed out. "So it couldn't have been Monk's body they were worried about."

"Right," Sean said. "Burning up Rivest's body means we can't tell if my theory on how he was killed was correct."

Michelle added. "Do we know if the ME had looked for that already?"

"If he did he didn't have a chance to tell us," Hayes said quickly. "I asked him to call me as soon as he found anything and he never did."

"We can follow down a lead Ventris doesn't have," Sean said confidently.

Michelle looked at him. "Which is?"

"Valerie Messaline."

Hayes groaned. "Damn. I was afraid you were going to say that."

49

Horatio Barnes shook hands with Viggie as Alicia Chadwick nervously watched. They were in the small parlor at the B&B where Horatio was staying.

Before Horatio could say anything Viggie sprang up and settled herself in front of the small upright piano situated in one corner of the room. She began to play. Horatio rose and joined her on the bench. As she played away, he said, "Mind if I jump in?"

She shook her head and he waited a moment, studying her rhythm and then began playing smoothly. They performed a duet for about five minutes and then Viggie abruptly stopped. "I'm done." She plopped back in the chair while Horatio resumed his seat across from her, studying her carefully.

"You're an excellent pianist," Horatio said. "And I hear you're quite the whiz at math too."

"Numbers are fun," Viggie said. "I like them because if you add the same numbers up you always get the same answers. There aren't many things that do that."

"Meaning life is too unpredictable? Yes, I'd agree with that. So numbers feel very safe to you?"

Viggie nodded absently and looked around the room.

Horatio continued to study her while she did so. Body cues were often as important as verbal communication in his field. He asked a few preliminary questions about her life at Babbage Town. Horatio had intended to tread carefully around the subject of Monk Turing, but Viggie's next words exploded that strategy.

"Monk is dead. Did you know that?" Viggie asked him. She plunged on before he could answer. "He was my father."

"I know, I heard. I'm very sorry. I'm sure you loved him very much."

Viggie nodded, picked up an apple from a bowl on the table next to her and began eating it.

"And how about your mother?"

Viggie stopped chewing. "I don't have a mother."

"Everyone has a mother. Do you mean she's dead?"

Viggie shrugged. "I mean I don't have a mother. Monk would've told me."

Horatio glanced at Alicia, who looked pained by this exchange. She shook her head helplessly at him.

"So you remember nothing about her?"

"About who?"

"Your mother."

"You're not listening. I don't *have* a mother."

"Okay, what did you like to do with your father?

He was good at numbers too, right? Did you play games with numbers, maybe?"

Viggie swallowed a bite of apple and nodded. "All the time. He said I was smarter than he was. And he knew about quantum physics. Do you know about that?"

"My IQ is not where it needs to be to understand that particular field."

"I understood it. I understand lots of things people don't think I do."

Horatio glanced over at Alicia, who nodded at him encouragingly.

"So people don't think you understand things?"

"I'm a kid. A kid, a kid, a kid," she said in a singsong voice. "At least that's what they think."

"I bet Monk didn't think that way about you, did he?"

"Monk treated me special."

"How did he do that?"

"He trusted me."

"That's very impressive, an adult trusting someone your age. I bet that made you feel really good." She shrugged noncommittally. "Do you remember the last time you saw Monk?" She shrugged again. "With a head like yours I bet if you try you'll be able to do it easily."

"I like remembering numbers better than anything. Numbers never change. A one is always a one and a ten is always a ten."

"But numbers do change, don't they? If you multiply them together, for example? Or add or subtract or divide them. And ten can be ten or ten thousand. And one can be one or one hundred. Right?"

Now Viggie focused squarely on him. "Right," she said automatically.

"Or is it wrong?" Horatio queried.

"It's wrong," Viggie said. "Wrong, wrong, wrong." She took another bite of her apple.

Horatio sat back. *Quite a mynah bird.* "You like number puzzles? There was one I learned in college. Would you like to play it? It's sort of hard."

Viggie put the apple down and said eagerly, "Not for me it won't be."

He said, "Suppose I'm a grandfather and I have a grandson who's about as many days old as my son is weeks old and my grandson is as many months old as I am in years. My son, grandson and I together are 140 years old. How old am I in years?"

Horatio glanced at Alicia, who was working out the problem on a piece of paper she'd pulled from her purse. When he looked back at Viggie he said, "Would you like some paper and a pencil?"

"What for?"

"To work out the problem."

"I've already worked it out. You're eighty-four years old, but you don't look it."

A minute later Alicia looked up. On her piece of paper was a series of calculations with the number

"84" written at the end. She smiled at Horatio and shook her head in a weary fashion. "I'm so clearly not in her league."

Horatio looked back at Viggie, who sat there expectantly.

"Did you see all the numbers in your head?" he asked and she nodded before resuming her apple eating.

He gave her two large numbers and asked her to multiply them together. She did so in a matter of seconds. He gave her a division problem, which she solved almost instantly. Then he quizzed her with a square root exercise. Viggie answered them all within seconds and then looked bored as Horatio jotted some notes down on a piece of paper.

"I have another problem for you to think about," he said.

She sat up straight though she still seemed bored.

Not a mynah bird. *A well-trained dog, aren't you, Viggie?* "Suppose you had a best friend that you did everything with. Now suppose this best friend moved away and you'd never see her again. How would you feel?"

Viggie blinked once and then again. She started blinking so hard that her face scrunched up with the effort. Horatio felt like he was watching a computer whose circuit board was overheating.

"How would you feel, Viggie?" he asked again.

"There aren't any numbers in the problem," she said in a puzzled tone.

"I know, but not all questions have to do with numbers. Would you be happy, sad, ambivalent?"

"What's ambivalent mean?"

"You don't really care one way or another."

"Yes," she said automatically.

"Or how about sad?"

"Sad, I'd be sad."

"But not happy?"

Viggie glanced over at Alicia. "There aren't any numbers in the problem."

"I know, Viggie, just do the best you can."

Viggie shrugged and resumed eating her apple.

Horatio wrote some other notes down. "Have you been thinking about the last time you saw your father?"

"Why wouldn't I be happy?" she asked suddenly.

"You wouldn't be happy because your friend went away. You do fun things with your friends. So if your *best* friend went away you couldn't do fun things anymore," Horatio explained. "Like I'm sure you did fun things with your father before he went away. You're sad that your father went away, right? No more fun things with him?"

"Monk went away."

"That's right. Were you doing something fun with him the last time you saw him."

"Lots of fun."

"What was it?"

"I can't tell you."

"Oh, it's a secret? Secrets are fun. Did you have lots of secrets with Monk?"

Viggie lowered her voice and edged closer to him. "It was all secret."

"And you can't tell anybody else, right?"

"Right."

"But you could if you wanted to."

"Right, if I wanted to."

"Do you want to? I bet you do."

For the first time she showed hesitation with a prompting like that. "I'd have to tell it in a secret way."

"You mean like in a code? I'm afraid I'm not very good at codes."

"Monk loved codes. He loved secret codes. It made him bloody. He told me so."

Horatio glanced questioningly over at Alicia, who looked equally confused.

Horatio said, "It made him bloody, Viggie? What do you mean by that?"

She smiled and said, "What do you mean by that?"

"I'm asking you, what did Monk mean when he said codes made him bloody?"

"That's right, that's what he said, codes made him bloody. Codes and blood, that's what he said."

Horatio sat back. "Did Monk get bloody the last time he saw you?"

"Yes," she said happily.

"So he told you a secret?" She nodded again. "Can you tell us what it is?"

Her smile faded and she slowly shook her head.

"Why not? Was it a super-secret?"

Alicia said gently, "Viggie, if you know something it's very important that you tell us."

"I don't think I like him," Viggie answered, pointing to Horatio. "I have to go now." She got up and walked out of the room.

Horatio glanced over at Alicia, who seemed to have been holding her breath. "I told you she'd be a hard nut to crack. Did you learn anything useful?"

He said, "I know her better than I did an hour ago. That's something."

"Well, the next time you meet her she could be someone else entirely."

After Alicia left with Viggie, Horatio called Sean and filled him in on the session.

"So is Viggie autistic?" Sean asked.

"Autistism is a broad term," Horatio replied. "But even so, I don't think she is."

"What then?"

"I think in certain ways she's so much smarter than the rest of us, that she can't relate. In other ways she's not very intelligent, or mature, I should say. It might be a perception problem. *Our* perception problem. We expect her emotional abilities to match her intellect, but she's still a little girl. And I got some strange vibes from her about her father."

"Like what?"

"Monk apparently treated her like an adult, at least

sometimes. But other times he treated her, well, like a
. . . device."

"A device?"

"I know I'm not making much sense. I wished I
knew something about her mother. Viggie apparently
doesn't believe that she even had one."

"So where does this all leave us?" Sean asked.

"Not much further, I'm afraid."

"Well, at least our results are consistent. Meaning
nil."

"So what are you going to do?"

"I'm going to swing at a pitch and see if I can get
on base."

50

Since the woman hadn't given Sean her phone number he checked the phone book and the Internet with no luck. Sean finally decided to head back to Williamsburg that evening and the same bar where he had seen her the previous night. Michelle wanted to tag along but Sean vetoed that idea as they sat in his room at Alicia's cottage.

"I'm not sure Valerie would appreciate your presence as much as I would."

"Sean, think about it, a guy like Ian Whitfield is not going to let his wife screw around on him. He probably has her followed 24/7."

"Well, then they've already seen me with her. And if they spot me a second time they might just get rattled and make a mistake that will trip them up."

"That's a little bit of a long shot, isn't it?"

"We don't have a lot of other options. The bodies are burnt to a crisp, Ventris is stonewalling us, nobody at Babbage Town knows anything and the only person who might be able to help us, Viggie, doesn't speak a language any of us can understand."

"I thought Horatio was meeting with her."

"He did." Sean quickly recounted what Horatio had reported to him about his session with Viggie.

"So apparently Monk did tell his daughter something, but it's in code."

"If she's to be believed. Codes and blood. What's that supposed to mean?"

Michelle shrugged. "No clue."

"That's the thing about this case. There are a few clues but they keep disappearing. And there don't appear to be any to take their place."

"Speaking of, any word back from the pit bull in a skirt?"

Sean pulled a piece of paper out of his pocket. "Monk traveled to England. Joan managed to track down his itinerary. He visited several places. London, Cambridge, Manchester and a place called Wilmslow in Cheshire. And one other place that makes the other locations make sense."

"Which was?" she prompted.

"Bletchley Park," he replied. "It's where his relative Alan Turing worked during World War II and, according to Champ Pollion, saved the world."

"And the connection to the other places?"

"Except for three years at Princeton, they basically track Alan Turing's life. He was born in Paddington in London, went to college at Cambridge, Ph.D. at Princeton in the U.S., back to Cambridge, on to Bletchley Park, then to Manchester University after

305

the war, and died by his own hand in Wilmslow, Cheshire, in 1954."

"So the guy was related to Monk and he decided to take a little stroll down history lane," Michelle said. "Or it could be more than that."

"Possibly."

"So while you're dallying with a married woman, what do you want me to do?"

"Tonight you have Viggie duty, but before that Horatio wants to talk to you. And if you can squeeze it in, it would great if you could look around for a secret room in the mansion."

"And what if I don't want to talk to Horatio?"

"I'm not forcing you to do anything. But he sincerely wants to help you."

"You mean by talking behind my back to my family and snooping into my past?"

"Here's the address of the place where he's staying."

"And what will you be doing in the meantime?"

"Getting ready for my date."

She scowled. "You really piss me off sometimes."

"Really? I wouldn't know how that feels."

51

Michelle spent the next hour going through the mansion's main floor as methodically and yet unobtrusively as possible. She made rounds through the billiards room, the vast library, a smoking room, gun room with ancient rifles and shotguns kept behind iron grille doors, a parlor, and a trophy room with the requisite animal heads on the walls. Yet nowhere did she see any indication of a room that wasn't supposed to be there. Tired of dark worm-eaten paneling, thick Persian rugs underfoot, the musty smell of another century grabbing at her twenty-first-century edges, and weary of making no progress she went outside to ponder her options.

It was too early to get Viggie, and yet it took another half-hour of fits and starts before Michelle climbed in her truck and drove to see Horatio.

"I'm doing this only for Sean," she said as they sat down in the same room where Horatio had met with Viggie earlier.

"I'm just glad you're here, whatever your motivation. You really left an impression on the psych

307

facility, I can tell you that. You caught a criminal and literally saved that woman's life. That has to make you feel good."

"Yeah, I was feeling really good until Sean said you wanted to talk to me."

"I'm just trying to do my job any way I can."

"Look, let's cut to the chase. I attended my little sessions, did my little exercises, answered your insulting questions, spilled my soul, caught a drug dealer and, like you said, saved a woman's life. I think we can conclude that I'm cured, so we can just stop spending Sean's money, okay? Now I'm going to go back to doing *my* job. And why don't you go back to whatever it is you do, I guess I've never really been clear on that." She got up.

The bark of his voice startled her. "You're not cured. You're not even close to being cured. You're totally and completely fucked up, lady. Things will continue to spiral down and the day will come when you're doing your *job* that you totally whack out and get yourself and maybe Sean killed. Now if you're cool with that, keep on walking, climb in that Dumpster you call a ride and drive off into the sunsets of a gathering hell. But don't sit here and think that you're *cured*, because that's the biggest load of crap I've ever heard. People who want to get better, they work at it. They don't lie to themselves and everyone else. They don't sit on their ass and sink deeper into a pathetic existence while denying anything's wrong at all. They have balls not bullshit. And I'm pretty much fed up with yours."

Michelle felt a blinding fury gathering inside her. Her fists clenched, her body tensed to strike.

He calmly continued. "See how much anger you have inside your gut right now? You see how quick it is to build, *Mick*? Just because of a few words I said. True words by the way, but still just words. That's called losing your self-control. You want to kill me, right? I know you do. I can see it in every molecule. Same way you wanted to kill that poor slob back at the bar. The difference is at the bar you had to get wasted *first* before the rage became so bad you just had to release it on another human being. This time you're stone-cold sober and that rage is taking control of you and makes you want to knock my head off. That's what I meant by things spiraling down. What next? Will the rage be triggered by the way some stranger looks at you on the street? Or bumps into you on the subway? Or maybe just the way someone smells? It all comes down to that inner rage, Michelle. And you have to deal with yours right now."

"And if I don't?" she said hollowly.

"You lose. And the demons win. It's your choice."

Slowly, by almost imperceptible degrees of movement, Michelle sat back down.

Horatio watched her steadily. Her gaze remained on the floor while a muscle tremor worked its way down her neck.

When she spoke, her voice shook. "I don't know what you want from me."

"I could be flippant and say the truth, but that's not really how the mind works. I want to talk, Michelle, that's all. I want to ask some questions, listen to your answers, but mostly I just want to talk to you. About you. That's all. You think you're up to that?"

A full minute went by as she white-knuckled the arms of her chair. "Okay," she finally said in a voice so small he could barely hear.

"I went to the home you lived in when you were six. Sean told you that."

"Yes."

"I met a woman named Hazel Rose. Do you remember her?"

Michelle nodded.

"Hazel certainly remembers you. She told me to tell you that she's very proud of you." Horatio waited a few moments but Michelle gave no reaction to this news. "Hazel said you used to come over to her house for tea parties with some of the other neighborhood kids. Do you remember those parties?"

"No."

Horatio continued to watch her closely. There was no manual on how to do this. Essentially Horatio read the body cues of the patient and hoped those reads were right.

"Hazel told me about this beautiful rose hedge you had."

As soon as he said it, Michelle's entire body went lax, as though someone had pulled the plug on her heart. At first he thought she was going to faint. Then she rallied and sat up straighter in the chair.

"My father planted that rose hedge," she said in an automatic tone.

"Right. An anniversary present. But someone cut it down."

"Some kids, mad at my dad."

"That's one theory."

She stiffened again, but didn't look at him.

"Hazel noticed a change in you too back then. Can you remember why?"

"I was six, how am I supposed to know?"

"Well, you remembered the rose hedge. And you remembered that your father planted it and that someone cut it down."

She snapped, "Maybe I brutally murdered someone when I was six and I'm repressing it. Would that satisfy your curiosity?"

"Are we going back to wisecracks already? I was hoping you'd hold off for at least ten minutes based on my big, pull-no-punches speech. I don't drag that one out very often."

Now she looked at him and her gaze was curious, hungry. "So why'd you use it on me?"

"Because I see you slipping away, Michelle," he said quietly. "And I don't want you to reach the point of no return."

311

"Dammit, I'm here, Horatio, I'm working, thinking, helping Sean *and* a little girl who needs someone right now. How bad can I be? Tell me, how bad can I be?"

"That's a question only you can answer."

For a moment Horatio thought he could see her eyes moisten, and then they became hard and dry. "I know you're trying to help me. I know Sean is too. I've got issues, I know that too. And I'm trying to deal with them. I'm trying to stay productive."

"That's all well and good. But while you're staying productive you're not addressing those issues. You're ignoring them, Michelle."

Her tone became defiant. "You say I changed at age six? Well my life hasn't turned out too badly. Were you ever an Olympian? Or a cop? Did you ever guard the president? Well, I did. Did you ever save someone else's life? I have. More than once."

"I'm not saying you haven't had an exemplary life. What you've achieved has been extraordinary. What I'm talking about is the future. What I'm talking about is self-destructive behavior. What I'm trying to make you understand is that at some point you have to pay the piper."

She stood. "Are you telling me that everything I've done in my life is tied to something that might have happened to me when I was a kid? Are you possibly trying to say that to *me!*" She screamed the last word at him.

"No, I didn't say that. *You* did."

Just as Viggie had, in an instant Michelle was gone. He heard her truck start up and shoot gravel out as she sped off.

Horatio rubbed his temple, walked outside, hopped on his Harley and followed her. This time he wasn't letting the lady go.

52

At the very least I think you should have me cover your back, Sean," Sheriff Hayes said. The men were in Hayes's personal car heading toward Williamsburg.

"That won't work, because Whitfield knows what you look like."

"One of my deputies then. Whitfield is not the kind of guy who's going to let you screw around with his wife."

"He doesn't seem to have a problem with his wife frequenting bars and getting hit on. It wasn't like it was the first time she'd been in that place."

"But he knows who you are too. If he sees you around her, he might think you're trying to spy on him."

"But he doesn't know that I know she's his wife. If he or his muscle shows up, I act surprised and go on my way."

"You really think a guy like Whitfield is gonna buy that?"

"Probably not, but if you have a better lead we can run down I'm listening. Hell, I have no idea if she'll even be there tonight. This could be a complete wild-goose chase."

"But even if Messaline knows something, why would she tell *you*?"

"I'm not exactly a novice at getting information out of people."

"But you said she blew you off the first time."

"That was the first time."

"So you really believe Whitfield had something to do with Monk's and Len's deaths?"

"Monk died on CIA soil. Whitfield made a special point of calling us off the case. Even got the DDO on my butt. And from that same plot of land somebody took a shot at me. And planes flying without lights land there in the middle of the night."

"Planes?" Hayes said.

"They come right over Babbage Town. And they're big jets, easily capable of intercontinental flight. No one knows who's on those flights. And there was hush money funneled through Congress to build what was termed a new dorm for agent trainees at the Camp, even though they have lots of housing there already."

"What do you mean 'termed'?"

"A building can be lots of things. Including an interrogation center. Even a torture chamber."

Hayes almost drove off the road. "Are you out of your damn mind? That's totally and completely illegal in this country."

"Maybe Monk saw prisoners no one knows about getting their organs tickled by electrical current. What better motive to kill the man?"

"I can't believe that. And what about Len Rivest?"

"Monk told him, or else he suspected, or found out somehow. Whitfield discovered that and no more Len Rivest."

"But if he knew something why wouldn't Len have gone to the police? He was ex-FBI for God's sake."

"Maybe he didn't want to go up against the CIA and Ian Whitfield. Maybe there are folks even higher up in the government who know about what's going on at Camp Peary. And maybe he did tell someone and that person was the wrong person to tell."

"Now you're talking some kind of major conspiracy."

"So what? They happen every day. If the stakes are big enough the conspiracies tend to grow large enough to accommodate them. And by the way, in D.C. they're not referred to as conspiracies, they're called *policies*."

Hayes said nervously, "This is getting way over my head, Sean, I don't mind telling you. I'm just a small-town cop looking to retire in a few years."

"Merk, you can just drop me off and don't look back. Our partnership can be dissolved with no hard feelings, but I am not letting this go."

Hayes seemed to consider this for a minute. "What

the hell," he finally said. "If I'm going down it might as well be over something important. But I still think somebody should be following you tonight."

If either of them had turned around, he would have noticed that someone already was following them tonight.

53

Horatio pulled his motorcycle to a stop next to Michelle's truck. The woman had turned off the main road and parked under some trees down near the river. She wasn't in the truck and Horatio followed a dirt path down to the water where he found her sitting on a fallen tree that extended partially over the water. She didn't acknowledge his presence as he sat down on the other part of the tree that was still firmly on land.

"Nice evening," he said as he tossed a pebble into the fast-moving York, which was carrying debris from an earlier thunderstorm down to the Chesapeake Bay.

She was silent for some minutes, just staring at the water until Horatio started to fear she might jump in.

Her first words definitely got his attention. "I cleaned my truck out once. I did it for Sean."

"Why?"

"Because I liked him and he'd been going through a bad time."

"Was it hard, cleaning out the truck?"

"Far harder than it should have been. Everything in there seemed to weigh a thousand pounds. But it's just a truck, right?" She swiveled around on her backside until she was facing him. "It's just a truck," she said again.

"Truck, bedroom, lifestyle. I can imagine it was very hard."

"I couldn't keep it clean. I tried. Well, I didn't really try. I just couldn't do it. Within a day I put everything back."

"Sean says your racing scull is pristine. You could eat off the hull, he claims."

She smiled. "He would say that. Although he's not exactly without his quirks. Have you ever seen anyone so neat and orderly? I mean, come on."

She snapped off a small branch from the fallen tree and tossed it in the water. As she watched it sail away she said, "I don't know why I changed, Horatio. I really don't. I don't even remember changing to tell the truth, but with so many people claiming I did, I guess I have to accept it."

"Okay. That's a good admission. A very positive step, Michelle. Yet when I mentioned the rose hedge you reacted to that. Why?"

She'd visibly shuddered again when he'd said it. Another few minutes of silence went by. Michelle stared at the tree trunk she was sitting on; Horatio's gaze was directly on her. He didn't say anything, fearful he might ruin the possibility of the first real breakthrough since he'd started seeing her. His patience was amply rewarded.

She said, "Can you be afraid of something and you don't even know what it is?"

"Yes. It can be buried so deeply within your mind that all you can register is the fear without realizing what the source of that fear is. Repression into the subconscious of past events that were beyond someone's ability to deal with at the time is the brain's failsafe mechanism to protect us. We simply block it out."

"Just like that?"

"Just like that. But it's akin to water in the basement that you try to fix by patching here and there. Eventually the damage becomes so severe that the entire foundation of the house is threatened as the water starts to seep into unexpected places, places you can't even see until the damage is done."

"So I'm a rotting house?"

"And I'm the best house fixer you're ever going to run across."

"But if I can't even remember why I'm so scared, how can you help me?"

"There's a tried-and-true method: hypnosis."

Michelle shook her head. "I don't believe in that crap. No one can hypnotize me."

"Usually the people who are certain they can't be are the easiest to do it to."

"But you have to want to be hypnotized, right?"

"That certainly helps. But you want to get better, don't you?"

"I wouldn't be sitting here talking to you about this stuff if I didn't. I haven't spoken to anyone about this, ever!"

"I'll take that as a compliment. Will you let me hypnotize you?"

"I don't like losing control, Horatio. And what if I tell you something that I can't handle? What if it's that bad?"

"That's why I went to all those schools and have all the certificates on my wall. I'm the professional. Just let me do my job. That's all I'm asking."

"That's asking a lot. Maybe too much," she added bluntly.

"Will you at least think about it?"

She rose, nimbly walked down the trunk and hopped to the ground next to him. As Michelle passed him she called over her shoulder, "I'll think about it."

Horatio looked after her in exasperation. "Where are you going now?"

"I've got Viggie duty."

54

Sean lucked out because Valerie was sitting at the same table as the night before. And like that time she was sending another would-be pickup artist on his way.

Valerie was dressed less provocatively this time, in slacks and a cashmere sweater. Her hair was pulled back in a French braid and her lipstick was muted.

When she saw Sean headed toward her Valerie quickly glanced the other way. When he sat down across from her, she still didn't look at him.

"I see you're still very popular here," he said.

"And I can see you don't get the concept of a brush-off very well."

"Tonight's a new venture."

"Not from where I'm sitting."

"Would you like to grab some dinner?"

"Do I have to call the bouncer to get rid of you?"

"Let me think about that one while you decide where you'd like to eat." She almost smiled. He was quick to pick up on it. "Okay, that's a tiny little crack, but I'll take what I can get."

"And why would you think I would want to have dinner with you?"

"Okay, now that I have your full attention, I'll tell you." He paused and said, "I just want someone to talk to. Traveling around by yourself gets really old really fast. I'm not looking for anything other than good conversation over a nice bottle of wine. And we can split the check, no favors owed on either side."

"And you're assuming I can provide this good conversation? And that I like wine?"

"The conversation I think is a given. My stupid and shallow radar is pretty damn good. It hasn't made a peep since I met you. As for the wine, I'm flexible, but I passed a place down the street from here that has a Cabernet on the list I've been dying to try."

"You know your way around grapes?"

"I used to collect wine."

"Used to?"

"Yeah, until somebody blew up my house and my wine cellar." Sean rose from the table. "Shall we?"

Sitting at a corner overlooking the street and sharing the bottle of Cabernet, Sean once more glanced at Valerie's wedding ring. He did so in such a way that she could hardly miss it.

"You're wondering why I'm having dinner with you while I happen to be a married woman?" she said.

"I was thinking if I was your husband I wouldn't let you go to bars by yourself."

"I can take care of myself."

"My worry would be that you might just take a fancy to one of those gentlemen."

"And you think I've taken a fancy to you?"

"I think you're wondering if I'm really sincere, or just another creep waiting to make his move."

"And which one are you?"

"Well, if I am a creep I'd tell you that I'm quite sincere."

"So where does that leave us?"

"At you making up your own mind based on observation. Sound reasonable?"

"What do we talk about so I can start observing?"

"Personal histories are an accepted protocol. I'll go first. Like I said, I'm divorced, no kids. I told you I was a problem solver and I am. I'm a lawyer, but don't hold that against me. I'm down here doing some due diligence for a client embroiled in some nasty litigation. You?"

"Married and never a mom like I told you before. I used to have a career. Now I sit at home or I sometimes go out. That's about it."

"Without your husband? I mean what part of beautiful and intelligent doesn't he get?"

She held up a warning finger. "You're treading the creepy line."

"Sorry. I'll retreat to a respectful position. What do you do for fun?"

"I don't do anything for fun. I think I've had my share of fun in life. Now it's all downhill."

"Come on, it's not like you have one foot in the grave."

"Don't I?"

"You're not ill or anything?"

"Not in the sense you're thinking, no."

He sat back and swirled the wine around in his glass. "Okay, you qualify at least in the top three of the most interesting women I've ever met. Just so you can put that in context, my ex never even made the top ten."

"Which tells me you're a poor judge of character."

"I've gotten better."

"My husband would make anyone's top five list. He's actually very interesting. At least what he does is very interesting."

"And what's that?"

She shook her head. "Loose lips sink ships, you know."

Sean appeared to be puzzled for a moment. "Sink ships? Is he in the military? I know they have a big presence down here."

"He's with the government, but not that branch; although he used to be. Vietnam."

"Vietnam! But you're not that old."

"He waited a long time to marry. Why he decided to go for it after all those years on his own, I can't tell you."

"What then? FBI? I've got some ex-Army buddies who joined up with the Bureau."

"Have you ever heard of Camp Peary?"

Sean slowly shook his head. "But it sounds familiar. Is it a camp like for kids?"

She smiled. "In a way, but the kids are really big with toys to match."

"What are you talking about?"

"Camp Peary is a training center for a government agency whose initials start with C and end with A. Does that spell it out for you, no pun intended?"

"CIA! Your husband works for the CIA?" he said in a furious whisper.

She looked at him with suspicion. "You're sure you never heard of Camp Peary?"

"I'm from Ohio. Maybe it's famous around here, but the news hasn't reached Dayton. Sorry."

"Well, my husband actually runs the place. Again, it's not exactly a state secret."

Sean appeared stunned. "Valerie, let me ask you one simple question."

"Why would a man like that let his wife go to bars by herself and have dinner with strange men?" Sean nodded. "Well, let me give you a simple answer. He doesn't care what I do. Some days I don't know why he married me. Well, I do. I make a terrific first impression. But with Ian, the effect wore off."

"So if *Ian* goes his way and you go yours, why not just divorce?"

She shrugged. "Divorces tend to get nasty and take too much energy. You said you'd been divorced. Isn't that true?"

"Very true," he admitted. "I guess he keeps pretty busy. I mean with the war on terror and everything."

"Or it just could be that I'm not interesting enough," she said.

Sean sat back and looked pensive. "It was love at first sight for my wife and me. But then she changed, or I changed, who the hell knows. She didn't like lawyers very much. I guess it was doomed from the start."

"Maybe that's what happened to me too."

"Why, how did you and Ian meet?"

"I was with a private contractor that worked with CIA. My field is or was bioterrorism long before it became so popular. Ian and I met at a conference in Australia. That was before he'd been promoted to run Camp Peary of course. I'd actually visited the place before I even knew Ian. But I got burned out and left. He still revels in that world. That's the difference between him and me. And it's become a big difference."

"Wait a minute. That's why it sounded familiar. Didn't they find a body at Camp Peary?"

Valerie nodded slowly. "The guy apparently climbed over the fence and shot himself."

"Damn, why would anyone do that?"

"Everybody has issues, problems."

"You sound like you speak from experience."

"We all speak from experience, Sean."

After dinner was over they walked down the street together.

"This was a great evening, Valerie, thank you."

"It was a depressing evening, due in large part to me."

Sean remained silent. He simply didn't have a good answer to this. Finally he said, "I'll be in town for about a week. Would you like to do this again?"

"I don't think that's a good idea," she said.

"Could I at least have your phone number?"

"Why?"

"Is there any harm in talking?"

"There's harm in everything." Even so, she reached in her purse, pulled out a pen and piece of paper and wrote a number down and handed it to him.

"You can leave a message there; if I don't call back, well, I'm sorry. Thank you for saving me from another night in that bar. Goodbye." She touched his arm, then walked off down the street, leaving Sean feeling very troubled. Valerie Messaline was probably what she seemed to be: a lonely woman treading water until something happened. His only viable lead to Camp Peary had just disappeared. Now where should he start looking?

The answer came to him almost as quickly as the question had. The only thing was, would he have the courage, or more accurately, the level of insanity needed to pull it off?

55

Michelle decided to combine her Viggie duty with a bold tactical move. There was still daylight left so she took the girl down to the boathouse after getting permission from Alicia. There she outfitted Viggie with a proper life jacket after ascertaining that the girl was only a fair swimmer. They pulled a kayak out and were soon on the water with Viggie in front with a paddle and Michelle guiding the craft from the rear while she instructed Viggie on the proper paddling motion.

She quickly mastered the correct motion and soon her cuts were smooth and efficient through the water. Viggie was certainly stronger than she looked, Michelle decided.

"This is fun," Viggie said as the wind whipped through her hair.

"I love it," Michelle said. It only took her two cuts in the water with her paddle before she was once more in the groove. When you've paddled, collectively, hundreds of thousands of miles in the water, the muscle memory is ingrained.

They quickly came, as Michelle had planned, to the area of the York across from Camp Peary. She stopped paddling and told Viggie to do the same. As they drifted in the current Michelle leaned back, and unobtrusively took in the shrouded-in-secrecy CIA installation. The perimeter fence gleamed back at her. There wasn't a guard in sight, yet Michelle's sixth sense told her that eyes were watching.

"That's Camp Peary," Viggie said suddenly. "That's where Monk died."

"You know about Camp Peary?" Viggie nodded. "Did Monk ever talk to you about it?" Viggie gave another nod. "What'd he say?"

"Stuff."

"Codes and blood?"

Viggie turned to stare at her. "You've been talking to that other man."

"Horatio Barnes, yes. He's a friend." Michelle had to bite her lip on that last comment.

"I don't like him."

"Well, he strikes some people the wrong way. So codes and blood? That sounds really interesting."

One good thing about being on a kayak in the middle of the river, Viggie couldn't just get up and leave, which was one reason Michelle had brought the girl here.

"Monk liked codes. He taught me about them. He was related to a very famous scientist."

"And you're related to him too of course."

Viggie nodded with a proud look on her face. "Alan Turing was a homosexual. And people back then didn't like that, so he ate a poisoned apple and died."

Michelle was at a loss for words with this change in direction of the conversation. *Monk really had treated her like an adult.* "That is very sad," she finally said.

"I hope I never have to eat a poisoned apple when people are mad at me."

"I'm sure you never will, Viggie," Michelle said firmly. "Taking your own life is never the right answer." Michelle felt a stab of guilt as she said this.

"It's like the wicked old queen in Snow White. She turned herself into a hag, got in an old boat and floated down the river to the cottage in the woods. Then she tricked Snow White into eating a poisoned apple. She didn't die, but she went to sleep. It took a prince kissing her to wake her up. Yuck!"

"Counting on handsome princes to make your life better is not very smart. Right?"

"Right, but it also shows that whoever has the apple is pretty powerful."

Michelle decided to change the subject. "Viggie, have you ever heard of a secret room at the mansion?"

Viggie turned around. "A secret room?"

"Yes. We were at another old house around here and we found some kids inside a secret room there. One of the kids said lots of the old places down here had secret rooms."

"I've never heard of one at Babbage Town," Viggie said.

"Okay." Michelle waited a moment and said, "Speaking of secret stuff could you teach me some codes?"

"There are lots of different kinds. You can make them up too."

"Did you and Monk make codes up?"

"Oh sure. Lots of times."

"I guess he wanted to keep things secret from other people. Do you know which people he wanted to keep secrets from?"

"Everybody," Viggie said. Then she turned and gave Michelle a sly grin. "Including you."

Michelle suddenly realized that Viggie knew exactly what she was trying to do and was having fun at her expense. Michelle decided to take a more direct tack. It carried risks but they didn't have many options right now.

"Viggie, we're trying to find out who took Monk away from you, do you understand that? That's the only reason we're here."

Michelle watched as Viggie's shoulders slumped. Not sure how to interpret that body cue Michelle plunged on. "If he was afraid of someone or kept secrets from people, it would really help us to know who. All we're trying to do is help."

"People who say they want to help, they have other reasons why."

"Not us, Viggie, believe me."

Viggie wheeled around and stared at her. "Are you being *paid* to help?"

The question caught Michelle off-guard, but she sensed lying to the girl would not be a good thing. "It's my job to help people. It's how I make my living."

"So you do get paid. That's why you're spending time with me. You wouldn't want to be around me except for that. I bet you'd just want to hang out with your real friends."

"Viggie, I don't have many real friends. In fact, other than Sean, I can't say I have any."

"I bet that's not true."

"Why, do you think everyone has lots of friends except you? And there are other children at Babbage Town, at the school."

"None of them like me. Everybody thinks I'm weird."

"Everyone is odd in a way. If you ever took a ride in my truck, you'd know exactly what I'm talking about. It's a trash pit that I can't seem to get rid of no matter how hard I try."

Viggie stared at her. "That's why they brought that Mr. Barnes down. Because I'm weird."

Michelle swallowed with great difficulty. "Actually, Mr. Barnes is also helping me. To get over some problems I have . . . from when I was a little girl."

"He is?" Michelle nodded. "You promise? You aren't just saying it."

"I promise. Poor guy, I kept getting up and walk-ing out on him when he was asking me questions, trying to make me better."

In a hushed voice Viggie said, "I did that too. Why did you walk out?"

Michelle hesitated. It wasn't because she didn't know the answer to the question. It was just hard to say it. "Because I was afraid."

"Afraid of what?" Viggie said breathlessly as she stared at Michelle.

"Afraid he was getting too close to the truth and I couldn't handle it."

Viggie picked up her paddle. She said in a very small voice, "Me too."

"See, I don't really remember what happened to me. That's why he wants to hypnotize me, to help me remember."

"Are you going to let him?"

"I don't know, what do you think?"

"You want my opinion?"

"Sure. You're really smart. So should I or shouldn't I? I mean I guess I could just keep on going and never find out what it is. Sometimes the truth is not so great."

"I think you should let him do it," Viggie said decisively.

"Really? Why?"

"It's always better to know, isn't it?"

Michelle didn't answer right away. "I think you're right. It is better to know."

"Can we go back now?" Viggie asked, sliding her paddle into the water.

"Sure. I hope this was fun for you."

Viggie nodded but didn't say anything. As they turned around and paddled away a man limped out of the woods on the Camp Peary side. Ian Whitfield lowered his binoculars but his gaze stayed on the small two-person craft. He'd been alerted to their presence by one of his men. He pulled a phone from his belt holder and punched in a number. His features were grim as he spoke. A few minutes later his aide, Six-Pack, joined him.

Whitfield said, "Ex-Secret Service? Both her and Sean King?"

"That's right. Michelle Maxwell, down to investigate Turing and Rivest on behalf of the Babbage Town folks."

Whitfield said, "Turing's daughter was in the kayak."

"What do you want to do about it, sir?"

Whitfield didn't answer the question. He just stood there staring through the chain link fence out at the water. Finally he turned to Six-Pack. "Sometimes it's a thankless damn job, son." Whitfield turned and limped into the forest.

Back at the boathouse Michelle and Viggie put the kayak and gear away. As they walked back to Babbage

Town Viggie placed her hand in Michelle's and squeezed. "I hope Mr. Barnes can help you remember stuff," she said.

"Thanks, Viggie. I appreciate your helping me decide."

When they got back to the cottage Viggie ran to her piano and started playing. When she finished performing the song she looked up at Michelle. "I like you, Michelle."

"I like you too, Viggie."

Viggie jumped up from the piano and raced up the stairs. At the top of the landing she paused and turned. "Codes and blood," she screamed and then ran down the hall to her room, leaving a stunned Michelle downstairs.

56

Sean had arranged for a rental car in Williamsburg and drove back to Babbage Town after dinner with Valerie. He crossed the bridge over the York and was passing Gloucester Point when the car that had been following him all evening caught up and forced him off the road. Before Sean could get out a man was at the driver's window.

"Get out of the car," he screamed at Sean, waving his ID.

FBI Special Agent Mike Ventris wasn't exactly exuding the warm fuzzies.

"Can I ask what this is in reference to?" Sean said politely.

"Shut the hell up and get in my car! Now!"

Sean followed him back to his federal-issued cruiser. He climbed in the passenger side while Ventris ducked in the driver's seat. When the doors slammed shut Ventris turned to him and snapped, "What do you think you're doing, you idiot?"

Sean said calmly, "I was driving back to Babbage Town when you ran me off the road. Is it time for your wheels refresher course at the Bureau or do you just do that for kicks?"

"Knock off the wise-ass crap. First, you went to see Ian Whitfield."

"Actually he summoned me and Sheriff Hayes."

"And after that you met his wife at a bar."

"No, we just ran into each other."

"And you just had dinner with her."

"Not a crime, at least that I'm aware of."

"What exactly is your relationship with Valerie Messaline?"

"We were drawn together by a common love of a good Mojito."

Ventris shoved a finger against Sean's chest. "I am this far from arresting your ass."

"Can I ask the charge?"

"I can lock you up for forty-eight hours no questions asked. In the meantime I can probably find something that'll stick."

"I'm down here working, just like you. Trying to find out who killed Monk Turing and Len Rivest. Remember the little competition I mentioned?"

"And I told you to stay out of my way."

"I wasn't aware that Valerie Messaline constituted being in your way."

"She has no involvement in this case and neither does Ian Whitfield. The man has more important things to worry about than a dipshit PI poking around where he shouldn't."

Sean looked at him in disbelief. "Since when is the Bureau the CIA's lapdog?"

"I'm telling you for your own good to back off. There are far more important issues here than a couple of murders."

"Care to share?"

"Get out of my car. And if we have to meet again, you really won't like it."

Sean climbed out of the vehicle and then tapped on the window. "By the way, any news on the 'gas leak' at the morgue?"

Ventris almost ran over Sean's foot as the car roared off.

Despite the smart-ass attitude he'd taken with Ventris, Sean wasn't smiling as he trudged back to his car. He was getting in deeper by the second and so far nothing made any sense at all. As he drove back to Babbage Town Sean knew what he had to do next.

"You can't be serious, Sean," Horatio said. The three of them were standing next to Michelle's truck and Horatio's Harley, which were parked along a dirt road about a mile from Babbage Town.

"Monk Turing went over the fence at Camp Peary and look what happened to him," Horatio continued.

"Trust me, I don't want to go over that fence, but I'm running out of options," Sean replied evenly.

Michelle leaned back against her truck and studied her partner. "When do you propose we do it?"

Horatio gaped at her. "You're planning on going with this nutcase?"

Sean looked at Michelle. "I go alone."

"Don't even bother. You go, I go."

"If we get caught we are up shit's creek," he told her. "I mean really up."

"You're never boring; I have to give you that," she replied.

"Will you two listen to what you're saying," Horatio pleaded. "This is the CIA for God's sake. You could be executed for treason."

"We'll go on Saturday," Sean said in answer to Michelle's previous question. "If we don't get a break in the case by then."

She said, "The next scheduled flight?" He nodded.

"I don't know if you noticed on the map in South Freeman's office, but the—"

She finished for him, "The runway is on the other side of the line of trees where they found Monk's body. So we're doing a recon on the flight?"

"At the very least it'll be interesting to see who or what gets off the damn plane."

"Okay, you are really freaking me out here, Sean," Horatio said. He added, "You know I can't let you two do this."

Sean turned on him. "If you don't want us to go over the fence then you come up with a way for us to get to the truth. You're big on the truth, aren't you? You've been working with Viggie and Michelle trying to do that, right?"

"That's different."

"It's not different to me. Three men have been killed. Every instinct I have tells me Camp Peary is at the center of it. Someone from there tried to kill *me*. I can't walk away from that."

"Then take it to the authorities."

"Sheriff Hayes would have a coronary if he knew what we were planning. Ventris would just shoot me and pretend his gun went off accidentally. I filled Hayes in on my dinner with Valerie and my little encounter with Ventris, but that's it. I let you in on this because I trust you. And I'd never do anything to screw you."

"What're you talking about?" Horatio asked nervously.

"If we get caught the cops will try to round up whoever they think's involved with us. That means you. So here's your chance to go home, right now. Michelle and I will swear you knew nothing about it."

Horatio leaned against the truck. "Well, I have to say, most felons I've worked with aren't nearly as considerate."

"And if we get through this and get back home, you can still see Michelle." Sean looked at his partner. "If she wants to," he hastily added.

Michelle remained quiet.

"And if I choose to stay?" Horatio asked.

"There's no problem if we don't get caught. If we do, the cops might start nosing around if you're still around. I can't guarantee you won't become a target."

"If you do get caught I can help build a great insanity defense for you both."

Sean smiled. "It's nice to have options."

Horatio said, "But you're risking your life, Sean."

"So? I've spent most of my adult life doing that."

Michelle added, "After a while, it sort of becomes instinctual, you know?"

Horatio watched as the two exchanged a very knowing look that only came between two people who'd put life and limb on the line on a regular basis. "Viggie knows something. Codes and blood. If we can just find out what it means, it might crack everything wide open without you two going over that damn fence."

"Any good investigator follows up multiple leads because most don't pan out. It's a simple numbers game. But right now my focus is on the plot of land across the river."

"In the meantime," Michelle said, "I can take a run at Champ."

Sean said, "And I can talk to Alicia too."

"What's the weather forecast for Saturday night?" Michelle asked.

"Cool and overcast."

"We have time to prep at least. We'll need some things."

"I've already called in for them."

"So Joan didn't ask questions?"

"I didn't use Joan, because I don't trust her, at least not with this."

"I don't want to hear any more of this," Horatio said, pretending to cover his ears. "I'm already an accessory before the fact as it is."

"Not to worry. Like I said, if we're caught we won't rat you out." He grinned. "Unless we can cut a better deal by selling your ass down the river."

"What I did to deserve friends like you I don't know."

Sean said, "Horatio, we *do* need to follow up with Viggie. Codes and blood. You're right, that's got to mean something."

"I can do another session with her," Horatio said.

"I've gotten pretty close to her," Michelle said. "Let me try."

Horatio looked at her. "Did she say she liked you?"

"Yes. And she said she *doesn't* like you."

"Your sheer enjoyment in communicating that fact is duly noted," the psychologist commented blandly.

Sean said, "The other thing that's puzzling is that if I'm right and Rivest was killed, no one saw anyone leaving his cottage. His place is on the main drag. Someone had to see something."

Horatio said, "You're sure your sheriff buddy is asking the right people the right questions?"

"I assumed he was. Maybe that assumption was wrong. Maybe we should do it ourselves."

"So what do I do while you two are preparing to be slaughtered?"

"Does that mean—" Sean began but Horatio cut him off.

"Yeah, I'm staying. I must be as nuts as you. But the good news is I'll have plenty of time for counseling inside the big house after we're all busted. So give me an assignment before I come to my senses, jump on my Harley and ride like hell away from you two psychos."

"You can go and talk to a guy named South Freeman over in Arch, Virginia. He runs the newspaper there and has a good handle on the local history. Tell him we sent you. Learn everything you can about the area from him."

As the meeting broke up Horatio whispered to Michelle. "Thought anymore about the hypnosis?"

"I'll make a deal with you. If I come back alive I'll let you hypnotize me."

"Just the fact that you two are seriously contemplating this means you're both certifiable. You know that, right?"

"Wish me luck, Horatio."

As she closed the truck door, he said grudgingly, "Good luck."

57

Early the next morning Michelle went on a walk with Viggie, eventually straying down by the river where they sat on the boathouse dock and put their feet in the water. She attempted several times to lead the conversation around to codes and blood, but Viggie just as cagily danced around those attempts.

"Can we go out on the kayak again?" Viggie asked.

"Sure, would you like to go now?"

"No, just asking." She pointed across the river. "I don't like that place."

"Camp Peary? How come? Because of what happened to Monk there?"

"Not just that," she said casually.

"What then?"

"Monk was gone a lot," she said, suddenly changing the subject. "He left me for a long time."

"When? You mean when he left the country?" Viggie nodded. Michelle couldn't believe she hadn't thought to ask the girl about this before. "Do you know why he left the country? Why he visited the places overseas that he did?"

"He talked a lot about Alan Turing when he got back. It wasn't the first time he went there. He liked Alan Turing a lot, even though he's dead."

"When was the first time he went there?"

"Before we came here. When we were living at the other place."

"What other place was that?"

"In New York City. I didn't like it there. We lived in an apartment building. Everybody there was old. I didn't like them because they smelled funny. All except one person. An old man. I liked him. Monk liked him too. They talked a lot. He talked funny though. It was hard to understand him."

"Do you remember what they talked about?" Michelle had little reason to believe this was important, but she wanted to keep Viggie engaged.

"Not really. They talked about old stuff from a long time ago."

"I see."

"I'd just play my piano really loud when they did that."

"But you said you liked the old man."

"I did. He was nice, but he only talked about old stuff and it was hard to understand him."

"Well, sometimes that's what elderly people like to do, remember their past. And apparently Monk found it interesting."

"The old man knew a lot about math and science. And he showed Monk some old maps and I saw him once writing all these letters down on a piece of paper and seeing if my dad could understand them."

"So like a code?"

"I guess."

"You said letters. I thought Monk was just into numbers?"

"Monk said history was full of numbers, important ones. Alan Turing used numbers a long time ago to help end a big war. Monk used to tell me about that. But they used alphabet letters too."

"Is that what he and the old man talked about? Alan Turing and what he did during the Second World War?"

"Sometimes."

Michelle, impatient by nature, was finding it difficult not to start screaming, "Just cut the bullshit games and tell me the truth, you little twerp!" Instead she said, as calmly as she could, "So what did they usually talk about?"

Viggie stood. "I'll race you home." She turned and sped off. Within five steps Michelle had caught her, but then fell back as though tiring.

Faking being out of breath she said, "I tell you what, Viggie, if I beat you back to the house, you have to tell me about codes and blood. If you beat me back I promise to never ask you another question about it. Deal?"

"Deal!" As soon as she said this Viggie kicked it

into another gear and flew down the path toward Alicia's cottage, leaving Michelle behind.

She rounded the last bend and there sat the cottage dead ahead. She squealed with delight and increased her speed. Ten feet from the front steps she watched in disbelief as Michelle, who'd been purposefully hanging back, blew by her, raced up the steps and sat down on the top step.

Viggie stopped short and stared in amazement at her. "You cheated," she said.

"Exactly how did I do that? You ran. I ran. I won. Now pay up."

"I like you, Michelle."

"Okay, Viggie," Michelle said warily. "But what about our deal?"

Viggie ran past her and into the house. Michelle quickly followed. By the time she got there Viggie was seated at the piano. She started playing frantically, beating the keys with her fingertips. The pace became so frenetic that Michelle couldn't even follow the music.

"Viggie, please, stop. Stop! VIGGIE!"

The next instant Viggie stopped, jumped up and raced to the stairs. She paused, turned to Michelle and yelled, "Codes and blood!" Then she shot up the steps. A moment later her bedroom door slammed.

A few seconds later a half-dressed Alicia Chadwick came rushing down the stairs. "My God, what is going on?" she cried out.

Michelle uncovered her ears and turned to her. "Hell if I know. She just went nuts on the piano."

"She doesn't usually do that unless something or some*one* has upset her," Alicia said in an accusing tone.

"Well, this time she did it all on her own."

Michelle tapped Alicia on the shoulder. "Tag, you're it. I need a break from the kid." She stalked out the door, slamming it behind her.

Michelle reported to Sean later that for now Viggie was a dead end.

"That makes getting into Camp Peary all the more important," he said. "The equipment I ordered will arrive tomorrow."

"Good. I'll check in with you later," Michelle said.

"Where are you off to?"

"I struck out with Viggie. I'm going to see if I have better luck with Champ. But I'm going to change first into something, you know."

"Michelle, I'm impressed at the depths you'll go to get to the truth."

"You'll be even more impressed when I put my foot through your mouth."

"And while you're seducing the world's greatest mind, I'm going to start canvassing Babbage Town and see if anyone saw anything at Rivest's place the night he was murdered. And then I'm going to take a look around for that secret room."

"I told you I already did that."

"Never hurts to have a fresh pair of eyes on it."

Two hours later Sean had finished his canvassing. No one reported seeing anyone suspicious, no one who shouldn't have been there. Puzzled, Sean walked over to the mansion for lunch in the dining room. He saw Viggie eating with some of the other children as Alicia sat alone at the other end of the room while waiters scurried around serving all the hungry geniuses.

He joined Alicia, ordered his food and said, "Factor any good numbers lately?"

Alicia frowned. "I'm glad to see how easily you amuse yourself. Where's your sidekick? She left Viggie in shambles this morning. That wasn't exactly my intention when I hired you."

He leaned forward. "See, the thing is, Alicia, you *didn't* hire us. We work for a firm retained by the owners of Babbage Town, whoever the hell they might be, to find out who killed Monk Turing."

"A task at which so far you've failed utterly."

"People who kill other people usually go to great lengths to make sure they're not caught."

"That's so very reassuring."

"I understand the session with Viggie and Horatio went well."

"Yes, if you call Viggie walking out in the middle of the session going well."

"What about codes and blood? That's what Viggie said, right?"

Alicia nervously fingered her cup of tea. "I'd never heard her use that phrase before. It was frightening the way she said it actually."

"And you have no idea what she could have meant by it?"

"No. I told Barnes the same thing."

"Come on, Alicia, you have an analytical mind, use it."

She sighed deeply. "There are lots of codes. Did Monk teach Viggie how to make a code? Maybe. Did they communicate via codes? Could be. How can you decipher a code if you don't even know what the code is? Find me a sample and maybe I can help you."

"What about the term *blood*?"

"Bloody enough the way Monk died."

"Right, but presumably Monk wasn't dead when he talked to her about it."

"Viggie is a very unstable, emotional young girl given to severe mood swings and hyperbole. If you're basing your whole case on something she said, well, I'm not sure that's wise."

"If you can think of anything else, I'm listening."

"I have a job to do here too, you know."

"Does Champ know who owns Babbage Town?"

"I don't know. I do know that he goes away once a month for a few days. Maybe he's meeting with them then."

"That's interesting. Does he drive or fly?"

"He flies his own plane."

351

"Really? Where does he keep it?"

"A private air terminal about five miles from here. I've been up with him once."

"Pretty nice to be able to afford your own plane."

"Well, I don't know if it actually belongs to him."

Sean fell silent. As he watched a waitress in uniform go by with a tray of food it finally struck him. He'd been asking the wrong damn question. He jumped up and raced out, leaving Alicia staring after him.

58

What Michelle chose was a pair of tight black jeans, open-toed sandals and a loose white blouse with the top two buttons undone. She didn't own a miniskirt and high heels were out of the question. She found Champ in his office, and the man almost fell out of his chair when she walked in, unannounced. At her request he gave her a tour of Hut Number Two and she made appreciative comments and noises about the "important" work he was doing. As he was showing her the Turing machine model, she leaned over to look more closely and placed a hand on his back, ostensibly to steady herself. She could feel the electricity rip through the poor guy's frame. She inwardly groaned. Men were so incredibly easy. And stupid. Even the geniuses.

They ate lunch in a small, private dining room in the mansion that was apparently reserved for the head of Babbage Town.

Michelle said, "This is quite an operation you have here. So how'd you end up running it?"

"I doubt you'd be interested in that," he said, glancing at her.

"If I weren't I wouldn't have asked."

"I had done some cutting-edge work in the field, first at Stanford and then later at MIT, that resulted in the issuance of numerous patents. And my doctoral thesis was on quantum mechanics and was considered groundbreaking. I think that cinched my appointment."

"Sean told me that the ownership of Babbage Town is a closely held secret."

"Very closely held. And they pay well for that confidentiality."

"Generosity is a great way to build loyalty."

"They have been more than generous. They even gave me my own plane to fly."

"Really? I'm not a pilot but I've certainly flown a lot. I love it."

"I could take you up sometime. Wonderful views of the area."

"That'd be great. So long as you avoid the airspace over Camp Peary, I suppose."

"Don't worry. Those parameters are programmed into my flight computer." He paused. "You seem to be showing me a lot of attention."

"You're an interesting person."

"And a possible suspect."

"I understand you have an alibi for the time Len Rivest died."

"I was working, yes."

"And how is it all coming?"

"With luck we'll have a rudimentary prototype ready early next year."

"And then the world ends, at least that's what Sean said he was told."

"Hardly. No, that computer will only be able to do very basic calculations. We're still several years away from really shocking the world."

"That's a long time to wait."

"In the world of physics that's actually pretty fast." He finished his wine. "And so how are things coming with Viggie?"

"She's a good kid. I like her. And I feel for her situation too. It can't be easy."

"Monk wasn't an easy fellow to read. As the Brits say he kept himself very much to himself."

"Speaking of the Brits, I understand he traveled to England recently."

"Right. He said he needed to attend to some family matters."

"Did he say anything to you when he got back? About what other countries he might have visited?"

"Not really. I guess if you have his passport that will tell you where he traveled." Champ snapped his fingers. "Wait a minute. I can't believe I didn't remember it before. He brought me a present. It was smart of him because his leaving at that point wasn't convenient."

"Present. From where? England?"

"No, it was a beer stein from Germany."

"Germany? You're sure?"

"I have it back at my cottage if you want to see for yourself."

Champ's cottage wasn't as sloppy as his office, but it wasn't exactly in the class of a Sean King operation either. She found herself giving the physicist high marks for his untidiness.

He led her into a small book-lined study. On one shelf sat a large elaborately decorated blue beer stein. He handed it to her.

"This is it. Pretty nice, although I'm not really a beer drinker."

Michelle examined the stein closely. It had a hinged pewter top with famous venues from major German cities painted on the side in raised relief. She turned it over and looked at the bottom. "It doesn't say where it's from. Just that it was made in Germany."

"Right. I guess it could have come from any-where."

"Can I hold on to this?" she asked.

"Be my guest, if it'll get us closer to the truth. I wish I could help somehow."

"There is something you can do," she said. He looked expectant. "You can let Horatio Barnes stay at Babbage Town."

Champ looked taken aback by this and Michelle added quickly, "Just room and board. It would mean a lot to me."

"Well, I guess it can't hurt," he said slowly.

"Thanks, Champ, I appreciate it. By the way I saw the martial arts outfit on the door of your office. Which one are you into?"

"Tae Kwon Do. Black belt. You?"

"No," she lied.

As they walked outside into the sunshine, Champ said, "I can pick you up day after tomorrow around nine if the weather holds." He adjusted his glasses. "Uh, on the way back I know a nice little restaurant that actually has a pretty decent menu."

Michelle eyed the man's tall, lanky frame. He would certainly have had the physical strength to kill Rivest by using a plunger to hold the drunken man underwater until he drowned. But as Sean had said, Champ had an alibi for the time of the murder.

Or did he?

59

You seem to be the resident expert on Camp Peary around here," Horatio said. He was seated across from South Freeman in the latter's office.

"Yeah, but these days nobody wants to listen," South said bitterly. "Let the CIA do whatever the hell it wants to. I just keep my head down now before it gets blown off."

"Well, most Americans want to be safe by any means possible."

"Yeah? Don't get me going on that logic; it won't be pretty."

Horatio went over briefly what Sean had filled him in on when he and Michelle had visited South Freeman. "Now he wants to know what other history there is about the place that might not be widely known."

"That fellow's interested in Monk Turing's death, right?" Horatio nodded. "Well, I am too. And if anything I tell you helps break that case, I want an exclusive. And I mean *exclusive*. Put my weekly rag back on the map, man, I'm telling you."

"I'm not sure I can speak for Sean on that."

Freeman immediately scowled. "Then you can get the hell out of here. I don't hand out favors for nothing; goes against all my principles."

Horatio hesitated only for an instant. "Okay, I'm making an executive decision. We break the case using something you gave us, you get the story first. I can put it in writing if you want."

"Writing doesn't mean shit with slick lawyers hovering around." South held out his hand for Horatio to shake. "I like to look a man in the eye and press the flesh on it. You screw me later I'll come and kick your ass."

"What a sweet-talker you are."

South said, "So what are you really interested in?"

"Well, why don't you go through it chronologically? I know some about the CIA and Camp Peary, but what about before that? I understand the Navy trained Seabees there for World War II but was there anything else going on?"

"Oh, yeah, a lot going on. Like I told your buddies, there were two towns over there, Magruder and Bigler's Mill. Magruder was named after, what else? A Confederate general; seems to have been a trend down this way." He snorted. "My parents obviously had different reasoning when they named me South."

"South *Freeman*," Horatio said. "Clever."

"Yeah. Anyway, Bigler's Mill was built on the site of a Civil War hospital. So the stage was all set when the Navy came knocking on the door."

"I wonder why the military picked that area?"

"You mean aside from it being occupied by colored folks who didn't have any voice? Well, you got a lot of cheap land, water nearby—we are talking the Navy after all, and the C&O Railway ran a spur track down from Williamsburg and made Magruder's Station."

"Why was that? For bringing sailors and supplies down?"

"Yep. Most folks don't realize that back then the railroad was how most troops got around in this country. But there was another reason for the spur."

"What was that?"

"When the Navy operated the place it also held a military stockade."

"Stockade? You mean a prison for American soldiers who'd committed crimes?"

"Nope. It was for *German* prisoners of war."

"Germans?"

"They were sailors mostly. They came from subs and ships that were sunk off the East Coast. Crazy man Hitler thought these fellows had been killed of course. That's why all the secrecy. The government didn't want anybody to know those Germans were being held there."

Horatio said, "Why? What was the big deal?"

South pointed at him and grinned. "Now that's the sixty-four-thousand-dollar question, ain't it?"

"You've obviously thought about it. What's your take?"

"Well, there's an obvious one. If we were getting those boys to talk, spill secrets or capturing them with Enigma codebooks the German navy was using, then Hitler and his cronies would move heaven and earth to kill them. And make no bones about it, there were a lot of German spies and assassins over here then. At the very least it seemed that the tide in the Atlantic war turned about the time those POWs showed up at Camp Peary, so I'm betting our boys got them to talk about the Enigma code."

"What happened to the prisoners after the war ended?"

"I figure some of them went back to Germany. I mean after the war what was the point in holding them? But I don't think all of them went back to Germany. What was back there except dust, rubble and chaos? And people thought they were dead anyway. So I think some of them just stayed in America."

As Horatio digested this information South continued his narrative. The war ended, the Navy left and the land was turned into a state forestry and game reserve. Then the Navy came back in 1951, shut it down and it had remained closed to the public ever since.

"The CIA took the place over in June of 1961 even though it was still officially listed as a military base. Pretty ironic when you think about it. That date."

Horatio jerked to attention. Sean had informed him

about Monk Turing's reference to "irony" as he and Len Rivest floated past Camp Peary while fishing.

"Ironic? How's that?"

"That was two months after the CIA fiasco at the Bay of Pigs in Cuba. At the time the Navy said it was officially opening a new facility in place of what they called a Seamaster base. And they transferred some of their training, like demolitions and unconventional weaponry, to another facility. But that was all bullshit. I'm sure June of 1961 is when Camp Peary became the CIA's main spy school. They were embarrassed after the Bay of Pigs screw-up and they should have been. Guess they needed a place to really train their people to do the job right. Yep, right after Bay of Pigs. But that's not the only irony."

"What else?"

"I told you the town was named after a Confederate general? Well General 'Prince John' Magruder was one of the true masters of deception during the war. Now the town that bore his name is home to people who make their living lying."

"I see your point. That *is* ironic," Horatio agreed. Although he couldn't see how it tied into what Monk had said to Rivest that day. "Anything else?"

South Freeman glanced around even though they were all alone. "Started to tell this to your friends, but then decided not to. But what the hell. There's a part of Camp Peary most folks have no idea about. Maybe even some people who work there."

"So how do you know?"

"Those folks have to eat and have their places cleaned, right? Well, I know lots of cooks and cleaners. Same old shit, a lot of 'em have my skin color, how about that?"

"Okay, go on," Horatio encouraged him.

"Well, the camp has a black area component. And I'm not talking about folks who look like me. That's where the secret side of U.S. diplomacy takes place."

"Secret diplomacy?"

"Yeah. Goes on all the time. Leaders of other countries, agents, rebels, dictators, even *terrorists* who happen to be on our side at least for now, are flown in on some of those planes you see landing at two A.M. They don't have to pass through customs or nothing. No one even knows they were ever here. And the meetings officially never happened. Before we invaded Iraq a bunch of Kurdish leaders were flown to the Farm to hold meetings about ways to topple old Saddam from the inside."

An impressed Horatio exclaimed, "South, how do you know all this?"

Freeman looked offended. "Hey, I'm a damn journalist, man."

Horatio sat back looking troubled.

Freeman grinned wickedly. "Scary shit."

"Scary shit," Horatio agreed.

60

When Sean and Michelle met later he said, "I didn't get a chance to search for a secret room earlier, you want to give it another shot together?"

A few minutes later they were in the main hall of the mansion. Waiting for it to clear out, they started making their rounds. They had cleared about a dozen rooms and had just finished with the library, when a voice startled them as they came out.

"You're not doing it the right way."

They turned and stared at Viggie, who was wearing a very superior look while perched on an ornate couch sitting against one wall in the main hall.

"Aren't you supposed to be in class?" Michelle asked.

"I'm sick."

"You don't look sick."

"I already finished all the work, including my homework. And I saw you snooping around."

"We're not snooping around," Sean objected.

"You're looking for that secret room you asked me about, but you're not doing it right."

"Okay, how would you do it?" Sean shot back.

In response Viggie held up several sheets of paper covered with numbers and equations. "I've already worked it out. Right after you asked me about it I spent a bunch of time measuring every exterior and interior dimension of the house and compared it with the actual physical configuration."

"You did?" Sean said, stunned. "You're only eleven."

Viggie ignored this. "And I came up with a very interesting discovery."

"What was it?" Michelle said.

"There's a twelve-by-twelve-foot square unaccounted for." She showed them the paperwork, which was too complicated for either Michelle or Sean to follow.

"Okay, little Miss Einstein," Sean said. "Where is it?"

"Third floor, west corridor, next to the last bedroom on the right."

Sean thought about this. "That's right next to the bedroom *I* was staying in."

Viggie put her hands on her hips and gave him a penetrating look. "Gee, you think you would have noticed then, *Mister* Einstein."

Sean headed up the stairs. Michelle and Viggie quickly followed.

A minute later they were standing on the third floor staring at what appeared to be a blank wall.

"Keep an eye out," Sean said, giving the hallway a searching look. He began probing the wall with his fingers, trying to find a gap in the wood or a hidden latch like at the other mansion. Ten minutes later he gave up. "I can't find anything, want to give it a try?" he asked Michelle.

After another ten minutes she said, "Nothing."

"Viggie, are you sure this was the spot?" Sean asked.

"Absolutely," she said tersely.

"Well, then either it's just wasted space and there's no secret room or there's another way to open the door."

"Sean, you said this is next to your old bedroom?" Michelle said. "Let's try from in there."

"Right!" He led them into the bedroom and started tapping on the wall. "Sounds hollow," he said. He probed the wall for a lever of some kind but found nothing. They went to the room on the other side of the blank space, but the door was dead-bolted.

"Okay, what now? You can't exactly cut a hole in the wall without anyone noticing," Michelle said. "And so what if it's a secret room. It's probably empty like the one in that old house."

"Michelle, we talked about this. If Rivest was right and there are spies here, they could be using that room for some reason."

"Spies!" Viggie exclaimed.

"Keep that to yourself," Sean warned.

"And what would spies be using this room for?" Michelle asked.

"If I knew that I wouldn't be trying to get in there," Sean snapped.

"Well, it doesn't look like we're going to be able to do that right now." She turned to Viggie. "Thanks for your help. There's no way Sean and I could have figured this out."

Viggie beamed at her.

61

Horatio thanked Freeman and headed back to the B&B. When he got there Horatio checked messages at his office. There were quite a few, but only one really excited him. He quickly called her back.

"Hello?"

"Mrs. Rose? Hazel Rose?"

"Hold on, she's in the next bed."

Horatio waited a few moments as the sounds of the phone being passed over reached him. Then a deep, southern voice came on the line.

"Hello? Who's calling?"

"Mrs. Rose. It's Horatio Barnes. I just got your message."

"Oh, yes, Mr. Barnes. I wanted to thank you for what you did. They're transferring me to that facility you talked about. I really can't believe it. They actually have a library with real books in it instead of just magazines."

Horatio's enthusiasm waned. He thought she'd remembered something about Michelle's childhood. "Right. Absolutely. I'm glad it worked out for you.

I know you'll be much happier there. Thank you for calling."

"Now just hold your horses. That's not the only reason I called."

Horatio immediately tensed. "It isn't?"

"I remembered something else. I don't know if it'll help you, but I thought I should pass it on."

"Right now, Mrs. Rose, I'll take anything I can get."

Hazel Rose's voice sank to a whisper, probably so her roommate couldn't hear. "Remember I said that Frank Maxwell went to college at night to get a master's degree so he could get onto a bigger police force?"

"I remember. With Michelle's brothers grown and gone by then, I'm sure it was pretty lonely for her."

"Well, I don't think Michelle was the *only* lonely one in that house."

"What do you mean?"

"You didn't hear this from me."

"I swear. Now please tell me."

There was a long sigh and then she said, "Around about the time we were talking about, at least once a week I used to see a car parked down the road a bit from the Maxwell place."

"A car?"

"I didn't think much of it to tell the truth. And it was never there in the morning when my husband went off to work. I'd know because I'd be up to make his breakfast."

"You ever find out whose car it was?"

"No. But I did see the car at another place once. It was parked outside a Dairy Queen."

"Did you see who was driving it?"

"Yep. A good-looking man. He was in uniform."

"What kind of uniform?"

"Army."

"Was there a military base nearby?"

"No, but there was a recruitment station in town."

"So you think he worked there?"

"Maybe. I never followed it up. It really wasn't my business."

"But why do you think the car had something to do with the Maxwells' house?"

"Back then it was the only house down that way other than mine. And the only other homes on the street were occupied by women whose husbands were home at night."

"And Frank Maxwell wasn't?"

"That's right. And the nights he *was* home, that car wasn't there."

"You're sure?"

"Absolutely."

"And you just thought of this?" he said skeptically.

"I thought of it while you were here. But why rake up muck? What good will it do?"

"What made you change your mind then?"

"The more I thought about it, the more I believe the truth, whatever it is, might help Michelle. She was just a little girl. Whatever might have happened back then it wasn't her fault."

"And what do you think happened, Mrs. Rose?"

"Mr. Barnes, that I just won't say. It's up to you now. I hope this helps. Did you tell Michelle I said hello?"

"I did and she remembered you very well."

Hazel Rose's voice cracked slightly. "I wish nothing but the best for that girl."

Horatio thanked her, hung up and slumped back in his chair. This put a whole new spin on everything that the psychologist didn't like at all.

62

Later that evening Horatio moved into an empty room in the mansion at Babbage Town after Michelle told him Champ had authorized it.

"I'm surprised," he said.

"Even geniuses change their minds," she pointed out.

"No, I'm surprised that you asked him to do it."

"How do you know *I* asked him?"

"I'm the head doc, okay? I just know."

After he was unpacked Horatio asked Sean to come to his room. There he filled him in on what South had told him about Camp Peary and German prisoners of war being held there. And also the phone conversation he'd had with Hazel Rose.

Sean mulled the latter part over. "What do you make of it?"

"Make of it? I *make* of it that Michelle's mother was having an affair with this Army guy."

"That part I figured out. I mean how does that fact tie into Michelle's personality changing?"

"I'm not sure," Horatio admitted.

"Did Hazel say when the Army guy stopped coming around?"

"No. Actually I didn't ask her."

The two men stared at each other. "You think Michelle saw something, don't you?" Horatio slowly nodded. "Like what?"

"It's only speculation, but something . . . bad. Like maybe her mother in bed with this guy. But what I'm really thinking is even worse. Her brother Bill didn't believe it was the case, but I'm thinking that maybe Michelle was sexually abused by him."

Sean looked skeptical. "And her mom would just allow that to happen? Come on!"

"Believe me I've seen it all. And maybe the mom didn't know about it, or didn't want to know about it so long as the guy kept coming around to see her."

"So what would that do to a six-year-old kid?"

"Seeing the mom in bed with another man? At that age she might not be able to understand anything other than a strange man is with Mommy. And if Mom was quick enough to explain it away? But the sexual abuse? That could be devastating. Particularly if her mother acquiesced in it."

"I can't believe this, Horatio. Michelle has been very successful in life. Could she have done all that carrying around that sort of baggage?"

"Sometimes the abuse history makes a person incredibly driven and that ambition allows them to achieve a great deal. But underneath the success lies a very different picture. It represents a stark imbalance in life. And at some point that imbalance can bring everything crashing down."

"That sounds like what happened to Michelle," Sean pointed out.

"I know."

Sean glanced out the window. "If Michelle saw her mom with another man or was abused by that guy and then told her *dad* about it?"

Horatio let out a long, troubled sigh. "Then you're getting into some serious mental shit. Hazel did say the Army guy just stopped coming around. Maybe he couldn't come around because he was dead."

Sean blurted out, "Wait a minute. Army guy! The guy she beat up in the bar. He was dressed in military style clothing when I saw him."

"Then that makes sense," Horatio said slowly.

"What do you mean it makes sense?"

"I talked to people who worked with Michelle over the years, as well as friends, athletes. Some of them spoke about the fights she'd gotten in."

"Let me guess. They were all military people?"

"Yes, as far as I could find out."

"Horatio, we need to find out if anything happened to the Army guy."

"I'm not sure that's such a good idea," Horatio said.

"When is the truth not a good idea?"

"This isn't one of your investigations, Sean. This is

about a person's head. Sometimes the truth can do more harm than good."

"At the very least I think *we* need to know so you can decide what to do next with her. She said you wanted to hypnotize her. If you do and you start asking questions you might end up somewhere you don't want to be. Better you know all the facts before you do that."

Horatio said, "Actually, you're right. But how do I find out?"

"I bet South Freeman knows somebody that knows somebody that could help us out in Tennessee."

"I'll give him a call."

A knock on the door interrupted them. It was Michelle. She immediately noted their gloomy faces.

"You two look like you're planning a funeral and getting ready to go to war at the same time," she said.

Sean said quickly, "Horatio was just filling me in on his talk with South Freeman. It appears those secret flights might be bringing in some folks that officially were never there. They have a black area there for secret diplomacy."

"And potentially fatal for Monk Turing if that's what he was witness to," Michelle commented.

Sean continued, "And that's not all. Before Camp Peary existed, the Navy held German prisoners of war there."

Michelle said, "German POWs? That's funny.

Champ showed me a beer stein from Germany that he said Monk brought him."

Sean sat up in his chair. "Monk Turing was in Germany?"

"Well, I can't be a hundred percent positive. But he brought the stein back with him on the trip he took overseas while he was working here. I can try and find out if Monk did go to Germany by talking to Sheriff Hayes. He might have convinced Ventris to let him have a look-see at Monk's passport."

"Germans at Camp Peary and Monk visited Germany," Sean said thoughtfully.

"What else did Champ tell you?" Horatio asked.

She filled them in on the rest and added, "And he very clearly has a schoolboy crush on me."

"Crush *him* if he tries anything," Sean said firmly, drawing an interested look from Horatio.

"Might not be that easy. He has a black belt in Tae Kwon Do."

"Yeah and the man flies his own plane. Alicia told me."

"Actually, it isn't his. It belongs to Babbage Town. In fact I'm going flying with him day after tomorrow."

"I'm not sure I like the idea of you alone with that guy at fifteen thousand feet."

"I have no interest in joining the Mile High Club if that's what you're suggesting."

"I know he has an alibi for the time Rivest was killed but still," Sean said.

"No, he might not."

"What do you mean? I checked the computer log," Sean said. "He was in Hut Number Two until three in the morning."

"Champ probably has override privileges on the security system. Plus he's a super-brain. Are you telling me someone like that can't manipulate a simple computer log?"

Sean looked chagrined. "I hadn't thought of that."

"Did you talk to a real person who was there that night to confirm what the computer log said?" Michelle asked.

"No, but I'm going to correct that mistake right away. Good catch, Michelle."

"I have my moments."

"Now I really don't like you going up in the plane with the guy."

"I know, but you'll get over it."

"And I found something else out," he said. "Remember I asked people if they saw anything out of the ordinary the night Rivest was killed?"

Michelle said, "And nobody did."

"Well, I went back and asked a slightly different question. I asked if they'd seen anybody around Rivest's cottage, including people who *should* have been there."

"I'm not following," Horatio said.

Michelle interjected, "He means other scientists, guards, etc."

"And cleaning people," Sean said. "And one of the guards saw a cleaning person in uniform pushing a laundry cart down the road toward Hut Number Three around one in the morning." They both looked at him. "Don't you see? What better way to carry off wet towels, bath mats and a plunger than in a laundry cart?"

Michelle was the first to speak. "There's no better way. Good catch right back at you."

Horatio spoke slowly, "So a cleaning person killed Rivest?"

"No, more likely someone dressed as one. And I checked the laundry building. No soaked towels, bath mats or plungers ever showed up there."

"But if that's the case it was a woman who killed Rivest then," Horatio said. "I mean it would be far easier for a woman to dress up as a woman, right?"

Sean shook his head. "I didn't say it was a woman. In fact the person said it was a guy. I checked with the cleaning supervisor. They have about as many men as women doing the cleaning work here. But a woman could put on pants and pretend to be a man."

"So we need to find out who was on duty that night," Michelle said.

"Yes and no," Sean said. "Certainly we'll get the list and run it down, but I'm thinking it could be an outsider disguised as a cleaning person who came here and did it. You show up in a uniform with a genuine-looking ID badge, who's going to question you?"

"Or it could be someone who works at Babbage Town disguised as a cleaner," Michelle added.

"That could be even more troubling."

Sean turned to leave.

"Where are you going?" Michelle asked.

"To find out if our resident genius, Champ Pollion, was actually in Hut Number Two or maybe pushing a laundry cart filled with evidence after drowning Len Rivest."

63

Sean couldn't find a live person who'd seen Champ at Hut Number Two until three in the morning the night Rivest had been killed. That resulted in Champ Pollion being put back on the suspect list for Len Rivest's murder. While he was walking back to Alicia's cottage he got a call from Joan.

"We got a communiqué from the owners of Babbage Town," she began.

"Who are they?" Sean asked quickly.

"Don't know."

"Then how do you know it's legit?"

"There are passwords and a secure channel access that was set up. It's them. Anyway, since Rivest was killed they've been rethinking our presence on the scene. Now if you were showing any progress . . ."

"Joan, I am busting my ass trying to do just that. You've never seen stone walls thrown up like the ones down here. And we don't even know who our client is."

"What *have* you found out?"

Sean hesitated and then filled her in on the German POW angle.

"You really think that might have something to do with Monk Turing's death?"

"It's possible. If you can get a list somewhere of the POWs held at Camp Peary during the war, and what happened to them, that would be very helpful. And you tracked his trip in England so any chance you could do the same for Germany? I can follow up on my end by trying to get a peek at his passport, if I can pry it from the Bureau's greedy hands."

"I'll see what I can do. Any idea where in Germany?"

"No."

"I see that you've requested funds for some equipment down there."

"That's right."

"However, you neglected to specify what the equipment is."

"Nothing out of the ordinary, I can assure you."

"Then you'll have no problem telling me what it is."

"Joan, if you won't approve the funds just say so. I got everything for a good price, and some of the stuff is just leased."

"I'm not debating the cost."

"So what's the big deal?"

"Just put it down to me feeling left out of the loop."

"When I have something to report, you'll hear about it."

"How's your *mental* sidekick?"

He stiffened. "What the hell do you mean by that?"

"I have my sources," Joan said cryptically.

"She's just fine."

"I'm sure. But if you want my advice, you don't need a fragile person covering your back in a crisis situation."

"My back is just great."

"Don't I know it, along with your other parts. But seriously, Sean, friendship is one thing, but would you bet your life on it? Three people have already been killed. I don't want you to be the fourth."

She clicked off leaving Sean hating himself for suddenly having doubts about Michelle, but doubts they still were. What if she cracked when they were on CIA territory? What if she did something that might end up getting them killed?

64

The following afternoon Michelle was trying to find Viggie, only no one knew where the girl was. Alicia was at her hut working, and the guard assigned to watch Viggie had somehow lost track of his charge. However, something Viggie had said earlier came back to Michelle and she set out at a dead run for the river.

Five minutes later she reached the boathouse and right away noticed that one of the kayaks was missing. Her gaze swept the river. A storm was rolling in, the wind was gaining strength and the water current was fast. A rumble of thunder reached her ears and the smell of rain coming swiftly was suddenly thick in her nostrils.

The next sound she heard froze Michelle.

"Help me! Help me!"

Michelle grabbed a two-person kayak and paddle from the holder next to the boathouse, threw a loop of rope in it and raced down to the end of the dock. A few moments later she was in the kayak and cutting through the frothing chop of the river with each stroke.

"Help me!"

She saw the speck of red in the distance. As Michelle drew closer she saw that Viggie's kayak had capsized. The girl was clinging to it, but she was being swept along by the accelerating river current. Michelle redoubled her effort and the kayak flew through the water. Michelle hadn't rowed this hard for many months and even for her, the pace was grueling. A moment later she had all the incentive she needed. A lightning bolt struck the other side of the river with such force that the ground shook. This was followed by a deafening crack of thunder.

Viggie's shrieks became louder now. Michelle kept her gaze steadily on the girl, letting the muscles of her arms, back and legs do the rest. Five minutes, and several hellish cracks of thunder and vicious lightning strikes later, Michelle pulled alongside the girl. As she put out her paddle for Viggie to grab the skies opened up and the rain came pelting down with such force it stung their faces and arms.

Viggie didn't even make a grab at the paddle; she clung stubbornly to the side of her overturned kayak.

Michelle said as calmly as she could, "Viggie, I've got you. You're going to be okay. Do you understand?"

The girl shook her head. She said in a trembling voice, "I'm going to drown. I don't have a life jacket on."

"You're *not* going to drown. Take your free hand and grab hold of the paddle."

"I can't."

"Yes you can, Viggie."

Lightning struck so close to them that the hairs on Michelle's neck stood up.

"Viggie, grab the paddle. Now!"

Viggie didn't make a move, but the current did. It ripped the kayak out of her hand and sent it spinning off. She screamed and started to go under.

Michelle tied the coil of rope she'd thrown in the boat around one of her ankles and attached the other end to the carry loop on the kayak.

"Help me!" Viggie screamed as she floundered in the water and then went under.

Michelle dove in and shot under the surface. The water was murky and Michelle was searching more with her hands than her eyes. Finally, she felt her. Gripping the girl by her hair, she pulled her to the surface. Viggie was kicking, screaming and coughing up dirty river water.

Michelle looked around. Her kayak was twenty yards away and moving fast. The length of rope attached to Michelle's leg was almost taut.

She forced Viggie to lie on her back, placed her arm around the girl's chest and said as calmly as she could, "I've got you, sweetie. You're okay. I'm going to get you to the kayak and then we'll be fine, okay? You just have to relax. If you fight me, it just makes it harder. Just relax. I've got you."

Realizing that she was not going under, Viggie

grew still. They were not out of danger yet, Michelle clearly understood, because the kayak was moving fast and pulling them along with it. She had two options. She could cut the line and swim back with Viggie, or she could try to pull the kayak to her with her one arm and attempt to get her and Viggie in it. Neither option was without its complications. Meanwhile, the storm was only getting worse.

Michelle was a very strong swimmer, but she could already feel herself growing a little tired. And it was a long way to shore. She could swim with the current, but at some point she'd have to cut against it to get to land. By then she might not have the strength to do it. She was not going to let this come down to choosing saving herself over Viggie. As soon as she had jumped in the water Michelle had made up her mind that it would be both or none.

The rope tied to her leg was pulled so taut that it made it impossible for her to keep a good grip on Viggie. She finally kicked the rope free and the kayak sailed away from them.

Michelle eyed behind her. She had to get them to shore, fast. She gripped Viggie tighter with one arm, kicked hard with her legs and pushed against the current with her free arm. It was no use. She simply couldn't swim across the current while holding on to Viggie.

The storm was right over them now. All she could hear were the cracks of the thunder, the swirl of wind and the groan of the trees as they were bent back and forth. Viggie started to squirm, perhaps sensing the rising panic in Michelle's tense limbs.

She never heard the sound of the motor until it was right on them. Strong hands reached down, grabbed Viggie and pulled her up. Then Michelle was being pulled in as well. As she perched on one of the seats, her arms around a whimpering Viggie, Michelle looked up at Champ Pollion, who had turned his attention back to piloting the boat. He set a direct course back to Babbage Town's dock.

After making sure Viggie was all right Michelle rose and stood beside him. "Thanks. It was getting pretty crazy out there."

"I was out for a walk; saw Viggie capsize first and then you heading out to rescue her. That's when I ran to get the powerboat. I figured the best way was to grab you both as fast as I could."

He smoothly docked the boat and helped Michelle get Viggie off. The girl was still pretty much dead-weight at this point.

"Sure she's okay?" Champ said anxiously.

"Yeah, just scared."

"Can't blame her."

Michelle took Viggie gently by the shoulder and led her up the path to Babbage Town. Champ walked with them to Alicia's cottage.

Michelle said, "If you pilot a plane as well as you do a boat, tomorrow should be very pleasant."

"Uh, do you mind if we push our flight back a day? Something came up."

"That's fine, Champ. Whenever."

Champ smiled shyly, mumbled something incoherent and hurried off.

"You saved my life, Mick," Viggie said after they had both changed into dry clothes.

"Mr. Champ deserves a lot of the credit," she said. "And what were you doing out on the river all by yourself?" she added in a scolding tone.

Viggie studied her hands, her face drooping like a rain-soaked flower. "I . . . I just wanted to be by myself."

"I can think of lots of ways to do that that don't involve putting yourself in danger."

"Thank you for saving my life," Viggie said.

"I'm just glad I was there."

Viggie stood, went over to the piano and started playing. Softly, not frantically, as she had last time. The notes were slow, almost mournful. She looked up at Michelle as she played, her features inscrutable.

After she finished, Michelle said, "Thank you, Viggie, that was beautiful. What was it?"

Viggie didn't answer. She turned and walked up the stairs. A moment later her bedroom door closed.

Back out on the York River, a twenty-foot RIB or rigid inflatable boat, the backbone of the military's light amphibious assault teams, was cruising around, Ian Whitfield at the wheel. The man seemed oblivious to the storm raging around him. On the deck of the RIB was Michelle's kayak, with the rope still attached to its stern ring. He hit the throttles and the RIB sprinted toward the Babbage Town side of the water. He docked the boat, climbed out and slid the kayak up onto the floating pier. He grimaced a bit as he jumped back into his vessel. He wore a yellow rain slicker and khaki shorts. His lower legs were muscular and deeply tanned. The right one, though, was also heavily scarred. Chilly rain always made it throb.

He hit the throttle and the RIB took a huge leap forward; its bow at a forty-five-degree angle as it rode up the wall of chop. In another minute the RIB and the head of Camp Peary were just a speck on the river as the storm continued to slam the area.

65

By early the next morning the bad weather had passed and Sean and Michelle convened at the same isolated spot about a mile from Babbage Town. When they had talked yesterday Michelle had recounted her experience on the river. In turn he'd brought her up to speed about Champ's lack of an alibi. They were meeting this morning to go over things in more detail away from prying eyes at Babbage Town.

He said, "Tell me again what was Viggie doing out on the water in a kayak all by herself?"

"She basically said she wanted some alone time."

"Or maybe she wanted to get a better look at Camp Peary?"

"Why?" she asked.

"I don't know."

"Did you find out anything on your end?"

Sean nodded. "I talked to Hayes. He got a look at Monk's passport and it shows that he *did* travel to Germany."

"Do we know where?"

"He entered by way of Frankfurt. That's all Hayes

could tell me. I've called Joan and she's trying to run down more specifics for us." He unrolled a large piece of paper and spread it out over the hood of Michelle's truck. "I took a picture of the satellite map of Camp Peary that Freeman had in his office and had it enlarged."

He pointed out various sections to her. "I've heard different numbers, but I believe the place is about ten thousand acres, most of it undeveloped. As we already knew, the runway is fairly near where Monk's body was found. A bit south are what appear to be a series of bunkers. Farther down from that is a boat dock." He traced another section with his finger that had names printed on it. "This looks like some of the neighborhoods Freeman mentioned. Bigler's Mill Pond is here, Porto Bello house there, Queens Lake behind it and Magruder there. The main complex is bordered on the west by Interstate 64 and to the south by Colonial National Historical Parkway. And the Naval Supply Cheatham Annex is there," he added, poking the paper with his index finger.

"There's an inlet from the York south of the runway and it carries you deeply into the grounds," Michelle pointed out.

"And we can be sure it's well guarded," Sean said. "Certainly on land and for all I know they have the inlet mined."

"So over the fence we go? Did the equipment come in?"

Sean nodded. "Yeah, all of it." He suddenly slumped back against the truck. "Michelle, I don't want to go over that fence, it's insane. Even if we don't get killed I'm not looking to spend the rest of my life in prison, and I'm not going to let you do it."

"But if you do go I can't let you go alone."

"Maybe we don't have to if Joan finds out where Monk went in Germany."

"Which may not tie into any of this."

"How about Viggie? Codes and blood?"

Michelle shook her head. "Nothing new. She was understandably subdued when we got back from the river. Her piano playing was very restrained which *is* unusual. Normally she says, 'Michelle, I like you', and then she plays like a banshee, screams 'Codes and Blood' and then runs up to her room. She didn't do it this time. She just thanked me for saving her life and then sat and played very slowly and beautifully, like she was thanking me again with music. It was actually very touching. And . . ."

Michelle's voice trailed off as she stared at Sean.

"Are you thinking what I'm thinking?" she said in a barely audible tone.

"Yes, and I'm also thinking how big an idiot I am for not seeing it before."

They jumped in the truck.

He checked his watch. "What about your plane ride with Champ?"

"Postponed until tomorrow."

"Good, maybe by then you'll change your mind. Call Horatio and tell him to meet us at Alicia's cottage."

"Why?"

"He's a piano player, that's why."

66

"After what happened on the river they kept Viggie out of school today," Michelle said as Horatio and Sean followed her up the walk to Alicia's cottage. "But I think she'll only play for me."

"Horatio brought his recorder," Sean explained. "We'll stay out of sight but we'll still hear the song."

"And then what?" Michelle asked.

"Then if it is code we can get some help decrypting it. I know at least one genius hanging around this place."

Horatio placed his sound-activated recorder near the piano, but hidden behind some books. Afterward he and Sean snuck out to the screened-in front porch. Through an open window they could hear the music from here.

Michelle went upstairs, got Viggie and asked her to play the song for her again.

The girl dutifully did and then went back upstairs. Michelle retrieved the recorder and joined Horatio and Sean.

Sean said, "I've contacted Alicia at work. She's

coming over shortly. Horatio, in the meantime can you write down the notes to the song she was playing just by listening to it?"

"Shouldn't be a problem."

"Wait a minute, you didn't recognize the song, did you? If you do we can just check around for the sheet music. She must have it here somewhere."

"Sorry, that stuff was a little too mellow for me," Horatio admitted. "I'm more into classic rock."

By the time Alicia arrived home Horatio had the notes written out. Sean showed them to her.

"So you think these are somehow a code?" she asked.

"That's right," Sean said.

"The thing is with musical notes you have only a few possibilities to work with."

Horatio nodded. "A, B, C, D, E, F, G. Of course you can break them down into sharps, flats, etc."

"Is that enough for you to work with, Alicia?" Sean said anxiously.

"I won't know until I know," she said. "Any idea what the subject matter might be?"

Sean looked at Michelle but remained silent.

Alicia, who'd been watching him, snapped, "Damn it, if you don't trust me enough to tell me what you're looking for, go find somebody else to help you."

"Okay, okay." He drew a deep breath. "You might want to think about Camp Peary, German prisoners of war and secret flights."

Alicia's eyes widened. "Just for the record, I'm a linguist and mathematician, not a cryptanalyst."

"But some of the world's best code breakers were linguists and math types," Sean pointed out.

"Well it would be nice to have some more context to work with. Monk Turing was a very smart man. I doubt it's something simple."

Sean cried out, "Turing! Codes and blood. That must be it."

"What must be it?" Michelle asked, staring at him in amazement.

"Monk Turing was related to Alan Turing, his *blood* relation. He visited England recently and went over the geographic locations of Turing's life. Alan Turing almost single-handedly broke one of the German Enigma codes. It must have something to do with that."

Alicia looked through the pages. "Well, that does help. I have some books on Alan Turing and his work. When do you need to know something?"

"Any minute now would be great."

67

Michelle, naturally always drawn to the water, decided to go kayaking. It helped her think and she wanted to take another pass by Camp Peary's river frontage. If they were going to try to break into the place at some point, a little extra reconnoitering couldn't hurt. When she got down to the boathouse she saw her kayak on the pier.

How did that get here? she wondered.

After a half-hour on the water she'd scrutinized the camp from several different angles. The chain link fence wouldn't be difficult to get past, but after that? For the first time she really thought about what would happen to them if they were caught. And what could they really expect to find amid thousands of acres of mostly undeveloped, forested land? Was that enough to give up her life for? And while it seemed that Sean was having second thoughts, what if he changed his mind and decided to go through with it? Would she stick by him or do the only logical thing and decline? And if he went by himself and was killed, when her presence might have made the difference? Could she live with herself?

These thoughts were interrupted when a boat's horn sounded nearby. She looked around. The RIB was puttering up to her from behind. Ian Whitfield was at the helm dressed in camie pants and a white T-shirt that revealed his chiseled physique. He was wearing a Yankees ball cap and a friendly expression.

He expertly drew the boat alongside her kayak and then shifted the throttle to neutral, as she slipped her paddle over the RIB's gunwale to hold her craft steady.

"Ian Whitfield," he announced, throwing up a hand in greeting.

Michelle tried to hide her surprise.

"Much nicer day to be out than yesterday," he said cheerfully.

"So you were out in the storm?"

"A little. I found that kayak you're sitting in floating downriver. Anything happen?"

"A friend of mine took a dunk in the water. We finally got her out."

"Good thing. The York's current can be a little tricky, Miss, uh?"

"Michelle Maxwell. Just call me Michelle." She glanced across the river. "So how are things on the other side of the York?"

"Don't recall saying I was from any side of the river."

"Just things you hear. And I hear more than most. I used to be with the Secret Service. But I'm sure you already knew that."

He continued to gaze out over the water. "My dream was to play shortstop for the Yankees, but the talent wasn't up to the dream. Serving your country wasn't a bad second option."

Michelle was a little taken aback by this tacit admission of the man's employment. "Riding on Air Force One and protecting the Man was one of the greatest honors of my life." She paused and added, "I knew some guys in Delta who were in Vietnam." He gave her a penetrating stare. "Like I said, I hear more than most."

He shrugged. "That was a long time ago."

"But you never forget."

"Some do; I never have." He pointed to Babbage Town. "So how goes it on your side of the river?"

"Slowly."

"I often wondered why they set up shop down here."

"You mean across from you?"

"You've got a partner here with you?" he said, ignoring her question.

"Yes."

"Monk Turing's death was unfortunate, but hardly the basis for a murder investigation."

"You told my partner it was a suicide."

"No, I told him there had been four other suicides

in and around Camp Peary. And I also told him that the FBI had concluded that Turing killed himself."

"I'm not sure they still believe that. And then there's Len Rivest."

"The local paper said he'd had a lot to drink and was found drowned in his bathtub. Doesn't sound all that sinister really."

"Two deaths so close together?"

"People die all the time in all different ways, Michelle."

He looked, Michelle thought, like a man who knew what he was talking about.

"That almost sounds like a warning," she said.

"I have no control over how you interpret my words." He swept his hand toward the other side of the river. "There's a big federal presence down here and that includes the Navy. People working for their country, doing dangerous things, risking their lives. You should understand that. You risked your life for your country."

"I do understand it," Michelle said. "And where exactly is this conversation going?"

"Just keep in mind that this stretch of the York can be very dangerous. Whatever you do, don't lose sight of that. You have a nice day now."

Michelle slipped her paddle off the gunwale as Whitfield put the throttle in reverse, turned and slowly puttered off. Michelle maneuvered her kayak so that she could continue to watch him as he headed downriver to the Camp Peary boat dock. The man never once looked back.

When he was out of sight Michelle turned around and paddled slowly away. Ian Whitfield had given her a lot to think about. And a good reason to be afraid.

68

Over coffee in the mansion's dining room Michelle filled Sean in on her conversation with Ian Whitfield.

"He strikes me as a guy who doesn't make empty threats."

"My skin was tingling the whole time he was talking to me."

"That makes me even less inclined to go over the fence."

"Then we need to find some new angles to work," she said. "I'm just not sure what they are."

"Let's go over what we know. Monk went to Germany and he died at Camp Peary. There were German POWs kept at Camp Peary during the war. Len Rivest wanted to talk to me about Babbage Town and now he's dead. He thought there were spies here. Alicia Chadwick was having a fling with Rivest and is Viggie's guardian. Champ doesn't have an alibi for Len's death but we have no evidence he had anything to do with it. Ian Whitfield warned me and then you off and his wife is a dead end. The morgue got blown up. To mess up the evidence that Rivest was murdered?"

"Wait a minute," Michelle said. "You suspected that Rivest was murdered because of the absence of towels, bath mat and the plunger."

"Right. I told Hayes and he asked the ME to check into whether any trace from the plunger was on the body."

"And?"

Sean said, "And we hadn't heard back before the ME died."

"If the morgue got blown up because someone knew you suspected murder, how would they have found out you did suspect something?"

"Well, Hayes could have carelessly let it slip to someone."

"Or deliberately told someone," Michelle countered.

"Why would he do that?"

"Just playing devil's advocate. What do you really know about him?"

"He's a county sheriff."

"But we don't know where his true loyalties lie."

"You getting paranoid on me?"

"With Babbage Town and Camp Peary right across the river I'd say you're totally screwed up if you're not paranoid."

Sean nodded. "All we can do is keep chipping away. See if Alicia comes up with anything. Run down the German angle. I don't see another alternative right now."

"And maybe it still comes down to us going over that fence," she said.

After Michelle left Sean pulled out a piece of paper with a phone number on it. He punched in the numbers, and after the beep said, "Valerie, it's Sean Carter. Can I see you?"

As Michelle was walking back to the cottage, she saw something up ahead that made her flat-out sprint.

"What the hell are you doing?" she screamed.

Viggie stopped and stared at her, the wide smile on her face melting away as she let go of the trash bag she was holding and it fell to the ground.

Michelle looked inside her truck. It was spick-and-span clean. She turned to the girl. "How dare you mess with my things? This is my truck. Who gave you permission to go inside my truck and touch my things? Who!"

Viggie fell back a step. "I . . . uh. You told me you could never get it clean, no matter how hard you tried. I thought you'd be happy."

Michelle grabbed the trash bag and started pulling things out and tossing them back in the truck. She screamed, "This is not trash. Get the hell away from my truck!"

Viggie turned and ran sobbing back to the house.

Michelle didn't seem to notice. She was busy picking things out of the trash bag and layering her floorboards with them.

"Catch you at a bad time?"

She whirled around to see Horatio staring at her and Michelle inwardly groaned.

"Just a misunderstanding," she said quickly.

"No, I think your meaning was crystal-clear."

"Get the hell off my back!"

"So do we just leave Viggie in the house crying her guts out, or what?"

Michelle glanced toward the house; Viggie's wails could be easily heard. Michelle slumped back against the truck and the tennis shoe and banana peel she was holding slipped to the ground. A tear trickled down her face. She sat down on the running board of her truck and stared at the grass.

"I'm sorry," Michelle said in a low voice. "But she was messing with my stuff. She had no right to do that."

Horatio came over to stand by the truck. "Well, in a sense you're absolutely right. People shouldn't mess with other people's stuff, but I think Viggie was just trying to help you, or at least she thought she was. You can see that, can't you?"

Michelle nodded her head curtly.

"Have you thought any more about the hypnosis?"

"I told you, if we come back alive—"

He cut her off. "Right, but let's skip the histrionics,

because I'm not sure you have all that much time left."

She slowly lifted her head to stare at him. "And what exactly is that supposed to mean?"

"Exactly what it sounded like."

She stood and tossed the garbage bag inside her truck. "What the hell good would it do? I'm obviously too far gone."

69

They were walking along the beach. Valerie carried her sandals while Sean slouched guiltily along, his head bowed, his loafers quickly filling up with sand. He had called Valerie because he couldn't think of another promising line of investigation, and because of her husband's conversation with Michelle. However, she'd pounced on him as soon as he'd stepped out of his car. She knew all about Sean Carter, including that his real name was Sean King.

"I take it you've talked to your husband?" he said.

"Oh yes! If there's one thing old Ian is really good at it's finding out stuff. You're ex–Secret Service and you're down here investigating those murders at Babbage Town. I can't believe I fell for your lines. I really can't believe it."

"Valerie, it wasn't exactly like that."

She whirled on him. "Are you denying you used me to try and get information on my husband? Are you denying that you didn't follow me to that bar after Ian told you to back off?"

"No, I don't deny that. But—"

"Then there are no *buts*."

"Yes I was fishing for information, but I was just doing my job."

"What you did was unforgivable."

"Valerie. I'm sorry if it hurt you. But when you're trying to find out how people were murdered. . . If I'd had any other way of getting info I would have."

She stared up at him, her arms folded across her chest, her sandals in the sand where she had dropped them. The ocean breeze whipped her white slacks against her legs. Slowly the look of fury on her face faded. "I guess I never expected it to happen to me. I never expected to be taken in. Not after Ian anyway."

"What do you mean?"

"I mean I thought he married me because he loved me. I was obviously wrong about that."

"Why then?"

"Who the hell knows? And then you come along and for the first time in my marriage I think, what would it be like to be with another man. You! You sonofabitch!"

Sean stared uncomfortably at her. "Valerie, I can only say that it was very difficult for me to keep a professional distance."

"Professional distance! Oh, that makes me feel so loved." Tears were sliding down her cheeks and she angrily wiped them away.

"I'm sorry, Valerie. I really am."

"Just save the lies for someone else. I don't need to hear them."

She stopped, stooped down, picked up a seashell and angrily flung it at a wave. She whirled around and grabbed his jacket with her hand. "And do you want to know the real kicker?"

Sean's expression showed that, no, he really didn't want to know the kicker. Yet he said, "Tell me, I deserve it."

"Maybe you don't."

"Valerie, if I could take it all back, I would, but I can't. So just tell me."

Her gaze finally broke off from him, but only for a second. "I can't tell you how much I want to go to bed with you. After all this shit. After everything you've done, used me, betrayed me. How much of a loser am I? How much! Because I want to screw your freaking brains out. What the hell does that say about me, Sean!"

She started sobbing. He went to hold her but she pushed him away. He took her in his arms again and this time she let him hold her.

A few minutes passed while the pair stood there, swaying in the sand together.

Finally, Valerie pulled away, took a tissue from her pocket and wiped her eyes. "Look, can we just go somewhere a little more private than this. I . . . I mean . . ." She took a deep breath. "I should hate you, but I don't. That first night in the bar when I blew you off, I left there thinking I was the biggest idiot in the world, because I could just sense there was far more to you." She added quietly, "Far more than I ever saw in my marriage. So can we please just go somewhere?"

"Sure, we can go somewhere, Valerie," Sean said. He took her hand. "But it can't be more than that. And I know this is going to sound crazy, but I don't think you want it to be more than that either."

"Why?"

"Because I think you're still in love with your husband."

"This is really wonderful," the voice said. "Really special."

They both looked up at the man as he walked toward them.

"Oh my God!" Valerie hissed.

Ian Whitfield limped across the sand.

Sean stepped in front of Valerie. "This is not really what it looks like, Whitfield."

Whitfield stopped directly in front of Sean. "You don't really want to go down that road, do you? Because bullshit lies might make me even more upset than I already am. And that would be quite an accomplishment, I can tell you."

"Ian, don't!" Valerie said frantically.

He didn't even bother looking at her. "You had drinks with my wife, then you had dinner with her and now you're walking on the beach holding hands. Are you suicidal or just stupid?"

"And if you knew all of that, why am I still standing here? Why didn't you have your goons take me out after the Mojito at the bar?" Sean took a step back and braced himself as the other man looked ready to start swinging.

"I'm not the mob, King. I don't have people whacked. I'm just a civil servant working for the American people."

"Okay, mister civil servant, piece of advice, work less and spend more time with your wife. The American people will understand."

Whitfield glanced over at Valerie, who shrank back. "So you're a marriage counselor now? I thought you were just an incompetent private investigator."

"Just trying to do my job."

"Your job includes seducing my wife?"

"I didn't seduce your wife. And your wife keeps brushing me off because I think she loves you. Why, I don't know. So maybe instead of playing the heavy with me, you and she might want to find some place private and talk it out. It's up to you, big guy."

Whitfield took a step back. Sean glanced at Valerie. "You want me to stay?"

She shook her head and mouthed the word, "No."

Sean looked back at Whitfield. "Don't blow it."

Sean marched off leaving Whitfield and Valerie looking at each other as the beach wind swept over them.

70

Michelle sat on the front porch steps of Alicia's cottage. Horatio had left and Viggie's sobs could still be heard from inside the house. Finally, Michelle rose, stepped inside and spent a minute plunking a nameless tune on the piano. The sobs finally stopped. Michelle took a deep breath and headed up.

She didn't bother to knock on Viggie's door, she just went in. Viggie was lying on the bed on her stomach, her head underneath a pillow. Her body was still shaking with grief. Michelle gently lifted the pillow off. Now Michelle could hear that Viggie was reciting numbers, very long numbers.

Michelle thought to herself, *She lost her father and I've treated her like shit. Never really bothered to understand how much she's hurting.*

She sat down on the bed, put a hand out and laid it on Viggie's back. The girl immediately tensed.

"Viggie, I am so sorry for what I did. I had no right to do it. I hope you can forgive me. I've, well, I've not been doing all that good lately. I have some issues, like we talked about before. Some days, well, some days are better than others. I guess this was just a bad day. But I shouldn't have taken it out on you. I know you were just trying to help."

Michelle was looking at the wall and didn't notice that Viggie had turned over and was staring at her. When Michelle did see her she reached out and took the girl in her arms, sobbing almost as hard as Viggie had been earlier. Now it was Viggie who comforted her.

"It's okay, Mick. I have bad days too. I . . . I get crazy sometimes. I can't seem to understand anything, which makes me so mad."

Michelle cried harder and Viggie tightened her grip on the woman. "It's okay. I'm not mad at you. I . . . really like you. You're my friend."

Michelle squeezed Viggie and whispered in between sobs, "You're my friend too, Viggie. I'd do anything for you. I will never hurt you again. I promise. I promise."

When Sean got back home he found a red-faced Michelle sitting in the living room of the cottage.

"You okay?" he said quickly. "Anything wrong with Viggie?"

"She's fine. I'm fine."

"You sure?" he said doubtfully.

She nodded slowly as though talking required an energy she simply didn't have.

He sat next to her. "Well, I'm not doing fine." He relayed to her what had happened on the beach.

"God, Sean, he could've killed you."

"He still could."

"What do we do now?"

"Go to sleep. Something tells me it's going to be a busy day tomorrow and a good night's sleep will do us both good."

Unfortunately, neither one of them would get it.

Michelle, always a light sleeper, slid her hand under her pillow and gripped her pistol as the door to her room slowly opened. Michelle eased her eyes to slit-wide until she could make out the person coming at her. Viggie was in a long T-shirt that hung past her knees. She was holding something in her hands.

She stood next to the bed for a moment and then slowly placed the item she was carrying on top of the bedspread. A few seconds later Michelle heard the door close. Moments after that Michelle heard Viggie's door close.

She immediately sat up in bed and turned on the light on the nightstand. Grabbing up the item Viggie had left for her she saw that it was a large manila envelope. In it were two articles: a letter in a regular envelope and a photograph. She was so excited that she slipped out into the hall still wearing only what'd she'd been sleeping in, panties and a short tank top.

She quietly knocked on Sean's bedroom door. There was no answer. She rapped again, a little harder.

She pressed her lips against the door. "Sean? Sean?"

Finally she heard a grumble, some muttering followed by the squeak of a mattress. Then a light was switched on, footsteps came her way, and the door opened.

He was sleepy-eyed and wearing striped pajamas.

"What is it?" he demanded.

A smile twitched across her lips. "You wear pajamas to bed?" she said, staring at him. "For real?"

He said nothing for a moment as his eyes cleared and he focused on her half-naked body. "And you wear nearly nothing when *you* go to bed? For real?"

She appeared startled, looked down at herself and quickly put a hand across her chest, holding the manila envelope in front of her even more private areas.

Now *Sean* was smiling. He said, "No, really, *Mick*, not on my account. Having been woken out of a dead sleep, it's hard for me to focus on things like breasts and . . ." He glanced down at the manila envelope. "Well, you get the picture." When she didn't say anything, and just stood there looking awkward, he added, "Is there something you wanted, other than to ridicule my choice of sleeping apparel?"

Michelle slipped past him and into his room, sat on the bed and motioned him to join her there. "Hurry up. I've got something to show you."

"I can see *that!*"

"I'm not horny, okay? I'm talking about something else. It's important."

He sighed, walked over and slumped down next to her. "What is it?"

She told him about Viggie's visit and showed him the items.

All weariness was now gone from Sean's features. He studied the letter and then the photo.

"Where did Viggie get these?"

"They had to come from her father. Wouldn't they?"

"So Viggie gave them to you; the music and now this. Why?"

"She likes me. I saved her life. She trusts me."

Sean looked at her curiously. "I think you hit it on the head, Michelle. She *trusts* you." He put the items back in the manila envelope. "You need to go and talk to Viggie, right now. This letter mentions something else, another piece of information, that we need to make sense of all this. She gave you this much, she should give you the rest."

"I'll try."

Michelle returned to her room, put on a bathrobe and went to Viggie's room. Ten minutes later she returned to Sean's room looking disappointed. "Not only would she not tell me anything else, she wouldn't even acknowledge what she had given me."

They spent the next hour trying to make sense of the letter and the photo. Finally Sean said, "Okay, not that I mind having a nearly naked woman in my bed, but you need to get dressed."

"What?" Michelle said, startled.

"You woke me up, now we're going to wake Horatio up. I want his opinion on something."

As she rose and left the room, Sean looked down at the envelope. Maybe this was finally the key they needed. He desperately hoped so, because they were running out of options. And he didn't want their only remaining option to be going over the fence at Camp Peary.

71

The sun was starting to rise as Sean and Michelle walked over to see Horatio in his room at the mansion. They checked in with the dour guard at the front security desk and then headed upstairs.

Sean had called ahead and Horatio opened the door immediately. The psychologist was fully dressed although he hadn't bothered to put his hair in its customary ponytail with the result that it was curled upward like a wave about to crash on the beach.

He started to say something.

"Not here," Sean said. "Let's take a ride."

Twenty minutes later they were standing next to Michelle's truck where it was parked under some trees near the banks of the York. The sunlight crept across the surface of the water as Sean and Michelle watched Horatio study the letter and the photo.

"Okay, the return address on the letter is Wiesbaden, Germany. Thankfully it's in English although the physical writing is that of a very old person whose first language is not English. And it's addressed to Monk Turing from . . ." Horatio squinted at the signature and adjusted the reading glasses he was wearing.

"Henry Fox," Michelle said helpfully.

Sean explained, "Basically Fox is thanking Monk for helping him get back home to Germany."

Horatio looked at the top of the letter. "Dated nearly a year ago. So *before* Monk went to England and Germany."

"At least the *last* time he went. Now check out the last two lines of the letter," Sean said.

Horatio read, " 'Now that you've helped me, I will, as agreed, return the favor. I have it. And it is yours when you come for a visit.' " Horatio looked up. "So Fox had something he wanted to give to Monk Turing in return for him helping Fox get back home?"

"Looks that way," Michelle said. "And Monk went to Germany to get it. And on the same trip he went for a jaunt through his family history with Alan Turing in England."

"So what did Monk get from Fox?"

"We don't know that yet," Michelle admitted.

Horatio said, "So Monk helped Fox back to his homeland, but Henry Fox doesn't sound like a German name."

"I have a theory about that," Sean said mysteriously. "But I have to wait for confirmation." He picked up the photograph. It showed three people sitting on steps in front of a large building. One person was Monk Turing; a younger Viggie was sitting next to him. The third person was a smallish, very elderly man with a white beard and shrewd, blue eyes. There was a date at the bottom of the picture.

"This was taken over three years ago," Michelle said. "Viggie told me that she and her father lived in an apartment in New York City then. She said they had no friends except for a very old man who talked to her father about old stuff. She also said he talked funny."

"Probably meaning with an accent, a German accent," Sean filled in.

"So presumably the old guy in the photo is Henry Fox?"

"Right," Sean said. "This explains a lot but it doesn't tell us what Fox gave Monk."

"Viggie said that the old man would write letters down on a piece of paper and challenge Monk Turing to, I guess, decipher them," Michelle added.

Horatio broke in. "Wait a minute. South Freeman said that one reason the military was keeping the presence of those German prisoners secret is because some of them might have had knowledge of the Enigma code. I did a little history reading after I talked with South. Each of the German military branches had different networks of the Enigma they used. The naval code was thought to be the toughest of all. The folks at Bletchley Park, Alan Turing included, couldn't make a dent in it. And the Germans and their U-boats were murdering the Allies in the Battle of the Atlantic. That is until some German naval codebooks were successfully obtained by the Allies. With that information the folks at Bletchley Park worked their magic and the tide began to turn."

"How does that help us?" Michelle asked.

"South also told me that the war in the Atlantic began to turn in favor of the Allies *after* those German POWs were taken to Camp Peary. And those POWs came from boats and subs that had been sunk. That means the POWs at Camp Peary could've had German naval Enigma codebooks and other intelligence the Allies could use."

"So you're thinking that this Henry Fox might have been one of the POWs?" Michelle said slowly.

"He's the right age, speaks with presumably a German accent, writes codes down on a piece of paper and talks about the war. Yeah, I think the probability lies in that direction."

Sean said, "And that's why I wanted to talk to you. Because we need to find out what Fox gave Monk Turing, the thing that's referenced in the letter."

Horatio looked puzzled. "Me? How should I know what Fox gave him?"

"Viggie slipped this letter and photo to Michelle while she was sleeping. I think she did it because she trusts Michelle."

"Okay, but where do I come in?"

"Might Turing have left all these clues with his daughter and told her to only give them out to someone she comes to trust?"

Horatio nodded. "That's entirely plausible. Viggie is highly intelligent, but quite capable of being manipulated. She'll sometimes give you whatever answer you put in her head. I saw that quite clearly in my talk with her."

"But Michelle spoke to Viggie after she gave her these items and the girl just clammed up. She wouldn't even acknowledge that she'd given Michelle anything. Why would she do that?"

Horatio didn't speak for a bit. When he did his words came slowly. "As funny as it sounds, I believe that Monk Turing hasn't simply manipulated his daughter but *programmed* her."

"Programmed her?" Michelle exclaimed.

"I'd suspected this before, but what you're saying now makes me think I'm closer to the truth than not. I think that brilliant father gave brilliant but naive daughter information, and he trained her to release that information only under certain circumstances. Viggie played the song for Michelle because she was nice to her and Viggie felt she could trust her. Then Michelle risked her life to save Viggie, so Viggie went a step further and gave her more information." Horatio looked at her. "It's curious though that she would give you this after what happened with the truck."

"Truck, what are you talking about?" Sean asked.

"Viggie and I worked it out," Michelle said hastily, averting her gaze from Sean's questioning look. She plunged on. "I doubt I'll be saving her life again, at least I hope I won't have to. So what else do I have to do to get her to give up the rest?"

"I don't know the answer to that."

Sean mulled this over. "So we're at a dead end for now, until Joan comes through, or Alicia decrypts that song." He put the articles away in his pocket, stretched and yawned. "Well, since we're up early we might as well go eat."

Michelle checked her watch. "Let's make it quick. Champ is picking me up at nine for our flight."

"You're still going?" Sean said harshly.

"I'm still going."

"But he doesn't have an alibi for the time Rivest was killed."

"I doubt we're going to get any good information from innocent people. So it makes far more sense to go after the ones we think might be guilty."

"My gut tells me to leave this guy alone."

"Yeah," Michelle said. "Well, my *brain* tells me we can't afford to do that."

Horatio glanced over at Sean. "Your turn unless you want to concede to the lady."

"Shut the hell up," Sean snapped as he climbed in the truck.

Horatio turned to Michelle. "Geez, could the guy be any more obvious?"

"More obvious?" she said, puzzled.

Horatio rolled his eyes, sighed deeply and got in the truck.

72

Horatio called South Freeman later that morning for two reasons. First, to see if the man had a list of any of the German POWs held at Camp Peary during World War II.

The man laughed out loud. "Oh, yeah, I got that right here on my desk. Pentagon wouldn't give it to me so I strolled on over to the CIA and the spooks printed me out a nice clean copy and then asked me what other secret shit I'd like to get my hands on."

"I'll take that as a *hell no*," Horatio said. Then he asked Freeman whether he knew any people with newspapers in Tennessee around the area where Michelle grew up. On this query Horatio struck gold.

"Man named Toby Rucker runs a weekly in a little place an hour south of Nashville." When he named the town, Horatio almost jumped out of his chair. It was the very place where Michelle had lived.

"What do you want to know for?" Freeman asked.

"I've got some questions about the disappearance of someone down there, say nearly thirty years ago."

"Well Toby's been there over forty years, so if it made the paper he'll know about it." Freeman gave Horatio the number and added, "I'll call him right now and tell him you'll be in contact."

"I appreciate it, South, I really do."

"You better. And don't you forget our deal. Exclusive! Or I strangle you."

"Right." Horatio hung up, waited twenty minutes and called the number.

A man identifying himself as Toby Rucker answered on the second ring. South Freeman had just gotten off the phone with him, Rucker said. Horatio relayed his request and Rucker agreed to see what he could find out.

As Horatio clicked off his phone, there was a sound from overhead. He poked his head out the bedroom window. It was a chopper buzzing over Babbage Town. As it sped away Horatio thought about Michelle thousands of feet up in the air with a man Sean King clearly didn't trust. So clearly in fact that he'd asked a special favor of Horatio that the man had granted.

"Come back in one piece, Michelle," he muttered under his breath. "We still have a lot to talk about."

The takeoff had been clean and smooth. The Cessna Grand Caravan was very roomy and luxurious, with a single aisle, seating fourteen counting pilot and co-pilot. It also had every navigation and communication bell and whistle, Champ had assured her.

"You take many people up?"

"I'm a solo kind of guy." He hastily added, "It's just that I like to think up here."

She looked back at all the seats. "Seems like kind of a waste then, all this room."

"Who knows, if things go really well, I could buy my own jet."

"You don't really strike me as all that materialistic."

He shrugged. "I'm not really. I went into science because I liked figuring out things. But it gets complicated, and I'm not referring to the science." He fell silent.

"Come on, Champ, talk to me."

He stared out the window of the plane. "Quantum computers have enormous potential to do good in the world and bad."

She said, "I'm sure the guy who invented the atom bomb had the same concerns."

Champ shuddered. "Can we please change the subject?"

"Okay, show me what this little old plane can do."

He put the plane into a steep climb, something it handled easily. Next he guided the Cessna through controlled dives, cutting tight banks and even doing a rollover. None of it bothered Michelle; she'd ridden in just about anything with two wings in some of the roughest conditions possible.

He pointed out the window. "The infamous Camp Peary. This is about the closest we can get without being shot down."

"Can we at least go a little lower?"

He eased them down to two thousand feet and circled back around. Michelle kept her eyes on the topography, taking in every detail she could. "So you can't get any closer?"

"Depends on how risk-averse you are."

"Not very. I take it you are."

"Funny, not since I met you."

He moved the flight wheel to the left and reduced their airspeed. The plane flew along on a straight line basically following the contours of the York River.

"This is really as close as we can get without having a missile up our butt," he said.

Michelle could see the boat dock that Ian Whitfield had presumably used to launch his RIB. Next to that appeared to be the bunkers that Sean had shown her from the satellite map. From the air they looked like a series of concrete boxes lined up side by side. To the north of that was the inlet from the York that seemed to bisect Camp Peary. And farther north of that she saw the massive runway. Her gaze next ran across the old neighborhoods South Freeman had described, then an old brick home, and a small pond. And south of Camp Peary was the Naval Supply Center and the Weapons Station.

"The feds have this area pretty well locked up," she said.

"Yes they do." He banked to the right, flew east over the York, staying at two thousand feet and passed over some of the most picturesque country Michelle had ever seen.

"It is beautiful."

"Yes, it is," Champ said, staring at her. Then he looked abruptly away.

"Come on, Champ, it's the girl who's supposed to blush."

He looked out the window. "I took Monk up once."

"Really? Did he want to see anything in particular?"

"Not really. Although he did want to fly pretty low over the river."

Michelle thought, *So he could do a recon on Camp Peary. Just like I am.*

"Um, would you like to take the controls?"

She took the wheel in front of her and eased it to the left. And then to the right. "Can we climb a bit?"

"You can go up to eight thousand. Just take it slow and easy." She edged the nose of the plane up and leveled off at eight thousand feet.

She said, "How about a controlled dive? Like you did?"

He stared at her a bit nervously. "Oh? Sure, okay."

She eased the wheel forward and the plane's nose

dipped. Then it dipped some more. Michelle could see the earth coming at them awfully fast. And still she kept the wheel pushed forward. Suddenly flashing through her mind were nightmares that had torn at her for nearly three decades. A child petrified, but what child? Her? Even in her mind's eye she couldn't be sure. And yet the terror she was feeling was very real.

They were diving nearly straight down and yet Michelle didn't seem to notice the altimeter reading plummeting or hear the warning horn in the cockpit. She also didn't see that Champ was frantically pulling his wheel back, screaming at her to let go; that she was going to crash the plane. And yet she couldn't pull her hands from the wheel. It was as though it had been electrified. For a second time she heard herself say, "Goodbye, Sean."

Finally, through the fog of her mind she heard, "Let go!"

Michelle glanced to the side and saw a white-faced Champ straining with all of his might to pull the wheel back, to free them from the death spiral. Michelle ripped her hands from the wheel. Champ managed to pull the plane level and then took them in for a bumpy landing, the tires kicking off the runway twice before settling firmly down.

They taxied to a stop. For several minutes all each could hear was the other's strained breathing. Finally Champ looked at her. "Are you all right?"

She could feel acid racing up her throat. "For nearly killing us both, yes, I'm fine."

"I've known other people to freeze up at the controls. I'm sorry, I shouldn't have let you take the wheel."

"Champ, you did nothing wrong. I'm sorry. I'm really sorry."

They were walking back from the plane to Champ's Mercedes when a motorcycle pulled up to them. It was Horatio Barnes's Harley. The rider pulled off his helmet, and Sean King said, "Beautiful day to fly, isn't it?"

"What are you doing here?" she demanded.

He tossed her a spare helmet. "Let's go."

"Thanks for the flying lesson, Champ. I'm afraid I'm not up to lunch right now." She climbed on the bike behind Sean.

After they'd left the private air terminal and been on the road for a couple of minutes Michelle told Sean to pull off.

"What's wrong?"

"Just do it," she urged.

He pulled off and Michelle ran behind some trees and threw up.

She came back a minute later, white-faced and wiping her mouth. She slowly climbed back on the bike.

"Skies a little unfriendly to you?" he asked.

She said slowly, "No, just chalk it up to pilot error. So what are you doing on Horatio's precious Harley?"

"Just went for a stroll."

"And just happened to arrive at the air terminal as we landed?"

He turned and said angrily, "You call that a friggin' landing? You guys were coming straight down. I thought you'd lost the damn engine. I almost killed myself getting to the runway even if it was just to spatula you off the tarmac! What the hell happened up there?"

"Some kind of engine trouble. Champ corrected it." She felt terrible lying to him, but would have felt even worse telling him the truth. And what was the truth? That she had frozen, nearly killing herself and an innocent person?

"I thought you said it was pilot error?"

"Just forget it," she said. "Any landing you walk away from is a great one."

"Excuse me for caring."

"So you've been riding this bike all over the countryside watching us fly around?"

"I told you I didn't want you to go up there with the guy."

"You don't think I can handle myself?"

"Oh hell, don't pull that crap with me. I was just—"

She smacked his helmet. "Sean?"

"What?"

"Thanks."

"You're welcome."

They rode on.

Michelle clung tightly to Sean's jacket. She didn't want to let go, for any reason. She had never been more terrified in her life. And this time the reason for the fear was not some external enemy. It was herself.

73

Sean drove them to the B&B where Horatio had originally been staying. "Joan is faxing me some info," he explained.

They got the documents and drove to a nearby restaurant. Michelle's stomach had settled down enough that they ordered sandwiches and coffee. She told Sean about Monk going up in the plane.

As they ate, they went over the pages Joan had faxed. Sean said, "Monk Turing did visit Wiesbaden."

"How'd they find that out so quickly?"

"Joan's firm has an affiliate in Frankfurt. They were able to track him via his credit card receipts. He bought that beer stein he gave Champ there among other things." He next looked at several sheets of paper. "This is the list of German POWs held at Camp Peary during World War II that I asked for."

"Okay, how the hell did Joan get *that* so fast?"

"One of their top executives is a former rear admiral and once headed the NSA. He was able to cut through the red tape. And it's not like this stuff is classified anymore. Just gathering mold in some office in the Pentagon."

They went down the list of Germans. Each name had the man's date of capture, rank and what had happened to him.

Sean said, "You can see that most of them were released at the end of the war or else died in captivity. But I don't see a Henry Fox listed."

"Wait a minute. Look at this guy." Michelle's finger pointed at a blank space. "There's nothing here that says what happened to him." She scanned the pages. "And he's the only one."

Sean looked at the man's name. "Heinrich Fuchs."

"Heinrich Fuchs," Michelle repeated slowly. "Anglicized, that might be Henry Fox."

Sean stared at her. "I think you're right, and for a very good reason."

"What's that?"

"Because I'm betting everything I have, little though it is, that Heinrich Fuchs was a German naval radio operator and that he was also the only man to *escape* from the naval stockade that is now the CIA's Camp Peary. That's why there's a blank in the space as to what happened to him. The Navy wasn't going to admit anyone escaped."

Michelle drew in a sharp breath. "Escaped and changed his name to Henry Fox?"

"And moved to New York, set up another life, grew old and ended up living in the same apartment building as Monk and Viggie Turing." He jumped up. "Come on. We need to see Viggie."

"Why?"

"Horatio says she was programmed. Well, the name Heinrich Fuchs may be the key she needs to tell us more. Maybe everything."

They drove to Babbage Town and hustled to the schoolroom where Viggie and the other children were. Only Viggie wasn't there.

"She said she was sick," the teacher said.

"She told you in person?" Sean asked.

"No, she sent in a note. It was on my desk this morning when I got in."

A few minutes later Sean and Michelle were rushing up the steps to Alicia's cottage. They burst through the door and Michelle called out, "Viggie? Viggie!"

She hurtled up the stairs and threw open Viggie's bedroom door. The room was empty and she clattered back downstairs. She and Sean searched the rest of the cottage.

"No sign of her," he said, his voice panicky.

"Where the hell is her guard?" Michelle demanded.

The door to the cottage opened and Alicia walked in. She was holding a bundle of papers and looked very tired. She seemed surprised to see them here and then said in a scolding tone, "Okay, you two, I've run every possible configuration of these damn notes through our strongest computer programs and came up with gibberish every time. So either the code is beyond our capability to decipher it, or it's not code at all, which is the conclusion I'm fast coming to. I did find out the name of the song. It's 'Shenandoah,' from the nineteenth century. Anyway, what do you know, it has *lyrics*, not many, none of it spectacular, but it has words. So I had the brilliant idea that perhaps the lyrics were the key to the code. I hit them with everything we had, in every conceivable combination. And do you know what? It was still all gibberish."

They just stood there staring at her.

"What is it?" she said suspiciously.

"Where's Viggie?" Michelle asked quietly.

Alicia looked at her watch. "She's in school. She's been in school since eight o'clock."

"She's not there, Alicia," Sean said. "The teacher said someone left a note on her desk this morning saying that Viggie was sick."

She gave them both searching looks. "I've been up all night trying to make sense of this garbage. *You* were supposed to look after her."

"She was fine early this morning," Michelle explained. "She came to my room a bit before dawn. Then she went back to her room."

"Then what?" Alicia said.

Sean and Michelle looked at each other. Sean said in an uncomfortable tone, "Then we left to run down some leads."

"Leaving her alone!" Alicia exclaimed. "You left Viggie alone? Again!"

"We thought you were here," Michelle explained.

Alicia threw the papers up in the air. "You *thought* I was here? How the hell could I be here when you gave me this mess to deal with?" She drew several deep breaths. "Her guard is supposed to escort her to school. I requested a new one directly after that other fool let Viggie wander away and almost drown."

Sean looked at her curiously. "Who did you request the guard from?"

"Champ."

Michelle said, "Champ picked me up at nine to go to the plane."

"What are you talking about, what plane?" Alicia said fiercely.

"Just calm down, Alicia. Viggie might have just gone off by herself," Sean said.

"Look what happened the *last* time she did that!"

"She's right, Sean. I'm going to check down by the river."

"I'll get a security team to start looking over the grounds here," he said.

They both headed out, leaving Alicia Chadwick staring helplessly down at the mess of papers.

74

Viggie was not on the river. All watercraft were accounted for. A search of Babbage Town had turned up nothing. The note that had been left with the teacher had been written on a computer. No one had seen who'd delivered the note.

The guard that had been assigned to look after Viggie said he'd gone to the cottage that morning at a few minutes before eight, but there had been a note on the door inside the screen porch saying that Viggie was ill and would not be attending school that day. So he'd left. He produced the note. Like the other, it had been written on a computer and was untraceable.

"So anyone could have done it," Sean said. He, Michelle and Horatio were standing outside the grounds of Babbage Town. The psychologist had joined them in the search for Viggie. They had just scoured the area with Sheriff Hayes and a group of volunteers and turned up not a single clue as to what had happened to the girl.

As they were standing there a black sedan pulled up.

"Oh, shit," Sean exclaimed. "Not him. Not now."

Special Agent Ventris climbed out of the car and walked over to them.

"I understand you lost the girl. Again!"

"What do you want, Ventris?" Sean demanded.

"I want you to get out of here. Your presence here is counterproductive."

"What exactly have you produced? Other than confusion?"

Michelle put a warning hand on Sean's shoulder. "Just stay cool, he *is* a federal agent," she muttered.

"Better listen to your friend," Ventris said, who'd overheard her warning. "If the girl has been kidnapped, we'll find her. It's a Bureau specialty."

"Would that be dead or alive?" Sean said bitterly.

Ventris got back in his car and drove off as Sean stared angrily after him. "You son of a bitch," he screamed after the departing FBI agent.

Horatio said, "Okay, I think we all need to take a deep calming breath."

Sean snapped, "I don't want to take a deep calming breath. I want to kick the shit out of *Special my ass Agent Ventris.*"

"Okay, venting violent thoughts can be positive," Horatio said awkwardly.

All three turned their heads toward the road as a line of passenger buses rumbled up, stopped at the front gate and then were allowed through.

Sean and Michelle hustled over to the guard stationed there. "What's going on?"

"We're clearing out Babbage Town, at least for now."

"Why?" Michelle asked.

"Two mysterious deaths and now a little girl's gone missing. The people working here and their families are scared. They're being transported to Williamsburg until things get cleared up."

"Who ordered this?" Sean demanded.

"Actually, I did," a voice said. They all turned to see Champ Pollion striding toward them. "Do you blame me?"

"Can we stay?" Sean asked.

"No! I'm not going to be responsible for anyone else getting hurt."

He turned to leave.

"Where are you going?" Michelle asked.

"I'm leaving too. Not even the discovery of quantum computers is worth my life."

75

Two hours later Babbage Town was empty except for a few guards. Michelle and Sean had continued to walk around the grounds looking for any clue to Viggie's disappearance, while Horatio had gone to his room to get his things together.

While they were at Alicia's cottage packing to leave, Merkle Hayes called Sean with news that was hardly surprising. "It's like the girl's vanished from the face of the earth." Then Hayes made a comment that caused Sean to nearly drop his phone. "Even the CIA pitched in, but they couldn't find her either."

"The CIA!"

"Yeah. Ian Whitfield said he'd heard about Viggie being missing and offered to send resources to help in the search. But they found nothing."

"Wow, who knew the CIA had such a big heart," Sean said. He clicked off and tossed his phone onto his bed in disgust. He went to Michelle's room and relayed to her what Hayes had said.

"We need to go get Horatio from his room and

441

clear out of here," she reminded him. In response, Sean turned and headed off. "Where are you going?"

"Down to the dock. To think. Come on. We'll get Horatio in a little bit."

They walked through the forest path to the boat-house and sat on the dock.

"Where could Viggie be?" Michelle asked miserably. "Where?"

Sean looked across the river. "I think she's there," he said, pointing at Camp Peary. "I think she's in the same place where her father was killed."

"And Whitfield offering to help was just a cover?" He nodded. "So you think she's dead?"

"It doesn't look good."

"But why, Sean? Why Viggie?"

"Because her father told her things, Michelle. She told us things and somebody found out. And they didn't want her telling us anything else."

"But how could they know?"

"Between Babbage Town and Camp Peary no secret is safe apparently."

She stared across the calm water. Calm at least for now. "I know they're the CIA, Sean. I know that. But killing a little girl?"

"You're kidding, right? In the interests of national security they'd kill their own grandmothers."

She said, "What could Monk Turing have found out that would make the CIA come after him? And then kidnap Viggie?"

"I don't know enough and I'm apparently not smart enough to figure it out from the little I do know. But this I'm certain of: Monk was murdered, and so was Len Rivest. I don't know the motives yet, and they might have been killed by different people or organizations and for different reasons but murdered they were. And Monk Turing knew an old man who it seems probable was a prisoner over there, and who told him something about that place. Something that led Monk to go there. And die."

"So Henry Fox escaped the place, but Monk didn't. That's ironic."

"Seems that way," Sean said miserably.

"And now Viggie." Michelle choked back a sob and Sean put his arm around her.

"I'm sorry, Michelle. I've really messed things up on this one."

"We both left her alone, Sean," she replied. "*Both* of us."

Sean looked thoughtful. "We left the cottage this morning around six. It was still mostly dark. Alicia was at Hut Number One working on the code. So basically anyone could have come and taken Viggie after that. In a fast boat she's across the river to Camp Peary in minutes." The tears trickled down Michelle's cheeks as he was speaking.

He handed her his handkerchief and she dried her eyes. "Now what?" she asked.

He stared across the river. "Now I go over the fence."

She pulled away from him. "What?"

"It's the only way, Michelle. I messed up and left Viggie unprotected. I can't sit by and not do anything. I have to try and save her."

"Okay, when do you want to go?"

"You're not going."

"Then neither are you."

"Michelle, I can't let you do it. Hell, I could be wrong about the whole thing. I can't let you throw your whole life away."

"What life, Sean? I don't even know who I am some days. The only life I care about right now is Viggie Turing's. So if you're going over that damn fence, so am I."

He stared at her, partly with pride over her refusal to abandon him. And partly with fear as Joan's and Horatio's warnings came back to him.

"Sean," she said, "the CIA flight will be coming in tomorrow night. Do you think they may try and get Viggie out that way? Maybe they'll keep her alive until then."

He didn't answer. Sean looked out at the river. Did he really want to mix it up with the likes of Ian Whitfield? Did he really want to take it to this guy? The answer was no. And, of course, yes.

An idea suddenly interrupted these thoughts. He jumped up. "Come on!"

76

Toby Rucker called Horatio back while he was packing up. He'd been successful, he'd told the psychologist.

"Around the time you're talking about, a car was found abandoned about an hour's drive from here, up in the Smoky Mountains. I was just a freelance reporter at the time, but after reading the story from the archives I remember it fairly well."

"Who was the car registered to?"

"A William Joyner, sergeant in the Army. He was assigned to the recruitment office they used to have down here. This was back in the late Seventies."

"And what happened to him?"

"Nobody knows," Rucker said. "They found the car, but not him. Local police investigated, and the Army sent its people down, but they never did uncover anything."

"Was Joyner married?"

"Nope. He was in his late twenties. Joined the Army at eighteen. Fought in Vietnam, stayed in the military and had been back in the States about six years when he disappeared."

Horatio said hesitantly, "Any romantic involvement? Girlfriend?"

"Nothing in the archives about that. Why, you know different?"

"No," Horatio said quickly.

"Can I ask what your interest in this is? South didn't fill me in on that."

"Just call me a curious soul. So the investigation simply hit a dead end?"

"It often does when you can't turn up a body. Maybe Joyner got tired of the Army and found a better opportunity somewhere else and went Awol. It happens."

Horatio thanked the man and clicked off. It looked like William Joyner had had an affair with Frank Maxwell's wife and then disappeared. His body, assuming he was dead, had never been found. What had Michelle seen all those years ago that had damaged her so badly? Horatio knew the only place he would get those answers was from Michelle herself. Even if her conscious mind had long since buried the memory, he also knew her subconscious would never forget it.

Sean and Michelle pinched some tools from the garage and hid them in a bag. They walked up to the mansion and explained to the guard there that they had come for Horatio. "We're clearing out, like Champ said to."

The guard let them through and Michelle and Sean raced up the stairs to the top floor and down the hall toward the room that Sean had first stayed in. Going inside the room, they stopped in front of the wall where Viggie had calculated the secret room, if it existed, would be located.

Sean said, "There has to be a door somewhere, but we don't have time to find it." Attacking the wall with their tools, they methodically cut a large hole in it. Shining a flashlight through Sean peered in the hole. "Damn!"

"What is it?"

"You'll see," he replied. "Hurry!"

With renewed vigor they attacked the wall. Soon they stepped through a large hole and stared at walls of electronic devices. On the other side of the wall there appeared to be a door. Sean pointed at it. "It's accessed from the other room, the one that was dead-bolted."

There was a bank of TV screens against one wall that was showing the interior of all the huts.

"That's Hut Number One," Sean said, pointing to one screen.

"And Champ's Hut Number Two," Michelle said, pointing to another screen.

She motioned to a bank of computer screens against

another wall. Streams of numbers were flowing across all of them.

"They're secretly recording the data on the computers in Champ's hut," Sean exclaimed.

"So Len Rivest was right. There is a spy at Babbage Town, an electronic one," Michelle said. She glanced up at a red light blinking on a device on one wall. "Oh, shit, is that what I think it is?" she cried out.

They plunged through the hole and ran toward the stairs as the silent alarm burned red.

"What about Horatio?" Michelle called out.

Sean stopped dead, turned back and raced down another corridor. He pounded on Horatio's door. When Horatio opened it Sean grabbed him and hustled him down the hall.

"Why are we running?" Horatio puffed.

"Avoiding death," Michelle snapped.

At that, the little psychologist put on an enviable burst of speed.

"How are we getting out of here?" Michelle asked. "The front entrance is guarded."

"By boat," Sean answered. "Come on!"

The three made their way quickly down to the boathouse catching only two glimpses of guards along the way and neither one seemed to know about the break-in at the secret room.

"Are we sure that silent alarm was even working?" Michelle said.

"Should we call Sheriff Hayes?" Horatio suggested.

"I'm not trusting anyone right now," Sean replied firmly.

They reached the boathouse and Sean broke open the storage shed, grabbed the keys for the Formula boat, lowered the lift and they were soon in the water and drifting down the York on idle throttle with their running lights off.

"Keep a lookout," Sean warned.

Michelle seemed puzzled.

"What's the matter?" Sean asked as he looked at her from the captain's chair.

"Why did Viggie come down to the boathouse, get in a kayak and paddle out into the river?"

"You said she didn't say why."

"We'd come down here once before and gone out on the kayak. She said it was one of the best times she'd ever had. Then we raced back to the house after making a bet: If I beat her she had to talk to me about codes and blood. I did win, she got a little ticked off and started playing the song crazy, but she did play it."

"So?"

"So why did she come *back* to the river?" she asked again.

Horatio warned, "It's a little dangerous to try and figure out what Viggie was thinking, Michelle."

"Why do I think she was trying to tell me something? Why do I think she was trying to get me to come down to the dock?" Michelle stood there looking across the water at Camp Peary. "Something else was really odd. Viggie told me this story out of the blue."

"What story?"

"That she knew that Alan Turing had killed himself by eating a poisoned apple. She told me how it reminded her of the Snow White story. You know the wicked old queen turns into a hag, takes a boat down the river and tricks Snow White into eating the poisoned apple and Snow White almost died. Like Viggie almost died on the river. She said something like whoever holds the apple is definitely powerful. Why would she tell me that?"

"I don't know, but how does that help us?" Sean said.

Michelle suddenly exclaimed, "Omigod! Boat? Apple?" She raced to the Formula boat's stern, leaned over and stared down at the name stenciled on the transom: "*The Big Apple*," she read.

"*The Big Apple* as in New York," Sean said.

"No, the apple as in Snow White," Michelle corrected. "Come on, we have to tear this boat apart."

"Why?" Horatio asked.

"Just help me! Help me."

An hour later, the three of them sat in the stern seats staring at it. The rolled-up paper had been hidden in the enclosed head of the boat, behind spare rolls of toilet paper in a storage compartment.

Michelle said, "She must've come down here that

day to hide the document. She probably planned to leave me another clue or maybe just bring the document to me like she did the others if I said the magic words. Only she never got the chance."

Horatio added, "And the fact that she thought she needed a hiding place suggests she was afraid."

"Well, her fears turned out to be well founded, didn't they?" Michelle said bitterly.

"It's old," Sean said, as he held the document. "Second World War old. This must be what Henry Fox aka Heinrich Fuchs gave to Monk Turing when he visited him in Germany."

"It's a map," Horatio said, studying it.

"Of Camp Peary or what it used to be when the Navy ran it. I recognize the topography from the map in South Freeman's office," Michelle added.

Sean pointed at a line that ran from near the river's shore into the heart of the facility. "The only thing is there's no inlet there. The map must be wrong."

"It's not wrong if the line isn't delineating an inlet of *water*," Michelle countered.

"A road then."

She turned the document over. There was written the initials "H.F."

"Heinrich Fuchs," Horatio said.

"And there's writing down here, but it's in German."

"Look over there," Sean said, pointing to fresh writing done in another hand.

Michelle added, "It's in English. Maybe Monk Turing's. Look, there are compass points, directions, everything."

"Right, but to what?"

Michelle flipped the map back over. "To that line, it has to be. Wait a minute. Sean, if you're right, Fuchs escaped from Camp Peary."

"Okay."

"So how did he do it?"

"I don't know. I guess the best way was to get to the river. If he went by road or even through the fields and forest the scent dogs could follow him. Water nearly always makes a clean escape, but you have to get to it first. And I'm sure they had a lot of guards back then."

"I'm sure they did, *above* ground," she said.

"Above ground?"

"Sean, that line may represent a *tunnel*, right into Camp Peary. Or in Heinrich Fuch's case, a tunnel right *out* of Camp Peary, and freedom. A tunnel is a pretty popular way of breaking out of prison."

"But why would Monk go to all that trouble to get a map of a tunnel leading into Camp Peary? He was killed."

"They didn't kill him in the tunnel. They must have caught him after he got *out* of the tunnel. They might not know anything about it."

"That doesn't answer why he would risk going in the tunnel in the *first* place."

Horatio spoke up. "Maybe Fuchs told him about something there. Something located at Camp Peary. Something, I don't know, something *valuable*."

"This all sounds crazy, Michelle, but the discovery of this map provides us with one very critical thing: a way to get into Camp Peary."

"So you really do think Viggie's there?"

"Even if she isn't, we might be able to find out something important. Important enough to use it as leverage with those people so they'll release Viggie."

"But what if I'm wrong and they do know about the tunnel?"

Sean looked at the other two solemnly as he carefully folded up the map. "Then I'm afraid we're dead."

77

They decided to take the boat downriver to pick up the equipment that Sean had ordered for their assault on Camp Peary. After that Sean led them on a detour to see South Freeman. Arch, Virginia, wasn't on the river, so they had to dock the boat at an old pier and hike about a half-mile inland. Sean used Michelle's cell phone to call ahead and although it was late they found South seated at his desk smoking a cigarette as usual, his hands flying over the keyboard. "Girl disappears from Babbage Town. It's all over the place. Hot stuff. And even better it's Monk Turing's little girl. Gonna bring out a special edition. Make my whole life and please tell me it's got something to do with the spooks across that river."

"It has something to do with a little girl who might be *dead*," Michelle said severely. "Do you journalists ever stop and think about that?"

He stopped typing, wheeled around in his chair and scowled at her. "Hey, I got nothing against that child. I pray they find her safe and sound and arrest whoever took her. But news is news."

Michelle looked away in disgust.

Sean said, "South, was there any talk of something valuable over at Camp Peary? I mean back when the Navy operated it during the Second World War?"

"Valuable? Not that I can recall. Except for the old neighborhoods and the CIA's facilities, it's just woods, mostly, and a few ponds. Why?"

Sean looked disappointed. "I was hoping you'd say there was buried treasure there, you know from a ship sinking or something."

Freeman cracked a smile. "Well, now there is a legend about that, but trust me, it's a load of bull."

Horatio said, "Tell us about it, South."

"Why? You sure as hell can't get to it if it's at Camp Peary."

"Humor us," Sean said.

Freeman leaned back in his chair and settled down to tell his tale. "Well, this takes us back, way back, into colonial times, in fact."

"Can you just get to the point?" Michelle snapped impatiently.

He jerked up straight. "Hey, lady, I don't *have* to tell you a damn thing!"

Sean held up a calming hand. "Just take your time, South." He sat down in a chair across from Freeman and glared at Michelle, who reluctantly perched on the edge of the desk and gazed stonily at the journalist.

Freeman looked appeased, sat back and began

455

again. "You remember me telling you about that Lord Dunmore character?"

"The last royal governor of Virginia, yes," Sean said.

"Well, local legend has it the British sent over tons of gold to help finance the war. They were going to use it to pay for spies, for the German mercenaries fighting for the Brits and also to get the population on their side. And Dunmore was supposed to get the Indians riled up against the Americans so they'd have to fight them at the same time they had their hands full with the redcoats. A lot of people don't realize it but back then most citizens kept flip-flopping on which side they wanted to win. Mostly, it was based on who'd won the last big battle and which army was in their backyard. So the gold Dunmore supposedly had could've caused a lot of damage."

"But Dunmore was in Williamsburg," Sean pointed out.

"But he got run out by the colonials," Freeman countered. "And he had to hightail it to his hunting lodge, Porto Bello, the same lodge that's on the National Register. It's located pretty much smack in the middle of Camp Peary." He stood and pointed to a map. "Right about there." He resumed his seat.

"If the gold ended up in Porto Bello what could've happened to it?" Sean asked as he started pacing.

"Who knows? But it didn't end up there, because it never existed."

"You're certain of that?" Sean said from across the room.

"Let's be realistic here. If that treasure was at Camp Peary somebody would've found it, and they would've told somebody. You can't keep something like that quiet."

"What if no one has found it yet?" Sean replied.

"I doubt Dunmore was smart enough to hide a mountain of gold so well that nobody could find it."

Michelle said, "Camp Peary is thousands of acres. There are probably some parts of it that to this day neither the Navy nor the CIA has even explored."

Freeman looked extremely doubtful about that. "Yeah, well even if it is there there ain't nobody gonna be able to get to it now. So unless the spooks find it, it's not gonna get found. Right?" He looked over at Sean, who was staring at something on the wall. "Am I right?" Freeman said again in a louder voice.

Sean's gaze was fixed on a piece of paper tacked to the wall.

Michelle looked concerned. "Sean, what is it?"

Sean spun around. "South, this list of places in Virginia that no longer exist, the one you showed us before, is it accurate? You're sure?"

Freeman rose and walked over to him. "Sure I'm sure. That list came right from the folks in Richmond. It's the official list."

"Damn, that's it!" Sean exclaimed.

"What's it?" Horatio cried out.

In answer Sean stabbed his finger at one name on the list. "There was a county in Virginia named *Dunmore*."

"Yep," Freeman said gleefully. "Only after they run the rascal out, they put an end to that. Now it's called *Shenandoah* County. Real pretty area."

Sean rushed out, the others following him. It wasn't the damn musical notes, or the lyrics. It was the *name* of the song. *Shenandoah*. That was the key.

Freeman ran to the door and called after them. "What's so important about Shenandoah County?" He fell silent and then yelled, "Don't you forget our deal. I want a damn Pulitzer! You hear me!"

78

The next night the boat crept along the river at under five knots, just enough to maintain steerage. Its running lights were on and a solitary figure stood at the wheel. Horatio Barnes zipped up his windbreaker as a wind from an approaching low pressure front chilled the air. A light chop, pushed by the wind, jostled the slow-moving Formula. Horatio had boated around the Chesapeake Bay for decades, so the York, even at night, wasn't much of a challenge for the man.

As he sipped coffee from a Styrofoam cup Horatio knew he had the easy job tonight, just moseying down the river. But human and electronic eyes were, without doubt, watching him and his vessel. But these were public waters and so long as he didn't stray too close to the opposite shore the CIA was powerless to stop him.

Then Horatio recalled that someone had taken a shot at Sean when the man was on *private* land. He immediately plopped down in his captain's chair and hunched forward. No reason to give the bastards too big a target. Then his thoughts turned to the fates of two people he'd grown to care about very much. "Be safe," he said in the face of the cold, raw wind. Then he looked to the sky. "And if we get caught, God, can you make it a minimum security prison?"

On the shore opposite Camp Peary, Sean and Michelle were in their wet suits and checking their gear.

Sean took a deep breath. "No mistakes, Michelle. One wrong move over there, we're dead."

She didn't answer him.

He glanced at her. "Michelle, you ready?"

Every time in her life that Michelle had heard that question the answer had been an immediate "Yes!" Now, she hesitated. The images suddenly flowing through her head were powerful ones. And they all pointed to potential disaster, to her freezing at some crucial time or suffering an overwhelming suicidal impulse that would result in her death. But far more terrifying was the mental picture of Sean King lying dead because of something she had done or failed to do.

"Michelle?" he touched her on the arm and she jumped. "Hey, are you okay?"

She couldn't meet his eye as she began to shake.

"Michelle, what is it?"

"Sean," she gasped. "I . . . I can't do it." He tightened his grip on her arm. "I am so sorry, but I just can't go with you. I know you must think I'm the biggest coward in the world. But it's not that. It's not. It's just . . ." She couldn't even finish the sentence.

"Stop that," he said, firmly. "Stop that. You're the bravest person I know. And it's my fault. Because I never had the right to allow you to do this in the first place. Never!"

She grabbed his shoulder. "Sean, you can't go, not by yourself. You can't. They'll . . . they'll kill you."

Sean sat back on his haunches and fiddled with his mask, not meeting her gaze.

"I have to go, Michelle. For a lot of reasons."

"But it's too dangerous."

"So are most things in life worth dying for." He glanced across the river. "Something bad is going on over there. And I need to find out what it is. And I need to stop it."

"Sean, please," she said, holding tight to him.

He slipped on his mask and readied his other gear. "If I'm not back by morning, get ahold of Hayes and tell him what happened." He gently removed her hands. "It'll be okay, Michelle. I'll see you in a while."

He slid into the river and was gone. Michelle sat there on the red-clay shore staring at the ripples of water until the surface grew calm. She had never felt more alone. And she had never felt more ashamed. Michelle slowly lay back on the wet earth, stared at the overcast sky and felt the tears trickle down her face.

In the clouds Michelle saw things, terrifying things from years ago. They took the shape of creatures dredged up from nightmares she'd had for years and could never understand or hope to explain. In those shapes she saw a little girl, scared beyond belief, reaching out to someone for help, but getting nothing in return. She had been a loner all her life, mostly because she could not bring herself to trust anyone, not completely. And yet there had been one person who had earned her respect, her absolute trust above all others. Who had proved to Michelle that he would never let her down, who had literally sacrificed everything he had to help her. And she had just allowed that man to slip into the waters of the York alone. To go off on what amounted to a suicide mission. Alone.

She could not let that happen. Screw whatever was going on inside her head. Sean was not going to face this without her. If they went down, they'd go down together.

The images in the clouds suddenly dissipated, returning to a grayish white of harmless puff. Michelle grabbed her gear and slipped into the water.

79

A few feet below the surface of the York, Sean moved through the water easily with the aid of a diver's propulsion unit while his flippers made efficient strokes. His oxygen came from a miniature air tank wrapped around the lower part of his face. He also carried a waterproof bag tied to his ankle. The assault tonight on Camp Peary had come together in a whirlwind of seat-of-their-pants improvisation. There were a million ways it could all go wrong, and very few ways for it to turn out all right.

The revelation about the title of the song "Shenandoah" had told Sean that he was on the right track. Shenandoah County used to be Dunmore County. It had been a subtle clue but once uncovered it pointed in one direction only: Dunmore's hunting lodge on the grounds of Camp Peary, Porto Bello. That must have been where Monk Turing had gone. The only way he would find out why was to follow the man's path. A path that had led to his death.

He reached shore, some distance down from where Monk Turing had made his own egress, even as Horatio's late night boat ride hopefully drew the attention of Camp Peary's perimeter security far away. However feeble, Sean was also counting on the notion that the Camp Peary folks probably wouldn't believe someone else would be so *stupid* as to try and breach their security so soon after Turing had been killed.

A flashlight was out of the question, so he pulled NV goggles from his bag, slid them on and fired them up. His line of vision instantly turned to an amorphous green, but at least he could see in the absence of virtually any ambient light.

Sean slid forward on his belly after hiding his propulsion unit under some shore brush. The fence, the point of no return, was dead ahead. Sean pulled out a small device that did one thing and one thing only: It registered the presence of energy of any kind. He aimed it at the fence and waited for a green light to appear. It did. The fence was not electrified, nor was it covered by monitoring sensors.

Sean had learned that the outer perimeter of Camp Peary was so immense that the CIA had not wasted time or budget dollars putting in elaborate security there. The inner defenses that covered every square inch of the facilities, operations and training areas were another story. It was state-of-the-art in its lethality. Which was why Sean was counting on Heinrich Fuchs, who'd apparently been the only person ever to escape from what Sean assumed was a very secure federal military stockade in its own right.

However, right this instant it seemed ludicrous in the extreme to bet his freedom and more likely his life on something that had happened over sixty years ago. And suddenly an overwhelming sense of panic hit him as he lay in the wet red clay of the York's shoreline preparing to break into one of the most heavily guarded facilities in the United States. Right now Sean wanted nothing more than to turn around, slip back into the inviting waters of the river and go home. Yet he couldn't move. He was paralyzed.

He nearly screamed out when he felt it. On his shoulder. Next he heard the familiar voice whispering in his ear in a calm, reassuring voice.

"It's okay, Sean. *We* can do this," Michelle said.

He turned to find her kneeling over him, a look on her face that told him everything he needed to know. He squeezed her arm in return and nodded. What a fool he'd been to even consider for a second that she was not up to this. Hell, she was more up to it than *he* was. His panic and paralysis gone, Sean drew a deep breath and then moved forward quickly with Michelle right behind. They were now directly in front of the fence. While Michelle kept watch Sean cut out a small section of the chain link. They slipped through this opening with their gear, Sean leaned the cut section of fence back into place and they plunged into the forest.

A minute later they knelt down and Sean pulled out the document that Heinrich Fuchs had given Monk Turing. The paper was now full of new writing and calculations that Sean and Michelle had worked out. They had to chance a light as they peered at the map.

Fuchs had left no helpful marks on trees or an X on the ground to mark the entrance to his tunnel, not that those would have survived over the years anyway. Yet they didn't have to rely on that because of Monk Turing. On the Fuchs document Monk had carefully noted directions, landmarks, compass points and, through his daughter, left one important clue as to their target. He also knew that Monk Turing had not braved death to cavalierly retrace the escape route of a German POW. Turing must've had another reason, a good one.

Following Turing's directions they headed north-west and reached a small clearing completely sur-rounded by birch trees. This was it. Sean started marking off paces but Michelle stopped him.

"How tall was Turing?" she asked.

"Five-seven."

"You're seven inches taller," she whispered. "Let me walk the paces." She did, using shorter strides than she ordinarily would. Monk Turing must have had the most meticulous mind, Sean thought, because when Michelle stopped walking around trees, and through bushes and other forest clutter, he knew they'd found it. They were in a part of the woods that seemingly had had no human intervention for decades if not centuries; and yet if you knew what Sean knew, it had.

He knelt down and traced the letter with his hand. It had been done with a long vine of kudzu pulled from one of the trees and laid on the ground.

X didn't mark the spot; the letter V did. V, Sean knew, for Viggie because Monk had written that on the document as well. The two of them dug their hands under what appeared to be the normal ground cover of deep forest. Yet their fingers finally found the edge of the weathered board and they pulled. A four-by-four square of wood rose up revealing the entrance to the tunnel.

They lowered themselves through the opening and then let go of the edges, dropping a few feet and landing on the tunnel's dirt floor. Standing on Sean's shoulders, Michelle reached back through the opening and replaced the cover over the entrance.

As she did so, Michelle saw a bit of rope encircling the support board that held up the tunnel's cover.

"Monk must have put a rope here before he got into the tunnel," she said, pointing it out to Sean. "He'd have to use it to climb back out. The hatch is too far off the ground."

"I brought some rope too," he said. "On the way out, I'll hoist you up and you can tie the rope up there. Then I'll use it to climb out."

With the hatch replaced, they risked turning on their lights. As they moved forward the tunnel wall sloped downward, forcing the tall people to bend over as they walked. The walls were solid red clay, dry and firm. Every two feet or so there were decaying timbers set into the ceiling and also wedged against the walls.

"Doesn't look like it would pass your basic mine safety inspection," Michelle said a little anxiously. "You think he built this all by himself? I mean that's a lot of work for one guy."

"I think other prisoners helped him, but he was the only one to actually use it."

"Why?"

"I think the other prisoners were released after the war in Europe ended, maybe about the time the tunnel was finished. But Fuchs wasn't."

"Why not?"

"Like Horatio I did a little history reading. If Heinrich Fuchs was a signal operator on his ship he would've had to be familiar with the Enigma code. Back then the Allies didn't release any prisoner with knowledge of that code. They kept them to exploit that information and also to keep them from returning to Germany."

"But Germany was beaten."

"Right, but there were still pockets of die-hard Nazis and German high command officers spread all over the world. The last thing the Allies wanted to do was give them back code operators who could help the Nazis develop another communications network."

"Which goes to show an appreciation of history can be very helpful in day-to-day living."

"I've always thought so. Okay, let's do it."

80

The Boeing 767 had the strengthened engines and other enhanced capabilities required for long hauls over the ocean. The wide-body jet banked left and reached the continental United States, passing over Norfolk, Virginia, and continuing the descent to its final destination. The 767 didn't belong to any domestic or foreign commercial airline. It was not owned by any business or individual, nor was it operated by the United States military. Normally a jet without one of those ties, when passing into U.S. airspace above one of the most important military installations America possessed, would have prompted the scrambling of fighter jets from Norfolk and an uncomfortable intercept in the air. However, no sirens sounded and no Navy pilots raced for their planes because the jet had clearance from the highest command levels to fly to any point in the United States it wished. The 767 continued on, just as it had every Saturday at this time for at least the last two years. In less than thirty minutes the pilots would engage the landing gears after setting the wing flaps for the final descent onto a runway fully paid for by the

American taxpayer, a long strip of concrete virtually no U.S. citizen would ever be allowed to set foot on.

Sean and Michelle reached the end of the tunnel and listened for any sound on the other side of the wall they were looking at barely six inches above their heads. They had just passed under some of the most intricate security defenses America had to offer. If they'd been above ground, the security detail would have already killed or captured them.

Placing their hands against the ceiling, they applied steady pressure, their bodies tensed to run if any noise signaled the presence of others. The silence remained, the ceiling was shifted aside and they clambered up into a room, and shone their lights around. The walls here were brick, the air damp and foul-smelling.

"It's like we stepped back in time," Michelle said in a hushed voice as she gazed around at ancient brick, rotting timbers and a partially dirt floor.

"Welcome to Porto Bello," Sean said. "The Navy must've used this place to hold Fuchs and the other POWs. And the Germans managed to dig a tunnel out right under the Navy's nose."

In one corner some of the brick had come off the foundation wall and lay in a pile.

"Not very reassuring," Michelle said, staring at the fallen brick. "This whole place might tumble down on our heads any second."

Sean picked up one of the bricks. "It's been standing for over two hundred years. It should be good for another hour."

Sean shone his light on the floor. The dirt had been disturbed. "Monk Turing, at least I hope so," he said.

"So where's the gold?" Michelle asked.

"We haven't searched the place yet," Sean reminded her.

"I'm more interested in finding Viggie than a treasure."

He checked his watch. "We have to hurry. The plane will be landing soon."

After poking around the cellar they made their way upstairs. The main floor was vacant of even a stick of furniture. And yet here and there they saw touches of faded elegance in the woodwork, the fireplace surround, ornately carved mantel and the crest of the British crown crafted into the wall over the front door. The centuries had diminished the impact of it all. Yet it still made them look around in a certain wonder as their feet trod boards that had been in place when Washington, Jefferson and Adams were fighting for American independence.

Clearly the dilapidated place was not being used by the CIA. As soon as they peered out one of the front cracked leaded windows they saw why. There wasn't much here. The only thing nearby was a small tributary.

Sean pointed to it. "The inlet from the York," he

said. Heinrich Fuchs and his fellow prisoners had obviously followed the inlet's contours when digging their tunnel, figuring, rightly as it turned out, that it would lead the way to the York and freedom.

For Sean and Michelle's plan the inlet was also critical because it ran close to the end of the runway.

They searched the house to make sure Viggie wasn't there. They didn't find any treasure either. After that they slipped out of the old lodge and headed toward the water. Michelle looked back at the dark house. It sat on a smooth patch of land with two massive trees out front. It had a flat roof with shingles covering the top third of the structure where a row of peaked windows was situated. A single chimney stack rose from near the center of the lodge. The house was all brick save for a small wooden front porch that was leaning at a precarious angle.

She said, "I saw this place from the air when I was with Champ."

Sean nooded. "I'm sure that's why Monk flew with Champ. He wanted to see if Porto Bello was occupied and what else was around it."

A minute later they had slipped into the inlet and were heading east, neatly reversing the path they'd taken in the tunnel. So far they hadn't seen any sign of another human being. Yet each knew this could change instantly, and the next human they did see would very likely carry a gun along with a strong desire to kill them.

81

The jet, lights out, swooped past the tree line on the outskirts of Babbage Town, passed over the York, cleared the security fence and kissed the reinforced surface of the ten-thousand-foot-long runway. It came to a complete stop well short of that length as its reverse thrusters and wheel brakes did their job.

The plane taxied to the end of the runway and the pilots turned the plane around in the wide stretch of concrete. A bus, Hummer and cargo truck were already waiting there. The engines were killed and the plane's aft door opened, portable stairs were brought up and people started walking off. The cargo door at the rear of the plane was opened and the truck backed up to it.

Sean and Michelle crawled forward on their bellies right up to a chain link fence surrounding the runway area. Their NV goggles easily picked up all the activity. Sean was also recording it using a special surveillance video camera that would deliver startling crisp footage regardless of the absence of light

Michelle flinched when the first man dressed in a

business suit and wearing a traditional Arab kaffiya on his head emerged from the plane. He was followed by a dozen more, all wearing similar garb.

Michelle pointed toward the back of the plane. Sean started as he saw the cargo being taken off. Along with luggage were piles of black plastic bales.

He looked at Michelle in alarm and whispered, "Oh shit. Is that what I think it is?"

As they continued to watch, a Range Rover pulled up next to the small passenger bus and a person got out.

As soon as Sean saw who it was, he froze.

Valerie Messaline was dressed in a beige pantsuit. She walked up to the Arabs and started speaking to them. Sean could make out around her neck what looked to be a white security badge. She was CIA. And a world-class actress; she'd made him believe every word of her sad story.

Michelle saw how stunned he was and said softly, "Valerie?"

He nodded dumbly.

Valerie continued to speak with the same Arab for a few minutes while the other men were led onto the bus with their luggage. Occasionally Valerie and the Arab would glance at the cargo being unloaded from the rear of the plane. Once Valerie strolled over with the Arab to one of the bales, touched it and laughed at something the man said.

A minute later Valerie climbed back in the Range

Rover with the Arab and they followed the passenger bus out, probably toward the nearby complex shown on the satellite map.

With the cargo unloaded all the men except two climbed in the Hummer and drove off. The remaining men jumped in the cargo truck and it pulled away. While the Hummer followed the path taken by the passenger bus with the Arabs, the truck drove off in the opposite direction and directly toward where Sean and Michelle were lying in hiding near the chain link gate.

"Get back," he whispered urgently.

They fell back, pressing themselves flat against the ground.

The truck stopped at the gate and one of the men got out, unlocked it and the truck pulled through with the man following. He locked the gate and started to climb back in the truck.

Michelle slipped off her backpack and turned to Sean. "Get back to Babbage Town, get ahold of Merkle Hayes and show him the videotape. Then wait to hear from me."

He stared at her. "Wait to hear from you? Where are you going?"

"The video's not enough," she said. "We need to make sure what that cargo is."

Before he could say anything or even reach out to grab her arm she exploded forward, approaching the truck from behind, threw herself under it, clamped her arms and legs around the metal of the truck's underbelly and held on as it rolled off.

Sean was so stunned he couldn't even move. He couldn't believe what she had just done.

As his partner disappeared into the night underneath a truck, Sean lay all alone smack in the middle of the CIA's most top secret facility and seriously wondered if he was having a heart attack. He finally seized an element of calm, from where he didn't know. He put Michelle's backpack in his, and started to slide on his belly back toward the ancient Porto Bello. By water it was less than five hundred yards away. It might as well have been five hundred miles.

Sean wasn't the only one wondering why Michelle had impulsively done what she had. The woman herself was having second thoughts and more than once she came close to letting go, dropping to the ground, watching the truck pass over her and sprinting back to Sean. Yet something made her hold on.

Noises other than the truck's rumblings reached her. They must be getting close to the main gate, she thought, as the truck slowed and then stopped completely. She panicked for a moment. Would they search the truck before it left Camp Peary? Then she realized no one was going to even lay as much as an eyeball on this vehicle. She was right; the squeak of motorized security gates reached her ears and the truck started up again as they left the Camp Peary grounds.

They turned out onto a street and the truck sped up. Michelle's arms and legs were growing tired, yet she had no choice but to hang on. Letting go now at this speed probably meant at the very least a cracked skull. A minute later she could see the wheels of other cars passing them.

After traveling for a while the truck pulled off the road and turned onto a gravel drive. The gravel soon gave way to asphalt and five minutes later the truck stopped. The doors opened and Michelle saw two sets of legs climb down from the truck's cab and walk off. When she no longer heard footsteps, she let go, dropped silently to the ground and rolled out on the opposite side from where the men had departed.

She glanced around. The area seemed familiar for some reason, though it was very dark and most of what she was seeing was indistinct.

Michelle heard them coming back and, using the truck as cover, ran behind a small building she'd just spotted. She turned the corner, stopped, and then risked taking a look. As she peered around the edge of the building, the breath caught in her throat. Now, Michelle knew exactly where she was.

82

Sean reached the grounds in front of Porto Bello without being seen. He crept up the rotted front steps and had no time to react as the board broke under him. Sean felt himself plummeting down; his leg hit something sharp and he involuntarily yelled in pain. He froze as his scream seemed to float up into the air and then, like a summer downpour, cascade down all over the damn place.

Was that a siren? Were those running feet? Had he heard the sharp bark of a scent hound? No, they were the products of his terror. He struggled to free himself from the wreckage of the front porch, silently cursing the royal governor for choosing unreliable wood over sturdy brick. He reached down and felt the blood flowing from a deep gash in his calf.

He limped into the house, and hurried down to the cellar. There he tripped over some debris and crashed against the wall, actually knocking a brick loose in the collision. Cursing, he rose up on his knees and rubbed at his scraped-up hands. Eye-level with the foundation wall he stared at the small gap the fallen brick had left. He flicked his light in the gap and something caught his eye. The foundation wall, he could see, was very thick with something behind it . . .

"Damn!"

Sean grabbed a broken piece of wood and jammed it in the opening, levering it around harder and harder until the mortar broke loose. He reached in and worked the object free, scraping up his hands as he did so.

A solid gold coin. He dug some more and what came out was a small, hard stone. He brushed the dirt off and shone his light on it. The stone was revealed as a gleaming emerald. Digging some more he saw what looked very much like a solid gold bar and then some more gold coins. It was Lord Dunmore's treasure and it was more than just gold. He'd found it, and by the looks of the disturbed site, so had Monk Turing.

This is what Heinrich Fuchs had told Monk about in return for the American's help in getting Fuchs back to Germany. Sean realized that it might be more than a king's ransom hidden here. South Freeman had been wrong. Dunmore *had* been smart enough to keep the treasure undiscovered all these years by using a false foundation wall. Until an enterprising German POW trying to dig his way to freedom came along.

As Sean looked at his hands, another mystery was cleared up. And it also had to do with Monk Turing.

He smiled in triumph, a feeling that was cut short by a sound.

Feet running. Feet running toward the house. Not his imagination this time; it was the real thing.

He grabbed a couple of bricks and jammed them in the gap in the wall to cover the treasure, slipped the gold coin and emerald inside his bag, raced to the part of the floor over the tunnel and removed it. He piled some of the bricks on top of the wooden cover, slid it partially over the hole, dropped through, reached back up and pulled the heavy cover closed over the tunnel entrance.

Then he started to run, bad leg and all.

When Sean reached the other end of the tunnel he realized he was totally screwed. He stared up at the exit to the tunnel that was three feet above his head. Even if he could jump that high on his bad wheel, there was nothing for him to grab on to. Michelle had had to stand on his shoulders to replace the cover. Their exit plan had consisted of Michelle being hoisted up on his shoulders and setting in place a knotted rope for him to use to climb out.

Wait a minute. If he was right, and Heinrich Fuchs had escaped *alone*, how had he done it? He dropped to his knees next to one of the fallen timbers they had passed on the way in. He managed to push the timber out of the way and frantically scraped away dirt until a rough-hewn ladder was revealed. It must have lain there undisturbed since Fuchs had made his escape all those years ago, until a fallen support timber had covered it along with decades of dirt.

He hoisted the ladder up and set it against the top of the tunnel entrance. Like Monk Turing, Heinrich Fuchs had also been a very precise man. It fit perfectly into a ledge of wood just below the tunnel's cover. He slung his bag over his back, gripped the ladder and clambered up as fast as he could. He pushed aside the cover, climbed up and then pulled the ladder up with him. Then he stopped. If Michelle hadn't gotten out of Camp Peary by truck she might need the ladder to escape through the tunnel. The next moment this thought was dashed from Sean's mind as the sounds reached him. There were other people in the tunnel now. Michelle wouldn't be getting out this way. He threw the ladder into the woods.

Sean put the tunnel cover back in place, turned and started counting off paces back to the clearing as a light rain started falling. Very troubling noises were coming at him now from all directions. Searchlights slit the black sky like a knife racing across a throat. *Oh shit!* He dropped to the ground, his hand fumbling in his bag.

A few seconds later the man almost stepped on him. Sean saw the MP5, the black-painted face, the eyes starting to swivel in his direction. He fired and the man stiffened and then dropped to the ground. Sean put the stun gun back in his bag, took the man's gun belt and checked it. A pistol, cuffs, baton and something that Sean could actually use: two grenades. He put the gun belt in his bag but, keeping one of the grenades out, crouched in the woods.

He would be heading to the right to get back to his gear. Unfortunately, the sounds he was hearing were coming from that direction. Sean hefted one of the grenades, pulled the pin and threw it as far as he could to the left. He hit the ground, covered his ears. Five seconds later all of Camp Peary came alive as the explosion rocked the night.

Sean could hear yells and feet running. And still he waited. Ten seconds, twenty seconds. A minute. Then he jumped up and ran flat-out.

Two minutes later he was through the fence and had located the propulsion units. He left Michelle's just in case she made it back this far.

Sean could hear a boat, its engines racing, coming from the south. He didn't wait to see what it was. He inserted the nozzle from the oxygen tank in his mouth and dove under the water. He went down far enough to avoid the boat's prop, engaged his propulsion unit and made a beeline straight across the York, emerging on the other side about two hundred yards down from the boathouse. It had been an exhausting trip back but he had no time to rest. He plunged into the woods, grabbed a bag they had earlier hidden there, stripped off his wet suit and changed into street clothes. He stashed most of his things in the bag and hid it back under a bush. His video camera had a copy function and he took a few moments to copy the video he'd taken onto another digital stick. Then Sean raced through the woods to Babbage Town. Somehow, he didn't know how, he had to find Michelle before it was too late.

83

The small plane was loaded with the cargo from the truck. There was plenty of room with the seats removed. Champ Pollion climbed in the cockpit and readied the Cessna for takeoff. Even with the rain starting to fall more heavily and the winds picking up he figured he'd have no problem meeting his schedule. The men finished loading the cargo on the plane, but, out of Champ's sight, kept several large plastic bales on the truck. They drove off and quickly disappeared into the darkness.

Champ nimbly went through his preflight checklist and next hit a switch; the prop roared to life. Champ had just put on his headset when the door was thrown open and Michelle poked her head in.

"Hey, Champ, got room for one more?"

He looked at her for several seconds, as though she couldn't possibly be real. A moment later his hand flew to the sidearm on his belt, only Michelle's fist was faster. The blow knocked Champ sideways in his seat, blood spurting from his nose.

He rolled over into the co-pilot's seat and then out

the other door. Michelle jumped across the seat after him.

Champ fell out onto the ground and Michelle was right on top of him. As he tried to get up she hit him with a brutal kick that caught the man on the side of his head and dropped him again. His leg shot out and tripped her. She went tumbling back against the plane. The Cessna was vibrating, its engine chafing against the plane's restraints.

Champ managed to pull his gun, but Michelle's well-aimed kick sent it flying out of his hand. A second later he landed a fist to her side and Michelle's ribs screamed in agony. The next second, a foot followed the fist and Michelle realized she was in for a real fight as she fell to the ground but just as quickly regained her feet.

The two faced off against the backdrop of the whirring plane.

"What the hell are you doing here?" Champ screamed.

"Making a citizen's arrest," Michelle yelled back as her gaze darted over him, looking for any opening.

"You have no idea what you're doing."

"Me! Since when does a respected physicist turn into a drug runner for the CIA? That's what's in the bales, right? Drugs?"

"Michelle, you don't understand what's going on here."

"So explain it to me."

"I can't, and I don't want to hurt you."

"Hurt me! What about Monk Turing? Len Rivest?"

"I'm just trying to do my job. You have to believe that."

"Sorry, Champ, I'm fresh out of trust." While they'd been speaking she'd been inching toward him. Now, Michelle whirled and connected a kick to his head sending the man flying backward. Yet before she could strike again, he'd recovered and slammed a foot into her shoulder, sending her back on her ass. She leapt up and avoided another blow, managing to duck under his swing, and delivered a hard shot to his kidney. Amazingly, it didn't drop him. He staggered back, breathing hard, but with his defenses still intact.

"You're good," she called out over the plane's engine.

"Maybe not as good as you," he admitted. He looked over his shoulder. "Michelle, you need to get out of here."

"Why, so you can fly off with the drugs?"

"I'm doing nothing criminal. You have to trust me."

"I told you, I'm fresh out." She leaped and her foot connected with his chest. He fell back and unfortunately landed next to his gun. He grabbed the pistol, took point blank aim and—

Michelle dove back into the cockpit and slammed the door shut as a round from Champ's pistol exploded through the glass. Michelle frantically scanned the controls. She'd watched Champ go through his flight checklist when they'd gone up. Now that attention to detail paid off. She released the foot brake, pushed the throttle ahead and the Cessna shot forward.

Another bullet came winging through the cockpit and this time Michelle could not get out of the way. She grunted in pain as the slug bit hotly into her arm leaving a bloody crease before exiting out the opposite window. She rammed the throttle ahead and the Cessna picked up speed, zipping down the concrete toward the main runway. Champ sprinted after her, his gun waving in his hand. He sent another shot at the plane's tail but missed.

"Stop," he screamed. "You don't know what you're doing. Stop!"

Michelle had no intention of taking the Cessna off the ground. She throttled forward at the same time she stood on the right foot pedal throwing the small plane into a one-eighty. Champ stopped dead as the plane turned directly at him. He raised his gun to fire but instead turned and ran. As fleet as he was Michelle had to throttle back to keep from running over him. As the plane bore down on him he screamed and threw himself sideways, rolled down an embankment and crashed into a set of gasoline drums.

Michelle cut the throttle, engaged the brake, jumped out and raced down the embankment. She didn't wait for Champ to attempt to get up. She launched herself from halfway up the rise and landed on top of him, her elbow slamming into the back of his head. Champ let out one groan and then his eyes closed and his body went limp.

"You're not dying on me, Champ," she said furiously as she rolled him over and checked his pulse. "Prison is calling, you stupid genius freak." His breathing was steady and his pulse strong and he would no doubt wake soon with a monster headache and an overpowering desire to call his lawyer. She looked around, spotted some cable hanging on the exterior wall of a storage shed, and used that to tie him up.

She searched his pockets, found his cell phone and car keys and ran back to the plane. Throwing the door open she climbed in, cut the engine, jabbed one of the keys into the bale nearest her and checked it. Heroin, she was almost certain. She stuffed some of it in a bag she pulled from a storage compartment in the plane. As she was turning to leave, a sound caught her ears from the back of the plane, behind the bales. Then she saw one of the packages move a bit.

She began heaving the bales out of the way. At the very rear of the cabin something was wrapped in a blanket. And that something was squirming.

Michelle pulled at the blanket and it finally fell away, revealing a tied-up and gagged Viggie.

Michelle quickly freed her and they raced off the plane.

"Mick—" Viggie began.

"Tell me later. Now, just run."

They reached Champ's Mercedes and climbed in. Michelle called Merkle Hayes at home, woke the man up and gave him a rundown of what had happened. "Get to Babbage Town with everybody you can," she screamed into the phone.

"Holy shit," was all the lawman could manage to say.

Michelle fired up the car and gunned the motor. With a wide-eyed Viggie hanging on to whatever she could, Michelle laid rubber down the entire length of the small parking lot before hitting the road, hanging a left and accelerating, leaving behind an unconscious genius ripe for a long prison sentence and a Cessna full of heroin courtesy of the CIA. She hit a hundred on the straightaway and kept her foot mashed to the floor.

84

Sean crouched down behind a low hedge. What he was seeing destroyed what little hope he had of surviving tonight. Men in black body armor with MP5s—clearly government guns from across the river—were talking with two of the security guards left at Babbage Town.

This group spread out and started heading Sean's way. He immediately skirted the tree line and plunged into the woods where he hoped he would be far to the right of the group. He emerged a few minutes later into a clearing directly behind the late Len Rivest's cottage. On the other side of the road from Rivest's cottage was the back of Hut Number Three. He crept from tree to tree, keeping low. He could hear shouts and the sounds of running feet as he made his way slowly along.

Using a rock, he broke the lock on the back of the door to the laundry and crept in. The smell of detergent and bleach hit him as he looked around at the large commercial machines. It didn't take him long to spot what he wanted. He grabbed the clothes and slipped back out.

Looking up ahead, he saw his destination: Alicia Chadwick's cottage. It was dark inside. He made it to the back door unseen and jiggled the handle. It was unlocked. He moved inside, stopped and listened. All seemed clear. He suddenly ducked down as shadows raced down the street.

He went up the stairs, found his bedroom door and slipped in. He wanted to get to his cell phone, which he'd stupidly left behind when they'd fled from Babbage Town. Yet he almost instantly realized that his room had been searched and everything taken. He left and moved to Alicia's door, opened it and crept in with the intent of trying to find a phone in her room.

A blow struck him in the shoulder.

"Get away from me. Get away!" a voice yelled out.

He caught her hand before she could hit him again. "Alicia, it's me. It's Sean."

She had been behind the door and had lashed out at him with, of all things, her prosthetic.

"Sean!" she said in amazement.

He held her tightly, trying to keep her upright on the one leg.

"What are you doing here? I thought you left," he said.

"I thought you did too. I came back here in case Viggie showed up. Then I heard someone sneaking around in the house."

"Alicia, we need to get out of here."

"Why, what's happened?"

"I can't take the time to explain right now, but it involves the CIA, possibly drugs and murder. The spooks are all over the place, but I have a plan."

She quickly strapped on her leg.

"Where's Michelle?" she asked.

"I wish I knew. She followed the drugs. I . . . I hope she's okay. Do you have a cell phone? I need to call the police."

"I left it in my car."

"Do you have a hard line phone here?"

"No, just the cell."

"Damn it!" He looked around. "Okay, here's what we're going to do. You're going to go to your car. I'm assuming it's parked in the front?"

"Yes."

He pulled out the clothes he'd taken from the laundry facility. They were a guard's uniform. He quickly changed into them. When she saw the wound on his leg Alicia cried out, "Oh my God, Sean, you're hurt."

"Forget it. I'll be in a lot worse shape if we don't get out of here. Now if anyone stops you, you just tell them you're scared, and you're leaving. I'll be shadowing you."

"You're wearing that uniform. Why can't you just pretend you're my escort?"

"The guards will recognize me if they get a look at

my face. But from a distance they and the CIA guys will just see a uniform. I'll join you in the front and we can get to the cops."

She looked panicked. "Sean, what if they won't let me leave? They might think I know something."

"Alicia, just act frightened."

She managed a weak smile. "That won't be hard because I'm terrified." Tears slid down her cheeks. "Do you think these men are the ones who took Viggie?"

He didn't answer right away. "Yes, they're the ones."

He looked around the room and handed her a heavy paperweight lying on her nightstand. "It's not much of a weapon, but it's the best I can do right now."

There were more noises from outside. He said, "Alicia, just take the main road past Hut Number Three and the pool and then out to the front court-yard." He gripped her shoulders. "You can do this. You can!"

She finally nodded, drew a deep, calming breath and followed him downstairs.

A minute later everything was going fine. Two guards passed by, but didn't stop her. She had just reached the pool when disaster struck. A team of armored men came rushing toward her. The lead man had his hand up for her to stop.

"Shit!" Sean muttered from his hiding place. He

looked around for anything he could use to get them out of this jam. And then he saw it. He reached in his bag and pulled out the grenade he'd taken from the guard at Camp Peary, slipped out the pin and tossed it over the fence surrounding Hut Number Two. It clanged against the metal silo and dropped to the ground. Sean had already raced away and climbed into the low branches of a tree.

Five seconds later, the explosion ripped a large hole in the base of the silo and tons of water came pouring out. It swept in all directions like a river flooding its banks. Sean heard screams and looked out from his perch in time to see Alicia and the men in armor get hit with the rushing water, knocking them off their feet.

Alicia was carried alongside the deck and into some chairs at the other end of the pool. The three armored men were knocked unconscious when they collided with the stone fireplace.

As soon as the silo emptied out Sean sloughed through the knee-high but rapidly receding water toward Alicia. "Sorry about the tsunami," he called out. "It was the only thing I could think of." As he drew closer he realized something was wrong.

Alicia was clutching at her prosthetic, writhing in pain.

He ran forward and knelt down next to her. "Alicia, what is it?"

She moaned, "When the water hit me. It feels like

a piece of steel is wedged in the top of my thigh. I can't walk."

"Oh damn!" Sean examined the leg. The next thing, he was tumbling headfirst into the pool water. His skull felt like it had been cracked. He settled down on the bottom of the shallow end and then propelled himself back to the surface. As soon as he did something settled around his neck and was pulled tight. He instinctively grabbed for whatever it was, but it was imbedded so tightly in his neck already that his fingers couldn't reach it. He looked behind him.

Alicia had a garrote around his neck. She was strangling him.

He couldn't breathe; his eyes were bulging out of his head. He tried to throw her off, but she wrapped her good leg around his middle and pulled on the cord with all her might. In a panic, he swung his fists behind him, trying to hit her, but missed. He aimed a punch at the leg wrapped around him, but she kicked him in the back with her other leg knocking the wind out of him. He toppled forward into the water, carrying her on his back. Yet unlike him Alicia was able to draw a deep breath. His brain was about to burst and the damn cord kept tightening. He had to take a breath. He felt himself failing. His body was shutting down.

Help me, Michelle. Help me, I'm dying. But Michelle wasn't here.

And then like a miracle the pressure was gone from around his neck. And then so was the weight of

Alicia. In a second he erupted out of the pool, taking huge breaths and retching in the water.

"Come on!"

His bursting brain could barely understand the words. Yes, it was Michelle; she'd gotten here in time to rescue him. She was safe. Safe!

"Now!" the hand grabbed him roughly.

He looked up into the face. Ian Whitfield stared back at him. Lying unconscious on the concrete pool surround was Alicia.

"We've got to get out of here," the head of Camp Peary urged as he hauled up Sean.

"What the hell are you doing here?" Sean managed to say, coughing up water and rubbing at his torn-up neck.

"No time to talk. Just move. This place is crawling with people."

"Yeah, *your* people, you sonofabitch."

"Not tonight they're not. They're two squads of paramilitary from the camp and they don't report to me. Come on!"

Whitfield fast limped toward the gap between Hut Number Three and the main garage.

Sean hesitated for an instant. He looked down at Alicia. The paperweight she'd slugged him with was lying beside her. She'd tried to kill him. But why? The next second he heard cries coming from behind him. He ran off and joined Whitfield, who was crouched down next to a tree.

"You going to tell me what's going on?" Sean demanded in a weak, scratchy voice.

"Not now," Whitfield snapped. He pulled a pistol from his belt and handed it to Sean while he picked up an MP5 he'd obviously hidden behind the bush earlier. "If you have to use it, make it a head shot. The body armor they're wearing will stop any pistol ammo."

"Where are we trying to get to?"

"I've got a boat tied up about two hundred yards down from the dock."

"Aren't they patrolling the water?"

"Yes, but once we get to the boat I'll hide you under some tarp. When they see it's me, they won't bother us."

"Let's go then."

Whitfield put up a hand. "Not so fast. I've seen the grid search they have in place. As soon as they clear one area we enter it. We'll work our way backward to the river."

"Where's Michelle?"

"No clue."

"She was under the truck when it left Camp Peary."

Whitfield looked stunned for a moment and then his features turned grim. "Shit."

"Was it heroin they brought in on that plane? And the Arabs? Who were they?"

Whitfield brandished his weapon threateningly.

"Look, King, I don't owe you or anyone else an explanation about jackshit. I'm here to save your neck and maybe right a few wrongs. Don't make me reconsider my decision."

85

Michelle ditched the Mercedes before hitting the main road leading to Babbage Town and struck out through the woods to the river with Viggie in tow. On the drive over Viggie had explained how someone had come into her bedroom and pressed something against her face. The next thing she knew she was tied up and in the back of the plane.

Before plunging into the woods Michelle saw a stream of black Suburbans hurtling down the road to Babbage Town; Merkle Hayes's police cruiser was leading the procession. At least the cavalry was here.

Michelle and Viggie skirted the banks of the York, keeping low because there was enough activity on the water to tell Michelle that something had happened.

The pair slipped and slid on the wet embankments of the York, but finally made it within the grounds of Babbage Town. Michelle looked to the sky as a plane soared overhead. It was soon out of sight and she turned her attention back to the enemies she faced on the ground. She had tried Sean's cell phone before remembering he'd left it at Babbage Town. Then she had an inspiration. She called Horatio. He answered on the first ring and she succinctly explained what had happened including the fact that she had Viggie.

To his credit he didn't ask a single question other than, "Where can I pick you up?"

They made it to the river and a few minutes later Horatio pulled up to the shore in the Formula Bowrider.

"I anchored down in a cove near here," he explained. "I was hoping somebody would call me. Where's Sean?"

"I don't kn—" Michelle had glanced over her shoulder back at the woods. "Sean!"

A wave of relief poured over her as Sean King emerged from the trees. An instant later this relief was replaced with terror as she spotted Ian Whitfield and his machine gun. She pointed her gun at his head. "Let him go!"

"It's okay, Michelle," Sean called out. "He's here to help."

"Bullshit," she roared.

"He saved my life."

Whitfield said, "I hear you're a hell of a shot, Maxwell." He stepped forward and tossed her the MP5. "You better be."

Michelle caught the gun in one hand, her pistol still trained on the man, but her look of suspicion had faded. She said to Sean, "What is going on?"

"Babbage Town is crawling with Camp Peary guys armed to the teeth and Alicia tried to kill me."

"I called the cops," Michelle said. "They're at Babbage Town."

Sean glanced over her shoulder. "Viggie?"

The girl shyly waved back at him.

Whitfield looked at Horatio and the Formula boat. "What's this?"

"Friend of ours," Sean replied. "Come on." He started to climb in the boat.

"No!" Whitfield exclaimed. "That boat won't cut it out there. Follow me."

They all made their way along the shore and boarded the RIB that Whitfield had tethered to a piling sticking out of the water. He had the four lie on the deck and put a tarp over them.

Sean popped his head back out and brandished his gun. "FYI, you try to screw us you get one right in the head."

The storm had quickly settled in with force; the river was starting to pitch and heave and the rain shot out of the dark skies. Michelle took a moment to pop out from the under the tarp, grab a life jacket and put it on Viggie.

They had not gone far when another boat approached them. From under the tarp Sean heard Whitfield mutter a curse, which he did not take as an encouraging sign. His hand tightened on his gun.

The other boat was far larger than the RIB Whitfield was piloting and there were ten armed men aboard, and someone else.

Sean flinched when he heard the person's voice: "Where have you been, Ian?" Valerie Messaline said.

"Babbage Town. Looks like someone called the cops."

"And who might have done that?" the woman said coolly.

"Whoever broke into Camp Peary would be my guess," Whitfield replied. "But whoever did it doesn't matter. The cat's out of the bag. You have to pull out. Now."

"I don't think so," she said. "Why don't you take some of the men and head down the river in your boat? Whoever breached us might have tried to get away in that direction."

"No, I think you should take your crew and head to Babbage Town. Looks like our boys will need all the help they can get. I'm going back to Camp Peary and try to do some damage control there."

While he was speaking Valerie had been looking at his vessel. As she glanced up there was a smile of triumph on her features. She said, "Your boat's riding a little low in the water to just have one person on it, Ian."

Whitfield throttled his vessel forward and smashed into the side of the other craft, knocking two of the men overboard and Valerie off her feet.

Whitfield rammed the RIB into reverse, props

spinning half out of the water, and the boat surged backward. He slammed the throttle forward and the craft shot ahead. Shots fired by Valerie's men pinged off the water and put holes in the RIB's hull.

"Could use some help up here," Whitfield called out.

Sean and Michelle threw off the tarp and came up while Horatio stayed low with his arms protectively around Viggie. The larger boat was racing after them. As gunshots zipped past them, Sean and Michelle ducked and then returned fire. Michelle strafed the other vessel's bow with her MP5.

Whitfield cried out, "Conserve your ammo, I've only got two extra mags for the MP and one for each pistol." He tossed Michelle another machine gun clip.

They were doing over a hundred kilometers an hour, the craft bouncing in nauseating leaps across the river as the wind picked up. The swells had quickly boiled to well over a meter in height.

Sean took careful aim and fired four rounds. Only at this distance and firing from what amounted to a trampoline, a pistol was not very effective.

"So can I ask a stupid question," Sean called out to Whitfield.

"You can ask," Whitfield called back.

"Can you tell us why your little woman is trying to kill you and us?"

Whitfield navigated across a particularly difficult wave and barked, "She's not my wife. She's my boss."

Sean gaped at him. "Your boss! What the hell are you talking about? I thought *you* were the head of Camp Peary?"

"You can think what you want," Whitfield snapped.

"And you guys are into drug running?"

Whitfield said nothing.

Sean said, "And what about the Arabs on the plane?"

Whitfield shook his head. "Not going there."

"And did Alicia kill Len Rivest?"

Silence.

Sean snapped, "The woman almost killed me, and would have except for you. Which is the only reason I'm not making a citizen's arrest on your ass."

"And Champ?" Michelle asked. "Does he work for CIA?"

Whitfield said, "Let's just worry about surviving the next ten minutes."

"They're gaining," Michelle cried out as she glanced behind them.

"Their engines are twice the size of mine," Whitfield said over his shoulder as he braced himself. "Now hold on."

"What the hell do you think we've been do—?" Sean couldn't finish because Whitfield somehow managed to cut a ninety-degree turn in the water while going full throttle. Sean would've gone over the side if Michelle hadn't clamped a hand on him as he slid by her. She had her legs scissored around Viggie just in case Horatio couldn't hold her.

"Mick!" Viggie screamed out.

"I've got you, Viggie, you're not going anywhere."

Whitfield put on a burst of speed and the RIB shot toward the opposite shore, heading directly toward the inlet into Camp Peary. They zoomed past a gauntlet of lighted beacons five hundred yards from shore that warned of *extreme* danger for persons trespassing here, and Sean had every reason to believe they meant it. They next roared past two boats stationed at the entrance to the inlet. The men on board leveled weapons at them, including a rocket-propelled grenade launcher, but when they saw who it was, they lowered their ordnance and just stared with bewildered looks. Whitfield actually had the gall to salute them.

Whitfield cut the RIB to the left and then the right, seemingly avoiding invisible obstacles in the water while he kept glancing at a lighted screen on his console.

"They're still gaining," Michelle called out. Then she paled even more. "They're going to fire a rocket," she screamed. The man in the bow of the chase boat was indeed putting them in the crosshairs of his weapon.

Viggie yelled in terror.

Michelle barked, "Horatio, do *not* let her go!"

Whitfield eyed one spot in the water and seemed

to be timing something. What he was timing was a wave. "Hold the hell on," he roared.

Sean and Michelle dropped to the deck and held on to anything they could find, including each other.

86

The RIB hit the wave, rode it straight up and went airborne, its twin props screaming as the water around them disappeared. Then the boat hit the surface of the inlet two feet farther down.

"Look out!" Valerie Messaline screamed from the chase boat. She had obviously realized what Whitfield had just done.

Michelle glanced back in time to see her dive off the boat along with a slew of others. The driver attempted to swerve around the place that Whitfield had managed to jump over, but it was too late. The boat hit the mine and exploded.

Whitfield immediately threw the RIB into a tight turn and shot back out of the inlet, passing Messaline and company as they struggled to get out of their body armor before it dragged them under.

"How the hell did you do that?" Sean asked in a stunned voice.

Whitfield tapped the screen in front of him. "It's easy, when you know where the mines are laid. I had them change the position of one yesterday. I try to be prepared."

The RIB roared back out on the York. None of them saw the missile launch from one of the patrol boats. It missed them but not by much. The RIB almost flipped over from the force of the explosion as the rocket hit the water ten yards away from them before Whitfield managed to get the boat back under control. The rain was coming down slantwise now, stinging their faces as Sean and Michelle slowly stood on trembling legs.

Michelle glanced around. "Viggie! Horatio!"

They looked behind them. In her life jacket Viggie was bobbing in the water already fifty yards away. To the left of her Horatio was sputtering and going under.

Michelle didn't hesitate. She grabbed a preserver, dove off the boat and swam for Horatio. She didn't see Sean dive off the other side of the boat and head to Viggie. Michelle reached Horatio and pushed the life preserver in his hands. "You're okay, Horatio, just don't panic. Can you make it to the boat while I go get Viggie?"

He nodded and Michelle headed off for Viggie. What she saw as she approached where Viggie had been struck her cold. The girl was being hauled into a boat driven by some of the men from Camp Peary. As Michelle strained to see through the rain and darkness, she saw another chilling spectacle. Two men on the boat were taking aim at Sean, who was still desperately trying to reach Viggie

"No!" Michelle screamed, but she had nothing to hurt them with.

An instant later she heard the sound behind her. She swung back around and saw Whitfield's boat coming at her fast. Horatio was already on board so Whitfield must have come back around and picked him up. As the boat drew nearer, Michelle saw Whitfield hand off the wheel to Horatio. Then the Camp Peary chief leaned over the side of the RIB and looped his leg through a bungee strap on the boat's gunwale. He extended his hand. Michelle instantly knew what he was doing. She'd practiced this particular maneuver in a joint training session with the FBI while at the Secret Service. As the boat zoomed alongside her she reached up and grabbed Whitfield's hand. The man placed an iron grip on her arm with his other hand and his strength and the speed of the boat yanked her right out of the water and onto the boat's deck. She didn't even bother thanking him. She rolled to her feet, grabbed a gun and pointed it at the other boat as they drew close.

Michelle knew Viggie was on board so she couldn't fire directly at them, but she did manage to place five shots in such a compact manner that the gunmen ducked down and gave Sean a chance to escape.

"Get close and we'll grab him," Michelle yelled.

"I don't think I can do this," Horatio called out from the helm.

Michelle slid over to the wheel while Whitfield lay across the gunwale again. As the RIB swooped by Sean was whisked into the boat.

"Hit it!" Whitfield screamed.

"What about Viggie!" Michelle screamed back.

"Hit it or we all die!"

Michelle slammed the throttle forward and the RIB shot ahead so fast Horatio and Sean almost fell overboard.

Michelle yelled over the howls of the storm, "We're going to round up an army and then we're going back across that fucking river and we're getting Viggie back."

She ran the RIB up on the shore on the other side of the York. They jumped off the boat and raced toward the entrance to Babbage Town. On the way, Sean stopped and retrieved his bag that he'd hidden behind a bush.

The caravan of Suburbans was parked at the entrance and Michelle led the way single file toward them. As soon as they showed themselves they were surrounded by agents. Merkle Hayes stepped forward. He wasn't wearing a police uniform. He had on a blue windbreaker with the letters "DEA" stenciled on it. Agent Ventris was right next to him.

Sean stared at him. "DEA?"

"It's a long story," Hayes said.

"Have you rounded them up?" Michelle asked.

"Who?" Ventris said angrily. "There's nobody here except a few guards."

"The place was swarming with CIA guys in body armor," Sean said.

"Well, they're not here now."

"We just had a gun battle on the river. They fired a rocket at us. Are you telling me you guys heard none of it?" Michelle asked incredulously.

Hayes said, "A siren's been going off just about the whole time we've been here. We just got the damn thing turned off. So with that and the storm we haven't heard anything."

"Did you at least find the plane at the private strip filled with drugs?" Michelle asked.

Hayes shook his head. "There was no plane and no Champ Pollion when my men got there."

"So—what drugs?" Ventris asked.

In answer Michelle reached in her pocket and pulled out the wet Baggie. "These. There was at least a ton of it on Champ's plane. Heroin."

Hayes took the bag and looked at it. "And where'd it come from?"

Sean pointed across the river. "From over there. At Camp Peary."

At that instant a fireball raced into the sky. It was clearly coming from the other side of the York.

Everyone turned their attention to the sight.

"What the hell is that?" Ventris yelled.

"Oh, shit!" Michelle exclaimed. "That plane I heard going over earlier. I bet that was Champ's plane. He must've escaped and flew it to Camp Peary with the drugs. They just blew it up to get rid of the evidence."

"So you're saying those drugs really came from Camp Peary?" Hayes said while nervously eying Ventris.

"Tell them, Whitfield," Sean said.

Only Whitfield wasn't there.

"Where the hell did he go?" Sean said.

Michelle said, "Sean, I don't think he followed us out of the woods."

"Ian Whitfield was with us. He saved my life."

"It's true," Michelle said and Horatio nodded in agreement.

"Dammit, you have to believe us," Sean said.

"We want to," Hayes said quietly.

"Hold on!" Sean shouted, pulling the video camera out of his backpack. "Look at this." He ran the tape for them, pointing out the plane, the Arabs, Valerie Messaline, and the bales being off-loaded.

Ventris said, "This footage *is* of Camp Peary. How the hell did you get it?"

"We're going to have to have some amnesty on that," Sean said uneasily.

Michelle pushed past Sean so she was directly in front of Ventris. "Listen to me," Michelle snapped. "They have kidnapped Viggie Turing. They took her in one of the boats and they're probably on their way back to Camp Peary."

"You saw this?" Hayes said quickly.

"Yes!" Michelle screamed. She grabbed Ventris's jacket. "Kidnapped. Remember the FBI's specialty? So let's get going."

Hayes said, "We can't just storm into Camp Peary for God's sake. We at least need a warrant."

"Then dammit get one. You're the local sheriff, Hayes!"

He sighed and said, "No, I'm not, I *am* with DEA. For the last two years Mike's been working a joint task force with us. I was just *planted* here as the local sheriff."

Michelle said, "Why here?"

"Because there have been a lot of drugs pouring into the East Coast. We narrowed it down to this area," Ventris interjected. "We thought the source was Babbage Town, but we didn't know how they were getting them into the country. We thought they were coming in by boat."

"You must have known Champ had a plane," Sean pointed out.

"We did. But that Cessna didn't have the range to bring in shipments from out of the country. We wanted the source of the stuff," Hayes said.

"We never suspected the CIA flights. They're a government agency," Ventris added, looking nervous.

Michelle snatched the tape from Sean and stuffed it into Ventris's hands. "Here's your damn proof. Now stop jawing about shit that doesn't matter, file for a warrant and take a frigging battalion of cops across the river before something happens to Viggie. Because I swear to God if they hurt her while you're standing here pissing around, I will hunt you down and kick the living shit out of you."

Without hesitation Ventris said curtly, "Let's go."

Hayes said, "Mike, it's the damn CIA."

"All we can do is try."

87

It took some time to get a warrant at that hour, and the judge who granted it didn't seem at all pleased about having authorized a search of Camp Peary. Yet the videotape and the testimony of Sean, Michelle and Horatio carried the day. Still, dawn was breaking as the line of Suburbans pulled to a stop in front of the entrance to the CIA's facility and Ventris and Hayes led two dozen federal lawmen and Sean and Michelle toward the guardhouses.

At Sean's insistence Horatio Barnes had been escorted back to northern Virginia by a pair of DEA agents to nurse his strained back, saturated lungs and a severely stressed nervous system. Sean had given him the copy of the video stick showing the plane, Arabs and drugs from Camp Peary with instructions for Horatio to make additional copies of it and to put them in separate safety-deposit boxes.

Ventris held up the warrant and his creds as three armed guards from the front gate approached him.

"You'd better get one of your superiors out here, gents," Hayes said, flashing his badge as well.

The guard said in a crisp professional tone, "Actually, sir, *your* superiors are here."

Two other men came out from the guard building. One wore a suit; the other was dressed in khakis with a blue DEA windbreaker.

Sean's heart sank as he saw Ventris and Hayes stiffen. The man in the suit said, "Agent Ventris, give me the warrant."

Ventris said, "But sir, I—"

"Now!"

Ventris handed it over. The man looked at it and then tore the paper up.

The man in the DEA jacket said to Hayes, "Now give me the video that was shot."

"How'd you know about that?" Hayes asked.

"You showed it to the judge to get the warrant. Now give it to me."

Hayes pulled the video from his pocket and gave it to his boss, who in turn gave it to one of the Camp Peary guards.

"Now get your men back in the vehicles and get out of here."

Hayes immediately started to protest but the man cut him off.

"National security interests are at stake here, Hayes. I'm not saying I like it, but that's just the way it is. Go!"

Ventris's boss nodded curtly at him as well. "You too."

The men turned back toward the Suburbans. Michelle and Sean started to follow, but the Camp Peary guards stopped them.

"You two are being detained," one of them said.

"What!" Sean exclaimed.

Ventris and Hayes started to intercede but their two superiors stepped in.

"Get in your damn vehicles and get the hell out of here. We have no jurisdiction at this place," Ventris's boss said.

"We had a warrant," Ventris said bitterly.

"Do *you* want to go to prison for obstruction, Mike?" The man glared at Sean and Michelle. "Or for harboring and aiding and abetting felons? Now get your ass in the truck and pretend this was all a nightmare. That's an order."

Ventris and Hayes looked helplessly at Michelle and Sean. Sean nodded. "Go on, guys, we'll work it out." He didn't sound too confident because he wasn't.

As the motorcade drove off, footsteps made Sean and Michelle turn around.

Valerie Messaline was standing there dressed in beige fatigues, her CIA ID on a lanyard around her neck.

"Welcome to Camp Peary," she said. "I understand you've been dying to visit."

88

The cell was six-by-six concrete, cold, damp and windowless. Sean's clothes were stripped off and he was ordered to stand at attention in the corner. After six hours, exhausted, he squatted on the floor. The door to his cell immediately banged open and hands lifted him back up. An hour later, his legs growing numb, he squatted again. The same thing happened over and over. Twenty-two hours later he was allowed to fall back on his hard cot. A minute later the cold water hit him in the face. Then he was forced to sit on the edge of a metal stool that was bolted to the floor. If he moved even a millimeter the door immediately clanged open and he was forced back to his original position. An hour later he was forced to sit so close to the edge he could barely stay on the stool. Thirty minutes later, he was forced even closer to the edge. Every time they moved him, part of the skin from his butt cheeks remained on the cold metal stool. His muscles knotted up after five hours. After ten hours he threw up everything in his belly. Sixteen hours later he was allowed to collapse on his bed covered in his retch. He was given a cup of water but no food.

As soon as he was drifting off to sleep the door banged open again and he was lightly smacked in the sides with wooden batons and ordered to remain awake. As soon as he started falling asleep again the same thing happened. For two days this occurred until he finally fell to the floor, his body twitching uncontrollably.

After three days of this treatment he found the strength to scream, "I'm a United States citizen, dammit, you can't do this. You *can't* do this."

He jumped up and charged the door, but strong hands shoved him back. He fell onto the concrete, ripping skin off his knees and hands.

"You can't do this," he said again. He tried to rise, to fight them, but he was too weak. "You can't do this. You have no right."

"We have every right," a voice said. Sean looked up to see Valerie standing there.

"You broke into a United States intelligence facility. You stole things."

"You're crazy."

"You are a traitor to your country. We have evidence that you came down here on the pretense of investigating a murder but with the real purpose of spying on the CIA."

"That's bullshit and you know it! I want a lawyer, right now!"

She went on calmly, "Based on our investigation we have classified you and Michelle Maxwell as persons who are materially aiding enemies of this country by spying on the CIA. Therefore you are not entitled to legal representation or to habeas corpus until we decide to charge you with a crime and bring you to trial."

He exploded, "You can't fucking keep me here just because you want to."

"The law allows us quite a bit of latitude."

"What do you want from me?" he shouted.

"Things you saw, things you heard. Even what you're imagining. But I'll talk about that once you're softened up a bit more. You gave us quite a rough time out on the river; it's payback now."

She turned to leave.

"You killed Monk Turing. And Len Rivest. And you blew up the morgue? All in the name of serving your freaking country? Do you know how many laws you've broken?"

Valerie said, "Monk Turing did what you did. Broke in here. He was shot for it. And we had every right to do it."

"Right. If that were the truth you wouldn't have made it look like a suicide. So people would think it was like the others. He saw the people getting off the plane, didn't he? He saw the drugs. So Turing had to die. But what you didn't know was he'd been over here before and he put it all down in a code. Alicia took the code and despite what she told us I bet she actually did crack it. So Viggie disappears. Am I right? Come on, Val, tell me!"

"You're hardly in a position to demand answers."

Despite being weak Sean was just warming up. "And Rivest. He was going to tell me things about Babbage Town before he was killed. Maybe he found out the CIA was spying on the place. Maybe he confided in Alicia, who was pretending to have a thing for him. Only he didn't know she was on your team. Bam, he's dead. Later you blow up the morgue to cover up some incriminating evidence. How am I doing Val? Batting a thousand?"

"You can speculate all you want."

"The FBI and the DEA know you have us here. There's no way you're going to get away with this."

Valerie looked at him condescendingly. "You just don't understand how this whole thing works, do you? In the grand scheme of saving millions of lives, what's a couple of deaths? I mean really? What's a couple of deaths? You're just a blip on the ass of history. Nobody will even remember you." She told the guard, "Hit it hard." And then she closed the cell door behind her.

89

Two days later Sean King could barely remember his own name. "Please stop," he kept asking them. "Please stop." They never listened.

Instead they picked him up and carried him to another room. He was placed in a long box resembling a coffin. He was packed in so tightly he could barely move. Wires were attached to his chest and arm. When the cover was put on, it rested within two inches of his face. The feeling of claustrophobia was extreme. What Sean couldn't see were the pipes attached to the chamber. At regular intervals the temperature in the chamber was lowered until Sean was pushed right to the edge of hypothermia. He struggled to catch his breath as the oxygen levels were reduced. Just as he was about pass out, they pumped more air in. For ten hours this process went on. And he grew weaker and weaker. Finally, thankfully, he lost consciousness.

When he awoke later in his cell he noticed he had another visitor.

"Hello, Sean," Alicia said.

"Come to gloat?" he answered weakly.

"No. I take no pleasure in seeing you in here."

"Really? That's sort of hard to believe." Sean sat up and leaned his back against the wall. "Drug smuggling, murder, kidnapping, torture. Have I left anything out?"

"I'm not sure what you mean," she said calmly.

"I mean you and Val are smuggling drugs in on planes."

"You may call it that. I don't."

"And what do you call murdering Monk Turing and Len Rivest?"

"Monk was shot for trespassing."

"But you did kill Len, didn't you? And I thought you liked him."

"We all have a job to do."

"So you're admitting you killed him?"

"There's a war going on. We all have a job to do," she repeated more slowly.

"And you almost killed me!"

"We knew it was you who broke into the camp. You saw things. You and Michelle. Just like Monk Turing. That's why you're here."

"So you torture us, find out what we know and then what? Let us go?"

"That's not my responsibility."

"Oh, good, just pass the buck along to someone else. So what'll it be? Gas explosion? Suicide? Will I die in my bathtub? By the way did you use the plunger or that metal leg of yours?"

"I simply follow orders."

"From Valerie? Is that all it takes for you to kill somebody? Orders from a psychopath? What about the morgue doc? What the hell did he do to deserve getting blown up?"

"There's always collateral damage. It comes with the territory. I don't like it, but there's nothing I can do about it."

"Sure there is. You can stop doing it."

"I don't know what sort of world you want to live in, but it's obviously not the one I'm envisioning."

"Does that world include killing Viggie?"

Alicia quickly looked down. "Viggie will be fine."

He roared, "No she *won't* be fine, Alicia. She's going to be collateral damage too. She probably already is. You know that and I know that."

Alicia turned to leave.

"What, you just came to see me before the hammer comes down? Is that it? Seeing another victim off to the great hereafter. I'm sure Len appreciated the gesture. Did he even know it was you? Did he think you came there to screw him? A little fun in the old tub?"

"Shut up!" she said sharply.

"No, I'm not shutting up. You're going to hear me out, lady."

As Alicia fled the cell, his screams of outrage followed her. "Are you gonna pull the trigger on Viggie? Are you?"

Alicia broke into a run, but she couldn't outrun the screams. The stone floor was slick and she stumbled. As she fell, her prosthetic leg hit her good leg, cutting into her skin. She slumped to the floor sobbing quietly as Sean's shouts thundered down the bleak hall.

"I'm so sorry, Viggie," she said. "I'm so sorry."

90

For three more days Sean was forced to stand at attention or squat. He was barely fed and a cup of water a day was his sole allotment, enough only to keep him alive. He was returned to the coffin three times. He was poked or hit with a water jet whenever he tried to doze off. Deafening music was piped into his cell without warning and stayed on for hours. They had rigged his cell with electricity that would give him a mild shock when he touched his bed or the wall, or certain spots on the floor. It got so he simply huddled in one corner afraid to move. His belly was empty, his skin was raw; his spirit was cracking in half.

After his last trip to the coffin he awoke two hours later in his cell and looked around. He didn't know how long he'd been in here. It could be days, weeks or years. His brain had simply shut down on him. As the cell door opened, he started sobbing, terrified of what they were going to do to him next.

"Hello, Sean, are we ready to be a good boy now?" Valerie asked.

He couldn't even raise his head.

"Your friend's made of tougher stuff. We never got *her* to cry."

Now he looked up. "Where is Michelle?"

"That's really none of your concern, now is it, *little* man?"

As Sean stared at Valerie Messaline, at the arrogant features of her face, at the confident tilt of her body, rage replaced his fear. He pushed his hand against the wall to steady himself. And then before anyone could react he pushed off the wall, lunged and was on top of her, his hands around her throat. He wanted to kill her, squeeze every molecule of arrogance, of superiority out of her ugly, filthy being.

Guards pulled him off and threw Sean back into a corner. When Sean sat up he looked at her. Valerie was standing against the far wall trying to appear composed yet he could see the fear in her eyes. And that small triumph was all he needed right now.

He stood on trembling legs, holding on to the wall for support, and said, "That's a nasty bruise, Val. You might want to take a session in the coffin. They say oxygen deprivation is good for strangulation marks, if you don't suffocate that is."

"You think it's been bad up till now," she hissed. "Just wait."

"Where's Michelle?"

"Like I said you should be concerned about yourself."

"She's my partner and my friend. But I guess you don't understand those concepts." He glanced at one of the guards, a young man with short blond hair and a muscular physique. "Hey, kid, you better hope to hell you don't do anything to piss this lady off. She might just decide to label you a *spy*, torture your ass, and apparently there won't be a damn thing you can do about it."

The guard said nothing, but Sean could see just the tiniest bit of doubt creep into his eyes as he shot a sideways glance at his boss.

He turned back to Valerie. "Where is Michelle?" he screamed, finding lung power he didn't know he had left.

"I can see we have some more work to do with you."

"I have friends who work at the CIA. There's no way in hell the Agency has authorized what you're doing. You'll rot in jail for this."

She stared at him coldly. "I'm *doing* my job. You're the one trying to bring this country down. *You're* the enemy. You broke in here. You are a spy. *You* are a traitor."

"And *you* are full of shit."

"We even have evidence of your participating in a drug smuggling scheme."

"Oh, that's a good one coming from *you*."

"By the time we're done with you, you'll tell us everything we want to know."

"You may torture me into saying what you want, but that won't change the real truth."

"And what's that?"

"That you're insane," he snapped.

She turned to the guard. "Take him to the next level. And take him hard."

Before the guard could react the cell door opened and another man wearing a suit came in followed by two other armed men.

"What are you doing here?" Valerie snapped.

The suit said, "Ian Whitfield sent me to deliver instructions to you."

"Instructions from Whitfield? He has no authority over me."

"Perhaps not, but *this* person does." He handed a piece of paper to Valerie. As she scanned the contents Sean, who was watching her closely, knew exactly what had just happened: The woman had been left as the scapegoat in a classic Washington power move that would be instantly recognizable to everyone operating within the Beltway and totally foreign to the *normal* population.

Valerie folded the paper and put it in her pocket.

One of the guards stepped forward, spun Valerie around and handcuffed her. As she was being led away Valerie glanced at Sean. Their positions had just been neatly reversed and he didn't intend to waste the opportunity. In a voice strained but clear, he said, "Better get yourself one *fucking* great lawyer, lady, because you're gonna need it."

91

The next day Sean and Michelle were flown separately to a private hospital where it seemed they were the only patients. They had no idea where the facility was and no one there would answer any of their questions. However, they were given top-notch care. After several days of IVs, and long, uninterrupted periods of sleep, followed by two weeks of solid food and limited exercise, they both were nearly back to normal.

The doctors had kept Sean and Michelle segregated, refusing to tell them anything about the other. Finally Sean would have no more of it. Wielding a chair before a cowering nurse and attendant, he demanded to see Michelle. "Now!" he screamed.

When Sean walked into her room, she was sitting over by the window looking out at a depressing gray sky. As though sensing his presence, she turned around, cried out, "Sean," and raced to him. They stood there in the middle of the room clinging to each other, trembling.

"They . . . they wouldn't tell me anything about you," she began as tears welled in her eyes.

"I didn't even know if you were alive," he stammered. "But it's all over, Michelle," he said. "We're safe. And they arrested Valerie."

"Did they put you in the coffin?" she asked.

"More than once. They said you never cried."

"I cried, Sean. Trust me. I cried a lot." She looked out the window. There was a bed of flowers below her window. Their blooms were done for the season; their stems drooping. "A lot," she added.

"I'm sorry, Michelle."

"For what? You got the same treatment in there that I did."

"It was my idea to go over the fence."

"I'm a big girl, Sean. I could have let you go it alone," she added quietly.

"I know why you didn't," he said. "I know." They sat in the window seat looking at the dead flowers.

After Sean and Michelle were sufficiently recovered they were flown by private jet to another location, driven by car with blacked-out windows to an underground parking garage and taken by secure elevator to an enormous office suite that had nothing in it except three chairs. While two muscular men with guns inside their suit coats waited outside they sat down across from a small, thin, impeccably dressed man with thick white hair and slender wire rim glasses. This gentleman put his fingertips together and gazed at them with a sympathetic expression.

"First, I want to extend to both of you the official apologies of your government for what happened."

Sean spoke up angrily. "Funny, I thought it *was* our *government* that was trying to kill us."

"Government can be an unwieldy thing, Mr. King, with certain parts of it overstepping boundaries of authority from time to time," the man replied evenly. "That doesn't make the rest of government evil. However, you *did* break into a CIA facility."

Sean was not in a conciliatory mood. "Prove it!"

Before he could answer Michelle said, "Do you understand what was going on there? Do you blame us for trying to do what we did?"

The man shrugged. "My job is not to assign blame, Ms. Maxwell. My task is to move forward from this point in a way that benefits us all."

"How exactly do we do that?" Sean demanded. "*Our* government kicked the shit out of us. A girl named Viggie Turing has been taken by *our* government. People have been murdered by *our* government. How do we move forward in a way that benefits us all from that!"

The man leaned forward. "Here's how. We have viewed the video that was used to issue the search warrant for Camp Peary. As you know it shows certain . . . compromising activity. Our technical people tell us that the video has been copied."

"You want the video that shows *our* government breaking about a hundred laws."

"It wasn't *our* government, Mr. King," the man snapped. "As I said, sometimes people overstep their boundaries of authority."

"In our case they didn't step, they *stomped*." Sean studied the man. "So that's why they sent you with your nice manners and white hair and glasses looking like an old Cold War warrior right out of a damn John le Carré novel to give us the pitch."

"I'm glad you understand the situation. And the fact that we need any and all copies of that video, Mr. King," the man added quietly.

"I bet you do. But I'm a lawyer and I need to see the quid pro quo and let me tell you it better be ten times bigger than whatever you might be thinking of right now if you really want to do a deal."

"I have authority to make certain concessions—"

"Screw that. Here're our terms. First, we want Viggie back safe and sound and if you tell me that's not possible the tape goes straight to a journalist friend of mine who'll take it and win the Pulitzer he so desperately wants. Next, Valerie Messaline, or whatever the hell her name really is, gets everything she has coming to her and I'm not talking a promotion. Third, Alicia Chadwick with the one leg gets the same treatment. And the shit that they're doing over at Camp Peary has to stop. I mean really stop. No more drugs. No torture. And consider yourself lucky."

The man sat back and considered this. "The two women have already been taken care of. You have my word on that."

"Your word means shit to me. I want real proof!"

"All right."

"What about Viggie?" Michelle blurted out. "Is she okay?"

The man nodded curtly. "But the actions you're talking about at Camp Peary; some of them will stop, Mr. King, indeed some of them already have. But I cannot promise that all of them will. Yet I can assure you that these activities are absolutely *essential* to preserving the security of this nation."

"Isn't that what you always say when you want to piss all over someone's rights?"

"How is drug running essential to our nation's security?" Michelle asked.

"We're not selling it," the man said impatiently. "We destroy it."

"Yeah, and I didn't inhale," Sean barked.

"Three people were killed," Michelle pointed out. "Murdered."

"A very unfortunate fact. But the sacrifice of three lives to save thousands, if not millions?"

"Well, I guess that's just great so long as you or someone you care about isn't one of the people sacrificed," Sean countered.

"Nevertheless, I cannot promise that *all* the activities you witnessed at Camp Peary will cease."

"Then I guess we have a problem," Sean said. "And if you're thinking of maybe eliminating the two *problems* you see sitting in front of you, think about this. I had *five* copies made of that video. And they're all in very safe places. Now unless Michelle and I die in our sleep at age ninety, one copy is going to be delivered to my aforementioned Pulitzer-hungry friend so he can write the story first, with other copies going to the *New York Times*, the *Washington Post* and the *Times* of London."

"That only makes four. What about the fifth one?"

"That goes to the president. I bet he'd get a real kick out of it."

"And yet as you pointed out we seem to have reached an impasse."

Sean stood and paced. "Good lawyers always think of a compromise so here's one for you. There's a hidden treasure at Camp Peary."

"Excuse me," the man said, startled.

"Just shut up and listen. It's hidden in the foundation wall of Lord Dunmore's Porto Bello lodge. Gold, silver, jewels. The whole thing's easily worth millions."

"My God!" the man exclaimed.

"Yeah, before you get permanent dollar signs etched in your eyes that treasure is to be taken and sold for the highest possible price. Hell, if the government wants to buy it they can. I don't really care. But the proceeds of those funds will be divided into three equal shares."

The man pulled out a pen and a piece of paper. "All right. Presumably with one share going to each of you."

"No!" Sean snapped. "One share goes to Viggie Turing. It won't make up for her dad getting killed but it's a start. The second share goes to Len Rivest's two kids. They're in college and could probably use the money. And the third share goes to the family of the medical examiner who was killed in that *gas* explosion. You got that?"

The man finished writing and nodded. "Got it."

"Good. Now I'm going to check on the amounts paid over to them so don't try to screw with me on the dollars. And I don't care if it takes an act of Congress, but all the money goes to them tax-free."

The man said, "That won't be a problem."

"I didn't think so."

"And we want to see Viggie, to make sure she's all right," Michelle added.

"That can be arranged."

"Then arrange it," Sean said. "Sooner rather than later."

"Give us one week and it'll all be done."

"Make sure it is."

"And you'll say nothing about any of this?" the man asked.

"That's right. I'm not looking to go to prison."

"And who would believe us anyway?" Michelle added.

"And then we get the copies?" the man asked.

"And then you get the copies."

"And we can trust you?"

"As much as I can trust you," Sean said.

92

A week later Sean and Michelle met with Joan Dillinger in her office, along with another man who gave neither his name nor affiliation. He would only say that the ownership of Babbage Town was grateful for the work done by them and he had presented them directly with a check. The amount, Sean quickly saw, would resolve all their financial problems for the foreseeable future and fund some vacation time as well. They certainly needed it.

"Hope you found someone to take Champ's and Alicia's places. Too bad you lost such valuable people."

"Oh, we have. But thanks to you our research won't be preyed upon by electronic eyes anymore," said the man.

As the fellow was leaving Sean couldn't resist a parting shot. "So why spend all this time and money on creating something that will stop the world in its tracks?" he said.

The man had looked at him quizzically. "Who told you that's what Babbage Town was doing?"

"A couple of real geniuses."

The man raised an eyebrow. "Well, let's just say that while what you described is certainly a possibility, it's a tad more complicated than that."

"And you're just ready to roll the dice with the whole world at stake?" Sean exclaimed.

"Well, if we don't, someone else will."

After he left, Michelle added glumly, "I'm sick of geniuses."

Joan smiled. "Good work, Sean." She paused and glanced at Michelle. "And you too, Maxwell. From what I've heard I don't think Sean would've made it without you."

She knew nothing of their ordeal at the hands of Valerie Messaline or their arrangement with the government, and never would.

The two women extended to each other a grudging handshake.

When they returned to their apartment and were getting out of their car in the underground parking garage a limo pulled up in front of them. Ian Whitfield leaned out and said tersely, "Get in."

They sat across from Whitfield, who said, "Sorry it took me so long to spring you."

"And how exactly did you manage to turn the tables on the wicked witch?" Sean asked.

Surprisingly, Michelle answered. "You found out

she was taking a cut from the drug shipments and selling them. You nailed her with that, right?"

Whitfield said, "How do you figure that, Maxwell?"

"When I was at the airport and they loaded the drugs on Champ's plane, I noticed they kept some bales back. That was Valerie's cut. The old guy from the government told us the CIA was destroying the drugs, but Hayes and Ventris said the area was being *flooded* with drugs."

Whitfield said sternly, "Not even Valerie was connected enough to dig herself out of that one."

Sean snapped his fingers. "That explains her going to that bar and pretending to get hit on. She was really moving her drug shipments."

Whitfield nodded. "I finally got one of her team to turn on her. I used his information to crack her plan open, spring you two and nail her."

"But why take the risk of Champ flying the drugs out? Why not just destroy them at Camp Peary?" Michelle asked.

"We don't have the facilities to do it there. But when Michelle caught Champ in the act, we didn't have time for anything else."

Sean said, "Okay, what happened to old Val and her homicidal sidekick, Alicia?"

In answer Whitfield held up a copy of the *Washington Post*. On page A-6 was a brief story about the unfortunate deaths of two State Department employees in a car accident near Beijing. There were two grainy photos of the victims.

Sean looked at Michelle and then back at Whitfield. "Damn, I didn't mean for them to be killed."

"And what exactly did you expect would happen to them? That we'd try them in a court of law where their stories would come out? Where highly sensitive programs they were involved in might possibly be revealed to the public?" He looked at the photo of Alicia. "I was riding in the Humvee with her in Iraq when we hit the IED. I was the one who pulled her out. That's how my leg got banged up. She used to be a good agent. Something just went wrong somewhere."

"What about the treasure?" Sean said.

Whitfield pulled out some documents and handed them to Sean.

"The full proceeds were split into thirds, tax-free, as you requested. A nice gesture," he added. "Most people wouldn't have been so magnanimous."

"And Viggie?" Michelle said.

"That's where we're headed right now. And she's absolutely fine. It was fortunate Valerie was so busy with you two she put her plans for Viggie on hold."

Sean hunched forward. "Ian, you took our side against your own agency. Why aren't you dead or under arrest?"

His features turned grim. "I was the technical head of Camp Peary, but Valerie really ran the place. She's done impressive work and her rise at the Agency has been amazingly swift. I didn't know that was the deal when I took the job, but I had to live with it if I wanted to continue my career.

"Very quickly I saw it was a mistake because she started doing things that were way over the line. She co-opted several of the paramilitary squads based at the camp. All I could do was wait for an opening, though it didn't look like one would ever come along." Whitfield glanced at Sean. "I know Valerie made a hard rush at you to get you in the sack."

"I didn't have much trouble resisting," Sean said almost truthfully.

"Good. Because you wouldn't have walked out alive. That's why I showed up on the beach. I knew she was concerned about how much you were finding out. I followed her and pretended to be the cuckolded husband. She was pissed at me for letting you get away."

Sean looked stunned. "Thanks for saving my life. Again."

"It's my job to protect Americans, even from my own agency."

"I'm surprised Valerie just didn't have us killed right away."

"I think she wanted to pay you back, for messing up her plans. And she also needed to find out how much you knew."

"So who killed Len Rivest?" Sean asked.

"The only thing I can tell you is that Alicia's interest in Rivest wasn't romantic."

Sean said, "And her and Champ being at Babbage Town was no coincidence?"

"Champ and Alicia were recruited long ago by the CIA. They were posted at Babbage Town when it first started. By the way, they were the real deal in the science world."

"And they were at Babbage Town to steal whatever technology they came up with on quantum computers?" Michelle said.

"Let's just say they were very interested observers. But what they were really working on at Babbage Town was a counter to the quantum computer."

"A counter?" Michelle said.

"It's a given that a commercially viable quantum computer will be a reality one day. The folks that owned Babbage Town were attempting to build a quantum computer so they could, in turn, construct an effective counter-device to it."

"So the owners of Babbage Town were the very ones who would be hurt by quantum computers?" Sean said.

"Like banks and multinational companies?" Michelle added. "Really deep pockets."

Whitfield nodded. "They had to do it on the Q.T. If the public found out, there would've been a panic. But the CIA wasn't going to stand by and let something like that take place right under its nose. I can't say we were interested in a counter-device though. We are spies, after all."

"So how close are they to stopping the world in its tracks?"

Whitfield shrugged. "If I were you I'd start paying in cash and stocking up on paper and pen for your correspondence."

"But was it a coincidence that Babbage Town was located right across from Camp Peary?" Sean asked.

Whitfield shook his head. "CIA owns the estate through a shell company. They bought it because it *was* right across from Camp Peary. Champ convinced the people behind Babbage Town to lease the place."

Michelle added, "And Champ was a pilot who could fly the drugs out for you."

"Be clear on this point: Champ is a good agent. He was doing what he was ordered to do. That's all. He wasn't working with Valerie or Alicia." He glanced at Michelle. "He told me to tell you that he was sorry how things turned out."

"Sorry! The bastard shot me in the arm!"

"If he wanted to kill you, you'd be dead."

"Viggie was in his plane. Was he going to kill her?"

"No. We were getting the girl away from Valerie. *You* just got in the way."

"Oh," Michelle said, looking chagrined.

"Champ also told me to tell you that you have a lot to live for. And to give up trying to fly planes. I'm not sure what he meant by that."

Michelle looked down at her hands. "So Champ is okay?" she said.

"Yes. And like me, he's been reassigned."

"Why was Viggie taken?" Michelle asked.

Whitfield said, "There was also code in the song's notes that Alicia managed to break using the computers at Babbage Town. It was actually based on the World War II–era Enigma code."

Sean said, "I knew it! She used my clue about the Enigma code to break it and then lied to us about it. And Viggie was also a code, a living, breathing one."

"And the song title was the big clue: 'Shenandoah,'" Michelle added.

"That's right," Sean agreed.

"What did the decoded song say?" Michelle asked.

"It described some of the things Monk Turing saw at Camp Peary. It was enough to make Valerie order Alicia to take Viggie."

"Alicia kidnapped her?" Michelle exclaimed.

He nodded. "I know it probably doesn't mean much after all she did, but Alicia helped me and Champ get Viggie onto that plane. I believe she really did care about the girl because it was a big risk, her doing it."

"It might mean a little bit," Sean admitted.

"Ian, how can you continue to work for a place that's dealing in drugs!" Michelle exclaimed.

Whitfield shrugged. "You need poppy seeds to make opium and you need opium to make heroin.

And right now in Afghanistan, the poppy crop is the only thing keeping the economy going. And if we don't buy it terrorists will and use the enormous profits from dealing the drugs to attack us. Lesser of two evils; sometimes it's the only choice we have."

"It's still wrong," Michelle persisted. "And what Valerie did was criminal."

"Valerie was a rogue clear and simple. As crazy as it sounds I believe she was going to kill you both after the torture was done, and she probably believed she'd get away with it. The role of the CIA she had in mind is not the same one I have, and never will be so long as I have anything to say about it."

"Ian, you have to tell us one thing: How did Monk Turing get across the river?" Sean asked.

Whitfield hesitated. "I guess I owe you that. It was an underwater propulsion device. We found it."

Sean looked at Michelle. He said, "No, that was—"

Whitfield cut in: "We found *two* of them, actually. One on the night all hell broke loose." He eyed them both. "Know anything about that?"

Sean smiled. "Great minds *do* think alike."

The limo slowed and then stopped.

"We're here," Whitfield said, opening the door. "Take your time, I'll wait outside."

93

When the woman opened the door, Michelle saw that Viggie Turing had indeed taken after her mother.

She'd been expecting them, the woman said, and ushered the pair inside.

"You're Viggie's mother?" Michelle said.

"No, I'm her aunt. My poor sister died years ago. But people have always said that we looked a lot alike." She led them into the living room. As soon as Viggie saw Michelle she started playing the piano. Michelle sat down next to Viggie and hugged her.

Viggie's aunt, whose name was Helen, said, "I didn't even know they were in Virginia. And I certainly didn't know anything had happened to Monk. And then Viggie just appeared one day. I nearly fainted."

"So Monk had custody of her?"

Helen lowered her voice so Viggie couldn't hear. "My sister had a very troubled life. Drugs, mental illness; we believe that she even physically abused Viggie. Monk finally got her away but maybe I should have tried to intervene more. But I have a way to make it up to her. I'm going to adopt Viggie."

"That's great, Helen," Michelle said out of Viggie's earshot. "She's a very special girl."

"I know that she needs counseling and other treatment. At first I was worried because the help it seems she needs is very expensive. But then very recently I've come to understand that Monk died a rich man. Viggie will have more than enough money for anything."

Sean said, "If you need a good psychologist, I have a name for you. And he's already seen Viggie."

Viggie pulled Michelle to the window and pointed outside at a nearby lake. "Can we go on the water again?"

"You think you're up to it? Remember last time."

"That's because I went alone. If I go with you everything will be okay, right?"

"Right."

As they were walking back to the limo later Michelle said, "It really was generous you giving the treasure away, considering you found it."

"Heinrich Fuchs really figured it out. But finding the treasure cleared up something else that had been bugging me."

"What?" Michelle asked.

"Remember Monk had those red stains on his hands?"

"Right, rust stains from climbing the chain link fence."

"No. That chain link was brand-new, it had no rust stains. I saw that when I was cutting through the fence. Monk got the stains from scraping at the bricks to get to the treasure, just like I did." Sean shook his head. "Codes and blood. I was wrong. It had nothing to do with Alan Turing and bloodlines. Monk was being literal. His hands looked *bloody* because of digging through the brick for the treasure."

"How many times do you think Monk infiltrated Camp Peary?" she asked.

"At least once too many. He obviously witnessed what we saw too. Only he didn't get away. The fact that he left a coded message in those musical notes about what he'd seen makes me believe he started out a treasure hunter and ended up trying to bust what he saw as illegal activity at Camp Peary."

"But how was he going to get the treasure out? Gold isn't easy to move."

"Maybe Monk just did it for the challenge of finding the treasure. But the guy was a genius. Maybe he was just planning to take the jewels. They'd be relatively easy to carry."

"And when Monk said to Len Rivest that it was ironic—" Michelle began.

"Right, it was ironic that the greatest secret-keeping organization in the world was clueless about a *secret* treasure right under its nose."

When they got back in the limo, Whitfield said, "We need to finish the deal."

"The copies of the video?" Sean said and Whitfield nodded.

Sean told the limo driver where to go. Sean had gotten the copies from Horatio and hidden them in various safe places. After they collected the copies, he handed them to Whitfield. The man looked at them and handed one back to Sean.

Sean said, "Ian, they're expecting five. If you only deliver four you could be having an accident in China too, not to mention what'll happen to us."

"I'll make another copy from one of these four. You didn't hear it from me but when dealing with CIA it's always best to keep an ace up the sleeve. I'll emphasize that we have no way of knowing if you made other copies. That should keep you both safe."

The limo took them back to their apartment and they got out of the car. Sean turned back. "Look, I know we probably won't be seeing you again, but if you ever need help, you've got a couple of friends in Virginia."

Whitfield shook both their hands. "If I've learned anything in this business it's that *real* friends are damn hard to come by."

94

It was a chilly day in early November when Sean drove Michelle to Horatio's office.

"I don't want to do this, Sean. I really don't."

"Hey, *you* came back from Camp Peary alive. And if I know one thing about you, you never go back on a deal."

"Thanks for your support," Michelle said bitterly.

Horatio was waiting for them.

Sean started to leave but Michelle gripped his hand. "Please stay with me."

Sean looked at Horatio. "That's not a good idea," the psychologist said.

"But I want him to."

"You're just going to have to trust me on that, Michelle. Sean can't stay."

After Sean left the room it didn't take long to perform the hypnosis.

Horatio spent a few minutes getting Michelle back to the age of six. And he took another few minutes placing her in that night in Tennessee when her life had changed forever.

Michelle's eyes were open, even though her conscious mind was no longer in charge. Horatio watched with great professional interest and also with growing pain as she recounted what had happened. Sometimes she talked as a child and other times with the reflection and vocabulary of an adult whose subconscious mind had grappled with that night and tried mightily to make sense of it.

The man in uniform had come that night. Michelle didn't remember seeing him before. She must have always been asleep when he came. But that night her mom was very nervous and kept Michelle with her. Her mother told the man she didn't want to see him; that he had to leave. He thought she was joking at first, and when it was apparent that she wasn't he turned angry. He started taking off his clothes. When he reached for Michelle's mother, she told Michelle to run. The man started pulling her mom's clothes off. Her mom was trying to stop him but he was too strong. He was forcing her down on the floor.

It had taken Michelle only a second to reach it. She had sometimes held her father's gun when it was unloaded of course. She pulled the soldier's gun from the holster he had thrown on the sofa with his other clothes. She had pointed it at his back and fired one time. A big red mark appeared on the man's back, dead center. He had died quietly, slumping over on top of Michelle's mother. The woman was so shocked she'd fainted.

"I killed him. I killed a man." Tears came down Michelle's face as she spoke about this long-buried event in her life.

She had been standing there with the pistol in her hand when the door had opened and her father came in. Michelle didn't know why he had come home early but he had. He saw what had happened, took the gun from Michelle and pulled the man's body off his wife. He tried to revive her, but she was still unconscious. He carried her up to bed, ran back down and took Michelle by the hand, whispering gently to her.

"He took my hand," Michelle said in a small voice. "He said he had to go away for a while, but he would be back. I started screaming, screaming for him to not leave me. I grabbed his leg, I wouldn't let go. I wouldn't. Then he said he was going to take me with him. That we were going for a ride. He put me in the front seat of his car. Then he went back inside and carried the man out and put him on the floor in the back."

"Why not the trunk?" Horatio said.

"It was full of junk," Michelle immediately answered. "So, Daddy put the man in the back. I saw his face. His eyes were still open. He was dead. I knew he was dead because I shot him. I know what happens when you get shot. You die. You always die."

"What did your daddy do next?" Horatio asked quietly.

"He put newspaper over the man. And an old coat

and some boxes, whatever he could find. But I could still see the man's eyes looking at me. I started crying and told Daddy. Daddy, I can still see the man's eyes, he's looking at me. Make him stop looking at me."

"And what did your daddy do?"

"He put more stuff on him. More stuff until I couldn't see him anymore. No more eyes staring at me."

"And your daddy drove somewhere?"

"Up in the mountains. He parked the car and went away for a bit. But he promised me he'd be back. And he did. He came back."

"Without the man?"

Michelle's breath caught in her throat and then she sobbed, "He took the man away. But I couldn't look down at the floor. Because he might be there. He might be there looking at me." She bent over in her anguish.

"Take a rest, Michelle," Horatio instructed. "Rest for a few moments, it's all right. None of this can hurt you. The man is not coming back. You can't see him anymore."

She straightened up and finally the cries stopped.

Horatio said, "Are you ready to continue?"

Composed, she nodded and said, "And then we drove home to Mom. My daddy drove me home."

"Was she awake then?"

Michelle nodded. "She was crying. She and Daddy talked. Daddy was mad. Madder than ever. They didn't think that I could hear, but I could. Then Daddy came and talked to me. He said he and Mom loved me. He said everything that had happened was a bad dream. A nightmare, he said. He told me to forget it. Never to talk about it." She started crying again. "And I never did. I promise, Daddy, I never did tell anybody. I swear." She sobbed heavily. "I killed him. I killed that man."

"Take another rest, Michelle," Horatio said quickly and she sat back in her chair with the tears dampening her face.

Horatio knew that what was destroying Michelle was keeping this all inside. It was like a wound that had never been cleaned; the infection just built until it became lethal. She'd carried the knowledge of her mother's adultery and her father's covering up a death with her all this time. And yet Horatio knew that paled in comparison with the guilt she must feel for killing another human being.

He recalled something she had blurted out when he had been at Babbage Town; that maybe her problem stemmed from her brutally murdering some-one when she was six. Horatio had thought she was being a smart-ass, but her subconscious had been talking to him. He'd just been too slow to see it.

Horatio didn't believe that Michelle saw the face staring at her from the floor of her truck or bedroom. He didn't believe she *saw* anything. It was more likely that she sensed something terrible, but didn't know what. Her reaction had been to cover it up, physically doing what she was also psychologically attempting.

Horatio waited a few more seconds and then said, "Okay, Michelle, can you tell me about the rose hedge?"

"Daddy cut it down one night. I saw him from my window."

Horatio sat back and recalled that Frank Maxwell had planted that hedge as an anniversary present for his wife. Apparently, the Maxwells had gotten through this nightmare by simply burying it. And yet somewhere out there a family had been wondering for nearly thirty years what had happened to the dead man. And all these years his bones had been lying somewhere up in the Tennessee hills. One day, the Maxwells would have to face what they'd done, at least in the complicated chambers of their own minds if not a court of law. He looked back at Michelle. "You just rest now. Just rest."

He left the room and spoke with Sean, but didn't tell him anything of what Michelle had revealed. "And I can't tell her either," he informed Sean.

"So what good has it done?"

"By her subconscious revealing what it has, it may relieve pressure on her conscious being. And I can tailor treatment that will more likely help her than not. In fact with another hypnosis session I can plant certain suggestions in her subconscious that may take care of the problem entirely."

"Why not do it now?"

"Doing it now could put a strain on her subconscious that might prove harmful."

"What can I do?"

"You can be more understanding of her little quirks. That would be a start."

Horatio returned to his office and slowly brought Michelle out of the trance.

"Well, what did I say?" she said anxiously.

Horatio said, "You know, I think we've made real progress today."

Michelle snapped, "You're not going to tell me, are you, you little shit!"

"Now there's the Michelle I've come to love and fear."

After leaving Horatio, Michelle said to Sean, "Are you or are you not going to tell me?"

"I can't because he didn't tell me either."

"Come on, do you really expect me to believe that?"

"It's the truth."

"Can't you tell me anything?"

"Yes. I will never kid you about being a slob again."

"That's it? I pour my soul out for *that*."

"It's the best I can do."

"I can't believe this."

He put his arm around her. "All right, I *can* tell you something else. But I need to give you something first." He reached in his pocket and pulled out the emerald he'd taken from Lord Dunmore's house. He'd had it mounted on a necklace for her.

When Michelle's eyes widened at the sight of it he said awkwardly, "Uh, it didn't seem right that you walked away with nothing from the treasure." He helped her put it on.

"Sean, it's beautiful. But what did you want to tell me?"

"It's a request actually," he said nervously.

"What is it?" she asked cautiously, her gaze locked on his face.

He paused, took her by the hand and said, "Don't ever leave me, Michelle."

AUTHOR'S NOTE

WARNING:

DO NOT READ THIS
BEFORE YOU READ THE NOVEL.

Dear Readers,

Babbage Town is completely fictitious but was inspired in part by Bletchley Park outside London where German military codes were broken by the Allies during the Second Word War. I have fudged certain geographic details and other facts where Babbage Town is set, created places out of thin air, totally fabricated a history for that area of Virginia, complete with abandoned mansions, and generally run amuck in a literary sense. However, readers knowledgeable about Virginia history will recognize in the story the influences of some of the "real" Tidewater estates along the James River (as opposed to the York River) of historical significance, such as Westover, Carter's Grove, and Shirley Plantation. Fortunately, this triumvirate of Virginia estates has *not* fallen into ruin.

That said, "making it up" and distorting the facts are legitimate tools of the novelist, so please disincline from writing to me to point out various factual and historical gaffes. I am not only aware of them, I tend to revel in them.

Now, the material concerning quantum computers is all true, or at least as true as a layperson such as yours truly can understand these baffling concepts and then communicate them to the reader in a narrative form that will not put one to sleep. There really are colleges, companies and countries in a race to get there first. And if someone does the world *will* change forever. To what degree and whether for the positive or negative depends, I guess, on who wins that race. One book that I found helpful in writing about quantum physics was *A Shortcut Through Time*, by George Johnson.

Since secret codes and the history of certain real-life cryptanalysts are tangentially explored in the book, I took inspiration from that field to create some of the character names. Here's the list:

1. Champ Pollion was derived from Jean-Francois Champollion, a brilliant French linguist, who was instrumental in the decipherment of the cartouches of Ptolemaios and Cleopatra. His work also enabled scholars to read the history of the pharaohs as set down by their scribes.
2. Michael Ventris was the name of the man who discovered that the so-called Linear B tablets unearthed on the island of Crete were written in Greek.
3. Alicia Chadwick's surname came from John Chadwick whose extensive knowledge of archaic Greek was instrumental as he and Ventris went on to decipher the Linear B tablets. As an interesting side note their findings were made public around the same time that Mt. Everest was first conquered, prompting their discovery to be labeled the "Everest of Greek Archaeology."

4. Ian Whitfield's surname came from Whitfield Diffie, who came up with a groundbreaking new type of cipher that used an *asymmetric* key, instead of a symmetric key. Symmetric merely means that the way one unscrambles the cipher is the same way one scrambles it.

5. Merkle Hayes's first name came from Ralph Merkle, who worked with Diffie and Stanford professor Martin Hellman on their world-changing work in conceptualizing public cryptography in a way that finally solved the key distribution problem.

6. Len Rivest's last name came from Ron *Rivest*, who teamed with Adi *S*hamir and Leonard *A*delman to create RSA, the system of asymmetric public key cryptography that is dominant in the world today.

7. Monk Turing's last name came from, of course, Alan Turing, whose actual history is set forth in the book. Charles Babbage and Blaise de Vigenère were real people as well, whose discoveries are also chronicled in the novel.

8. The inspiration for Valerie Messaline's surname (with a slightly different spelling) didn't come from the world of cryptanalysts. However, students of history may spot the significance. One clue: Unlike RSA, which is brilliantly asymmetrical, Valerie's name and character are beautifully symmetrical.

So as they say, what's in a name? Well, with *Simple Genius*, a lot!

The history of Camp Peary revealed in the novel is based on the research I was able to do and is factually accurate as well. However, the descriptions of what goes on there in the book are entirely products of my imagination. This was necessary since it's doubtful any novelist will ever be allowed there to do research. In that vein, anyone who works at Camp Peary who reads the novel, please keep in mind that I just made up what happens at the place; the characters and the dialogue, and nothing in the story is a reflection on you or the work you do for your country. A rogue agent is just that. Known as the "secret place" by some locals, it's worth a trip down just to drive by Camp Peary. No, you can't tour the place; the CIA won't even acknowledge it exists.

The idea for *Simple Genius* came to me, or at least part of it did, after reading about the Beale Cipher. The Beale Cipher is one of those oxymoronic phenomena— a famous secret. It concerns an enormously complicated code, three pages worth of numbers, and an alleged treasure worth tens of millions of dollars that was supposedly hidden by Mr. Thomas Jefferson Beale in the early 1800s. One page of the cipher has been—at least allegedly—successfully deciphered long ago by a friend of a friend of Mr. Beale's. The page was decrypted using the American Declaration of Independence as a source of letters corresponding with the numbers on the cipher. For example, the third number in the cipher is 24, which means, you'd look up the 24th word in the Declaration. That word is "another," so you'd take the first letter of that word, or "a," and plug it into the ciphertext in order to form words.

The decrypted page tells the general vicinity of the treasure—somewhere in Bedford County, Virginia—as well as the type and amount of the treasure—gold, silver and some jewels—and that it's buried in stone-lined caves stored in iron pots. Based on today's precious metals prices the treasure would be worth well over $20 million. It's impossible to calculate the value of the jewels, really. However, the deciphered message says they were worth $13,000 in 1821, so presumably they're worth a lot more today.

Easy, you might say. One page broken, two pages to go, put me down for the private jet. Well, here's the catch. Apparently everyone who is anyone in the cryptanalyst field has tried to decipher the other two pages, using cutting-edge technology and supercomputers, and they've all failed. Indeed, it's estimated that one out of ten of the best cryptanalysts in the world have tried to crack the Beale Cipher and not a single one of them has succeeded. The difficulty is that if the ciphertext is tied to a particular document—e.g., the Declaration of Independence—you need to know which document is the right one. And even in 1820 there were a lot of possibilities. The more obvious ones, like the U.S. Constitution and the Magna Carta, have already been tried.

However, at least one Web site *has* claimed to have solved the cipher and includes photos of the alleged vault found on the site. The folks running the Web site also claim that the treasure vault was empty when they got to it. Hmm. Maybe, maybe not.

The Beale Cipher has achieved such mythic status that another Web site offers specialized Beale Cipher software that can be used to decrypt the code and discover the location of the treasure. It makes you wonder why *they* don't use the software to decrypt the code and find the treasure. Yet, it could be they're selling a lot of that software and are perfectly content with those profits.

There is even a Beale Cypher and Treasure Association founded in the 1960s to stimulate interest in the mystery, not that enough people aren't stimulated already. It's said that there's hardly a farmer or land-owner in Bedford Country, Virginia, that hasn't had part of their land dug up by eager treasure hunters, often without their consent.

Below I've reproduced the three pages of the cipher for you, including the plain text of the decrypted one. The first page of numbers supposedly reveals the exact location of the treasure. The third page lists the parties who are legitimately entitled to the treasure. I would imagine that virtually all interested treasure hunters would not even bother to look at page three!

To find out more information about the mysterious Mr. Beale and how and why he did what he allegedly did, read *The Beale Treasure: New History of a Mystery*, by Peter Viemeister, or check out the Wikipedia free encyclopedia entry. Another tome you aspiring crypt-analysts might want to check out is *The Code Book*, by Simon Singh.

Is it all a complete hoax as many believe? It certainly could be. If so, someone went to extraordinary lengths to carry it off. Just so you know, I've tried a few times to break the code but I'm far from an expert. It will take a better cryptanalyst than your humble novelist to pull it off, if it is genuine. Piece of advice for those of you thirsting for instant wealth: Don't quit your day job while you're hunting. The odds of cracking the Beale and finding the treasure, if it does exist, are probably longer than winning the Powerball lottery. Another piece of advice: Never go digging on anyone's land without their consent. You might get sued or shot at, neither of which is particularly healthy.

For those of you who, despite the incredible odds, still want to pit your wits against perhaps the most impenetrable puzzle of them all—I wish you good luck.

And I hoped you enjoyed the return of Sean King and Michelle Maxwell in *Simple Genius*.

Take care and keep reading.

Sincerely,
David Baldacci

simple genius

The Beale Cipher

#1 The Locality of the Vault

71, 194, 38, 1701, 89, 76, 11, 83, 1629, 48, 94, 63,
132, 16, 111, 95, 84, 341, 975, 14, 40, 64, 27, 81,
139, 213, 63, 90, 1120, 8, 15, 3, 126, 2018, 40, 74,
758, 485, 604, 230, 436, 664, 582, 150, 251, 284,
308, 231, 124, 211, 486, 225, 401, 370, 11, 101, 305,
139, 189, 17, 33, 88, 208, 193, 145, 1, 94, 73, 416,
918, 263, 28, 500, 538, 356, 117, 136, 219, 27, 176,
130, 10, 460, 25, 485, 18, 436, 65, 84, 200, 283, 118,
320, 138, 36, 416, 280, 15, 71, 224, 961, 44, 16, 401,
39, 88, 61, 304, 12, 21, 24, 283, 134, 92, 63, 246,
486, 682, 7, 219, 184, 360, 780, 18, 64, 463, 474,
131, 160, 79, 73, 440, 95, 18, 64, 581, 34, 69, 128,
367, 460, 17, 81, 12, 103, 820, 62, 116, 97, 103, 862,
70, 60, 1317, 471, 540, 208, 121, 890, 346, 36, 150,
59, 568, 614, 13, 120, 63, 219, 812, 2160, 1780, 99,
35, 18, 21, 136, 872, 15, 28, 170, 88, 4, 30, 44, 112,
18, 147, 436, 195, 320, 37, 122, 113, 6, 140, 8, 120,
305, 42, 58, 461, 44, 106, 301, 13, 408, 680, 93, 86,
116, 530, 82, 568, 9, 102, 38, 416, 89, 71, 216, 728,
965, 818, 2, 38, 121, 195, 14, 326, 148, 234, 18, 55,
131, 234, 361, 824, 5, 81, 623, 48, 961, 19, 26, 33,
10, 1101, 365, 92, 88, 181, 275, 346, 201, 206, 86,
36, 219, 324, 829, 840, 64, 326, 19, 48, 122, 85, 216,
284, 919, 861, 326, 985, 233, 64, 68, 232, 431, 960,
50, 29, 81, 216, 321, 603, 14, 612, 81, 360, 36, 51,

62, 194, 78, 60, 200, 314, 676, 112, 4, 28, 18, 61,
136, 247, 819, 921, 1060, 464, 895, 10, 6, 66, 119,
38, 41, 49, 602, 423, 962, 302, 294, 875, 78, 14, 23,
111, 109, 62, 31, 501, 823, 216, 280, 34, 24, 150,
1000, 162, 286, 19, 21, 17, 340, 19, 242, 31, 86, 234,
140, 607, 115, 33, 191, 67, 104, 86, 52, 88, 16, 80,
121, 67, 95, 122, 216, 548, 96, 11, 201, 77, 364, 218,
65, 667, 890, 236, 154, 211, 10, 98, 34, 119, 56, 216,
119, 71, 218, 1164, 1496, 1817, 51, 39, 210, 36, 3,
19, 540, 232, 22, 141, 617, 84, 290, 80, 46, 207, 411,
150, 29, 38, 46, 172, 85, 194, 39, 261, 543, 897, 624,
18, 212, 416, 127, 931, 19, 4, 63, 96, 12, 101, 418,
16, 140, 230, 460, 538, 19, 27, 88, 612, 1431, 90,
716, 275, 74, 83, 11, 426, 89, 72, 84, 1300, 1706,
814, 221, 132, 40, 102, 34, 868, 975, 1101, 84, 16,
79, 23, 16, 81, 122, 324, 403, 912, 227, 936, 447, 55,
86, 34, 43, 212, 107, 96, 314, 264, 1065, 323, 428,
601, 203, 124, 95, 216, 814, 2906, 654, 820, 2, 301,
112, 176, 213, 71, 87, 96, 202, 35, 10, 2, 41, 17, 84,
221, 736, 820, 214, 11, 60, 760

#3 Names and Residences of Beale Associates, Relatives, etc.

317, 8, 92, 73, 112, 89, 67, 318, 28, 96, 107, 41, 631,
78, 146, 397, 118, 98, 114, 246, 348, 116, 74, 88, 12,
65, 32, 14, 81, 19, 76, 121, 216, 85, 33, 66, 15, 108,
68, 77, 43, 24, 122, 96, 117, 36, 211, 301, 15, 44, 11,
46, 89, 18, 136, 68, 317, 28, 90, 82, 304, 71, 43, 221,

198, 176, 310, 319, 81, 99, 264, 380, 56, 37, 319, 2,
44, 53, 28, 44, 75, 98, 102, 37, 85, 107, 117, 64, 88,
136, 48, 154, 99, 175, 89, 315, 326, 78, 96, 214, 218,
311, 43, 89, 51, 90, 75, 128, 96, 33, 28, 103, 84, 65,
26, 41, 246, 84, 270, 98, 116, 32, 59, 74, 66, 69, 240,
15, 8, 121, 20, 77, 89, 31, 11, 106, 81, 191, 224, 328,
18, 75, 52, 82, 117, 201, 39, 23, 217, 27, 21, 84, 35,
54, 109, 128, 49, 77, 88, 1, 81, 217, 64, 55, 83, 116,
251, 269, 311, 96, 54, 32, 120, 18, 132, 102, 219,
211, 84, 150, 219, 275, 312, 64, 10, 106, 87, 75, 47,
21, 29, 37, 81, 44, 18, 126, 115, 132, 160, 181, 203,
76, 81, 299, 314, 337, 351, 96, 11, 28, 97, 318, 238,
106, 24, 93, 3, 19, 17, 26, 60, 73, 88, 14, 126, 138,
234, 286, 297, 321, 365, 264, 19, 22, 84, 56, 107, 98,
123, 111, 214, 136, 7, 33, 45, 40, 13, 28, 46, 42, 107,
196, 227, 344, 198, 203, 247, 116, 19, 8, 212, 230,
31, 6, 328, 65, 48, 52, 59, 41, 122, 33, 117, 11, 18,
25, 71, 36, 45, 83, 76, 89, 92, 31, 65, 70, 83, 96, 27,
33, 44, 50, 61, 24, 112, 136, 149, 176, 180, 194, 143,
171, 205, 296, 87, 12, 44, 51, 89, 98, 34, 41, 208,
173, 66, 9, 35, 16, 95, 8, 113, 175, 90, 56, 203, 19,
177, 183, 206, 157, 200, 218, 260, 291, 305, 618,
951, 320, 18, 124, 78, 65, 19, 32, 124, 48, 53, 57, 84,
96, 207, 244, 66, 82, 119, 71, 11, 86, 77, 213, 54, 82,
316, 245, 303, 86, 97, 106, 212, 18, 37, 15, 81, 89,
16, 7, 81, 39, 96, 14, 43, 216, 118, 29, 55, 109, 136,
172, 213, 64, 8, 227, 304, 611, 221, 364, 819, 375,
128, 296, 1, 18, 53, 76, 10, 15, 23, 19, 71, 84, 120,
134, 66, 73, 89, 96, 230, 48, 77, 26, 101, 127, 936,

218, 439, 178, 171, 61, 226, 313, 215, 102, 18, 167,
262, 114, 218, 66, 59, 48, 27, 19, 13, 82, 48, 162,
119, 34, 127, 139, 34, 128, 129, 74, 63, 120, 11, 54,
61, 73, 92, 180, 66, 75, 101, 124, 265, 89, 96, 126,
274, 896, 917, 434, 461, 235, 890, 312, 413, 328,
381, 96, 105, 217, 66, 118, 22, 77, 64, 42, 12, 7, 55,
24, 83, 67, 97, 109, 121, 135, 181, 203, 219, 228,
256, 21, 34, 77, 319, 374, 382, 675, 684, 717, 864,
203, 4, 18, 92, 16, 63, 82, 22, 46, 55, 69, 74, 112,
134, 186, 175, 119, 213, 416, 312, 343, 264, 119,
186, 218, 343, 417, 845, 951, 124, 209, 49, 617, 856,
924, 936, 72, 19, 28, 11, 35, 42, 40, 66, 85, 94, 112,
65, 82, 115, 119, 236, 244, 186, 172, 112, 85, 6, 56,
38, 44, 85, 72, 32, 47, 73, 96, 124, 217, 314, 319,
221, 644, 817, 821, 934, 922, 416, 975, 10, 22, 18,
46, 137, 181, 101, 39, 86, 103, 116, 138, 164, 212,
218, 296, 815, 380, 412, 460, 495, 675, 820, 952

#2 Contents of the Treasure

115, 73, 24, 807, 37, 52, 49, 17, 31, 62, 647, 22, 7,
15, 140, 47, 29, 107, 79, 84, 56, 239, 10, 26, 811, 5,
196, 308, 85, 52, 160, 136, 59, 211, 36, 9, 46, 316,
554, 122, 106, 95, 53, 58, 2, 42, 7, 35, 122, 53, 31,
82, 77, 250, 196, 56, 96, 118, 71, 140, 287, 28, 353,
37, 1005, 65, 147, 807, 24, 3, 8, 12, 47, 43, 59, 807,
45, 316, 101, 41, 78, 154, 1005, 122, 138, 191, 16,
77, 49, 102, 57, 72, 34, 73, 85, 35, 371, 59, 196, 81,
92, 191, 106, 273, 60, 394, 620, 270, 220, 106, 388,

287, 63, 3, 6, 191, 122, 43, 234, 400, 106, 290, 314,
47, 48, 81, 96, 26, 115, 92, 158, 191, 110, 77, 85, 197,
46, 10, 113, 140, 353, 48, 120, 106, 2, 607, 61, 420,
811, 29, 125, 14, 20, 37, 105, 28, 248, 16, 159, 7, 35,
19, 301, 125, 110, 486, 287, 98, 117, 511, 62, 51, 220,
37, 113, 140, 807, 138, 540, 8, 44, 287, 388, 117, 18,
79, 344, 34, 20, 59, 511, 548, 107, 603, 220, 7, 66,
154, 41, 20, 50, 6, 575, 122, 154, 248, 110, 61, 52,
33, 30, 5, 38, 8, 14, 84, 57, 540, 217, 115, 71, 29, 84,
63, 43, 131, 29, 138, 47, 73, 239, 540, 52, 53, 79, 118,
51, 44, 63, 196, 12, 239, 112, 3, 49, 79, 353, 105, 56,
371, 557, 211, 515, 125, 360, 133, 143, 101, 15, 284,
540, 252, 14, 205, 140, 344, 26, 811, 138, 115, 48,
73, 34, 205, 316, 607, 63, 220, 7, 52, 150, 44, 52, 16,
40, 37, 158, 807, 37, 121, 12, 95, 10, 15, 35, 12, 131,
62, 115, 102, 807, 49, 53, 135, 138, 30, 31, 62, 67,
41, 85, 63, 10, 106, 807, 138, 8, 113, 20, 32, 33, 37,
353, 287, 140, 47, 85, 50, 37, 49, 47, 64, 6, 7, 71, 33,
4, 43, 47, 63, 1, 27, 600, 208, 230, 15, 191, 246, 85,
94, 511, 2, 270, 20, 39, 7, 33, 44, 22, 40, 7, 10, 3,
811, 106, 44, 486, 230, 353, 211, 200, 31, 10, 38, 140,
297, 61, 603, 320, 302, 666, 287, 2, 44, 33, 32, 511,
548, 10, 6, 250, 557, 246, 53, 37, 52, 83, 47, 320, 38,
33, 807, 7, 44, 30, 31, 250, 10, 15, 35, 106, 160, 113,
31, 102, 406, 230, 540, 320, 29, 66, 33, 101, 807, 138,
301, 316, 353, 320, 220, 37, 52, 28, 540, 320, 33, 8,
48, 107, 50, 811, 7, 2, 113, 73, 16, 125, 11, 110, 67,
102, 807, 33, 59, 81, 158, 38, 43, 581, 138, 19, 85,
400, 38, 43, 77, 14, 27, 8, 47, 138, 63, 140, 44, 35,

22, 177, 106, 250, 314, 217, 2, 10, 7, 1005, 4, 20, 25,
44, 48, 7, 26, 46, 110, 230, 807, 191, 34, 112, 147,
44, 110, 121, 125, 96, 41, 51, 50, 140, 56, 47, 152,
540, 63, 807, 28, 42, 250, 138, 582, 98, 643, 32, 107,
140, 112, 26, 85, 138, 540, 53, 20, 125, 371, 38, 36,
10, 52, 118, 136, 102, 420, 150, 112, 71, 14, 20, 7,
24, 18, 12, 807, 37, 67, 110, 62, 33, 21, 95, 220, 511,
102, 811, 30, 83, 84, 305, 620, 15, 2, 108, 220, 106,
353, 105, 106, 60, 275, 72, 8, 50, 205, 185, 112, 125,
540, 65, 106, 807, 188, 96, 110, 16, 73, 33, 807, 150,
409, 400, 50, 154, 285, 96, 106, 316, 270, 205, 101,
811, 400, 8, 44, 37, 52, 40, 241, 34, 205, 38, 16, 46,
47, 85, 24, 44, 15, 64, 73, 138, 807, 85, 78, 110, 33,
420, 505, 53, 37, 38, 22, 31, 10, 110, 106, 101, 140,
15, 38, 3, 5, 44, 7, 98, 287, 135, 150, 96, 33, 84, 125,
807, 191, 96, 511, 118, 440, 370, 643, 466, 106, 41,
107, 603, 220, 275, 30, 150, 105, 49, 53, 287, 250,
208, 134, 7, 53, 12, 47, 85, 63, 138, 110, 21, 112, 140,
485, 486, 505, 14, 73, 84, 575, 1005, 150, 200, 16,
42, 5, 4, 25, 42, 8, 16, 811, 125, 160, 32, 205, 603,
807, 81, 96, 405, 41, 600, 136, 14, 20, 28, 26, 353,
302, 246, 8, 131, 160, 140, 84, 440, 42, 16, 811, 40,
67, 101, 102, 194, 138, 205, 51, 63, 241, 540, 122, 8,
10, 63, 140, 47, 48, 140, 288

The deciphered message from #2 reads as follows:

I have deposited in the county of Bedford, about
four miles from Buford's, in an excavation or

vault, six feet below the surface of the ground, the following articles, belonging jointly to the parties whose names are given in number "3," herewith:

The first deposit consisted of one thousand and fourteen pounds of gold, and three thousand eight hundred and twelve pounds of silver, deposited November, 1819. The second was made December, 1821, and consisted of nineteen hundred and seven pounds of gold, and twelve hundred and eighty-eight pounds of silver; also jewels, obtained in St. Louis in exchange for silver to save transportation, and valued at US$13,000.

The above is securely packed in iron pots, with iron covers. The vault is roughly lined with stone, and the vessels rest on solid stone, and are covered with others. Paper number "1" describes the exact locality of the vault, so that no difficulty will be had in finding it.

The #2 cipher can be translated using any copy of the Declaration of Independence, but the deciphering requires some editing for spelling.

ACKNOWLEDGMENTS

To Michelle, here's to lucky 13! What a ride so far.

To Frances Jalet-Miller, for another superb editing job. Glad we're a team again.

To Aaron Priest, Lucy Childs, Lisa Vance Erbach and Nicole Kenealy, for all you do every day for me. And to Abner Stein, who does a great job for me on the other side of the Atlantic.

To David Young, Jamie Raab, Emi Battaglia and Jennifer Romanello at Hachette Book Group USA, for all your support and friendship.

To David North, Maria Rejt and Katie James for all your input and support from across the pond.

To Patty and Tom Maciag for being such great friends.

To Karen Spiegel and Lucy Stille for getting Hollywood jazzed again.

To Spencer, for the musical assist in the story. And to Collin, who every day and in every way shows me the power of rapid-fire dialogue.

To Alli and Anshu Guleria, David and Catherine Broome and Bob and Marilyn Schule for always being there for us. A special thanks to Alli for the Indian material, and to Bob for his thoughtful editorial comments.

To Neal Schiff, for helping me to get to places I need to go.

To Deborah and Lynette, the true heads of the "Enterprise."

extracts reading groups
competitions books new
discounts extracts extracts
competitions discounts
books new events
events books reading groups
extracts extracts
new titles reading groups
interviews
events extracts
discounts events
new books events
events new

www.panmacmillan.com

extracts events reading groups
competitions books extracts new